Epi
The End of Eternity

Daniel Rohn

Acknowledgements:

Special thanks to George, Sarah, Patty, Steve, Mom and the rest of my family for their invaluable assistance and patience with this book.

Chapter One

White drapes fluttered in the breeze that came through the open windows, filling the long chamber with cold, November air. Sonia Moreno shivered and clutched her daughter's hand tightly between her own. "How are you, darling?" she asked softly. She did not expect an answer, even as Mary shifted beneath the thick blankets on her too-large hospital bed. Sonia knew that her daughter would not answer; she never spoke, not in the dreams. Looking away from Mary, Sonia's eyes lingered on the row of empty, white beds stretching away from her for what seemed like forever. It was always so cold, Sonia thought, squeezing Mary's hand as her eyes began to water.

However, unlike the real ward, it was perfectly quiet in Sonia's dream-world. She steadied herself and closed her eyes, listening to the faint sound of Mary breathing in and out. If it wasn't for the peaceful silence, Sonia would have considered her recurrent dream to be more of a nightmare. But in the real world, she found it hard to enjoy her time with Mary in the long, miserable cancer ward. There was too much noise, and death seemed to linger everywhere, reminding Sonia that it would not be long before she lost her only child. Not long at all.

At first, Sonia did not hear the footsteps behind her; the sharp snapping noise of boots on marble tile was lost amongst countless drapes fluttering in the icy, whispering wind. Yet even with Sonia's eyes closed and her head buried in her daughter's chest, she couldn't fail to notice the light. She sat up with a start, glancing to the side at the window over Mary's bed. The dark glass glowed softly, and Sonia squinted her eyes – somewhere, impossibly far in the distance, she thought that she could see the rising sun. Only then did she hear the approaching footfalls, and Sonia tried to turn to face them. "Who is – *ahh!*" she gasped and threw a hand up to shield her eyes as her dream exploded with light. A fanfare of trumpets sounded in the air and the ward filled with the golden light of day, pouring in through illuminated windows.

"Sonia Moreno," spoke a deep and mellow male voice, touched with a hint of an Arabic accent. "You have been chosen. You have been called to service." The blaze of light around Sonia diminished slightly, and she trembled as she pulled back her hand. Sonia made the sign of the cross and fell to her knees, prostrating herself before a divine and radiant power.

"I am Michael, faithful child. And I have come in the name of the Lord of Hosts to charge you with a holy mission." The archangel smiled down at Sonia as she looked up to behold him; his perfectly white teeth were all the more noticeable behind his dark, chestnut-colored skin. Michael wore a simple, glittering alabaster robe bound with silver clasps and held his immense wings folded behind him.

Sonia opened her mouth to speak but choked on her words. She swallowed hard then tried again. "H-how...how may I serve?" she whispered and a shiver ran through her despite the warmth of Michael's presence on her skin. Nearly eight feet fall, Michael towered over Sonia as he fixed her with his luminous eyes – golden orbs set deep in a flawless face. Despite Sonia's great faith, she could not help but think that Michael's power was as terrible as his figure was beautiful.

Michael stretched out his right hand and waved it in the air, calling forth a confusing whirl of sparks beside him. "You will bring a man to me," he commanded as the shower of light coalesced into a lifelike image of a male in his early thirties. "This man." Sonia's eyes raced over the figure as she tried to take in every detail: he was tall, perhaps six and a half feet, even as he seemed to shrink away beside the resplendent archangel. He wore his brown hair short and messy beneath a well-worn U.S. Navy baseball cap, and he clutched a bloody brown jacket tightly about his chest.

Suddenly, the image beside Michael threw back his head and laughed, reveling in his madness. As his hollow, awful laughter echoed throughout Sonia's dream she knew with utter certainty that he was a dangerous man. A very dangerous man, she feared, but one whom she could remember. Sonia needed only to think her next question before Michael continued, dismissing the frightful picture with a wave of his hand.

"You will cross paths with this man tonight, and you will bring him to me in Ashevale Park," Michael explained, crossing his broad arms in front of his chest. "Say *nothing* of me and he will do as you say without resistance." Sonia nodded obediently, and Michael stepped forward to put his strong hand on her head of thick, curly black hair.

"Do this in the service of the Lord thy God and you shall be reunited with your daughter."

Sonia gasped in surprise; she had not hoped—not dared to ask—for such a boon. Behind her, Mary stirred in her bed and sat upright. "Does that mean I can come home from the hospital, mommy?" she asked in a weak, hopeful voice. "I thought the doctors said I would have to stay here…"

Sonia sobbed aloud and turned to embrace her daughter, hugging Mary tightly against her chest as she wept. "No, no," Sonia answered in a trembling voice. "You don't have to stay, *mi hija preciosa*, you can come home with me."

Filled with light and warmth and—for the first time in three years, *hope*—Sonia held Mary by her shoulders and looked deeply into her eyes. Mary smiled a broad, toothy smile and clapped her hands together excitedly. "I'd like that," she said quietly. Her voice lingered in Sonia's dreamscape until it was shattered by the crass roar of her mother's alarm.

Sonia's hand came down on the alarm harder than she meant and the frail plastic device bounced violently off of her nightstand. Sitting up in bed drenched in sweat and tears, Sonia grasped the tiny silver cross she wore about her neck. She would see her daughter home safely—alive!—from that awful hospital, the rows of beds for the not-quite-yet-dead.

Eager to begin her mission, Sonia looked down to where her clock laid blinking on the floor; it was 10:45pm and her shift was going to start soon. She still had time enough to shower and put on her uniform, to brush her teeth and say a silent prayer. No, Sonia thought with a sudden rush of emotion, *today* I will not pray silently. On that windy Friday night in November, Sonia Moreno would rejoice in her faith.

"Of *course* we have shitty weather tonight," Pete Machal muttered under his breath, staring out his apartment window at the rustling trees below. "Nice and warm so I can haul my ass to the office all week, then…" His words trailed off as he paused to stare at the stars. They were barely visible through the smothering ground-light of the city, yet the far-off lights still twinkled in amusement at Pete's misfortune. Pete grunted defiantly and presented the heavens with his middle finger.

The stars continued on as they were, unperturbed. Shutting the blinds on his only window, Pete tugged his brown leather jacket up over his broad shoulders and snatched his ragged Navy cap from atop his bedpost. He rifled through the top drawer of his nightstand for a moment to find his keys and a few twenty-dollar bills – both of which Pete stuffed into his jeans' pockets. He had every reason to believe it would be a typical Friday evening; drinking, grousing and…stupidly losing the directions to where he was going. Pete rubbed his temples, sighed, and surveyed his cramped, messy apartment for the tiny scrap of paper.

"If I were the directions, where would I be?" he asked aloud, looking back and forth between his desk and nightstand. "You can't have run very far…" Pete continued as he checked beneath his blankets and inside his jacket. Still, he couldn't find the directions and his patience was quickly running out. "Where *are* you, goddammit?!" Pete didn't get an answer other than the uncomfortable rustling noises of his next-door neighbors. He always thought they might be afraid of him—or *for* him—or perhaps both. In fairness to them, Pete couldn't blame his neighbors; he wasn't particularly stable.

But Pete had good reasons for being a little bit on the crazy side. Damned good ones, he reminded himself as he checked the kitchen's aging tile countertop for the elusive directions. "Anyone else…anyone…would be in an asylum if they had to deal with this shit," Pete muttered. It wasn't exactly a reassuring thought. "How is it possible…" he peered under a pile of old mail, "…for everything to go wrong? Really. How?" Pete took a deep breath and ran his fingers through his prickly, close-cut brown hair.

"Screw it." Pete pulled open the door of his fridge and gave a resigned smile at the black plastic bag within. "I can drink here." He reached inside the bag and his fingertips slid over smooth, cold glass – then against a folded piece of paper which crinkled noisily from the disturbance and bit into Pete's finger right below the nail. "*Son of a bitch!*" He yelped loudly and pulled a set of neatly folded—albeit slightly bloody—set of directions out of his bag from the liquor store.

Typical, Pete thought as he wiped his finger off on a paper towel and unfolded the directions. Just typical.

The lights in Pete's tiny apartment flicked out as he hit the switch and closed the door behind him. As was often the case on Friday nights, Pete Machal was heading out to a bar with his friends. Despite his persistent bad luck and the appropriately bitter worldview that came with it, Pete still had a few friends from the office at the Evening Post. And with dutiful regularity these friends would always go out with Pete on Friday night, collectively washing away their sorrows in the cheapest liquor money could buy. That is, with the exception of Rachel Lores; being a lawyer, she drowned her sorrows in the most *expensive* liquor money could buy. Sometimes Pete wished he made that kind of money.

Usually, however, Pete wished he could have his old job back. He just wanted to fly again. His silver aviator watch poked out from under his jacket as Pete tapped the button for the fifth-floor elevator, and he smiled sadly. It had been over two years since his discharge from the Navy. Two years of loading newspapers into trucks to make ends meet. Pete scolded himself silently; he had been lucky as hell—for *once* in his life—to survive the accident.

Nobody had expected him to walk again after Pete's ejector seat threw him directly into a bullet-proof cockpit that had failed to open. But Pete Machal had dreamt of flying a fighter jet since he was six years old and he wasn't going to let a bit of catastrophic spinal damage stop him. And if the universe was a just universe, it *wouldn't* have stopped him. Pete's officers always told him that he was the toughest damned pilot in the fleet, and they weren't the least bit surprised when Pete made a full recovery after only six months in physical therapy. But fate had one more trick to play on him; it always got the last laugh.

It was never easy for Pete to recall that final meeting with his captain and the attending physician; the memories floated as bits and pieces amidst a sea of grief. Concussion. Color blindness. Vision impairment. Never going to fly again. The elevator finally arrived in front of Pete with a half-hearted ding. *Never.* He stepped inside the dull metal box with a bland orange carpet, staring down at his old watch as the doors creaked shut. The Navy gave him an honorable discharge and a decent pension, but Pete hadn't taught himself to walk again so he could get a check in the mail every month.

Pete growled as he pulled himself from his memories and redirected his bitterness elsewhere. "How is it possible for this goddamned piece of junk to be so slow?" he grumbled as the ancient machine creaked around him, slowly descending. Taking the stairs would have been faster, Pete thought, but damned if he paid a grand a month for rent and had to use the stairs. "So why can't they replace you, huh?" Once again, Pete pressed the yellowed plastic button for the lobby. "What *exactly* are they using my money for? Gold-plated limousines that run on cocaine?" The elevator didn't answer; perhaps it was reflecting on the possibility of a life fueled by narcotics. If nothing else, drugs would probably make it faster.

At long last, the elevator shuddered and came to a halt. Tapping his foot on carpeting which he suspected was made before the First World War, Pete stared at the doors. "Well?" He reached forward and tugged at the metal doors without success. "Don't you dare," Pete hissed angrily, "don't you fucking dare, elevator! Argh!" With what Pete imagined was a twisted delight in his misfortune, the machine gave a feeble ding and opened its doors. "That's more like—*goddammit!*" The bottom four feet of the carriage peeked out into the building's lobby while the rest stared into the darkness of the elevator's shaft.

Pete knelt and surveyed his options. He was pretty sure that he could make it out—and to the floor—safely enough, assuming that the elevator didn't start back up and cut him in half. Despite his cosmically bad luck, Pete wasn't too worried by that possibility. The universe seemed more interested in crushing his dreams than simply killing him; it had certainly passed on the opportunity quite a few times. Tugging his jacket tightly around him, Pete wiggled his way out of the elevator carriage and dropped to the floor. "Not too hard…" He stood and smoothed out his clothing, already imagining the tale he would spin for his friends. None of them would be surprised, of course, but he knew that they would at least be amused.

Pulling the directions out of his jacket's inner pocket, Pete gave a disdainful look around the foyer of his apartment building. There was never a shortage of things for Pete to complain about and that night was no exception. Gaudy Halloween decorations from a month ago still covered the walls. Faux-marble Greek columns stood around the mail boxes complete with artificial ivy. And finally, a large sign proclaimed that 'Luxury Towers'—*hah!*, scoffed Pete—was both the finest and the most affordable building in the city. Still, all of that would wait until after Pete drank what he anticipated would be a couple gallons of cheap liquor. If he stopped to gripe about everything little thing, after all, he'd never even make it out the door.

Walking past a cheery cardboard vampire, Pete stepped out of the Luxury Towers into the surprisingly windy and unseasonably cold November night. He paused under the nearest street light and narrowed his eyes at the directions in his hand. Incomprehensible gibberish. Pete stared harder at Robert's hand-written directions. By all accounts, Robert Euhe was a great guy, one hell of an accountant and a genius at anything involving numbers. He could not, however, write legibly to save his life. Pete turned the crumpled paper sideways; it didn't help. If a picture was truly worth a thousand words, Pete dared not imagine the twisted unreality which a thousand of Robert's words might describe.

On most Friday evenings, Pete and his friends from work—a failing newspaper called The Evening Post—got together at their favorite local bar. The Sticky Ichor wasn't the cleanest or the nicest place in town, but it was absolutely the cheapest. Unfortunately, it was also the scene of an unpleasant altercation two weeks prior, after which the management had not-so-politely suggested that the crew from the Evening Post find a different venue. As it so happened, the new location was named Ockham's Kegger, words which Pete mouthed silently as he deciphered Robert's inscrutable notes.

The directions could not be read—not by any sane, mortal man—but they could be deciphered. Pete reached the end of his block and turned north on to Raca Avenue, concluding that first line of scrawled characters more likely meant 'Raca' than any of the other local roads. "At least the measurements are clear," Pete said, followed by a soft laugh. He wasn't entirely sure why walking directions to a bar required precision to the tenth of a meter, but Robert was *particular* about such things – "numbers matter," that's what Robert always said. Numbers annoyed Pete. But in truth, most things annoyed Pete.

After two more turns and through what Robert claimed was 161.7 meters of travelled distance, Pete Machal was thoroughly ready to get drunk. Making a final bend eastwards, Pete hoped it would not be too difficult to find the street number. Most of the buildings in the neighborhood were quite run-down, he thought, and – "woah." Pete stopped in his tracks and his eyes went wide as he took in the street. There on the left was a grey, nondescript store. A few boarded-up row-homes came up next. Then, completely out of place, Ockham's Kegger stood proudly in a cascade of lights. Bright red brick and slick wood paneling was adorned with flashing, twirling lights and…the sign. Pete looked up at the gaudy, heady silver panel hanging over the mirrored doorway; it depicted a cheery monk hoisting a wooden keg of gigantic proportions.

"Pete!" Robert's voice fell on deaf ears. "Pete, snap out of it!" Pete blinked in surprise, only registering his friend's presence once Robert grabbed his shoulder.

"It's…it's *beautiful*," whispered Pete reverentially, the reflection of neon signs proclaiming ludicrous drink specials dancing in his wide eyes.

Grabbing Pete by his arm, Robert tugged his much larger friend towards the entrance. "Good, but I'm going to freeze to death out here," he explained as he guided Pete through a short, mirrored entryway. Robert was a good foot and a half shorter than Pete and probably seventy-five pounds lighter; there was little doubt that the thin accountant would be a block of ice before Pete finished marveling at the exterior décor. "You know, I was prepared for you to start whining about my directions."

"Don't worry, I'll get to it," Pete said through a grin, gazing around the interior of the bar.

Robert pushed his glasses up his thin nose and surveyed the crowded main room for their mutual friends. "Ah, over here," he said and lead Pete through the teeming and mostly soused masses.

Slowing for a moment, Pete examined the tablecloth on one of the few empty tables. Again there was a picture of the same monk, the bar's name, and a small line of text. Pete leaned over the table and read aloud. "'The simplest explanation…is to get drunk and forget about it.' Rob, what the hell is this place? I've never seen anything like it."

Robert shrugged emphatically as he glanced over Pete's shoulder at the tablecloth. "I don't know. I saw a flier on the way home from work on Tuesday, and it looked like a nice place, despite the neighborhood. Kind of upscale, you know?"

"I don't know if I'd call it upscale, but…hell, I don't know *what* I'd call it," Pete admitted. "It's a damn bit nicer than the Ichor, though."

"I thought the Ichor was plenty nice before you and Wilfred decided to trash the place," Robert muttered. "Swinging barstools, really?"

Pete made a loud *harrumph*-ing noise. "They started it."

"And you escalated it," Robert countered as he tried to push through the crowds with his small frame.

"You sound like my mother. And hell, at least she could write legibly."

Robert groaned and rolled his eyes. "What does that have to do with – no, you know what? Everyone else made it here just fine and they *all* had the same directions. I'm not getting into this with you again; at least not until I'm properly drunk." Shaking his head, Robert guided Pete the rest of the way through the sprawling forest of wooden tables to the back corner of the room.

Pete smiled widely when he caught sight of three more of his friends; all of them were busily engaged in conversation while nursing a wide array of multicolored drinks. In view of his otherwise abysmal luck, Pete particularly appreciated the company of his friends – they represented one of the rare, small bits of the universe that didn't seem inexorably set again him. The moment Pete's tall figure broke through the crowd a loud cheer went up from his friends. Wilfred and Patty waved at him enthusiastically; the former noisily banged his mug of beer on the table, splashing the dark amber liquid everywhere.

"Augh!" Rachel exclaimed as ice-cold beer splattered all over her face, rousing her from a drunken stupor. "Wha…where?" Finally registering the source of her sudden dousing, she turned and smacked Wilfred soundly on the back of his head. The short, stocky Asian man laughed loudly and shrugged off her reprisal with a grin.

"Pete! You made it!" Once again he slammed his mug on the table before he stood and pulled a chair out for his friend. "After Rob told me he wrote the directions for you on his way out of work…" Turning serious, Wilfred stared at Robert and shook his drink menacingly. "I told him that if you didn't show up, I'd have to murder him with this very mug."

Robert chuckled nervously and shrugged; that was his default reaction to Wilfred's threats. Accustomed to the fact that Wilfred threatened massacres on a near-daily basis, all of his friends had decided that the best course of action was to merely assume he was kidding. After all, leaving aside Wilfred's violent bluffs, he was a remarkably decent guy to hang out with. It was a matter of consensus amongst the rest of the party that if and when Wilfred finally lost it, it was probably better to be his friend when it happened.

Sliding around the table past Wilfred, Pete clapped his stout coworker on the back. "Yeah, well, I guess Rob gets to live and crunch numbers for another day," Pete said with a laugh. "At least these chairs are comfortable," he continued as he slid in to one of the wooden chairs with red leather pads.

Rachel nodded, slouching forward on the chair, her hair nearly brushing on the tabletop. "They're even more comfortable…when you're drunk!" She commented, quickly sitting back upright as her face dipped dangerously near the beer-soaked table.

"I wonder if they're any good for swingin'…" Wilfred mused aloud, reaching aside to Pete's chair to give it a firm shake. Unsurprisingly, Wilfred bore no small degree of responsibility for the fight at the Sticky Ichor. "Looks solid enough for – *ach!*" Rachel smacked him upside his head again.

The petite, thoroughly drunk lawyer tried to scold Wilfred even as she stumbled drunkenly over her words. "No more…fighting! You two dumbasses are lucky…lucky you didn't get arrested last time." She blinked at Wilfred, groaned softly and tilted her head back to stare at the ceiling lights.

Patty laughed loudly. "You'd better get caught up, Pete, you're late! Rachel's already a few drinks in…as you can probably tell." Patty said with a smile, jabbing Rachel lightly in the side and eliciting a loud giggle from the lawyer.

"Heeeey, I can hold my liquor." Rachel slurred, swaying a bit from side to side. That statement was doubly untrue; not only was she quite a light-weight, Rachel was too drunk to even lift her glass with one hand. Seated at Ockham's Kegger, Rachel wore a dazzling red top along with a black skirt. Her very short blonde hair bounced lightly as she giggled, reflecting the light from above.

Patty shook her head and turned back to Pete. "Yeah, sure. So why are you late? I'm guessing it was either that elevator or Rob's directions…" She grinned knowingly. Having dated Pete for awhile in the not-so-distant past, Patty was well-acquainted with Luxury Tower's antiquated lift.

Pete's eyes opened wide; he had nearly forgotten about his earlier tribulations and dramatic escape. "Oh my god!" he exclaimed, slapping his forehead. "You will not believe what happened to me on the way out the door today! That damned machine tried to kill me this time!"

"Lord, not the elevator again," Robert sighed, returning to the cocktail he had left unattended while waiting outside. Pete's friends knew more about his elevator woes than about his family.

Pete gave a frustrated hrmph-ing noise, grinding his teeth for a moment. "Look, Rob, the elevator is serious business. There's no reason it should take three minutes to move five floors." Tapping his watch, he repeated himself for emphasis. "Three…minutes. Hell, I bet that probably violates some sort of code, and it's illegal. It's illegal…right, Rachel?" Rachel merely gave a drunken cackle as she took another pull on her neon red drink, and then began to stare off at the ceiling lights. She thought that they were amazingly sparkly.

"I could always take care of the management for you, Pete," said Wilfred sternly.

"Wilfred, I don't want you to *kill* anybody, I'm just saying someone isn't doing their job, and for all the money I'm paying…"

"What about just their knees?" suggested Wilfred, cracking his knuckles for unnecessary emphasis. "They're made for breakin', you know." Wilfred had a highly peculiar theology – he reasoned that if the good Lord didn't intend horrific injuries, He wouldn't have made such delightfully breakable mono-directional joints.

Thinking quickly, Robert intervened in the conversation before Pete got really worked up and actually agreed to put out a hit on his apartment managers. While common sense might not dissuade Pete from his rants about the Luxury Towers, Robert knew that alcohol could succeed. "How about you go get a drink, Pete?" he suggested, shaking his deep green martini in Pete's general direction. "They're cheap!" he added, as if his friend needed any further inducement.

"Oooh," Pete replied with a smile. "Hold that though, Wilf," he added as he squeezed back out from his seat against the wall to head for the bar. Weaving his way through the crowds and walking towards the bar, Pete searched around for an opening – the entire length was teeming with customers. At last, Pete found a hole in the mob next to two elderly gentlemen; Pete squeezed himself in and caught the bartender's attention. When his whiskey sour finally arrived, Pete barely managed to grab his drink around the expressive motions of the two older men; a jolly Scotsman and an elderly German were deep in a heated philosophical debate over something entirely beyond Pete's understanding.

Navigating the mobbed floor once again, Pete arrived back at the table and slid in to his seat. Stretching his legs, Pete relaxed and took a long pull on his drink. "Ahhh... *much* better. That's the best thing about new bars; they never go light on the good stuff!" he remarked. "It's actually a competent whiskey sour, Rob. I mean, lack of a cherry aside."

Robert rolled his eyes slowly, sipping at his own dark green drink. "That's a pretty remarkable comment coming from you, Pete. Compliments before you've even started drinking..." he remarked with a grin.

Pete guffawed, sipping his drink while he curiously inspected Robert's glass. "Now," he asked curiously, "what exactly is that you're drinking? I don't think I've ever seen a drink that *green* before, barring St. Patty's Day jokes."

Lifting his glass up, Robert gave it a little shake; the liquid, deep and sparkling green like malachite, swirled around lazily. "It was one of their specials," Robert said, examining the glass himself as he stared at it, "the bartender said it was called a 'Grue.' It was bright blue when I got it, but its green now...as you can see."

Cocking an eyebrow, Pete wondered aloud. "Wouldn't that be better as some sort of kid's cereal? Seems kind of gimmicky."

"Well, perhaps, but there's nothing kiddy about how this tastes. I really don't care what color it is; it's freaking delicious." Robert rebutted, taking another swallow before shrugging. "I think it's a nice trick. It seems like magic."

"It's a miracle!" suggested Patty, waving her hands around a bit over Robert's drink. "The Lord works in mysterious ways, not the least of which involves making some math nerd's drink change colors."

At that Rachel was somewhat roused from her stupor, leaning forward as she shook a finger at Patty. "The 'Lord'…does not exist. And that's a good reason for Him not to give a damn about Rob's drink. I'm sure it's just, um, heat-sensitive. Or something." She hiccupped loudly.

Rachel and Patty had developed an antagonistic—yet friendly—relationship regarding religion. While Rachel normally remained quiet about her atheism, alcohol would always spur her into blasphemous remarks. Consequently, Patty would invoke God at every opportunity during their Friday night outings, guaranteeing an argument, or at the very least, a snarky comment from Rachel.

Pete snorted indignantly, finishing off his drink and wiping his mouth clean. He looked down, making sure that he had gotten the last of the liquor out of his small glass. "Really, who cares?" he asked impiously. "Even if there is a God, he's doing a damned lousy job."

Wilfred laughed as Robert merely shook his head. "I bet," Wilfred asked sarcastically, "that God would be responsible for your elevator, too?"

Patty smiled deviously. "If that's the case, maybe you would have to reconsider your offer of knee-breaking, Wilf," she teased. Wilfred looked surprised then furrowed his brow in thought; he appeared to be seriously wondering if he could take God in a fight.

Stroking his chin slowly, Pete nodded at Wilfred and set his empty glass aside. "Actually," said Pete seriously, patting the table for emphasis, "that's a really good point. Would a loving God allow a world with my elevator? That's certainly better than any of that nonsense Rachel goes on about after two beers." Rachel coughed indignantly, staring at Pete while he responded with a helpless shrug.

Robert sighed deeply and rubbed his temples, unsure whether to be aggravated more by the blasphemous discussion, or the fact that it somehow, despite all reason, managed to include Pete's obsession with the Luxury Towers elevator. "Enough about the damned elevator," Robert groaned. "Go get something else to drink, and make it exciting. You could even try a 'Grue;' I promise you'll like it." Patty nodded enthusiastically at the suggestion, even as she was disappointed that her attempt to provoke Rachel had dead-ended into another recital of Pete's apartment grievances.

Pete kicked back from the table and stood up, leaning down and taking a look at the remnants of Robert's drink before making a disgusted face. "Ok, I'll try one of their specials," answered Pete, shaking his head at Robert, "but I'm not touching one of *those* things. Who knows what color it'll be in my stomach? I bet whatever they put in that causes cancer. Or headaches."

"We know all about headaches, Pete! Now go get a drink!" exclaimed Patty, pointing insistently back towards the bar area.

Throwing his hands up in exasperation, Pete turned briskly and strolled back over to the bar. Again squeezing himself in next to the two foreign gentlemen, Pete waved his hand and attempted to get the bartender's attention. After a few moments a new bartender caught sight of Pete's waving hand, heading over to serve him. Leaning across the counter, the bartender stared Pete straight in the eye as he adjusted his thick glasses and asked for an order with an unusually authentic French accent. "What will it be, monsieur?" he asked pleasantly. Pete stammered for a moment, temporarily confused by both his indecision regarding what to drink and his immediate feeling that the Frenchman was wildly out of place.

"I'll, um...er, I'll have a...I don't know, ok, just one of your specials," Pete finally coughed out, internally trying to decide whether the outrageous French bartender or the ridiculous looking monk display was more offensive to his tastes. Relatively certain that the cartoon monk was less likely to stop serving him drinks after being criticized, Pete bit his tongue and waited for the bartender to pour something.

"Ah, yes, the specials! You will love the Grue then, eh? It is blue when you…" the Frenchman began, pulling out what looked like a foaming beaker straight from a Hollywood horror film gone wrong.

Pete quickly came back to his senses, waving his hands wildly. "No, NO!" He protested, "I mean, I want to try something else. That looks too…" Pete stared at the beaker for a moment, only further convinced that the substance probably caused cancer. "Too interesting," he concluded, giving the bartender a ridiculously fake smile.

The Frenchman sighed, adjusting his glasses once more. He looked over Pete carefully, sizing him up. "Ah, ok, how about…hrrm…this?" The bartender drew a heavy, black bottle up from under the counter, then another smaller bottle, white and polished to a shine. Placing a hand on top of each bottle, he leaned forward and gave Pete a sly wink. "This…is the 'Existential Dilemma,' hmm? It's the best drink we have here, made from our own *secret* ingredients." The bartender patted the bottles again for emphasis, and then broke into a wide grin. "And…it's only $1 tonight! It's the best special we have."

Next to Pete, the pair of suited gentlemen suddenly dropped their argument, leaving him in an awkward lull of silence. For a moment, Pete swore that half of the bar had suddenly begun to stare at him. Pete gazed briefly at the two unlabelled yet entirely too fancy looking bottles, giving a silent moan as he remembered that he *had* promised to try one of the specials. "It doesn't…change colors, does it?"

The bartender laughed the kind of outrageous laugh Pete had expected a Frenchman would make, shaking his head and grinning. "Anhhh hah hah! Oh no," he reassured Pete, "it doesn't change. Not colors, that is." That supposed comfort was paired with the kind of cheesy smile that most people would usually associate with used car salesmen or televangelist. Pete deeply regretted that he hadn't simply asked for a beer.

Caving against what he felt was his better judgment; Pete pulled out a one dollar bill and slid it across the counter. "Alright, I'll take it," he said resignedly. Once again, Pete felt eyes on his back and a curious silence around the bar. Slipping the bill into his apron, the bartender quickly took out a small, spiraled double shot glass, tilting the obviously heavy white bottle as he filled the glass two-thirds of the way with what looked like milk. Popping the cap off of the smaller bottle, he then topped off the drink with an inky black substance. After only a moment, the two colors had swirled together into a completely uniform grey, the kind of color one would expect of a government office building and not of a late-night drink special.

Before he could complain—something which Pete wanted to do mightily—the bartender had already waltzed off down the row of customers, leaving Pete stuck with the drink. Gingerly lifting the small glass, he gave the drink a sniff; it smelt of lemons. Concluding that nothing which smelled like lemons could be entirely bad, Pete turned and headed for his table. Despairing over his drink, he didn't notice the young woman in front of him until it was too late.

"Oh, excuse me!" She chirped as Pete walked into her, jostled by the collision. Pete blinked in surprise, blushed a deep red, and tried to steady himself; he was shocked that he hadn't dropped the Existential Dilemma. That, he thought, would have been ideal. He couldn't have dropped it, he immediately realized, feeling the woman's hand around his wrist. She had an unusually strong grip for a young woman.

"You wouldn't want to spill *that*, love," she whispered, letting go of his hand with deliberate sensuality, her fingertips tracing against his skin. "Do take care of yourself." Before Pete could so much as collect his thoughts she was gone again, a blur of deep brown hair and the dazzling purple fabric of her dress. He looked around through the crowds, but she had disappeared entirely.

Once he regained his focus, Pete navigated the rest of the barroom floor and returned safely to his seat and his friends. Once there, he found that Patty had finally managed to successfully goad Rachel into an argument, despite the fact that the latter woman was almost wholly occupied with not falling out of her chair.

The two were engaged in a passionate debate, which revolved almost entirely around whether God could do the logically impossible. More specifically, they were having a fight over whether He could make calculus fun. Having suffered through an abortive attempt at a mathematics degree before changing majors then heading to law school, Rachel was particularly incensed by Patty's insistence that it was within the Almighty's power to render integration by parts enjoyable. Needless to say, Robert objected to the entire discussion, pointing out that he had plenty of fun doing math; that admission earned him universal contempt at the table.

"Now look," Rachel mumbled, pointing one of her many empty glasses at Patty for emphasis, "it doesn't matter what you think, nobody can do logically impossible things, even if they're God."

Patty laughed, shaking her head. "That's silly. God is God. He can make two plus two equal five and happiness at the same time. But what you don't understand is..." she trailed off, raising an eyebrow at Pete as he sunk lethargically into his seat.

"What the *hell* is that?" mocked Wilfred, leaning in close to stare at Pete's still mournfully grey drink.

"That is exactly what I'd like to know," Robert chimed in and the entire table went silent to take in the 'Existential Dilemma.' Pete opened his mouth, but even his usually sardonic nature failed him at the moment. Merely looking at the drink was depressing; seeing such a dreadfully dreary mixed drink seemed to strike the very chords of human discontent.

Pete shrugged, pausing for a moment before answering. "It's the 'Existential Dilemma,' that one dollar special they were advertising," he said slowly, also gazing into the drink's bland depths.

"Wow," replied Patty, laughing again, "no wonder it's only $1. It looks like boring paint." It was just like Pete, she thought, to pick the one depressing drink special in the entire universe.

"Yeah," Pete said glumly, "you don't need to tell me. At least it smells like lemons?"

"Oh good," Wilfred chuckled, "lemon paint is so much better."

Pete glared at his friend, tapping the drink lightly on the table and looking around at the group. "Well, let's just have a round and get this over with," he said, already steeling himself for what Pete expected to be the worst drink of his life.

"Alright, but what are we going to drink to?" Robert wondered, having picked up another 'Grue' while Pete was gone. "I want to drink this one before it turns green," he said, smirking at Pete as he jiggled his glass, the ocean-blue liquid already starting to turn into a mild turquoise.

"How about we let Rachel decide?" Patty suggested, looking over at the thoroughly-plastered lawyer. "She isn't going to be having another drink anyways, so we might as well let her pick."

Slouched backwards, Rachel continued to stare at the delightfully shiny lights until she was roused from her stupor. Upon hearing her name, Rachel perked up, leaning forward in her chair. Blinking, she rubbed her face as she thought of an appropriate toast and looked around at her friends. Finally seizing upon the opportunity to get back at Patty, she grinned widely and sat up straight in her chair. "Well," she began, trying to sound as serious as possible. "I do know what we can drink to: we can drink to the proposition that, if there is a God," she coughed, adding under her breath that there was not, "that we could all do a better job of things than Him. Especially," she added, "in light of Pete's apartment building."

Patty rolled her eyes as Rachel gave Pete a thumbs-up, while Wilfred and Robert sighed simultaneously. "You know I'm not going to drink to that, Rachel," Patty said dryly. "Me neither," chimed in Robert, frowning a bit himself, "I don't feel like going to hell over a toast."

Rachel stared glumly at her friends and shrugged slowly. "Oh, you're a bunch of spoil-sports," she said. "As if the *Lord Almighty* would care about what you toast to."

"I agree," said Pete, having been put in a particularly heretical mood by both the color of his beverage and the invocation of his elevator-induced woes. "I'll drink to that, even if nobody else will. What about you, Wilf?" he asked, looking over at him. Wilfred only shook his head silently, perhaps cognizant of the fact that his apparent homicidal tendencies would not make for a very good deity.

"Let's do it, then!" exclaimed Pete as he hoisted his glass, waiting for Rachel to get a grip on her water.

Rachel clapped excitedly, steadying herself before lifting her own glass. She didn't want to fall off of her chair mid-toast. "To our potential as exceptionally clever gods!" she offered, tapping her glass against Pete's with a loud *clink*.

"Gods who don't allow crappy elevators!" Pete enjoined, pausing to grimace only for a moment before quickly drinking the 'Existential Dilemma.' Immediately, Pete knew with utter certainty that it was, by far, the worst drink he had ever ordered. It was not that the drink tasted bad; in fact, the Existential Dilemma had a smooth texture and a subdued lemon taste that was actually quite enjoyable. Pete wished that the drink had simply been disgusting.

As Wilfred, Patty, and Robert tried to think of something more appropriate to which they could toast, Pete slumped back into his chair with a shocked look on his face, staring blankly across the room. His worries about cancer or color-changing drinks suddenly seemed very insubstantial—something much, much worse had happened. Specifically, Pete had become God. Now, it was commonly thought that turning into God would not be bad thing. Unfortunately, that reflected a lack of consideration, as very few people commonly turned in to the Almighty after a toast. Pete knew, in the depths of his still considerably cynical heart, that he was God. The Creator. The Big Cheese From Whom No Slice Can Be Cut. That made Pete quite upset, for the simple reason that most people who knew they were God happened to be completely insane.

Pete blinked his eyes slowly, lost in his own thoughts. Everyone, after all, had seen the crazy people on TV; there was no shortage of nut-jobs at street corners, court rooms, or mental hospitals that were thoroughly convinced they were God, Elvis, or both. Right then, Pete was sitting in his chair at Ockam's Kegger, wondering if all those crazy people felt exactly like he felt. "No!" he suddenly muttered out loud, shaking his head quickly as his friends turned to look at him.

"Was it really that bad?" questioned Patty, leaning over the table as she examined Pete. "We thought you went in to shock."

Wilfred chuckled softly and leaned forward to punch Pete lightly in the arm. "Come on, Pete, you're a big guy, can't you handle your liquor?" he teased, nodding over at Rachel. "Don't tell me you're as bad as she is!"

Pete stared at his friends with a blank expression on his face, shaking his head once more as he tried to dispel the remarkably persistent notion that he was the Lord. "It's nothing," he said shakily,

"I just didn't expect *that*. Let's have a round of tequila." He reasoned that whatever was wrong, more alcohol could surely make it better.

Hoping that a shot of tequila might dispel his problems—or at least distract his friends long enough for him to screw his head back on right—Pete squeezed shut his eyes and tried to clear his mind. At that point, Pete was struggling with another common—yet entirely forgivable—misconception about people who turn into gods. Newly minted gods did not, in fact, spring fully-formed into godhood. While Pete was still, very disturbingly, certain he was God, he did not have access to all of the perks traditionally associated with the position. He could sense, ever so vaguely, the vast sea of omniscience and omnipotence around him, brimming with untold mysteries. But those waters were dammed back and inaccessible. Still, the smallest drops of knowledge leaked into his mind, trickles of insight which nearly made Pete soil himself in abject terror.

For instance, Pete suddenly knew with absolute certainty how many fibers were in his pants, the exact distance between himself and the Orion Nebula, and the unsettling fact that exactly twenty-three people in a 100-mile radius were convinced that the Communists would be coming at any moment. Furthermore, it was no longer ludicrous to imagine himself leaping up to his fifth-floor window to avoid the elevator, or ridiculous to think that he could turn his chair in to a delicious cheeseburger. Still, Pete dared not seriously entertain these notions, clinging to his sanity.

"Success!" Robert proclaimed, his voice mercifully distracting Pete from his ruminations. The accountant carried aloft a small platter with four shots of tequila and a fresh glass of water for Rachel. "Drinks for all!" he said as he lowered the dull plastic tray to the table and retook his seat. One by one he passed out the drinks until he at last handed Pete a small shot glass full of sparkling yellow liquid.

"I tried to get one of those 'Existential Dilemmas' myself…" Robert began, eliciting a small choking noise from Pete. "But they said you got the last one. Just my luck, eh? I wanted to see what the big deal was."

"Yeah, you poor bastard," said Pete flatly. He stared down into the tequila, wondering if it would help him clear his head. It wouldn't. Pete knew that with miserable, utter certainty.

Somewhere nearby yet far beyond the focus of Pete's brooding mind, Robert proposed a new toast. Pete heard himself say a few words and lift his glass, a rush of burning alcohol in his throat. The tequila itself was an afterthought, for Pete was lost in other things – he was watching the sun fall behind the horizon in Mexico, many years ago when his drink had been bottled for shipping. There were little cacti all over the rocky earth, Pete noted as he instantly traced the plant's entire evolutionary history backwards to the dawn of life.

"Pete?" He didn't respond; he was busy watching whorls of nothingness churn in tiny, yawning chasms between realities. "PETE!" Patty's voice snapped with urgency and Pete felt her warm hand press against his cheek. "What's wrong with you?"

"Pete, what's going on?" asked Robert, his voice carrying the same notes of concern and fear. "Should we call for help, or…?"

"No, no, it's ok," replied Pete, wiping off the sweat that had formed on his brow. He hesitated for a second as he refocused on the present time and place. "I'm…I'm just not feeling so hot." His words came out slowly and uncertainly. "I should probably…ah…get back to my place and lay down for a bit." Patty narrowed her eyes at him skeptically; it wasn't like Pete to head back to the Luxury Towers and his nemesis-elevator so soon.

Wilfred frowned, worried about his usually indefatigable friend. "Do you need me to walk back with you, Pete? I'll even whip that elevator in to shape for you." Pete waved him off, managing a weak smile as he felt Wilfred consider calling an ambulance.

"Pete, I'm going to walk you back whether you like it or not," Patty insisted. "You're…really out of it. I'm sure Robert and Wilfred can take care of our drunk." Rachel muttered something barely audible in response, her head still buried in her arms.

"Yeah, we can get her back to her place," said Robert with a nod.

"Do you want to go home now?" Patty asked as she gently squeezed Pete's shoulder. "Or do you want to sit for a little bit? I could get you some water…" All of Pete's instincts wanted him to object strenuously to being walked back to his apartment. However, aggravating him only further, he knew without a doubt that Patty would adamantly refuse not to accompany him. Thus, with a long sigh, Pete gave in.

"Alright...fine. Let's get going, then." Pete quickly stood up from the table, eager to get out into the fresh air as soon as possible. He looked around the table and waved once to his friends. "Sorry I'm out of it tonight, guys. I'll see the rest of you on Monday." Not even waiting for a response, Pete grabbed his jacket and headed for the door.

Pulling his coat over his shoulders, Pete froze mid-step in the bar's short, mirrored hallway. He stared into the glass and exhaled slowly, staring deep into his reflection. Examining himself, he didn't think he looked crazy; he didn't have wild eyes, unkempt hair or a manic twitch, the kind of traits usually associated with psychopaths and physics professors. Pete thought he looked perfectly normal. Not mad at all, he thought. Divine. "No!" he hissed under his breath, tearing himself away from the mirror and barging through the door into the cold night.

The wind was blowing hard outside, and the former pilot leaned against the wall, staring up at the night sky. An empty soda can bounced and rolled by him on the sidewalk, driven by the wind as it clinked and clanked down the street. Pete ran a hand slowly through his short, brown hair, his eyes drifting from star to star as he shivered. "Is this it?" he thought soberly, "Have I gone crazy?"

Unbidden and unwanted, a reply surged up from Pete's subconscious with a force that made him physically gag. "No, you aren't crazy," the voice inside him said, "God can't be crazy." He slapped his hand against his forehead, tears watering in his eyes. Pete wanted to run away screaming but he knew that it wouldn't do any good.

"Feeling ill?" Pete spun on his heel to face the unexpected voice. He found himself face to face with a lithe young woman in a purple dress. The same woman he had nearly knocked over earlier. And, Pete noted curiously, someone that he had not sensed sneak up behind him. "Well? You look awful..." She clicked her tongue on her perfectly white teeth and shook her head, her shoulder-length hair bouncing back and forth. "I know how to make it better," she cooed, stepping in close to Pete and pressing against him as she put both hands on his chest. Faint purple smoke drifted from her open mouth as she smiled indecently, staring into Pete's fearful eyes. She licked her lips, patting Pete's chest softly as he inhaled. "That's a good boy." He coughed as the violet mist filled his lungs, leaving an acrid, metallic taste in his mouth.

"Pete…" Patty's voice leapt at Pete from nowhere. "What are you staring at? Pete?"

"Ah!" Pete yelped and jumped as Patty's hand touched his back. The seductress in purple was gone, vanished so completely it was as if she had never been there at all. "You…what…" Pete quickly looked up and down the empty street. "Gone? How?" A sharp pain cut through his chest and he doubled over, coughing violently. Patty rushed to him and put her arms around him as he coughed and gagged.

"My God, Pete, what's wrong with you?" she asked quietly, the concern in her voice turning to fear. "I think you need to go to the hospital…Pete?" Patty looked up at Pete's face searchingly, eliciting only a sigh from him as the pair stood in silence on the street.

Turning to look past his friend, Pete looked blankly down the row of businesses – mostly bars – that lined the street. There was no sense in mentioning the other woman, he thought; he looked crazy enough as it was. "I don't need to go to the hospital. I just feel really…strange. Maybe I'm coming down with something," Pete responded at last. He felt quite unnatural lying to Patty, especially since Pete knew *exactly* what his problem was at the moment. His stomach turned unpleasantly and Pete stifled another cough. "It'd be best if I got some rest."

Patty shook her head sadly, silently examining Pete. She took a hold of his arm as they began to walk down the street, heading back towards his room in the Luxury Towers. She had always cared about Pete; the two of them had once been in a relationship a few years ago. Pete had been too erratic; he was too emotional for Patty to deal with. But it was *that* very energy that was missing from Pete, Patty thought. He was never so withdrawn.

Pete did not say a word as he walked westwards with Patty, his eyes set and brow furrowed in thought. He did not even avoid the street grates which he usually took great care not to step upon. Biting her lip, Patty tried to keep her composure as Pete dragged his feet over yet another steaming grate. She had thought that he might open up to her once they were alone, but he remained utterly silent. Patty couldn't take the sight any longer as she stopped the both of them abruptly. She grabbed tightly onto Pete's arm, forcing him to turn and face her.

"Pete, I'm really worried about you. Do we need to go to the hospital?" she suggested again, her eyes meeting his. He did not respond. Patty held onto him defiantly; she needed an answer. "Pete. I'm not going to let you do this to yourself. What's wrong? I know this can't just be about some shitty drink."

Pete stared back into Patty's eyes, his hands stuffed into his jacket pockets. But Pete was not lost in her deep green eyes; he was lost in her mind. He felt Patty's concern, her fear, her every emotion rushing through his head. Already a god, Pete was still too much of a man; too human for the experience. Turning to the side of the street before it was too late, Pete wretched violently into the gutter, falling to his knees with a loud sob. Pete felt like a rapist as the whole of Patty's being flooded into him; a sparkling rush of knowledge and secrets he never wanted and never should have had. He had to stop it and Pete leveraged all of his will against the intrusion.

Soft hands pressed against his back while Pete gagged and coughed, struggling to return his mind to the world in front of him. He saw Patty kneeling next to him, holding him close as he wiped his mouth clean. Slowly, she pulled back and dug her hand into her purse, searching for her phone. Pete shivered and reached out to her, grabbing her thin wrist with more force than he intended. She cried out softly.

"Ow! Pete, stop it that hurts!" Patty didn't remember him being so strong, ex-military or not.

"I'm sorry, just…*don't*," Pete insisted as he turned to her, still down on one knee. "You don't need to call for help. I'll tell you, okay? I'll tell you what happened…" She nodded quietly and Pete released his grip. He rose to his feet and held out his hand to Patty. Her eyes darted to Pete's face then back to his hand, and Patty hesitated. Then, she grasped his hand and stood.

The fledgling deity stared up into the sky, watching the stars twinkle far above. "That drink changed me," Pete began slowly, trying to decide how to best explain his predicament. Realizing there wasn't any *delicate* way to phrase a sudden ascendancy to godhood, he took the most direct approach. "I'm not human, anymore. I think...I might..." His expression changed, becoming suddenly more serious. "No, no. I *am* a god." Patty stared at him with her mouth agape.

"...what?" Patty mumbled as she took a step backwards, her mind spinning as she tried to assess the situation. She had thought Pete was sick—maybe depressed—but not crazy. "Pete, you're scaring me," she said, her voice quaking, "I...I'm going to help...you need help." Pete was substantially larger than Patty, but he had never intimidated her before; it was always Wilfred's job to be scary. But then, on a cool street in the middle of the night, Pete loomed large over Patty.

"Don't tell me what I need!" Pete snapped at her, his humanity ebbing. "I am a *god*! I...ack!" He coughed up a mist of fine purple smoke and Patty backed away, staring wide-eyed at the dissipating, violet fog. She quickly reached into her purse and pulled out her cell, frantically dialing 9-1-1. Nothing happened. Again, more carefully, her fingers pressed the right buttons. And again, nothing happened. "You don't understand," he cooed to her as the coughing ceased, "I can do anything..."

Patty dropped her phone from her trembling hands, the plastic shell striking the pavement with a sharp cracking noise. She looked back and forth down the deserted street, searching in vain for a police car or a pedestrian, anyone who might help her. Her heart racing, Patty wanted desperately to run away but her body was paralyzed by fear. No, she told herself, not fear – something *else* held her in place. "P-please...*please*...don't hurt me, Pete," she whimpered.

The tension in the air vanished, life returning to Patty's limbs as Pete slapped his face and shook his head vigorously. "Oh god, I'm sorry," he mumbled, realizing the effect he has having on her. "I didn't mean to...wait, wait...I can show you! You'll like this, I promise." A wide, warm smile spread across Pete's face as he reached into the gutter and picked out a dented, discarded soda can.

Patty stared warily at Pete, even after his face had softened into a calming smile. "What...do you mean?" she asked, clutching her purse to her stomach, feeling the throbbing of her pulse slowly subside.

He knew that he didn't need a huge miracle to prove himself and his powers were still undeveloped. Pete wanted something small but convincing. "Ah!" he exclaimed, holding up the can for Patty to see. Across the crumpled and somewhat faded label she could barely make out the words 'Lemon-lime Soda.' "I know you love kittens, Patty, so…" Time slowed down for Pete as he reached beyond the veil of the world, traversing the bridge between reality and mere possibility. The empty can began to shift and change in the palm of Pete's hand. It grew larger and furrier, limbs then a tail sprouting as the young god demonstrated his authority over reality.

"Holy shit…" Patty breathed, awe-struck by the transformation. A tiny kitten with an otherworldly green coat sat in Pete's hand, staring at her new world with sleepy, watery eyes. The kitten blinked once at Patty before rolling over onto her back, waggling her paws briefly in the air, and falling asleep for a nap. "That's…wow…" Words failed her.

"Look what I found in the litter," Pete said with a smirk, holding out the fuzzy, drowsy kitten to Patty. The substantial parts of Pete that were still human swelled with pride at his power; the divine portions found his tasteless pun decidedly unbecoming of his stature.

As gently as she could, Patty took the kitten from Pete, eyes wide with wonder as she looked between the cat and her friend. Patty tenderly stroked a single finger down the kitten's back, and she responded by cuddling affectionately against Patty's hand. "Lime, huh?" she said as she lifted the kitten up to eye level for a closer look. "That's a pretty cute name."

Pete crossed his arms in front of his chest and admired his work, glad that he managed to prove his godhood without ruining Patty's mind. Still flabbergasted by Lime, Patty continued to stare at the kitten and scratch her head. Roused by Patty's constant attention, Lime squirmed back onto her stomach and stared back at Patty with sparkling sapphire eyes. "Pete," said Patty at last, moving closer to him again, "this is…amazing. Unbelievable." She shook her head and smiled at Pete, her earlier fear totally dispelled by Lime's almost unbearable cuteness. "How did the drink do this?" The purring miracle in her hand rolled onto her back again; Lime hoped that her newfound reality included belly rubs.

Pete laughed then shrugged. "I don't know, Patty," he admitted, stepping in close to Patty and gently rubbing Lime's fuzzy stomach. "But it did. Everything will be different now. Everything. There is so much I can do…" His first thoughts were of world peace and a cure to cancer, but it didn't take more than a second before he imagined a towering, terrible temple built in his honor. The spires would pierce the clouds themselves, draped with velvet banners. He stifled a cough and shook his head clear of the imagery.

Patty looked up at Pete, beaming with happiness as she cuddled Lime against her chest. She grinned as she too considered the potential uses of Pete's shocking power. "Haha!" laughed Patty, her first idea coming from their employer and shared source of misery. "Maybe you could even make the Post turn a profit?"

"Heh, I don't think even *I* could manage that," Pete snorted derisively before laughing with her. He was still human enough to appreciate Patty's humor, after all. Slowly, their mutual laughter subsided into silence. "You don't think I'm crazy?" he asked quietly.

"Well, of course I *did*, until this," Patty responded, holding up Lime. She meowed with an impeccable sense of timing. "Now…I don't know what to think. This is amazing. You're amazing."

Pete nodded happily at her, looking back down the street. For the first time since drinking the 'Existential Dilemma,' he felt somewhat comfortable. He wasn't crazy; he knew that and Patty accepted it. "Let's keep going then, OK?" he suggested. "I'm sure you're cold out here, and I think there would be a panic if I suddenly brought out the sun."

Laughing again, Patty sat Lime down in her purse, the kitten peeked her head over the edge of the bag as Patty took Pete's arm. "That sounds wonderful," she said, cuddling against Pete's side. "Let's head home." Pressed close together, they started again towards the Luxury Towers. Too absorbed in relief and wonder, even Pete did not notice the two figures that followed behind them in the darkness.

Chapter Two

Of all the things that were wrong with the Luxury Towers, the fact that the building was situated in a relatively unsafe urban area would rank near the top of most people's lists. Armed robberies were not nearly as infrequent as most people would like and the Luxury Towers had been burglarized more than once during Pete's time there. Unsurprisingly, those facts were paid little mind by Pete, who was quite convinced that the elevator was far more of a threat to his life than any crack fiend with a firearm.

More than once Pete's friends had suggested that he move to a safer location, but their advice was always rebuffed. Pete enjoyed the rock-bottom rent and—while he would never admit it—his endless rivalry with the elevator. Only once had he considered a move and that was during his relationship with Patty; while Pete rarely worried for his own safety, he understood Patty's trepidation in his sketchy neighborhood. Yet in fairness to Pete, he was far from an ideal target for robbery. Tall, broad-shouldered and always wearing his Navy cap, Pete walked with the confidence of a man who had been blasted through a bulletproof cockpit – and survived.

Nevertheless, on a usual night, Patty would have been nervous as she walked through the narrow streets near the Luxury Towers, even with Pete at her side. But that night was not even *remotely* usual and Patty nearly skipped along beside Pete as they walked. She wondered what Pete would do if someone harassed them, smirking at the myriad possibilities. If he could turn a can into a cat, she thought, surely he could turn a mugger into…what? Patty rubbed her chin. Probably a mug, she concluded silently, given Pete's terrible sense of humor. He'd probably say something like "looks like *you're* the one getting mugged!" Patty laughed aloud, drawing Pete's attention.

"Something on your mind?" asked Pete, arching his eyebrow curiously at her.

Patty grinned playfully. "I was just thinking…what if someone tried to mug us tonight?" she mused. "Wouldn't that just be *such* terrible luck? Of all the nights and all the people to harass…"

"Ooh, you're right," chuckled Pete. "Could be fun, though." Almost as soon as the words had left his lips, Pete stopped in his tracks. "Did you hear that?"

"Hear what?" Patty asked. Moments later a second scream drifted by on the breeze and it was not nearly as quiet as the first. "Oh my god, what was that?" Another scream came, followed by the sound of feet scuffling in the darkness.

"This way," whispered Pete as he lead the way forward, heading for a dimly-lit alleyway less than a block to their west. As he had always imagined, criminals were usually sensible enough to pick softer targets; those less liable to know ju-jitsu or throw bolts of divine lightning. Unfortunately for Stephen James, he could do neither of those things; all he could only yell and pray that someone came to help. He was a slight black man in his late fifties; all of his assailants were larger, younger and stronger than Stephen. At first, Stephen hadn't fought back—he knew better—but when the beating continued long after the thugs had taken his wallet he had begun to scream for help. Pete rushed around the corner, finding Stephen slouched against the wall with four young men pressed close around him.

Despite a black eye and a concussion, Stephen was the first to see Pete's arrival. "Help!" he cried out, doing little but drawing the attention of his attackers to the newcomers. Two of them stepped away from Stephen and the largest of them, a burly man older than the rest pulled out a short knife. He waved it at Pete, cursing.

"Fuck off, man, 'less you wanna get cut," he hissed, glowering beneath a dirty red hoodie. Pete didn't move. "I said *fuck off!*"

"Oh my god!" cried Patty, clinging to Pete's left arm. "Do something, Pete! Help him!" The dim glow from the streetlight barely reached back between the buildings, but she could see the blood on the ground and the ugly wounds on Stephen's face. She moved behind Pete instinctively, pushing him in front of her as Lime ducked down inside Patty's purse.

Still, Pete stood frozen in place, even as the man advanced towards him, knife in hand. "You're *gonna* get it now," growled the mugger before he broke into a run towards Pete. As a mortal, Pete would have undoubtedly sprung into action. He didn't particularly enjoy fights—not like Wilfred—but he wasn't one to stand by and see people suffer. But Pete was not his usual self, to say the least; he felt oddly constrained. Despite Patty's screams and her hand tugging furiously on his jacket—not to mention the blade dancing in the air before him—Pete couldn't bring himself to fight.

With a loud grunt the mugger barreled into Pete and the two men went down together. Pete didn't resist in the slightest, even as he felt the knife piercing between his ribs. Why couldn't he stop the evil that was right before his eyes? He furrowed his brow in thought, oblivious to the violent, smelly man on top of him. Saving Mr. James would hardly require any effort at all; it would be practically effortless compared to the minor miracle Pete had needed in order to create Lime. But his gut twisted painfully at the thought of forcing the muggers to stop; something about it did not sit right with his newfound godhood.

Pete's head bounced on the concrete with a dull *thunk* as the mugger let go of him and stood, panting from exertion. "Wha…what the fuck are you man? Retarded?" he spat, delivering a swift kick to the side of Pete's face. "Don't know how to scream?" Still, Pete did not respond, staring off into the sky as he bled profusely onto the sidewalk. Turning to face Patty, the thug twirled the knife artfully in his hand. "I bet you're gonna be a hell of a lot more fun, huh?" he said with a leer.

Patty screamed. She tried to turn and flee, digging both hands into her purse to try and find her phone beneath Lime's squirming body. Only then did she remember leaving it on the sidewalk back by the bar. A strong hand caught her shoulder and stopped her in her tracks. "Now who the fuck are you two?!" yelled the thug behind her, and Patty looked up. A portly, middle-aged gentlemen held her by the shoulder, clad in a spotless brown suit with a glittering red silk tie. He stared past Patty with his deep green eyes, narrowing them at the scene in the alleyway. From behind him stepped a tall, gaunt man, his grey hair pulled back into a short-cropped ponytail. The second man's angular face looked all the more menacing for the grave expression upon it as he swung a polished wood cane up from his side, pointing it at the mugger.

"I'm Immanuel Kant, *motherfucker*," he said mockingly, imitating the thug's dialect. "And you should know better than to treat people as a means to an end."

His larger companion grinned widely, nodding his approval. "In this case, for monetary gain and your own sadistic pleasure."

For just a second, the unkempt mugger gave the two strangers a bewildered look. "Are you two fuckers *crazy*?" he asked, hesitating in his attack while his knife dripped Pete's blood onto the dark pavement. His beady eyes stared out from underneath a hoodie, flickering back and forth between Kant and his larger companion. Neither of them looked nearly as physically intimidating as Pete; both of them were grey-haired and built like librarians.

"Crazy?" Kant scoffed, advancing on the mugger. "We're philosophers. The *craziest*." He danced to the side as the thug charged forward knife-first. Kant's cane snapped downwards and found the younger man's kneecap with a resounding *crack*. The thug screamed and fell gracelessly to the ground, clutching at his ruined joint. Without a word, Kant hopped over his body and turned into the alleyway. Four sets of eyes met his entrance; three terrified and one hopeful.

Patty broke free and ran to Pete, falling to her knees as the second gentlemen followed behind. Her hands went to Pete's bloody chest, searching and finding…nothing? "You're…okay?" she asked with surprise, catching Pete's eyes. There was plenty of blood, but she couldn't find any wounds. Blinking slowly, the new god stared blankly at his friend.

"…what?" Pete paused, looking down at Patty's hands on his bloody chest. "Oh. *Oh*. Yeah, I'm fine. I was just thinking, but…you interrupted me." He seemed annoyed with her, and Patty recoiled from him. Tilting his head upwards, Pete looked past Patty to the large man standing behind her. "How can you interfere?" he asked, nodding at the darkness of the alley. "Free will…" he murmured under his breath. In the shadows, Kant's cane danced back and forth and three boys screamed.

The larger man laughed heartily, shaking his head. His face was clean-cut and smooth, and his cheeks glowed red in the cold of the night. "They have been free for long enough, I think, Mister Machal," he replied. "None of us are truly free. Not even you." Pete wore a baffled expression. "But I forget my courtesies," he added, bowing deeply. "I am David Hume. It's a pleasure to make your acquaintance, although I must apologize for all of his." He gestured breezily towards the alley and at the crippled man behind him. "In truth, I had been watching for...ah, hm, more serious complications. The possibility of *this* kind of trouble skipped my mind." Hume shrugged.

"A welcome diversion," Kant said as he strode from the darkness, Mr. James' beaten body held in his arms. "This man should be thankful for our help, at least." He knelt next to Hume, lowering Mr. James to the sidewalk. "Do you have time to heal him before Russell gets here?"

Hume's eyes scanned over Mr. James and he nodded. "Yes," answered Hume as he lowered himself to one knee, pressing his hands against the semi-conscious man. Mr. James' flesh began to knit and heal, bruises faded and his eyes flickered with awareness. "That should do it. Good as new," he said with a sly smile. "Perhaps even a little bit better." Patty watched Hume with amazement. Pete, on the other hand, felt more than a bit jealous; he had thought that his power was *special*.

"Thank god," Stephen croaked, pulling himself to his feet with his own strength. He looked between the four strangers in front of him and glanced only for a moment back at the broken bodies in the shadowy alley.

Kant dipped his head. "The *god* was of little help to you, I'm afraid, but I was happy to help."

Stephen didn't understand, but he knew better than to linger in the company of such terrible, powerful men. "I appreciate it," he said, gathering his coat around him and checking his pockets for his belongings. He had seen many an ass-kicking in his day—even participated in more than a few brawls as a young man—but Stephen James had never seen anything like the short, ugly fight in the alley. Kant had to be older and smaller than Stephen, but he moved too fast for it. Far too fast, Stephen thought to himself, too fast to even be human. Nobody moved like that. He cleared his throat. "Thank-you again, but I have to get home to my wife," he explained. "I'm sure she's worried sick for me." Nobody objected as he hurried away towards the bus stop far in the distance, clutching his briefcase close to his chest. Stephen James was old, but he was also wise enough not to meddle in things far beyond his understanding.

Once Stephen was gone, Kant and Hume both focused their attention on Pete. He looked back at them awkwardly, unaccustomed to such scrutiny. Even more worrisome to Pete was his inability to read the strangers; his godly knowledge failed to yield anything about the two men before him. Pete could not help but wonder if, perhaps, they were also gods. But gods or not, he knew that their arrival could not be accidental. Pete cleared his throat. "You did this, didn't you?" he asked accusingly, narrowing his eyes.

David Hume shrugged his heavy shoulders. "Yes," he admitted. "We did."

"Why? How?" pressed Pete, rising to his feet before the two men. He didn't trust them.

Hume looked down at the ornate silver watch on his wrist. "Soon," he promised. "It will be safer once we are on our way. I suspect others will come looking for you now." Slowly, he tapped the glass face of his watch twice and the world itself seemed to give a little jump. "There. Better. Russell should be here momentarily to pick us up."

"No," grunted Pete and everyone turned to look at Pete. His refusal had been sharp and sudden. Uncharacteristic, thought Patty. "I'm not going anywhere. Tell me what you did to me. *Now.*" Kant straightened up, drumming his fingers against the black wood of his cane, but did not respond. "I said," Pete repeated icily, "*tell me wha...*" He doubled over and gagged violently. Purple smoke spilled from his mouth and twisted in the breeze, stinking of perfume and lies. Hume was beside him in a moment, holding the young god as he wheezed and choked.

Kant's left eyebrow arced curiously, but that was all of the thin man which moved. "That's not right," he said, studying Pete from where he stood. Another puff of smoke dissipated into the air as Hume thumped Pete's back. "Although it does smell lovely. Like fine perfume."

"Get off of me!" exclaimed Pete as he shoved Hume away. "You did this," he said accusingly. "I *know* it."

Hume waved his hands in front of him and protested. "No, no. Your godhood, yes. But this strange smoke..." he trailed off and shook his head. "This is not our doing."

"I think he's telling the truth, Pete," said Patty. Her voice softened. "They saved my life when…" She looked down at the ground and didn't finish her thought aloud.

Pete stared at Patty. "You're right," he conceded at last. "They did." Hume gave a long sigh of relief. "But I still want to know why—and *how*—they made me into a god." Arms crossed in front of his chest, Pete gave Hume a wary look. "When is your man going to get here?"

A smile on his face, Hume tapped the face of his watch once more. It made a soft *whirr*-ing noise then stopped with a sharp *click*. "Right about now." Headlights cut through the darkness as a polished black Aston-Martin sedan turned the corner. Patty held her hand up to shield her eyes as the car rolled to a stop next to them and the driver's side door opened.

The man that stepped out of the sports-car looked almost nothing like his colleagues. Bertrand Russell wore a suit like Kant and Hume, but his was of modern design and exquisitely tailored; the charcoal grey fabric fit his body snugly, accented by a deep lavender tie. Moreover, he appeared to be a few decades younger than Kant, the only hint of his actual age lay in Russell's magnificent and well-groomed moustache, a style never seen in the modern era.

"I see we have some guests," began Russell as he strolled around the front of the car, his dark eyes lingering for a moment too long on Patty. "You should have told me to bring a bus, Hume."

"I did, however, tell you to be discrete," said Hume matter-of-factly. "How many people in this city can afford a car like this?"

Rolling his eyes, Russell shook his head. "And I suppose you'd expect me to show up in some beat-up Volvo?" Hume smiled; he liked that idea.

Kant strolled over to the curb, leaning down as he inspected the car. "It is *quite* nice," he said, turning to look back at Russell. "You reproduced it with great fidelity. You're improving." He nodded to himself, a wide grin spreading across his face. "And I'm driving."

"My pleasure," replied Russell, tossing the keys through the air to Kant. "It took a few intimate hours test-driving one of these before

I could get the design right. If all else fails, I think we could make great money selling these, eh?"

Patty's eyes were wide. "You…made it?" she asked, staring at the car then Russell in turn. "With magic?"

"I wouldn't call it magic, per se, but yes," answered Russell, twirling his finger in the air before Patty. From nowhere a red rose appeared, dropping gently down into her hands. She gasped then applauded.

Reaching aside, Patty held up her purse for Russell to see — Lime peeked her head over to top, studying the newcomer's mustache with her bright, emerald eyes. "Pete made this for me," she explained as Lime mewed proudly.

"Why, we're just two peas in a pod then, aren't we Pete?" Russell laughed. Pete glared at him with a mixture of rage and intense jealousy. Russell's smile faded. "I did neglect to introduce myself, however. I am Bertrand Russell." He extended his hand to Pete, who reluctantly grasped it. They shook hands for only the briefest of moments. "We do need to get moving. There are other things out here in the night, and most of them are far less charming than I."

Pete grunted unhappily. Becoming a god had been a shock, but ultimately a pleasant one — it had been hard for Pete not to think of himself as quite special. But then he had run in to Kant, Hume and Russell. Pete's omnipotence was incomplete yet he knew that the three strangers were not mere mortals. They had power — real power, perhaps even greater than his own. That fact itched uncomfortably in the back of his mind; no god was without his pride.

"Fine." Pete looked warily at the car. Through the window, he saw Kant fiddling with the controls in the driver's seat. "We'll go with you for now. But I expect answers."

"Yes, yes, of course," Russell said, holding open the rear door for Patty and making to sit next to her.

Hume grabbed his partner's shoulder, pulling him back and pointing towards the front seat. "Up front."

Russell protested. "Oh come on, do you really think they want you squeezed in the back?" He gestured expansively at Hume's figure. "You're, ah…"

"*Robust.*" Hume finished his sentence for him, leaning in close to whisper. "And I'd be happy to sit up front if I thought you could behave yourself around a woman. Up. Front." Russell grumbled but complied, and Hume wedged himself in to the back seat after Pete.

Pete found himself wedged uncomfortably between Patty and Hume in the rear; holding onto his knees and ducking his head, he tried unsuccessfully not to block the rear-view mirror. Not a position suited to a god, Pete thought, before bitterly reminding himself that he simply wasn't that special. The three gentlemen around him were at least his equals; despite his budding omniscience, all that Pete knew of them were their names and the fact that Hume had no business whatsoever sitting in the back seat of a sedan with two other passengers.

Kant turned the wheel to the left and pulled out from the curb, humming a tune under his breath as they accelerated and made for the west. The rest of the passengers sat in an awkward silence; only Patty seemed undisturbed. She sat turned to the side, holding Lime up between her hands as they both watched the city lights roll by outside the tinted windows.

However, Pete's cramped and undignified position sorely tried his already thin patience. "You promised me answers," he said, looking sideways at Hume, who had the poor luck of being squashed between an irritable godling and the door. "Who are you? What did you *do* to me?" he asked angrily. Patty lowered Lime back in to her lap and reached over to put a hand on Pete's knee. She couldn't remember him *ever* being so confrontational. He ignored her gesture.

"That's quite complicated, Pete," Hume began. "However, if everything goes as planned...we made you into a god." Outside the car, the familiar landscape of downtown began to fade away as Kant merged on to the freeway.

"No, really? A god?" fumed Pete sarcastically. "I didn't fucking notice." Russell turned from the front seat, looking warily at Pete.

Hume held up his hands defensively. "I'm sorry; I didn't mean to offend you..."

"By treating me like a child? Even Patty could see what you did and she's the least of all of us!" Offended, Patty gave Pete a cross look and quickly withdrew her hand from his knee. "I want to know *how*. And I want to know *why*. I have been patient long enough! You're going to tell me or I'm *stopping* this car."

Russell spoke up before Hume could respond, his voice low and deadly serious. "You aren't in any position to make demands of us," he said, pointing a finger back at Pete. "We are here to help you – and hopefully, convince you to help us. But if this is how it's going to be, don't think we won't pull this car over and take *back* what we gave you." Pete ground his teeth, staring back Russell with fury in his eyes – but he didn't move.

"We do desperately want your friendship," Hume added, looking to Pete and nodding. "And I promise you that all will be explained once we get to safety."

Pete coughed slightly – more purple smoke. He swallowed hard, trying to get the bitter taste out of his mouth and clear his mind. "I...yes, I'm sorry," he said at last, hanging his head. "I don't know why I'm acting like this. I feel so sick..." Hume frowned.

Russell looked to Kant. "Was there anything unusual about those kids in the alley?"

Kant shook his head. "Not *that* sort of unusual, no. They were just a bunch of punks."

"Did you interact with anyone else after leaving the bar, Pete?" Russell asked, studying him.

"Ah..." Pete winced and coughed slightly, screwing up his face in thought. "I think...someone? It's hard to remember." His eyes narrowed and he looked up suddenly. "Why do *you* want to know?"

Russell ignored the question, afraid of provoking him further. Instead, he looked to Hume. "Someone got to him. This isn't right."

"I'm inclined to agree." Hume leaned forward, looking around Pete to address Patty. "He isn't...usually like this, is he?" She shook her head. "And did you see anyone with him?" Again, she shook her head.

"Don't you *dare* ignore *me!*" Pete bellowed. The car shook with his voice and Patty made to reach out to him but drew back, afraid. "I am a god!" His eyes glimmered weirdly and he spoke in an ancient tongue. "V'rash ag it—*hrrrk!*"

In a split second Patty screamed, Hume reached across to grab Pete's wrist and Russell gestured towards the backseat. The material of the cushion behind Pete's head twisted and sprang in to fluid motion, wrapping around his face and stifling him utterly. The godling struggled for a moment then fell still, the lower half of his face covered with an impenetrable black mask.

Russell let out a long, shaky sigh. "That...was close. Fucking close."

"Where did he learn *that?*" Kant hissed anxiously, glancing between the road and Pete.

"Get us to the mansion immediately," Hume ordered, reaching around Pete to take Patty's hand. She looked at him fearfully. "He's going to be fine, Patty, I promise. Pete was going to say something *very* bad." Both of them looked to Pete. His face spoke well enough even though his mouth was stilled; tears ran down Pete's face as he stared at Patty with an expression of utter horror. Slowly, he shook his head back and forth.

"Are you sure you didn't see anyone with him, Patty?" Hume asked gently, squeezing her hand. "Anyone at all?"

"N-no," Patty said, shaking her head and wiping the tears from her eyes. "I didn't see anyone. But...maybe..."

"Maybe...what?"

"When I came out of the bar after Pete, he was staring down the street into the distance. And...he jumped when I touched him," she explained. "He said something like: 'What? Gone?' I didn't think anything of it then; he was just acting so strange in general..." Hume nodded for her to continue, his face bearing a grim expression. "But I couldn't have been away from him for more than thirty seconds. And there *wasn't* anyone out there on the street."

"Not that you saw," Kant interjected. "But *somebody* got to him." Patty looked to Pete, snuggling up against him and giving a little sob. Still silent, Pete leaned his head against her and closed his eyes.

"We will make this right, I promise," Hume offered. "I don't mean for either of you to come to any harm."

"Why Pete?" Patty turned her eyes back to Hume. "Why did you do this to him?" Beside her, Pete fluctuated unpredictably between tears and rage, all the while struggling furiously against Russell's bonds.

"We didn't do *this* to him," Hume replied, watching as a whiff of purple smoke seeped out from under Pete's mask. "But…I imagine that's not what you meant. We chose your friend because he is a genuinely good man, Patty. He has strength of will uncommon in mortals, yet he remains virtuous. With the power we can grant him, he may turn the tide of battle in our favor."

Patty's expression hardened. "Battle?" She ground her teeth together. "You think he's going to agree to be your weapon?"

"Our weapon?" Hume shook his head. "No. Not *our* weapon – humanity's weapon. We exist to protect you," he explained, reaching out to put a hand on Patty's shoulder. "And his power will serve the same purpose."

"Protect me? From what? From who?"

Kant laughed suddenly. "From the gods." The car bounced suddenly as Kant turned it on to a gravel pathway, stone crunching noisily outside. Patty leaned back towards the window, watching as they rode past a set of ornamental gardens – and towards an imposing stone mansion. To her eyes, the building was ancient; pale green moss snaked up marble columns and through the deep, shadowy clefts in the cut-stone walls. At last the car rolled to a halt.

"Welcome to the Philosoplex," Kant said proudly, wasting no time as he opened the rear door and dragged himself out of the cramped rear seat. "It is my greatest creation and, more importantly, our base of operations." Clutching her purse—and Lime—to her chest, Patty stared at the grounds in awe.

"It's beautiful, but…" She looked back at the car, empty except for Pete. Still tied down in the back seat, he stared out the window silently. "What about Pete? I know there's nothing I can do, but please don't hurt him." Hume met her eyes and nodded.

"I won't hurt him, you have my word." He looked to Russell then back at the car. "Would you help him out, Bertrand?"

"Sure." Russell leaned in to the back seat and came out with a remarkably compliant Pete, who stood on his own next to the philosopher.

Hume smiled and approached the pair, holding his hands up in front of him. "Pete, listen to me," he said seriously, a dull *thrum*-ing noise slowly rising from the earth. "I mean you no harm, but someone has poisoned you. I am going to extricate the toxin and cast it beyond the dimensional well of the Philosoplex." The pulsing sound in the air waxed stronger as Hume put his left hand on Pete's chest. "All that you need to do is stand still."

Pete's body quaked once as Hume touched him, but then became as still as stone, frozen in space and time. Momentarily, the purple smoke began to seep from his every pore, hissing and twisting in the enchanted pulses of the air. As it rose, it coiled against itself and swelled into an orb of gaseous lavender. For just a second, it seemed to Patty as if the smoke tried to break free – it churned against Hume's magic, fighting the invisible chains cast about it.

Hume was unmoved by the resistance, and he spoke a deep note, deeper than any sound Patty had ever heard or even thought she *could* hear. He touched the thumb of his right hand to his ring finger and spoke the note once again – and suddenly, the mass of malignant purple fog froze. In a blink of an eye, the smoke vanished and Pete sagged forward against Hume's left hand, breathing hard through his constricting mask.

"Undo the binding," Hume ordered and Russell quickly obliged. The black mask made a soft *pop*-ing noise and fell away from Pete's face. "I trust you feel substantially better?"

Pete groaned, still trying to catch his breath as he leaned on Hume. "Fuck's sake," he whispered, holding on to the philosopher for balance. "I feel…like I just vomited…for days…" Before he could even finish his sentence, Patty was at his side, throwing her arms around Pete.

"Are you okay?" she asked, squeezing him tightly. "You were scaring me, Pete." Patty turned to look at Hume. "Thank you so much." The philosopher nodded with a smile on his face.

Pete slowly regained his balance, returning Patty's hug. "Yeah, I'm sorry," he said, shaking his head. "I don't know what they did to me, but…wow." Reaching up, Pete rubbed his head slowly. "I've still got a hell of a headache. But I guess that's true after every Friday night." Everyone shared a laugh.

"I imagine you're as eager to hear an explanation for all of this as I am to give it," said Hume, gesturing behind himself towards the grand oaken doors of the mansion. "We'll be more comfortable inside. If you would follow me?"

"Sure thing," Pete answered. He followed the three men up the polished marble stairs with Patty on his arm, looking all around him at the scenery. "Where exactly *are* we?" Pete Machal had lived in the area for nearly a decade, and not once had he ever heard of such a fantastic old mansion. "Some sort of…dimensional bubble? We can't be in the real world."

"Heh, gods are such quick studies," Kant laughed, pulling open the front door and holding it for the assembled party.

"You're half correct," answered Hume, stepping aside as he let Russell, Pete and Patty enter before him. "The Philosoplex exists within a dimensional construct of my own design; it is both within the real world, as you call it, and without." Pete paused next to Hume, reaching out to run his hand over the smooth wooden door. "I trust that since even you, a nascent god, are having difficulty with it…you will believe me when I simply say that it's *quite* complicated."

"I don't doubt it," Pete laughed, falling in beside Hume as the door *creak*-ed shut behind him. "I heard what you were telling Patty in the car, you know. A war against the gods, huh?" He shook his head. "I feel like an idiot even saying that out loud." Up ahead, Patty was engrossed in Russell's explanation of the oil paintings which lined the entry hallway. Pete tapped Hume on the shoulder, stopping him as the rest went on without them. "Look, before we go any further, I want you to know something."

Hume raised an eyebrow in curiosity, stopping with Pete. "Hm?"

"You saved my ass back there – and if I was going to do what I think I was going to do, you saved Patty too." Hume gave a slight nod of his head. "So I just want to be straight with you: I'm willing to help you out, but you know better than I do how this is going to go. So…"

He took a deep breath. "So make sure nothing happens to Patty, okay?"

"You have my word," Hume said solemnly, offering Pete his hand. "On my life and the lives of my colleagues, I will not let any harm come to her." Pete took Hume's hand and shook and firmly. "Good. You *are* the man I thought you were, Pete. Follow me," continued Hume, turning to lead the way towards the open door beyond. "We need to speak of gods, and of life and death. And of the end of eternity."

By the time Pete and Hume caught up to Patty, she was already seated with Russell and Kant on the near side of a grand oak table. The room stretched far overhead to a thirty-foot ceiling and two stories of balconies overlooked the large chamber. Patty twisted around in her chair to smile at Pete at he entered.

"Isn't it beautiful?" she asked.

Pete nodded, letting his eyes—and his mind—flicker over the room. The walls were lined with endless bookshelves holding countless tomes; while some of the books were new and neatly-bound, most were ancient and tattered works. He inhaled slowly, letting the titles and contents of the works spill over his mind like a wave. "Impressive," he said, returning Patty's smile and approaching the table.

"That would be an excellent trick," snapped a deep voice from the hallway behind Pete, "if you were a librarian." Pete gave a jump and turned, finding himself face to face with a magnificently mustachioed man in a silver wheelchair. "I trust our creation can do better than reading quickly," the rude man said to Hume, wheeling himself past Pete without an introduction. "Or we are all well and truly screwed."

Irritation flickered across Pete's face, but he straightened himself up and offered his hand. "I don't believe that I've met you," he said. "I'm Pete Machal. And you are...?"

The wheelchair stopped with a sudden *click*. Its occupant looked up and fixed Pete with an incredulous, withering stare. "Has your omniscience gone *dull*, child?" He laughed and shook his head, snubbing Pete's hand and rolling himself to the far end of the table. "You know perfectly well who I am."

"Nietzsche!" Russell shouted, slamming the flat of his palm on the table. "Behave yourself with our guests."

Friedrich Nietzsche chuckled at the rebuke, the whiskers of his moustache bristling. "You bring me a *god* and a *woman*, and you expect…what? Polite words and a curtsey?" He shook his head. "But enough of that. I promised to see this idiot plan through to the end." Everyone at the table frowned at Nietzsche, who obliged them with a smile as he drank in their displeasure.

"Nietzsche," Patty said slowly. "Weren't you…I mean, aren't you a famous philosopher?"

Hume interjected before Nietzsche could open his mouth again. "Yes," he replied, "he is quite famous. No doubt you've heard his name a great many times before." That seemed to placate Nietzsche somewhat, and he held his tongue.

"Actually," Pete said to Patty, "they're *all* famous philosophers."

Patty made a surprised noise and blushed. "Oh! I'm sorry. I thought all of your names did sound vaguely familiar."

Two seats to her right, Kant slapped his forehead with his hand and groaned. "A lifetime of work, and…" He sighed. "That makes me feel wonderful, thank you." Patty stammered an apology under her breath.

Hume cleared his throat, drawing everyone's attention. "I believe we have all been introduced," he suggested, drawing himself up to his feet. He walked slowly to the head of the table, his hands clasped behind his back. "Before we address our immediate strategic problems, I owe Pete an explanation for turning him in to a god and otherwise ruining his Friday night." Pete smiled politely at Hume, even as he felt a little itch in the back of his throat.

"As you heard before," Hume gestured broadly at the assembled philosophers, "we are at war with the gods. And we are *losing*. Up until tonight, we sought to match our strength against theirs. We are not without our own power. While we have won many victories, we have also lost most of our original number." Pete and Patty felt suddenly, acutely aware of the dozen empty chairs sitting around the conference table. "Our ability to continue in this way is…reaching its limit. I fear that another battle gone badly will see the end of us and with that, the end of humanity as you know it. We need to strike a final, decisive blow against the gods."

"Killing the gods, one at a time, was a misguided strategy. Humanity constantly invents new gods for itself, raising up another twisted paragon which we must then strike down. In order to win this struggle, we must not only destroy the gods which still walk the Earth – but more importantly, guarantee that no god will ever rise again." His exposition paused, Hume chuckled. "Ironically, *that* requires the power of a full god. So we have made you, Pete, into a god for that very purpose. We need you to re-weave the fabric of the universe and forever deny divine power any foothold here."

Pete leaned back in his chair, his arms crossed in front of him and a vaguely dissatisfied expression on his face. "That's part of an explanation," he said slowly. "But I still have a hell of a lot of questions. One big one, though…*why do you have to kill the gods?*"

Kant laughed dismissively, as if Pete's question was the stupidest he had ever heard. "Why do we have to kill the gods?" Kant repeated, arching an eyebrow at Pete. "Because they are *gods*. They hold the power to destroy the universe on a whim, to unmake time and unravel the history of countless billions of human lives. They are abominations: creatures that can turn mere *desire* into *reality*."

"Plus, they tend to go quite mad," added Russell casually. Pete made a little choking noise and Patty looked suddenly alarmed.

Hume spoke up quickly. "Don't worry," he reassured Pete, "you are at no risk of madness. We will be done with this before you are in any danger."

"What about that crap I was coughing up earlier?" Pete asked pointedly. The mere thought of the purple smoke made his stomach turn in painful, familiar ways.

"Indeed, Russell mentioned your difficulties," Nietzsche interjected. "How was our security compromised so quickly? And who was it?"

"I don't know!" Hume protested in frustration. "We spoke with Socrates before setting off after Pete, and he seemed to think everything was just fine." Under his breath, Nietzsche muttered something derogatory about his Greek colleague. Hume glared at him with uncharacteristic anger.

"And you don't remember anything, Pete?" Kant asked, his fingers pressed together in front of him. "Anything at all?"

"No! I already told you, I don't remember anything!" Pete shot back. "I thought we already dealt with that. Right?"

"Right," Hume answered, although he did not sound entirely convinced.

"Then how about we get back to explaining what the hell is going on," argued Pete. "I'm still not sure why you need to kill the gods. Or why there are gods to begin with. And what are you?" He waved his hand around the table at the assembled philosophers. "You turn me into a god—without bothering to ask my permission—then carry me off to a hidden dimension and ask me to destroy the rest of the gods. Could I please have some fucking answers? How do I know you aren't the bad guys in all of this?"

For six tense seconds, nobody spoke. "That's a good question," Hume reluctantly admitted. "It is no excuse, but you have to understand that this is a battle we have been fighting for a long, long time. You are the culmination of a plan that has been centuries in the making; Sartre's transformative potion, which you consumed, took over two hundred and fifty years to perfect." Pete did not appear satisfied. "I beg your patience while I explain. What I mean to say is that we take much of the present situation for granted; all of this, while new and shocking to you, is utterly familiar to us. Your questions are perfectly sensible, but...ah..." Hume trailed off, looking somewhat befuddled as he searched for the right words.

To everyone's surprise, Nietzsche spoke up to assist Hume. "It is as if you were to ask a fish what it is like to be in water," he explained, reaching up to give his moustache a few thoughtful tugs.

"Precisely, Nietzsche, thank you," Hume said appreciatively. "I did not anticipate how difficult it would be to summarize for you, Pete, and in a comprehensible way, what it is we do. And why, if you care anything for humanity's survival, you must help us."

"Actually, we don't have to *summarize* it for him," pointed out Russell. "He is a god now, after all. Why don't you simply let him have a brief peek in to your mind?" Kant nodded approvingly. "I think our history is self-explanatory, and quite convincing."

Like the rest of the philosophers, Pete had overlooked that possibility. "That would make things a lot easier," he admitted. "If you don't mind, that is?"

Hume laughed and shook his head from side to side. "No, no," he chuckled, "I don't mind at all. We have nothing to hide from you. I wish you had thought of this sooner, Russell." Pulling himself out of his chair, Hume walked around the table to stand behind Pete. The young god turned sideways in his chair, looking up at Hume's outstretched hand. "Take my hand, Pete. Drink deep of my knowledge, and I trust that your questions will all be answered." Pete Machal hesitated for only a second before he reached up to grasp Hume's hand. Immediately, Pete began to pour through the memories of the philosopher.

"No…no…NO!" The Creator slammed both of her fists on the desk, shaking the floor of the library. "This isn't right! I still…this still changes everything!" She looked around at the philosophers sitting before her, her face twitching as the assembled men exchanged concerned looks with each other. "I made you, and then you fix the world! But then *I* fix the world! I can't! *I can't do anything!*" The Creator suddenly howled, throwing her face into her hands. She sobbed into her hands, her grey hair hanging about her head in a mess.

Hume cleared his throat. "My lady, *someone* has to do *something*. If you don't put an end to this cycle of godhood and madness, then it is only a matter of time before humanity is snuffed out," he argued cautiously.

Three seats to Hume's right, Descartes was the next to speak. "He is right, my lady. Pure luck is all that has kept the mortal world alive thus far. Resurrecting us was a step in the right direction, but you must take decisive action *now*." He knew, as the others did, that the Creator's sanity was quickly unraveling.

"Action?!" The Creator howled the word, shaking her head violently. "You speak of action – but what of consequence? If I do something, then I may do everything! NO!" She kicked her chair backwards, rising to her feet and surveying the assembled philosophers. Her ancient, wrinkled face twitched and shuddered erratically. "This was a mistake; *you* were a mistake! I must unmake you, before…" She froze in mid-sentence, her entire body trembling. No-one dared to speak.

Then, with a flash, her eyes opened wide. "That's IT!" The Creator laughed, slapping her forehead. "Why did I not see this sooner? I know the answer now…*yes*! It's so clear…so very clear." Her creations watched silently, alternating between hope and dread as they waited for her revelation. "There is a way to end this…all of this…without violating free will! I only need to return to the beginning! Don't you see it?!"

Hume swallowed hard, but there was no time for him to respond before his Creator continued. "If I prevent…yes…if I prevent humanity from ever existing, so too do I prevent free will! I cannot violate that which does not yet exist! I can go back and unmake everything—everything!—at the very beginning, and there will be nothing left to *ruin* with my touch." Abruptly she stopped, staring down the long table at the philosophers. "…what? I am right, am I not?"

"I'm sorry, my lady," Hume said quietly, the eyes of the other philosophers bearing down on him. "This has gone too far already." Around the table, his colleagues nodded their assent. "You brought us back for our wisdom, but there is only one answer left. Forgive my insolence." The Creator stared at Hume blankly, lost somewhere in the chasm between confusion and madness. "Kill her."

David Hume leaned heavily on Russell's shoulder, staring over the field of corpses. Thousands of them were spread amongst the courtyard of the Masjid al-Haram, the broken bodies all dressed in white. He coughed violently and something twisted in his chest; a broken rib, by the feel of it, perhaps more than one. "Did he get inside?" Hume asked, staring at the elaborate black architecture of the Kaaba. All around him, the clear midday sky flashed with deep blue, otherworldly lightning. Russell made to answer, but his voice was lost amongst the rolling thunder.

She had beautiful, deep brown eyes that glistened with tears. Tanya stared up at the ceiling and sighed. "So I don't have any choice about this, do I?" she asked at last.

"I'm afraid not," Hume replied, his voice nearly shaking with emotion. "I hate to ask this of you. Especially given the circumstances."

Tanya looked back at the philosopher, then towards the window outside her Johannesburg flat. Two more of them were waiting outside, she knew, just in case she was not moved by Hume's words. "Funny how it ends this way, isn't it?" she asked, looking down at where the sharp fluorescent light shone off her dark skin. Hume made a painful smile. "You promised me that she won't come to any harm. All I wanted to do was bring her back."

"We don't want anything with her," Hume explained for what felt like the fifth time. "A single resurrection is not going to end the world. Your sister is free to enjoy her renewed life."

"Without me." Hume didn't answer, and looked as if he was going to burst in to tears at any moment. "That wasn't fair," apologized Tanya. "I understand why I have to go. It's just…" She bit her lip. "No, I can't say it isn't fair. A life for a life."

Two minutes later, Hume strode through the apartment door out in to the warm summer evening. He hurried past Russell and Kant, ignoring them entirely as he made to lose himself in the crowd. Still, their voices caught up to him as he walked away.

"Poor bastard," sighed Russell.

"You'd almost think it would be easier on him if *we* just killed them," Kant observed. "I cannot imagine how he sits there and convinces them to do it themselves…"

"It will *work* this time, David, I swear it," Sartre promised. He gestured at the two containers on the conference table. Hume leaned forward in his seat, staring at the bottles: one, a large, heavy wine bottle as black as obsidian and the other, a tiny, fluted vial of unblemished whiteness. "The effect should be immediate, although it will take some time for the subject to reach its full potential."

"But," cautioned Hume, "the subject has to drink this concoction of their own free will."

Sartre nodded quickly. "Yes, that was part of the problem before. Free will is essential to the transformation; we cannot force godhood upon someone."

"But we can trick them in to it."

A grin spread across Sartre's face. "Yes."

"And how do you propose we get someone to drink this?" Hume asked. "You told me there are *very* specific criteria for the subject. We will need to survey a great number of people, and then selectively administer this draught to the ideal candidate." The philosopher shook his head dejectedly. "People are not going to line up for a chance to drink some strange, exotic mixture."

Sartre laughed loudly. "You haven't read much about the modern night life, have you?"

Pete let go of Hume's hand almost immediately, sucking in a deep breath of air. He made a little, wordless noise then closed his eyes; his mind was not yet entirely used to learning in such a manner. The rest of the table watched him, all except Hume – he knew that it had worked, and casually returned to his seat at the head of the conference table.

"Amazing," mumbled Pete quietly.

"Your questions have been answered, then?" Russell asked.

Pete smiled affirmatively. "Yeah," he admitted. "There's still a lot I don't know, I'm sure. But…" He stopped mid-sentence, snapping his fingers as he suddenly remembered something. "One thing. All of Hume's memories – how long was that? It seemed...too long? I have no sense of when any of those events took place."

"You're very observant, Pete," Hume said, clearly impressed. "While I tried to present you with a narrative of sorts, the events you saw cannot be neatly placed in a timeline." Pete mulled Hume's words and nodded thoughtfully, as if the explanation made perfect sense.

"Excuse me," interjected Patty. "What does that mean?"

"Oh!" Hume chuckled. "Pardon me. Gods are notoriously fond of playing with time. I have done my best to keep this universe as it would be without their interference, but...there have been *many* revisions. More than even I can keep track of."

"Revisions?" she asked, only slightly less confused.

"He means to say," Russell chimed in, "that the timeline of this universe is utterly fucked. You see, when a god changes the history of the world, we change it back and try to paste things back together as if nothing happened. Hume is quite talented in the manipulation of time and causation, but even he can only do so much. I am not talking about one or two little changes – gods have *repeatedly* attempted to rewrite the history of the world to their liking. Entire alternate timelines. Mass deletions of whole epochs." He shook his head sadly. "Madness. So much has been lost."

"Indeed," agreed Hume. "I have salvaged as much as I can, but the fragmentary nature of the timeline should be proof enough of the danger of the gods." A grim expression crept across his face. "But we have pressing business, now that our aims have been explained."

"The interloper," said Kant. He had been sitting quietly the entire time, seemingly uninterested in the tedious job of exposition. "If Pete does not remember who assaulted him, then we must discover the truth through other means. This individual not only discovered our plan, but laid in wait to ambush Pete – and infected him with *extremely* dangerous magic."

"Even if I don't remember anyone speaking to me," Pete suggested, "couldn't we use the same trick as before? If Hume reads my memories, would he be able to discover anything?"

"Hm." Hume grunted thoughtfully, pulling at his chin. "Perhaps. It would be difficult, after all, to completely erase your memory of any encounter. Gods are not so malleable. But it would be far simpler to hide your memory from you. If it is hidden then, perhaps, I could uncover it."

"Then let's do it," pressed Pete, rising to his feet and walking over to Hume before the philosopher could finish his thought. He extended his hand. "I know what I nearly did to all of you. To myself. And to Patty. That shit isn't going to stand." For the second time that evening, Hume grasped Pete's hand and their two minds met.

Hume stood on the cold street outside Ockham's Kegger. Next to him stood Pete Machal, frozen in place as he stared across the pavement to the darkened apartments beyond. The philosopher reached out and gingerly pressed on Pete's shoulder – there was no response. "What did you see, Pete?" he asked, following Pete's eyes to the apartments. Hume looked searchingly at the buildings. "No, not there," he concluded, turning to look back at the bar. "Inside?"

His hand wrapped around the door handle and pulled, but the door did not open. "Curious," mumbled Hume and tried again. It remained stuck, but the iron handle grew icy to the touch and Hume drew back. "No, no," he growled, quickly looking back to Pete. "NO!" Pete was gone -- along with the city beyond him. All that remained was a starlit emptiness, stretching off beyond Hume's sight. "This isn't a memory!" he cried, feeling Ockham's Kegger growing over him, stretching towards the sky as its thousand lights twinkled with foul intent. Hume grasped his lapel with his left hand and made an elaborate motion with his right, making to sever the connection with Pete's mind. Nothing happened.

The philosopher staggered back away from the bar, watching as it began to bulge like an overinflated balloon. "What is this magic?!" he howled. "I purged the corruption from him!" Ockham's Kegger gave a long, hissing laugh as it began to rupture at the seams, purple gas venting violently. Hume called forth his power, casting his considerable will against the swirling, noxious tendrils that sought for him. The smoke staggered and was driven back, but the pillar of gas before Hume had waxed larger than he had thought conceivable. It shuddered on the wind and twisted, changing into the form of a shimmering purple dragon. The beast threw back its head and swallowed the moon, its tremendous wings blotting out all the stars in the sky as they swept around Hume.

"Verdammt!" Kant cursed as he sprung from his seat, the chair clattering to the floor as he reached for Hume. Within moments of connecting with Pete for a second time, Hume grew deathly pale and Pete began to cough. There was more purple smoke than before—much more, and thicker—and Kant staggered through the cloud. His hands closed on Hume and grabbed the seated man by his jacket, hauling him backwards away from Pete's grasp. As Hume fell, pulled away from the Pete, the link between their minds was severed.

Patty cried out as Hume and his chair hit the floor with a loud crash. Vaulting over the table, Russell tackled Pete sideways and both men went down into the whirling fog. Pete was belching more smoke at an alarming rate and Russell did the only thing he could; Russell clasped both hands firmly over Pete's mouth and nose, holding his jaw shut to stem the flow. Pete gagged violently on the sickness within him, his eyes went wide, and he slammed Russell hard in the chest with his right fist. The philosopher was launched bodily through the air, trailing purple smoke as he collided with a bookshelf on the far end of the room and went down covered in a heap of leather-bound tomes.

When Pete spoke, the voice that came out of his mouth was not at all his own. "Weaklings!" he yelled in a woman's voice, high and full of fury. "He is mine. *MINE!*" Pete wheeled around, clutching at his head while Russell staggered to his feet. Pete made a gurgling noise, choked, and spoke again in his own voice. "Too...strong..." he gasped, reeling. "Stop me!"

Nietzsche rose effortlessly from his wheelchair and spread his arms wide. There was a deep rumbling all about him and the smoke drew back, hissing and retreating towards Pete. "Stop you?" he asked in a voice filled with rolling thunder. "I will *end* you."

"NO!" Patty screamed, helpless.

Russell grabbed Nietzsche by the shoulder, pulling him backwards. "Do not kill him!" he demanded. Nietzsche snarled and tried to push Russell aside, but the Englishman held his ground.

The two men were equally matched, and Nietzsche struggled to remove himself from Russell's grasp. "Idiot, you don't—" Nietzsche howled.

Pete's scream drowned out the words, shaking the very earth beneath them. He fell backwards and as his feet slipped out beneath him, Pete struggled to see a path out of the mansion. There *was* no path backwards, Pete immediately discovered, no way to retrace the way he had come. His mind spun as he searched desperately for an exit, keenly aware that he had only a fraction of a second before he lost control again. Pete could not feel his heart hammering in his chest; he was working in the moments between beats, building a bridge out of Hume's hidden dimension.

Every possible exit demanded a million calculations and a million exits failed him. He needed an anchor in the real world to return; some *place* with which he was intimately acquainted. Yet Pete had only just become a god and had not spent much time considering the intricacies of inter-dimensional travel. Then the answer came to Pete: his creation of Lime. That miracle had left him with a particularly robust knowledge of that point in the real world. He focused his will on that lonely piece of sidewalk and his corporeal body followed.

The sudden, cold wind surprised him and Pete shivered in a very ungodly fashion, squeezing his arms around him. He was back again on the empty street and alone in the darkness. More importantly, Pete noticed, his head was clear and the smoke was gone – something about his sudden departure must have eased the sickness' hold on him. He was not foolish enough to think he was cured, but it was a welcome reprieve.

Standing on the edge of the sidewalk, Pete chewed thoughtfully on his lip; he could not find the location of the Philosoplex again. It was lost to him. That fact alone did not concern Pete greatly, but Patty was gone, stuck with the philosophers. "God dammit," he grumbled angrily. The irony was lost entirely on the discarded sheet of newspaper drifting by on the wind.

Chapter Three

Who was she? That question ran through Pete's head again and again, always unanswered and unanswerable. She was the voice within the purple smoke, full of an evil and terrible power. For the briefest of moments—when his strength nearly failed in the Philosoplex—Pete had sensed the malefic entity behind the dark magic. But it had been a glimpse and nothing more; Pete gleaned nothing of the creature or her nature.

Yet now that Pete stood far beyond the protection of the philosophers, the sickness within him had eased its grip, its task complete. Pete did not need the power of premonition in order to know what would happen next. She was coming for him. "Fuck, fuck, fuck," he whispered under his breath, his eyes scanning over the darkened buildings looming overhead. "Where are you?" The shadows didn't answer; they were content to wait.

Perhaps, Pete thought, she did not know exactly where he had gone. That had to be true, he concluded immediately. If she knew where he was, then Pete felt certain that she would have come to claim him – for what purpose, he dared not guess. In the earlier moments when her magic touched his mind, Pete understood that she did not fear him in the slightest. She possessed a power far beyond his ability to resist, and all that kept Pete safe was the fact that she had not found him yet.

He broke into a swift walk down the silent streets, chewing thoughtfully on his lip. It was almost certainly too dangerous to use his power again, Pete reluctantly concluded. Even with only a few miracles under his belt, he recognized that the exercise of supernatural power left an unmistakable mark. The woman that pursued him would surely be looking for such tell-tale signs. Pete felt a bead of sweat roll down his forehead, despite the fact that it was half past three on a November morning. He had to calm down.

"Don't panic," Pete whispered, desperately trying to reassure himself. That was no easy task, as his mind whirled through the possible outcomes of his dire situation. He had not yet reached the high pinnacle of omniscience, but Pete was already smarter than he had ever been—smarter than *any* mortal had ever been—by hundreds of times. There were not any happy endings for him; at least, none that were within his own power to achieve. Pete slipped between the moonlit buildings, lost in thought until he found himself once again on the corner of Raca Avenue.

It was only a few short blocks from there to Ockham's Kegger, where Pete might find the rest of the philosophers and perhaps his friends. He paused on the street corner, watching a single blue van pass in front of him. The philosophers were his best chance to resist the woman's power, even if they had been thoroughly outmaneuvered thus far. But returning to Ockham's Kegger was an obvious choice. So obvious, Pete calculated, that it could not have escaped his enemy's preparation. She would be waiting for him at the bar. So why did he hesitate?

"Oh, fuck me," Pete gasped as his eyes widened with understanding. "You're still there, aren't you?" Forgetting his earlier caution, he cast his mind's eye towards Ockham's Kegger, hoping silently that things were not as he feared. The bright and gaudy building sprung up before him, all blinking lights and obvious magical artifice. A thousand strings of spell-work, he thought, all held by…who? An unassuming bartender that wore thick glasses with rounded frames – Jean-Paul Sartre. He silently polished a wine glass, lost in the reflection and his own thoughts.

Pete refocused his vision, pushing aside the convoluted magic of the building itself and confirming his suspicions. His friends were still there, alone in the bar but for the philosopher and the apparitions of fellow patrons. Robert and Wilfred bickered playfully while Rachel slept face-down on the table. Yet there was another man, Pete saw, waiting outside on the street. He stood nearly seven feet tall and had arms the size of small trees, wearing a brilliant white beard that trailed halfway down his chest. And when Pete let his mind's eye rest on Socrates, the ancient sage's eyes lit up and searched through the dark as if to find who watched him, ever-vigilant.

But Socrates was not alone. The shadow beneath his feet twisted in weird ways, a deepening pool of utter blackness. Pete screamed through the psychic void, trying to warn the philosopher. Socrates looked downwards – down into the yawning depth of ten thousand ethereal mouths. Then he fell into the churning dark, disappearing beneath the earth. A fist rose up through the depth and Pete watched the shadow strain against it, drawn thin by Socrates' raw strength. But the philosopher could not prevail as the darkness poured over him, blotting out his resistance and covering the entire street in an unnatural twilight.

Pete Machal watched in horror as the swelling darkness washed up against the wall of Ockham's Kegger, trickling upwards over the red brick. It would take time for the shadow to penetrate the building, time enough for Pete to rush to his friends. But he did not move and one by one, the protective enchantments around Sartre's bar flickered brightly then died. They were his friends, Pete howled inside his head, the closest thing he still had left to a family! He watched them sit inside the bar, oblivious to the creeping doom. Robert. Wilfred. Rachel. Mortals. *Mortals.* So Pete turned south, tears still in his eyes as he walked away.

"He'll come back for you," Hume said earnestly. Patty took a long sip on her cup of tea and looked up at him without a word. "We just have to figure out what happened to him. Some sort of magic, but…" He glanced upwards towards the lights far above them in the vaulted, wooden ceiling of the library. Hume had absolutely no idea what had been done to Pete or by whom.

"You don't need to treat me like a child," Patty mumbled.

Hume looked away from the lights, startled. "What?"

"I said, you don't need to treat me like a *child*," she answered forcefully. Their eyes met. "I'm not some sort of demi-god like you, but I'm not a naïve child or an idiot. Is Pete going to live?"

Hume swallowed uncomfortably. "I have no idea," he admitted, looking away from Patty's cold stare. "The magic that has taken hold of Pete is strong." He waved his right hand dismissively and turned his eyes back to Patty. "But that doesn't matter. I know I can undo what was done to him, if I have a second chance. What worries me is that I haven't seen that *kind* of magic before. Ever. It was completely different than anything I have ever experienced, and I have been in this business for quite a long time."

"Ah." Patty took another slow drink of the tea. The frail porcelain mug shook slightly in her hand. "And what about me? What about Rachel and Wilfred?" She paused. "How do we figure in to your plans?"

"It would be for the best if you stayed here, inside the Philosoplex. The same goes for your friends, who were supposed to arrive with Socrates and Sartre," Hume answered.

"They didn't come."

"No, they did not. I would imagine that Sartre is simply taking longer than anticipated disassembling the bar." Hume took a deep breath. "However, in light of what happened to Pete, I sent Nietzsche to make sure everything is progressing smoothly. Russell will find Pete in the meanwhile."

Patty shot him a sharp look. "I'm not so sure. Nothing else has worked out for you tonight..." She trailed off then stared down into her tea. "Not for Pete, either. What if he's dead? What if *all* of my friends are dead?"

"They aren't. We won't let that happen."

"God! Half of me wants to throw this tea in your face and walk out of here." She took a deep breath. "So supposed to just...sit here and wait? Hope that my friends aren't all dead?"

"Unfortunately, there is nothing else we can do. I regret bringing you into this," Hume acknowledged. "I truly do. Pete did not ask for this burden, nor did any of you. But we needed a human vessel to use the Crisis. It was unavoidable." He reached across the table and took Patty's hand, their eyes meeting. "All I can ask is that you face this bravely, and swear to you, with all the power left in me, that I will see all of you safely through this." Patty nodded quietly and moved to withdraw her hand, but Hume held on and persisted. "You must understand this, Patty: we are losing this fight. Every new god that we must fight, every legion of god-spawned monsters..." Hume squeezed her hand. "We are nearly depleted. It is this or nothing. This, or surrender humanity forever. Do you understand?"

"Yes..." Patty answered softly as Hume let go. "I have to believe you. But it's a lot to take in. Earlier today I was living in a normal world, where the only time I ever even *thought* about gods was when I'd sit in church every Sunday. I don't even know if I really believed. Maybe I did. But now you're telling me that gods exist, they're going to kill us all, and you transformed my ex in to some sort of god-damned magical superweapon." Suddenly she laughed loudly, shaking her head back and forth. "It's ridiculous. All of this."

Hume smiled. "It is quite ridiculous."

"Do you need to go...do something?" Patty asked, looking down at her tea then around the cavernous mansion. "I don't want to keep you with stupid questions if you could be helping Pete."

"I wish I could be doing more," Hume said before draining what remained in his cup. "But I'm a lousy fighter. I give the orders—sometimes—and protect the integrity of the Philosoplex. Valuable roles, perhaps, but frustrating ones in times of crisis." He shrugged. "I'm happy to answer your questions. It might help make this ordeal, to some small extent, easier on you."

"I guess, well..." Patty thought aloud, reaching up to rub her head. "I've got a lot of questions. Pete read your mind and it all seemed to make sense to him, but I'm still lost." Hume motioned for her to continue. "Well, you make it sound like new gods just keep...popping up. Like they just *happen*."

"Ah, yes. Traditionally, you think of one or many gods that have been around forever – ones who are usually responsible for creating the universe and mankind itself."

"Yeah. I'm guessing that isn't how it works."

"Precisely. Our reality is a complicated one; the lawlike and naturalistic universe you're used to is underlain by a complicated supernatural framework. While the specifics are far beyond even me, the basic idea is that *will* and *consciousness* are fundamental parts of the world, not simply byproducts of physical phenomena. Conciousness is a thing, so to speak, that exists as surely and independently as does this table." He gave the table a demonstrative *thump*. "And will is the force that a consciousness exerts on the world around it. Does that make sense?"

Patty nodded slowly. "Yeah. I think so, at least," she agreed. "It sounds a lot like what I've always been taught...that souls exist separate from the body."

"Yes, that's close enough," Hume replied. "Most souls exert their will only through command of their associated physical body. You may will to raise your arm, twitch your nose, or what have you. And while this is arguably only my opinion, that is how things are *meant* to be. Souls are unproblematic so long as they bound to a limited physical vessel, obeying restrictive physical laws."

"And the ones that...aren't bound? Those are the gods?"

"Mhmm. Some souls – do not ask me why *them* and not others, for I do not know – awaken a power to do more than control a body. They bend and eventually break the laws of the universe, untethering themselves from ordinary existence. Not all of them become gods; as with all things, some souls excel more than others. There are petty wizards and psychics, there are even souls with such little power as to be just a bit luckier than probability demands. And of course, there are those who go further – they style themselves as angels or demons, monsters or divine kings. All of these souls are dangerous, but they are still limited and to be brutally honest, usually quite easy to kill." Patty grimaced slightly.

"The dangerous souls," Hume continued in a low voice, leaning across the table towards Patty, "are the ones who break the most fundamental rules. The laws of action and reaction, causation, and finite existence. Given enough time, these souls will elevate themselves beyond all consequence and repercussions. Once a soul has been so unleashed, it will draw the entire universe into itself and remake it in its own image."

"That sounds bad," Patty admitted. "But how do you kill something like that? It sounds impossible."

"And it would be, if a soul were to get so far," Hume concurred. "Our only saving grace in this battle is that the very last thing souls tend to discard is their sense of mortality. It is easy enough to imagine yourself living a long time, or being highly resistant to disease or harm. But you can imagine your existence as a necessary precondition for the universe? True, uncontested immortality?"

"...wow. No. I can't even imagine that."

"Indeed. It violates our sense of self, our notion of individuality, to think in such a way. Even the most powerful, dangerous souls struggle to discard this way of thinking. Most gods develop quite an ego, you can imagine, and they struggle mightily to overcome the idea of 'being part of the universe' rather than 'being the universe.' Absolute power obliterates the self. This truth is one of the reasons gods go mad." Hume sighed. "That is our only saving grace. So long as a god believes—and exists—as a part of the universe, that part can be destroyed. Often at a terrible cost, but it can be done."

Patty chewed on her lip thoughtfully, running her finger around the rim of her empty teacup. "So…one of these gods," she wondered aloud, "is responsible for what happened to Pete?"

Hume shook his head. "Unlikely," he stated. "There are not currently any active gods with that kind of power. Some old deities still remain, but they are for the most part dead or dying. Ngai, Bridgid, Nidhogg and the others…they will not trouble us. Most likely, our problems are due to some pet of a long-dead god. The Created. Pernicious bastards with nearly the power of a god, but with none of the gods' predilection for self-imposed exile or madness." Patty listened quietly. "Angels, demons, monsters and mythic heroes…while some of them were once human souls in their own right, most were created by a greater power. And all of them, every last one, hungers for the divine power that birthed them. Most of the new gods born into this world are found and devoured by one of these creatures."

"…devoured?" Patty's face was pale.

"That will not happen to Pete," Hume insisted. "Russell and Nietzsche will locate him and return him here, to the safety of the Philosoplex."

"Christ, I hope they hurry."

Pete wove through the streets and alleyways of the darkened city, meandering towards the city center. He hoped to lose himself in a club or bar and make himself one nameless face amongst hundreds. The woman in the smoke was coming for him, he knew, with a certainty that outstripped mere premonition. She would find him, wherever he hid, and any mortals unfortunate enough to be nearby would be burnt to ash like so many flies too close to a blinding light.

"No, no, calm the fuck down," Pete muttered, giving his head a violent shake. "There's a chance. Always a chance."

Every use of his power made it easier for her to find him and Pete had already been stupid enough to scry Ockham's Kegger. He had given her a lead on his location and given himself something else not to think about. Pete reminded himself he couldn't afford another mistake as he stepped from the alley's darkness. Traffic rolled by in front of him on a major downtown boulevard and for a moment, he paused to watch the passing lights. The sight was comfortingly ordinary to him.

"Hold up, pal," spoke a female voice from behind Pete. Every nerve in his body lit up as he turned on a dime and called to mind the most terrible power he could imagine. "Are you okay? Take it easy. *Take it easy.*" The policewoman kept her left hand on her holster, the right held out in front of her. She was a thicker, middle-aged woman of Hispanic descent whose dark eyes darted from the twitch in Pete's face, to his hands, to his blood-covered jacket and shirt. "I'm not going to hurt you, okay?"

Pete had forgotten about the blood. Too late now, he thought, holding up his hands in the expected gesture. "No need to worry, officer," he responded with obvious relief. She wasn't the one who hunted him. "I'm not looking to cause any trouble."

"That's good. That's real good," she replied, her gun hand steady as she slowly approached him. "Step into the light." She gestured sideways, towards the street light a few meters to Pete's left. He complied and Sonia Moreno's eyes went wide as the lamp illuminated his features. He was the man from her dream. No, she realized it was not a dream; the Archangel *had* come to her and charged her with a sacred mission. "Mary..." she whispered beneath her breath.

"Officer?" Pete asked, studying the woman in front of him. She had been staring at him for a good minute, seemingly lost in thought. "Are you alright?" It would only take a second to read her thoughts, Pete knew, a second to unravel her surprise. But he did not dare. His next mistake would be his last.

Sonia's eyes narrowed as she broke from the trance, her left hand snapping free her pistol with practiced grace, bringing the firearm up and level to Pete's chest with a sharp *click*. When she spoke again, her voice was different. Harder, and without a trace of fear. "Get on your knees and put your hands behind your head," she ordered. Pete hesitated to comply. "*Now!* Do it!" He fell to his knees.

"Officer, I can explain the blood," Pete said quickly, holding his hands behind his head as instructed. "My friends and I, we were having a season premiere party for that new zombie show, you know, the one on—"

"I didn't ask for an explanation," Sonia snapped, stepping close as she readied a set of metal cuffs. The Archangel had told her what he was; she didn't near to hear his lies. She was a woman of faith. "Padre neustro que estas en los cielos, santificado sea tu Nombre…"

Pete stared incredulously at Sonia as she approached him, mumbling the Lord's Prayer beneath her breath. Of all of the times to be arrested by a mentally unstable cop, he thought dryly, feeling her hands pull his wrists into the handcuffs. Still, Pete could escape her at any time. Would central booking be a worse place to hide than a club? "I'm not going to resist, you don't need to—*hrrngh*—make the cuffs so tight," he protested with mock discomfort. "I told you, I'm not looking for trouble, we all dressed up as zombie victims, and it isn't real blood."

Sonia was hardly even listening to him. "…sino que libranos del malo. Amen." She knew Mary was going to be with her again soon. Better. Healthy, like a child should be. "Stand up. We're going for a ride." Pete staggered to his feet and walked in front of her towards the squad car.

"That's fine," Pete agreed, perhaps too cheerily. "I don't have anything to hide, but I won't turn down a free ride from a kind woman." He flashed Sonia a winning smile as she pulled open the rear door of her car and pushed him inside. For just a moment, their eyes met.

Her brow furrowed, Sonia held Pete's gaze in silence. The man from her dream was supposed to be crazy. *Evil.* But faith did not doubt, she reminded herself. "What is your name?" she asked briskly, stepping back from the car. Mary could not wait.

"Pete Machal." There was no reason for him to lie. "Nice to meet you, Officer..." he squinted at the badge on her chest. "Officer Moreno. If you're having a rough night, I don't want to—"

"Mister Machal, I'm placing you in custody. You have the right to remain silent, and anything you say can be used against you in a court of law. You have the right to an attorney, and if you cannot afford one, one will be appointed to you," she stated dryly, going through the mechanical exercise of reading the Miranda warnings. Sonia tried to reassure herself; even if her premonitions were wrong, Pete was clearly disturbed, or on drugs. Nobody in their right mind smiled like that from the back seat of a police cruiser. "I have reason to believe you are a danger to yourself or others."

"Ain't that the truth," Pete admitted under his breath.

Sonia gave him a steely glare. "Excuse me?" Was he mocking her?

"Nothing, Officer, I'm sorry," he replied. "I've had a bit to drink tonight. S'why I'm walking, you know? I'm sorry if I'm being inappropriate." It was as plausible as an excuse as any, Pete figured. "I didn't plan on getting arrested tonight." He hadn't planned on a whole lot of things, truth be told, but the arrest might work to his benefit.

"Apology accepted," grumbled Sonia. She shut the door in his face.

"I'm glad we've reached an understanding," Pete continued as Sonia re-entered the car and took her seat on the driver's side. "I didn't want to get things off on the wrong foot between us." His chattiness was only half an act; Pete was admittedly desperate for an opportunity to take his mind off of his friends, doomed to die in Ockham's Kegger, and the woman who danced with a knife in the smoke.

"What part of 'remain silent' don't you understand?" Sonia asked sharply, turning her head to stare back at Pete through the protective metal screen.

"I waive my rights," Pete replied with a shrug. He nodded his head at the large, elaborate crucifix hanging from the rear view mirror. "Is it Constitutional to have that in a cop car, though?" Sonia gave him a hateful look. "Woah, woah, I didn't mean to offend. I don't know! I've never been in a cop car before. Separation of church and state though, right? I'm just asking."

Sonia sighed as she turned the key and the ignition fired. "I don't know," she lied, knowing full well that her supervisor would not approve. That didn't matter, of course; she wasn't planning on taking him back to the station where he might have an opportunity to complain. "I keep it for my daughter. She was very sick."

"Oh. I'm very sorry," Pete apologized, feeling rude for even bringing it up. "Did she...?"

"No. She's fine, now," Sonia replied confidently as they pulled away from the street. Lights and windows rolled slowly by outside of the car. "God has answered my prayers. Faith is a beautiful thing, Mr. Machal."

Pete smiled inwardly at the irony of the conversation. "Oh, yes. I'm a believer myself," he agreed. What would she think, Pete wondered silently, if she knew a *real* god was sitting in the back of her cruiser?

Sonia gave Pete a skeptical glance through the rear view mirror. Something did not feel right to her about him, about her mission. He was supposed to be an evil man. It was not, she reflected, his warmth or apparent sanity. Something else bothered her. It was not anything that Sonia could put her finger on, but deep in her gut, he did not strike her as a wicked man. "Sometimes belief is all we have left," Sonia replied after an awkward silence, a strange insistence in her voice. Again, she looked into the mirror to see Pete looking out the window at the passing buildings. It was him or Mary.

Why would a god heal her daughter? The question was bothering Pete more than it should have, but there were too many children that suffered in the world. Far too many. If a god saved one innocent child, then would he not have to save the others? Yes, Pete acknowledged, he would have to save them all. A parent's lack of piety was no cause for a child to die of malaria or cancer.

Yet surely saving so many lives would create new evil; what if the world's next genocidal dictator was lying in a hospital bed? Of course, Pete could know that, he would simply have to look deeply enough. But then, how could he refuse to save the children whose lives led to greater harm? Such a path would obligate him to terminate all lives with similarly ill fates. Pete felt a drop of sweat run down his forehead as he bit his lip, trying to see a way around the conundrum. He shook his head, telling himself that he would find a solution eventually.

Pete lost himself in thought for too long; it was not until the car went over a speed-bump that he snapped back to reality. Outside the car, the trees were dark and thick on either side of the road and gravel crunched beneath the car's tires. They weren't at a police station – hell, Pete thought, they weren't even downtown anymore. "Where are we?" he asked immediately, a note of urgency in his voice. In front of them, he could see a dark parking lot, dotted with inactive lampposts. "*Answer me!*" Pete banged on the grate in front of him, but Sonia drove onward in stony silence.

The patrol car thumped over another speed bump, rolling an open gate into the lot. Pete screamed loudly, thrashing violently against the restraints he could no longer break. His power had left him in an instant, vanishing the second the car entered the parking lot. "Auugggh! Fuck! What did you do?" he cried, slamming both of his fists against the grate. Pete screamed as he banged his body against the protective screen, fully overtaken by fear. "What did you do?!" He did not know *how*, but suddenly, Pete was powerless and utterly terrified.

Tears rolled down Sonia's cheeks as she gently unfastened her crucifix from the mirror, caressing it in her hands. There was hope for her daughter after all; Pete's screams reinforced her belief that she had been right to trust her dreams. Yet she was still human, and couldn't help but feel empathy for the panicked stranger behind her. "I'm sorry, Mr. Machal," she said meekly, squeezing her relic tightly as a man walked into the glare of her headlights. "It's for my daughter."

The stranger in the park was a tall man – far taller than even Pete – but he did not have the characteristic lankiness of a basketball star. Broad-shouldered and solidly built, he resembled the statue of David come to life. He had a smooth, bald head, his face clean-shaved and sculpted. A man of Middle-Eastern descent, he wore a perfectly white suit which attained nearly blinding luminescence in the stark light of the high beams. As he approached the driver's side of the car, Sonia opened her door, stepping out and immediately falling to her knees. The man – no, the *angel* – was exactly as she had dreamt earlier that day, and she could not even bring herself to look upon his beauty. "I –

I have done as you asked, Lord Michael," she said piously, the crucifix trembling in her nervous hands. "Please…" Sonia choked up, her tears falling on the pavement. "Please save my daughter."

Pete tried to calm himself down, tried to think despite the incessant throbbing of his pulse. Where had his strength gone? Had the policewoman brought him back to the philosophers? He craned his head, trying to get a better look at the man who stood in the shadows before Sergeant Moreno, now outside the illumination of the headlights. Pete hardly had a moment to register the man's name before the rear passenger-side door suddenly opened, causing Pete scream in a very ungodly fashion.

Drained of his power and with his hands bound securely behind his back, Pete couldn't avoid the hand reaching into the car for him. Fingers clasped roughly around his neck, squeezing him as if he was a toy; Pete was dragged unceremoniously across the seat and thrown down on to the pavement. Half screaming and half gasping for breath, Pete felt—and heard—his nose snap loudly as he hit the ground face first, the pavement tearing his skin. He howled in pain.

Sonia winced as she heard his screams, opening her mouth before Michael placed his hand gently on her head. "Be at ease, child," he said in a melodic voice, gently stroking his fingers through her hair. "It is necessary so that this world might yet be saved. You have performed well in the service of God." Shivering at his touch, Sonia nodded silently as she shut her mouth. Still, she could not help but glance over as the second stranger walked around the car to join them, dragging Pete by his hair across the ground.

Her eyes moved from Pete's shattered face to the sharp lines of the second man's black suit. Looking up, Sonia inhaled sharply as her eyes met his and she felt suddenly, terribly afraid. Her face registered shock; Sonia instinctively knew who stood before her, his form nearly fading into the dark. The second man looked nearly the same as Michael -- most humans would have mistaken the brothers for twins. But Sonia could not make that mistake. She had just been touched by an angel, and she knew that the man in black was not like Michael. He was not an angel; not anymore. Her head spun back to the archangel, her heart racing as she cried out. "How could you? Him?!" she said, not noticing as her chest throbbed dangerously. Michael's partner chuckled.

"Necessity breeds many oddities," Michael said regretfully, taking his hand off Sonia's head. "But I made you a promise in good faith, and I shall keep it. Once Heaven is restored, I shall reunite you with your daughter." Sonia barely had time to gasp as her heart trembled, then stood still. The officer clawed helplessly at her chest and her crucifix dropped to the ground only moments before she did. "A pity," Michael commented, reaching down to pick up Sonia's relic. Polishing it slightly with his hand, Michael tucked it into his pants' pocket for safe-keeping. "She would not have spoken of this evening to anyone, Lucifer," he said, turning to his once-estranged brother.

Lucifer gave the sort of grin that only the Devil could, and unceremoniously dropped Pete back to the ground. He wore a thin, neatly-cut goatee; the perfect choice for a man who spent much of his time looking evil. "Maybe, maybe not," he said with a shrug, his voice slightly deeper than Michael's. "But I believe I have a better understanding of human imperfection than you, brother. The stakes are too high for us to gamble on the strength of her *faith*." He sneered, the last word rolling off his tongue like a curse.

"Uggghhhh..." Pete groaned as Michael stepped closer, turning Pete onto his back with his foot. Michael leaned forward and peered down at his captive, noting that he had managed to get some of Pete's blood on his shoe. His disdain for Lucifer's excesses had no limit, especially when they sullied his wardrobe. Every successful partnership required sacrifices, however, and Michael would tolerate the inconveniences for now. If everything went as he planned, the two brothers would soon enough be at war with each other yet again.

"Hello, Pete," Michael said, looking down at him. "You're going to working with us from here on out. I trust that you'll be cooperative?" Pete coughed up some blood in response, groaning in pain. Such comparatively minor injuries would certainly not kill him, but that fact was little consolation given his inability to even slow the bleeding from his broken nose.

"Now that we don't have to worry about mood lighting for your delivery girl, I'd prefer to get a good look at our new friend," Lucifer said, snapping his fingers as the lights ringing the parking lot lit up. As both men stood over him, Pete rolled his head to the side, looking around the lot. They stood inside a wide red ring painted onto the ground, and Pete grimaced as the bloody circle glistened under the harsh light. He did not know what the ring was, but assumed it was what had sealed off his powers. It took little time to find its source; half a dozen pale, desiccated bodies were piled haphazardly in front of the nearby dumpster. Michael shook his head, obviously uncomfortable with the choice of décor as Lucifer laughed, following Pete's gaze. "The Red Cross would be proud. Do you know how much *squeezing* it took to finish the seal with just six?" Lucifer boasted, crossing his arms and giving a nod. "Hell, one of them was even a kid."

"Enough," Michael said tersely, trying to commend himself for insisting that his brother at least be efficient. The archangel looked back at Pete, nodding slightly. "He should make an acceptable Father, in time. We need to leave immediately. Our would-be partner will not appreciate this change in plans."

"Yes, yes, you're quite the hot commodity," Lucifer said playfully as he got down on one knee beside Pete, patting his battered cheek. Moving his hand to Pete's chin, he inspected Pete's face. "Mm, he will do," he said, addressing his brother. "I'm already starting to hate him! Get the chains."

Pete tried to pull his hand from the Devil's touch, the hand painfully cold. Straining to think through the throbbing injuries to his face, Pete struggled to come up with a plan of escape. His situation could not have been more hopeless; Pete had no power within the binding seal and he was in the hands of two of the greatest Created to ever walk the world. Pete's chances for escape rated somewhere between winning the lottery jackpot five games in a row and successfully negotiating a fair lease price for his downtown apartment. "Fuck," he muttered simply, resigning himself to captivity. At least it wasn't the woman in the fog.

Chapter Four

After Patty and Pete left Ockam's Kegger, the remaining three members of their group from the Post—Rachel, Wilfred, and Robert—spent another hour waiting for Rachel to sober up enough that she wouldn't throw up in a taxi. They had not taken note of the two gentlemen from the bar that had left in a hurry after Pete and they paid little attention to the rest of the rapidly-emptying establishment.

"I'm sure he'll be alright," Robert said with a shrug, taking a sip of his water. "You know how Pete gets sometimes, yeah?" He looked across the table at Rachel and Wilfred, the latter of whom seemed terribly bored now that Pete was gone. The accountant smiled at Wilfred, giving a little laugh. "Don't look so glum, Wilf," he said. "I'm sure Pete isn't off smashing anything without you."

"Yeah, I'm sure," Wilfred replied. "But this place is pretty dead. Everyone else must have gotten a crappy drink like Pete." He looked around the now empty bar, the last other group having left a good ten minutes ago. Their only company was the French bartender, who seemed to have been polishing his glasses clean for an inordinately long time. "Are you about to close, or what?" Wilfred asked him, not even needing to shout across the deserted room.

"An excellent question," the bartender replied as he hopped over the counter in a surprising display of athleticism. "We need to have a little chat, now that we're alone." Pushing his heavy glasses slightly up his nose, the Frenchman strolled over to the table. Casually pulling out Pete's now-empty chair, he took a seat next to Robert and gave a contented smile, happy to be off his feet. "Much better. I'm Jean-Paul Sartre, it's a pleasure to meet you all."

All three of the friends had heard his name before; Sartre's forays into literature and time as a public intellectual gave him the sort of name recognition that made many of his colleagues jealous. Robert and Wilfred both stared at him incredulously then shared a look with each other. Neither of them was *that* drunk. On the other hand, Rachel was slightly less stunned. Situated in the unique state of mind that can only be found at the intersection between serious intoxication and an undergraduate degree in philosophy, she peered across the table at Sartre. He certainly looked like Sartre, Rachel thought. "Who was the main character in *La Nausee*?" she asked pointedly.

Sartre gave a warm laugh, pleased at her familiarity with his novel. "Antoine Roquentin," he replied, recalling his story. "What a pleasant surprise that you've read my work! I admit it's somewhat awkward, given the situation. This certainly isn't where you would have expected to run into me, eh?" Rachel cocked her heard, still examining him curiously.

"That is true, seeing how you're dead..." She felt surprisingly convinced by the bartender's performance, but she reminded herself that she was still suffering through the aftermath of half-a-dozen too many tequila shots.

"Some of us can hold our liquor," Wilfred interjected, shaking his head in disbelief. "I think it's time for us to leave," he continued as he stood up, wondering what peculiar sort of lunatic would want to impersonate a dead French philosopher.

"Don't be hasty, I think you'll find this quite convincing," Sartre said, giving a flourish with his hand. Nestled in a plain paper wrapper, a baguette appeared in the middle of the table accompanied by a small dish of butter. "*Voila!*"

"What the hell?" Robert exclaimed in surprise, leaning forward and giving the baguette a tentative poke. Finding the bread not only real but nearly fresh out of an oven, he turned to Sartre and stared. For her part, Rachel giggled approvingly and clapped her hands together lightly at the performance. Wilfred gingerly sat back down, also turning to the alleged philosopher for an explanation. He had his answer: the bartender was a *magical* sort of lunatic.

"It's from my favorite bakery in Paris," he explained with a smile, wasting no time in cutting off a slice for himself. "Your lady friend – pardon me for not knowing your name – could use something in her stomach, and I'm starving too."

"My name is Rachel," she answered happily, taking a piece of bread for herself and buttering it lightly. "Mm!" Rachel commented through a full mouth, chewing eagerly on the snack. Clearing her throat with a mouthful of water, she nodded at her friends. "You should try it; it really is wonderful."

Wilfred shrugged as he and Robert each ripped off their own piece of bread, munching happily as Sartre continued his introduction. "Now, my partner will be showing up shortly, so I'll have to be brief. My colleagues and I are servants of a dead god. Our mission is to bring an end to the pernicious influence of supernatural beings on this world." He paused, taking a sip of water. Sartre resumed his explanation, speaking in an dry tone one would use to list the ingredients in a house salad. "To that end, I made your friend a drink that will eventually transform him into a god."

"Hurk!" Robert coughed violently, nearly choking on his piece of baguette. After a moment of wheezing he swallowed and caught his breath, earning a sigh of relief from the table. Sartre made a mental note that in the future it would be wise to serve food only *after* the dramatic and startling revelations. "The drink did *what*?" the accountant asked; after all, he had tried to order the Existential Dilemma himself.

"It was a necessary measure," Sartre explained. "We concluded that in order to accomplish our mission, we would need to harness the full power of a god. As we are simply derivative creations of a power that is now – sadly – gone, we agreed that a controlled experiment would be our best strategy."

"So you are...an angel?" Wilfred asked curiously, finding a middle-aged man with glasses outside the usual picture of the heavenly host.

"In a sense," Sartre answered, looking to Rachel who listened intently. "We are the Created left by one particular deity; angels are the servants of an entirely different divinity. Hopefully we won't have the misfortune of running into them."

"There is more than one god?!" Rachel suddenly asked. As a staunch atheist, she was more than slightly upset by the news. Finding out that not only one—but many—gods existed was a pretty crushing blow. In a way, it was much like betting on a horse in a race, only to find out that not only did her horse lose, but every other horse won.

"At the moment, there are not any major gods, although your friend Pete should achieve that level of power soon enough," Sartre clarified. "The occurrence of gods is a rare enough phenomena that there is almost never any overlap between their existences. However, starting as humans, all gods seem to have the same penchant for making minions. They have left the planet littered with fragments of a dozen, long-dead pantheons as they pass. Like me." Sartre smiled.

"When they pass?" Robert asked, not accustomed to the idea of gods expiring like deli meat.

"Do they need a nap, or what?" Wilfred added sarcastically. "Isn't part of being God the whole exists-for-eternity shtick?"

Sartre frowned, not from the questions but due the time on his watch: Socrates was supposed to have returned from watching the perimeter almost five minutes ago. "I appreciate your curiosity, but we may have a problem," he said, standing up as he looked out the window to the street. Sartre knew that the Greek would not be late unless something had gone wrong; Socrates took his duties with utmost seriousness. "Please enjoy the bread, and…don't move," he requested as politely as possible.

When food, water, and time fail to sober a person up, fear nearly always works. Rachel sat up straight in her chair, watching the philosopher. Sartre walked cautiously towards the door, his eyes narrowing. Instinctively, he stopped a few feet in front of the wall, examining the side of the building. Reaching onto an empty table, Sartre grabbed a spoon and flipped it towards the door. The silverware hit the door and fell to the ground with a clang, behaving exactly the way that any ordinary person would expect a spoon to act.

Needless to say, Sartre was not a particularly ordinary person, and the spoon's brief interaction with the wall was precisely not what he *had* expected. He had planned to make the spoon stick to the wall; that would have been a trivial feat if the bar's entrance had not been altered. "Illusion," he muttered as he quickly took a few steps back from the exit. "I must amend my earlier advice; please get behind the bar immediately," Sartre called out, clasping his hands together in front of him as he focused. The three were wise enough to quickly take his advice, dashing behind the far end of the counter. A man who could conjure baked goods from thin air demanded a certain degree of respect, after all. "Look away!" They didn't need to be told twice.

With the entirety of Sartre's will focused on the wall, the image began to waver. Ripples ran across the seemingly solid material, and the wall began to laugh. "Ahahaha," the chorus of voices echoed through the room, "I should not have expected you would make this easy on me." Wilfred, Robert, and Rachel all huddled together; the voice alone would have been unnerving even if had it not been emanating from a wall.

The illusion promptly shattered, and the three ordinary humans left in the room fell to the floor and shut their eyes tightly. What remained was enough to unhinge a mortal mind; even the philosopher felt a shiver run down his spine. In place of the door hung a gigantic mouth; glittering silver teeth wreathed in darkness. The entire wall had taken on a similarly inky black color, and Sartre felt as if he was staring into an abyssal trench. Multiple smaller mouths floated in space, all grinning and laughing in turn. Yet even more terrifying was what lay behind the mouths: floating in the infinite depths of blackness could be seen dozens of bodies, all in various states of decomposition, save one.

"Goddamit, Socrates," Sartre muttered under his breath, seeing his Greek partner suspended and unconscious within the nightmare creature. Seemingly just a few meters behind the creature's large mouth, the philosopher floated helplessly, bound in tendrils of nothingness inside the monster.

"And you said there aren't any major gods left on this pitiful world," the large mouth said with a terrifying smirk. "That really hurt, Sartre."

"Don't delude yourself, Yaggoth," Sartre hissed in response, desperately trying to assess his options. The horror in front of him was very old; even if he did not have to protect the three mortals behind him, Sartre knew he could never win in a direct confrontation. Yaggoth had been around for millennia; it had existed since the earliest days of humanity. In the depths of evolutionary history—long before what would become humans were aware enough to understand their dreams—Yaggoth had begun as a nightmare that had the good sense not to go away when the dreamer awoke. It had festered in the minds of countless generations, inducing a fevered madness that always ended with suicide.

Nightmares such as Yaggoth fed off the subconscious fears and anxiety present in every human mind; the inevitable suicide of its hosts was simply a by-product of harrowing mental parasitism. Hiding in the world of thoughts and dreams, the nightmare rarely manifested itself in the physical realm. For that very reason the philosophers had found exterminating Yaggoth to be a particularly challenging task.

The nightmare was well-aware of that fact; Yaggoth realized that its continued existence in the material world risked its safety. By their very nature, nightmares were the sort of things ideal at overpowering a single individual through fear, deception, and all of the other psychological tricks with which every dreamer is well-acquainted. With Sartre's partner immobilized, Yaggoth knew it held the upper hand against the philosopher. But it understood that Sartre had other friends, and that his prolonged absence would surely bring them looking.

"*Tremble*," spoke the countless mouths of Yaggoth, and its word shook both the building and Sartre's sanity. The philosopher was not mortal, but he still had hopes and fears. And there, Yaggoth had power.

Jean-Paul Sartre quaked, his hands clasped tightly together as he absorbed the full force of the nightmare's psychic assault. Keeping himself between Yaggoth and the humans, he served as a bulwark against the corrupting influence. If the nightmare managed to possess the minds of Pete's friends, Sartre knew that the situation would only become increasingly unstable. Present both in space and in Pete's emotions when he drank the Existential Dilemma, his friends were linked inextricably to his transformation. With the nascent god still highly vulnerable, one of Pete's friends under the dominion of Yaggoth would in turn grant the nightmare a subtle yet terrible control over Pete himself.

"Fear is the mind-killer," Sartre intoned quietly, struggling to keep his mind free from the flickering terrors that Yaggoth sent against him. Freeing Socrates while protecting the three behind him was surely impossible and Sartre doubted he could stand against Yaggoth for long. He felt himself shivering, a cold sweat beading on his forehead as he stared into the horror before him.

Yaggoth moved slowly against Sartre's mind, gently erasing the man's sources of hope one after another. In practice, breaking one of the Created was simply a more tedious version of corrupting an ordinary human. Sartre's only advantage was that he was aware of Yaggoth's movements and immune to the more primal sorts of terror.

The nightmare sought out Sartre's mental refuges and erased them: his friends, his colleagues, and his duty. Once all hope was gone, only terror would remain. Sartre struggled mightily, trying to remember his purpose and stave off fear, but even he could only endure the torture for so long. Soon enough, he too was engulfed in darkness.

Staring resolutely at the floorboards, Wilfred heard Sartre collapse to the ground with a dull thud. Robert had his eyes squeezed shut, and Rachel hid her face in her hands, ironically attempting to escape a nightmare by shutting out reality. This was not the fight that Wilfred had longed for his entire life, but as the laughing shadow expanded towards the rear of the bar, he knew that he had no choice. Clenching his fists and springing to his feet, Wilfred turned to face Yaggoth. He froze.

"What will your hands do to me?" it laughed, moving across the room and rolling over Sartre. "You are *alone*." The philosopher lay on the floor shaking, his glasses laid broken on the floor beside him as he sobbed. One of Yaggoth's mouths suddenly expanded, swallowing him whole. Wilfred could do no more than stare, his face going white as he looked into Yaggoth. His hands gripped onto the edge of the bar counter with enough force to splinter the wood, mouth hanging open in shock. Convictions slipping away in an instant, Wilfred welcomed the shadow's embrace.

But the end did not come for Wilfred. In front of him, Yaggoth's physical form bent violently then exploded outwards. Thrown backwards from the blast, Wilfred crashed into the bar and fell to the ground, covered in liquor and broken glass. Flying through a hail of stone and dissipating shadow, Friedrich Nietzsche landed in the middle of the dining area atop a Harley-Davidson. Behind him, Yaggoth howled in pain. Recoiling from Nietzsche's forced entry, the nightmare left a clear view through the smoking hole in the building's wall to the street outside.

Casually hopping off of his smoking, skidding ride, Nietzsche landed on his feet before the motorcycle collided with the rear wall. Yaggoth's remaining mouths cursed in a hundred dead languages as it struggled to retain control over both Socrates and Sartre. "That's what I wanted to hear," Nietzsche said as he brushed a few pieces of broken drywall off of his suit. "Scream for me, beast." Nietzsche had not been particularly fond of the philosophers' plan; he was of the opinion that creating gods in order to destroy gods was an obviously stupid idea. In life, he had once written that "god is dead" and his rebirth charged him with a particular, sadistic zeal to see the gods perish by his own hands.

Having spent too much of his original life confined to a wheelchair—bizarrely, he often still used it despite his perfectly-functional legs—riding a motorcycle through a brick wall was precisely the sort of thing Nietzsche wanted to do on his Friday nights. Whether through an ironic twist of fate or—as he would argue—sheer force of will, Nietzsche was the most capable fighter of the remaining philosophers. While all of the members were endowed with the last act of their Creator's power, this gift manifested itself in dramatically different ways. For Nietzsche, the task of his reincarnation was simple: to destroy.

Yaggoth struggled to reconstitute itself, drawing back from Nietzsche. Suppressing the power of two of the philosophers had already pushed the nightmare's limits; it could not possibly contend with a third. Not with Nietzsche. Immediately releasing its hold on Sartre and Socrates, the two men fell from their awkward suspension within Yaggoth and hit the ground. The nightmare threw a wave of fear at Nietzsche and the philosopher staggered backwards but did not fall.

Yaggoth was too old and too wise for panic, but it needed an immediate exit back into the dream world. Nietzsche threw off another psychic assault, forcing himself forward. Time was running out. The nightmare scanned feverishly through the abandoned streets and alleys around Ockham's Kegger; at two in the morning, the deserted commercial district offered Yaggoth few opportunities. It had to find someone, anyone – *there!* Two blocks north, a homeless couple slept in the alleyway. Yaggoth needed only to delay Nietzsche for a minute.

Over its millennia-long existence, Yaggoth had gathered onto itself most of humanity's terrors, from the subtlest frights to the goriest monstrosities. From demons to mice to high school math teachers, the black abyss possessed the power to call forth any of these lesser nightmares in its service. Yaggoth would have to part with some portion of its power to bring such a creature into existence, but as

Nietzsche broke through the nightmare's psychic barrier and charged, it had little choice left.

"*Gasp and DROWN!*" the nightmare screamed, its voices high with murderous fury. Yaggoth's shadowy figure stretched outwards like an amoeba towards Nietzsche, a single mouth riding a wave of darkness. The congealed shadow took humanoid form as it separated from Yaggoth with a loud *pop* and collided headlong with the charging philosopher. A deafening shockwave rocked the room, filling it with a weird purple light.

Nietzsche had not yet adjusted to the sudden flash when his nose was filled with the putrescent smell of rotting flesh. Before him towered a noxious specimen of the drowned undead; a mass of bandages and seaweed hung about the eight-foot-tall monstrosity, dripping befouled water onto the floor. It gave a gurgling scream and rushed forward.

A swift right hook met the mummy square in the face, smashing through bone and flesh. Nietzsche deftly dodged the shambling horror, its arms flailing about wildly. He struck out again, putting the whole of his weight behind the blow. Thunder echoed around the small room as Nietzsche's fist struck home, sending the mummy flying aside. It landed with a crash amidst the wooden tables of the dining area. Glassware and chairs shattered beneath its fall, the mummy left a slimy trail of seaweed and grime as it slid across the floor.

"So weak!" Nietzsche laughed at Yaggoth. The nightmare had only barely gotten itself beyond the door, oozing like a great sheet of ink across the tiled floor. "It's g—*aughh!*" Nietzsche was ripped backwards off of his feet, slamming to the ground. Twisted ropes of bloodied bandages and seaweed wrapped around his chest and neck, binding him in place. He threw out his arms and the bonds broke, snapping from his raw strength. But for every rope that broke another found its hold, snaking out of the mummy as it staggered towards Nietzsche.

Yaggoth was not a fool. The drowned corpse had lived from centuries in the nightmares of river-folk, dragging unwary children beneath the shallow water to its stone tomb. It was not as fast or as strong as Nietzsche, nor did it have any but the basest cunning. But it was resilient and single-minded, and that was all Yaggoth required of it.

The nightmare was escaping him and Nietzsche knew it, struggling against the grasp of the tangled, dripping ropes. His fingers twined in the sodden material, struggling to get a hold on the slippery mass. Squeezing tight, Nietzsche unleashed a torrent of electricity against his attacker. The mummy crackled and popped, its half-rotten muscles contracting uncontrollably from the sudden charge. Nietzsche seized the initiative and threw himself against the creature, tackling it to the floor with his hands around its neck.

The philosopher's eyes gleamed with a terrible fury as he increased the current a thousand-fold, feeling the mummy convulse beneath him helplessly. Seawater turned to steam, bandages smoked and decayed flesh caught fire. The mummy reached up with shaking, burning hands but they crumbled to ash and blew away. "Enough!" Nietzsche cried, releasing his hold and standing. Sparks still raced across his body and all his hair stood on end as the mummy smoldered and burned, broken beneath his feet.

Nietzsche raced for the door and out into the street, but arrived too late – Yaggoth was already gone from sight. He could not know that two blocks away, a man sleeping in the street was slowly engulfed in an undulating pool of blackness. The shadow crawled over his patchwork clothes, slithering into his eyes, into his mind, and into the freedom of darkened dreams.

Inside the building, Robert rose to his knees, choking on the smoke. "Sweet god," Robert said, coughing violently. Ockham's Kegger was silent other than the gentle crackling of fire, the room slowly filling with smoke. Looking between each other, Wilfred winced from the bruises sustained hitting the bar while Rachel glanced around the edge of the counter, covering her mouth.

"I think it's safe," she said, looking warily between the gaping hole in the wall, the two unconscious philosophers, and the still-burning nightmare. "What *is* that smell?"

Robert quickly stood up, holding his shirt sleeve up over his mouth and nose as he gagged. Not especially worried about his safety, the accountant was more concerned by the unspeakable smell issuing from the dining area. In his defense, there were few smells worse than that of slow-roasted undead.

Their eyes tearing up, Wilfred and Rachel followed Robert around the floor, pausing halfway across the room beside the two fallen philosophers. While Socrates had the great luck of continuing unconsciousness, Sartre began to cough as he woke. Experiencing a scent that could knock out a dinosaur, he struggled to his feet. "*Mon dieu!*" he exclaimed as he reached around awkwardly on the floor, having been reincarnated with his mortal need for glasses.

Helping Sartre to his feet, Rachel nodded to the gaping hole in the wall. "Outside," she gasped urgently, the bar's atmosphere quickly becoming toxic. Robert wasted no time dashing outside while Rachel followed as quickly as possible with the still-wobbly Frenchmen. Wilfred followed slowly, hauling the massive and unconscious Socrates across the floor. Despite being a mere mortal, Wilfred was far from weak; he spent three nights a week terrifying fellow gym-goers by throwing around weights while singing loudly along to German heavy metal. But contrary to most contemporary depictions of Socrates, the philosopher was not a slim old man in flowing robes. Wearing ragged blue jeans and a grey tank-top, Socrates was built like a tank and—to Wilfred—seemed to weigh nearly as much. Finally pulling Socrates outside, he gasped for air as he laid the philosopher flat on the sidewalk. Looking down, Wilfred could not help but admire the Greek's massive, curly beard. It at least tied Nietzsche's moustache for the title of "Facial Hair Most Likely to Kick Ass."

Sensing the superiority of his whiskers being called into question, Nietzsche rolled over to the group as they savored the fresh, cold air. Seated in his wheelchair once again, he puffed on a cigarette, immunity to horrific lung cancer being one of the more enjoyable perks of a supernatural existence. Finally regaining enough composure to summon himself a new pair of glasses, Sartre pushed the frames up his nose as he looked to Nietzsche.

The German philosopher slowly pulled the cigarette from his mouth, leaning forward towards Sartre with a wide smile. "Thank you?" he suggested teasingly.

Sartre simply nodded and straightened out his jacket before turning and hurrying over to Socrates. Rachel, however, was considerably less tolerant of Nietzsche's attitude. "Asshole," she muttered, loudly enough to be heard. Fortunately for her, Nietzsche was too occupied brooding over Yaggoth's escape to be drawn into an argument. She walked over to join Robert and Wilfred, both of whom were seated with Sartre besides Socrates' prone form. "Is he going to be OK?" she asked, looking to Sartre expectantly.

"It may take a while to extricate him from this fugue state," Sartre said slowly as he examined his partner, "but he should come out of it. Yaggoth was too preoccupied with the rest of us to do any lasting damage to him."

"Thank you," Wilfred added, awkwardly patting Sartre on the back. He was a proud man, but he gave credit where it was due. Having looked at Yaggoth for a few terrible moments, Wilfred had a special appreciation for the philosopher's courage in standing against the nightmare alone. Nietzsche snorted derisively, but was taken aback when Wilfred turned to him. "And thank you..." he trailed off, not knowing the other rescuer's name as he extended his hand.

"Friedrich Nietzsche," he replied, taking Wilfred's hand and shaking it firmly. Nietzsche enjoyed the appreciation; he was rarely thanked in light of his abrasiveness. While he was not a particularly friendly—or entirely sane—individual, some of Nietzsche's demeanor was simply an attempt to reject the tragic helplessness that had characterized the end of his life.

Sartre had pulled out his phone, and turned back to Nietzsche as he checked it for messages. "Where are the others? And where is Pete?" he asked urgently. Hearing his name, Pete's friends also looked to Nietzsche expectantly.

"Your little experiment decided to run off and cry because I hurt his feelings," Nietzsche replied, taking a long pull on his cigarette. Being unusually forthcoming, he continued. "Either that or your potion screwed up. He was coughing up a purple smoke."

"Purple smoke?" Sartre asked, shaking his head. "That couldn't have been my work." Something had gone seriously wrong; the philosopher needed to examine Pete immediately. "Where did he go?"

"We don't know where he is. Russell and Kant are off looking for him, and Hume is lounging around at the mansion with the girl he dragged along." Sartre gritted his teeth, not even remotely surprised by the outcome. He had strongly lobbied to leave Nietzsche at the bar in place of Socrates. While having to work alone with him for a few hours would have proved a fitting reminder of why Sartre famously stated that "hell is other people," it would have been less troublesome than their present situation.

Unfortunately, Nietzsche was the sort of individual who could not be deterred once he made up his mind. This trait sometimes yielded a few good laughs at Nietzsche's expense, such as when he insisted upon eating the peppers that the Chinese carryout menu specifically said not to eat. Most of the time, however, Nietzsche's obstinacy was simply a pain in the ass. Shaking his head, Sartre tried to stop himself from reflecting on the past. "What is our next move, then?" Sartre asked. Ockham's Kegger was an uninhabitable shambles.

"Presumably you should take these three back to the mansion, so Hume can keep hosting a slumber party while I'm out doing work," Nietzsche replied, dropping the butt of his spent cigarette to the ground. Reaching his right foot off of the footrest of the wheelchair, he stamped it out.

Sartre turned and faced the street, giving a dejected sigh as he looked up and down the empty road. Of all the philosophers, Sartre was the least capable at material transmutation; his glasses and the occasional loaf of bread were the limit of his competency. "And how am I supposed to do that?" he asked to nobody in particular. Even though Nietzsche had no difficulty summoning up a motorcycle for his use, Sartre wasn't even going to bother suggesting that he play chauffeur.

However, he was not without his own specialties. Able to manipulate human psychology and emotions with ease, Sartre was the genius behind the Existential Dilemma. And while most taxi drivers would not bother driving through an empty commercial district at 2:30 in the morning, with the philosopher's influence it quickly became inevitable that one would feel the sudden urge to pass by. Waiting for a ride, Sartre turned back to Nietzsche. "I assume you're going after Pete with the others?" he asked, having already tried and failed to get an answer from Russell on his phone. While all of the philosophers were legendary thinkers, none had fully adapted to the modern era; cell phones were often inexplicably left off for long periods of time.

"Of course," Nietzsche said, stretching his back as he stood up from the wheelchair. "Pete has already attracted enough attention to convince Yaggoth to risk taking physical form; it is a certainty that the other major players will be looking for him, if they haven't already found him."

"Who are *they*?" Wilfred asked curiously, concerned about his friend's safety.

Nietzsche shrugged, giving his wheelchair a gentle kick and transforming it into a new motorcycle, his old ride still smoldering in the back of the bar. "It is hard to know," he admitted, seating himself. "The few Created that I haven't been able to kill are very careful. Many of them disappear for decades at a time, vanishing until they see an opportunity. I won't know who has come out of the woodwork until I see them."

"Will Pete be alright?" Robert said, looking to the intimidating philosopher as he started up his motorcycle. The bike gave a pronounced roar in the quiet night.

"No," replied Nietzsche brusquely, "he won't be 'alright.' But maybe I can find him before they do anything *irreversible* to him, if you stop pestering me with questions." Nietzsche hit the gas and the bike sped off onto the road, tires howling in protest as he spun sharply. "Auf Wiedersehen!" Blazing away at a speed that demonstrated wanton disregard for highway safety regulations, Nietzsche's "UB3R-M3NSCH" license plate faded into the darkness.

The three friends turned back to Sartre, who had taken a seat on the curb next to his unconscious partner. "Why Pete?" Rachel asked, breaking the silence. "Why did you have to do this to him?"

"He was simply the right man at the right time," Sartre replied with a shrug, understanding the unfairness of the situation. "Someone was going to drink the Existential Dilemma tonight. I simply had to wait for a customer with the proper emotional make-up." He turned to his side, towards his anxious listeners. "The Existential Dilemma would only work on an intelligent individual with perception of both his surroundings and his emotions. Your friend is far more aware of his emotions than most people, and introspection is a necessary prerequisite."

"And you expect him to just kill himself because you ask nicely?" Robert said angrily, trying to understand how the philosopher planned to use Pete to destroy the supernatural.

"Oh, no, no," Sartre replied defensively as he shook his head. "Not suicide, certainly not. We simply want him to permanently remove the fabric of the supernatural that is woven into this world. Just like that," he snapped loudly, "and there would be no more gods, angels, or demons. He would make himself, me, Nietzsche and the others irreversibly mortal. More importantly, such an act would foreclose the possibility that any future gods would arise."

"What about…things like Yaggoth?" Wilfred asked quietly, the name alone conjuring up memories that he would never forget. A few seconds glancing into the consuming, hungering darkness had been more than enough to convince him of the rightness of Sartre's plan. Things like that could not be allowed to exist.

Sartre smiled widely; he was entirely sympathetic to Wilfred's concern. "Yaggoth and other monstrosities like him—things that have no analog in the physical world—would simply be erased," he said. Catching sight of a bright yellow cab turning the corner, Sartre sprung to his feet and waved. As he pulled his car to a stop in front of the party, the cab driver looked out the window, glancing skeptically down at Socrates.

"I don't think I can take five," the young man said with a frown. Brushing a hand through his short brown hair, Jim shook his head. "I could call for another cab, if you want?"

Sartre walked over to the window, looking down at the driver. Making eye contact and speaking in a slow, level voice, the philosopher worked his magic. "Jim, this *is* the fare you're looking for," he stated, foregoing the usual but unnecessary wave of his hand. Jim stopped for a moment, staring blankly into Sartre's eyes. "This is the fare I'm looking for," he slowly repeated, unlocking the car. "Hop in!"

"Holy shit, Obi-Wan," Robert said in awe as he helped Wilfred and Sartre heft Socrates' incredibly unwieldy body into the back seat. Sartre slid in next to his partner, wrapping his right arm around him to keep him from keeling over. Robert and Rachel managed to squeeze in after Sartre, the four of them fitting in the back seat only because of Socrates' quiet acquiescence to being spread out across everyone's lap.

Hopping into the front passenger's seat, Wilfred looked back at the pile in the rear. Jim turned as well, grimacing slightly as he realized that any sudden stops would see him crushed to paste by a flying, unconscious giant. "Where to?" he asked simply, flicking off the light on top of his cab.

"The mansion," Sartre said as he made eye contact with the driver again, using the same commanding tone as earlier.

"The..." Jim began to question, before trailing off. "Oh, yeah, the mansion. Sure thing! Sit back and, uh, relax." He tried to strike up a conversation to keep from falling asleep like Robert, who snored quietly despite bearing a substantial portion of Socrates' weight. "Quite a miracle that I ran into you guys at this hour, huh?"

Rachel blinked at Jim's comment, her eagerness to be distracted by a debate only heightened by the crushing force of Socrates' legs on her lap. "You shouldn't believe it was a miracle; it was simply very unlikely," she offered, using the argument of another philosopher whom she would soon meet.

"Uh," Jim replied hesitantly, recalling Rule #7 of *The Cabbie's Guide to Not Getting Shot*: do not argue with passengers about philosophy. "I guess you're right," he agreed with a forced smile and a nod.

Sartre, however, was not nearly as inclined to avoid the challenge. He was blissfully unaware that in the present year, philosophizing while driving had become the third leading cause of motor vehicle-related fatalities. This lamentable statistic—a source of both strange pride and horror at philosophy departments nationwide—was due primarily to the Dekalb Catastrophe. Two truckers heading west out of Chicago on I-88 had gotten into a heated argument about solipsism on their CB radios. As the trucks came alongside each other, the few surviving witnesses reported seeing the driver of the Burny's Discount Kerosene truck lean out of the window, hurling accusations of gross fallacies at the driver hauling high-performance gasoline.

The situation was brought to an ironic but horrible climax as the driver of a red sports car zipped in front of the two trucks and then braked, acting as if nobody but him really existed on the road. In the resulting cataclysm of fire and twisted steel, a good half-mile of the highway had to be shut down in both directions for months. While a subsequent push in Congress to ban philosophy on the roadways failed to garner a majority, a number of state legislatures which normally spent their time cheerleading for creationism voted to slap warning labels on every book using words in excess of two syllables. Unbeknownst to him, Sartre was fortunate enough to be in a state that had not followed Kansas' lead with the "Protect Our Drivers from Thinking Act."

"And why shouldn't we believe in miracles?" Sartre asked of Rachel. He wasn't a believer in miracles himself, but like any good philosopher—or ordinary lunatic—he enjoyed arguments for their own sake.

Rachel paused awkwardly, looking over at the philosopher. She had not expected to get into an argument with *him*, of all people. Rachel took a deep breath and tried to summon forth the full, terrible powers conveyed upon her by her B.A. in philosophy. "We shouldn't believe in miracles because they are—by definition—the most improbable sort of event," she replied smoothly.

"So you're arguing that we should condition our belief on the probability of an event's occurrence?" Sartre questioned, raising an eyebrow. Before Rachel could respond, he quickly followed up. "If that were the case, how could we ever believe that a six-sided die landed on '1?' After all, it's much more probable that it would have landed on '2' through '6,' yes?"

Glancing back and forth between the two combatants, Wilfred rightly wondered why such exchanges had never been given a prime-time slot on ESPN. Rachel sat in silence for a moment as she digested Sartre's rebuttal, chewing on her lip gently. "That's not what I'm arguing," she finally said as she decided to rephrase her position. "I'm saying that if you have two causal explanations for a given set of facts, it is only rational to believe the less improbable one. If we observed a die falling on '1,' or are told that it had done so by a reliable source, that would be evidence enough to believe an otherwise improbable outcome."

"Perhaps," Sartre said, pleased that she had seen through that difficulty. "But don't we still believe in a variety of improbable explanations? After all, improbability is certainly not the same as impossibility. Situations occur all the time whose explanations genuinely are improbable. Let me suggest a new example. Imagine you see a lady driving a red Mustang down the street. You're interested in an explanation for how she got the car. Let's say the only two options are first, she bought the car, and second, she won the car in a sweepstakes. Should we always believe that she bought the car and not won it simply because the latter explanation for ownership is vastly more improbable?"

Rachel furrowed her brow as she thought, trying to remember a decade ago when such questions used to occupy her for most of the night. Closing her eyes, she considered the question carefully. "Aha, I see now," Rachel said, her eyes opening as she grinned widely, sensing victory. "Both yes and no. Seeing the woman drive down the street in a Mustang, it's unquestionably rational to assume that she bought that car and did not win it; far more people have bought Mustangs than won them in contests. That does not mean that, in light of future information, we might not instead believe that she won the car. If we were to pull up beside the lady and ask her, and she was to say that she won the car in a contest, it would be perfectly rational to believe as much."

"…but isn't," Sartre tried to follow-up before being cut off by Rachel.

"I'm not done yet," she interrupted, feeling a bit of an adrenaline rush. "Your car example is actually a perfect example of why we can never rationally believe in miracles. We can be convinced that the car was won—the "miracle" option—only because it's possible that we could be exposed to additional facts that would change the relative probability. It is even more improbable that a woman who bought a Mustang would lie about winning it in a contest than that she actually did win it. Miracles, as opposed to Mustangs, are precisely the sort of things for which there are not additional confirmatory facts."

Rachel prepared to cinch the argument, and took a deep breath. "The only way to confirm a miracle is additional miracles; by their nature, you couldn't verify a miracle through the scientific method. And each additional miracle would face the same problem as the first. The only way to make miracles rationally believable would be for them to be probable explanations in their own right, which is precisely what miracles are *not*."

Jim stared straight ahead into the road, thankful that he hadn't gotten involved. Robert snored gently, his head tilted backwards against the seat. Wilfred looked at Rachel, his jaw hanging open in shock as if he had just watched a professional boxer punch out a hippopotamus. Sartre shook his head gently, putting his hands up as he clapped a few times, acknowledging defeat. "Ah, yes, you've got me," he said, smiling at his adversary. "After you recognized me in the bar, I was curious how much you knew of philosophy. Hopefully I did not offend you."

"Nah, it's fine," Rachel replied, feeling pretty good about herself, even if Sartre had only been playing devil's advocate. "It's been a while since undergraduate," she said, performing a karate-chop in the air, "but my philosophy kung-fu is still pretty fast. Sparring is always fun."

Sartre laughed loudly, unaccustomed to such a characterization of philosophical debate. "I should be glad I didn't get any bones broken then," he chuckled, even as he considered the possibility of such an outcome if he had to hold Socrates in his lap for much longer. Looking out the window, he wished that they were closer to the Philosoplex.

"I guess I'm a bit adversarial," Rachel admitted with a shrug. "That's probably why I'm comfortable in law. Although it's not exactly the same thing…" Her expression darkened a bit as she looked down at the ground. Wilfred frowned as she said that; he knew that his friend's dream had always been to lecture as a philosophy professor. Unfortunately, the likelihood of finding gainful employment in philosophy was about as probable as the miracles just discussed.

Chapter Five

Cruising down the city streets as daylight began to break through the sky, Bertrand Russell peered searchingly out of the tinted windows of his car. He turned to his left, glancing over at Kant. "Head further east! I think I may have found something," he said, quickly focusing his attention outside the car once more. A thoroughgoing naturalist in life, Russell commanded nearly complete mastery over the physical world and the forces of nature. Curiously enough, this made him even more sensitive to the supernatural than the rest of the team. Where Kant saw the metaphysical world as a pervasive gradient laid across reality, Russell understood such power as breaks in an otherwise seamless universe.

"It's been long enough," Kant said, accelerating as they moved towards the eastern limits of the city. Nonetheless, his senses were not nearly as sharp as Russell's and he could not be too critical of his navigator; Kant would have difficulty noticing the difference between a poltergeist and a god at any substantial distance. Still, after a few hours of driving Russell in expanding circles out of the city, he worried that they were far too late.

Russell merely shrugged; he was too intent on his search to worry about Kant's growing frustration. As trees began to appear alongside the road, Russell quickly became convinced that they were closing in. A few blocks away, he had only felt a slight disturbance in the world. They might have been following nothing at all. But as he urgently motioned for Kant to turn into Ashevale Park, that possibility vanished entirely. The breaks in reality he felt were too neat and too careful to be the footprint of some passing oddity; deliberate concealment could never be made to look truly inconspicuous.

Driving into the park, Kant had little need for further direction from Russell. Approaching the visitor's center, he stopped as roadway rapidly turned un-useable; the pavement was shattered in countless places, downed trees had fallen everywhere, and little pools of fire still simmered in the ground. Both philosophers immediately exited the car, following the trail of destruction toward the parking lot. The sun pulled itself slowly over the horizon as the two philosophers reached the eye of the now-passed storm, morning light illuminating the chaos before them. "We're too late," said Kant in a whisper, eyes scanning over the torn earth. Despite the ruination, he could make out the remnants of a bloody binding seal written upon the ground, the name 'Pete Machal' repeated again and again between lines of a demonic script. Of the seven bodies he saw nearby, he was at least thankful that none were Pete's; six poor souls were piled off to the side, and a police officer lay inside the circle next to a half-crushed cruiser.

Russell stepped inside the bloody circle, surveying the destruction around him. "We've been had," he said, clenching his fists at his sides. "Someone had all of this planned out to the very last detail!"

"Indeed," Kant replied, his figure crouched as he knelt over the magic seal painted on the concrete. "Dark magic like this takes time…and bodies," he continued, nodding at the pile of corpses on the far end of the lot. "But how could anyone have known Pete would be here?" Russell did not reply. "Pete disappeared in front of us; nobody could have gotten a head start on finding him."

"Even a head start wouldn't be good enough," Russell added, scuffing his shoe against the dried blood. "This seal was made hours ago, before Pete had even left the Philosoplex. His assailants knew his name, they knew that he was going to flee from us, and they knew he was going to end up at this very spot."

Kant gave a deep sigh, trying to keep his cool. "At least we know who took him." He reached down and picked up a blackened feather from the ground, turning it over in his fingers. "Michael's feathers are unmistakable."

"As is the demonic script used to draw this circle," Russell continued. "But Lucifer and Michael could not have done this alone. They are not subtle creatures; the two angels do not have the power to peer into the future. How could they have seen so far in advance?"

Kant nodded. "That is puzzling enough. But even though the brothers had the foresight to set this complicated trap, it seems apparent that they were ambushed. Angelic blood and feathers are all over the lot…" He paused, squinting as he lifted up another item from the broken concrete. "And these serpentine scales."

"Everyone seemed to know Pete would be here but us," Russell said with a growl. "How the hell is that possible?!" He took a breath, pulling his cell phone out of his jacket. "We need to confer with the others." He dialed back to the Philosoplex, hoping that the five calls from Hume that he had missed had not been particularly important.

"Would you *please* learn to leave your phone on?!" Hume hissed into the line, keeping his voice down in an effort to not wake up Patty. "The last time I was alive, we were still using goddamned carrier pigeons – and I've still figured this out." He made an exasperated noise while Russell waited in silence. "Should I assume that you haven't checked your messages?"

"…uh, perhaps?" Russell replied, rubbing the back of his head while Kant snickered in the background. His face blanched as Hume hurriedly explained what had happened at Ockham's Kegger. "Are they going to be alright?" he asked of Sartre and Socrates, immediately receiving a concerned look from Kant. "I hate to say that I don't have even a little bit of good news. Pete is gone; it looks like Michael and Lucifer lured him into a trap." Russell glanced up at the sky, tapping his foot. "No, I don't know *how*; that's why I'm calling you."

"Do you have *any* idea whatsoever where they went?" Hume pressed anxiously.

"Look, it's worse than that," Russell continued. "Something attacked the brothers; this parking lot looks like a goddamned war zone. And no, I don't know what attacked them either. Something with scales, but that doesn't really narrow things down." Shape-shifting creatures aside, serpentine forms were remarkably popular amongst the gods. "At the moment, I don't even know who won, or who took Pete." He gestured towards Kant, handing him the phone. "Hume wants to yell at you too."

"I'm not yelling at anyone," Hume said to Kant, rubbing his head as he leaned back against the kitchen counter. "I just don't have any clue how this happened. The attack at Ockham's Kegger and this trap for Pete bespeak an incredible amount of coordination and planning."

"I agree," Kant replied. "Is it possible that someone infiltrated our operation at Ockham's Kegger? Frankly, my feeling is that the brothers—and whoever else is behind this—were simply waiting for us to succeed with the Existential Dilemma and then claim the new god for their own purposes."

"As do I," Hume continued as he returned to the Philosoplex's foyer and collapsed in one of the couches. "So we've been had from the start. Yet I am at an absolute loss as to how anyone discovered our plans and then managed to outmaneuver us with such precision." He furrowed his brow in thought. "Still, our immediate concern must be recovering Pete. The brothers—or whoever else might have him now—will surely move quickly and consume his power for themselves. That outcome must be prevented at any cost."

Kant nodded solemnly. "Where do you suggest we begin?" He looked back towards Russell, who had spent the last few minutes thoroughly inspecting the scene. Kant's partner frowned and made a thumbs-down gesture; he had not discovered anything of value. "There are no clear leads to be followed here."

"Given our urgent need to recover Pete, I hesitate to suggest such a detour...but if Russell cannot follow the brothers' trail, you may need to pay a visit to Nidhogg." Hume knew that Nidhogg, the old Nordic serpent, would assist the philosophers as he had done so before. Nidhogg was the last survivor of the Nordic pantheon; he lingered on long after Odin and the others had perished. The ancient wyrm still possessed great power over the land; Nidhogg surely would have felt what transpired in Ashevale Park. Yet Nidhogg lived deep, deep down, coiled on a pillar near the molten heart of the Earth. Even with the philosopher's power, such a journey would consume precious time. "Make haste! I will direct Nietzsche to wait at the park for your return."

Kant snapped the phone shut as Russell returned to his side. "Hume suggests that we seek guidance from Nidhogg," he said briskly. "*Quickly.*"

"Oh, you know I get things done quickly," Russell said with a wide grin. That was precisely the reason why Kant never let him drive the car.

Kant snorted dismissively. "...that's what *she* said."

"I love when you get sassy, Kant," Russell said with a loud laugh, stepping close to his partner. Kant did not have much time to prepare himself before Russell stiffened up, drawing in a deep breath. "OPEN!" he yelled at the ground, fists clenched at his sides. While screaming at the ground would ordinarily be a model exercise in futility, the ground began to crumble around the two men. As a gaping hole opened beneath him, Russell flattered himself by thinking that he was simply hilariously persuasive. However, despite whatever truth to this assertion could be found in his philosophy, Russell's mastery over the physical world provided the true explanation. Kant clutched his cane to his chest as the philosophers fell downwards, through Russell's seemingly endless tunnel in the planet.

Falling to the center of the Earth is not, however, as simple as movies have led people to believe. The planet has an average radius of almost four thousand miles and even a spectacularly aerodynamic diver could only reach a maximum terminal velocity of around two-hundred miles per hour. Since suit jackets and Russell's moustache would hardly help that figure, the philosophers could expect to fall to the center of the Earth in around twenty hours. To Russell, that sort of a wait was completely unacceptable. He was a punctual man and Russell was not about to spend a day waiting behind uncooperative air before he fell to the center of the Earth. Not needing to breath, and completely unconcerned by Kant's distaste for extreme sports, Russell purged his tunnel of atmosphere. No longer held back by the meddling forces of wind resistance, the philosophers were soon free-falling at nearly twenty times the speed of sound.

When the cab finally pulled up in front of the philosophers' mansion, Hume was already waiting outside for the group. He hurried down to the car, pulling open the rear door. "Good god, is he alright?" he asked, looking down at Socrates. Not wasting any time, he helped pull the Greek out of the back seat.

Sartre hurried out of the car, assisting Hume in holding up Socrates while the rest of the passengers unloaded. Almost as an afterthought, Sartre tossed a small wad of bills up to Jim, who gratefully received at least ten times more than he was owed. "He should be fine," said Sartre breathlessly as he hoisted Socrates aloft. "Let's get inside." Rachel ran ahead to open the door – Socrates' broad shoulders barely fit through the door frame. Wilfred and Robert followed sleepily behind them, not used to dashing around on adventures in the dead of night. As Jim turned away from the mansion and sped off, he found himself already forgetting where he was; the strange route quickly began to fade from his mind.

Setting Socrates down on the large rug in the foyer, Hume wiped his brow before turning to introduce himself to the newcomers. "I'm David Hume," he said with a smile, "and your friend Patty is asleep upstairs." Before he could continue, Rachel gave a squeal and clapped excitedly, looking for a moment like a teenage girl at a concert.

"Hume!" she exclaimed, taking the philosopher's hand and shaking it firmly as she beamed at him. "You're one of my favorites, Sartre didn't tell me you'd be here! This is just too much, ohhhh." She clapped her hand over her mouth, blushing a bit at her outburst. Looking away from Hume, she smiled bashfully. Sartre felt a bit disappointed that he hadn't gotten such a response.

"I, um, well," Hume said, taken back by her enthusiasm. "Well, thank you. Thank you." He felt a bit like a collectible toy, and considered briefly the lucrative possibility of a line of plush philosopher dolls. "Let me show you up to your rooms; I'm sure you are all thoroughly exhausted from the night," he continued, beckoning to the party as he headed up a long, winding flight of wooden stairs. Walking down the hallway, Hume spoke in hushed tones so as to not wake Patty. "Please use any of the last three rooms on the left," he said, gesturing at the doors. "The bathroom is at the end of the hallway. I'm sure you all have many questions, but you will be safe here for the night. I'll endeavor to explain everything more thoroughly in the morning, but for now I must focus my attention on Socrates."

The three friends glanced at each other before choosing their rooms, nearly inside before Sartre came bounding up the stairs. "Wait, wait," he said, walking over to Wilfred and patting him on the back. "I need to talk to you for a moment." Sartre smiled casually, not wanting to alarm anyone.

"Uh, sure," Wilfred said. He was too sleepy to recognize right away his unique situation amongst the three. Turning to Rachel and Robert, he gave them a confident thumbs-up. "Get some sleep. I'll see you all in the morning, alright?" Nodding in assent, both of his friends went inside to get some much needed rest. Rachel was still deeply curious about the mansion, Hume, and what they wanted with Wilfred, but thought better than to be nosy.

Hume looked over at Sartre questioningly as the three men went back downstairs, taking a seat on the long couch next to Socrates' body. Habitually adjusting his glasses, Sartre turned towards Wilfred with a serious expression. "You looked into Yaggoth, didn't you?" he asked bluntly. Hume's eyes widened, immediately understanding why Sartre had detained Wilfred from sleep.

Wilfred swallowed hard, wondering if his hair had gone white as a result. "Yes, but only for a moment," he said quietly, not enjoying even the brief, involuntary recollection. "How did you know?"

"I have power over the mind and human emotions; I can feel your fear of that experience lingering around you," Sartre explained, patting Wilfred on the shoulder. "Nothing is wrong with you; don't worry. I should have said that at the start." Wilfred gave a long sigh of relief, having felt a deep terror of being alone in the darkness of his room. "Quite the contrary, in fact. You are, I believe, the only mortal to have ever looked into the depths of Yaggoth and survived the experience. As a result, you should be thoroughly immune to any effort by the nightmare to enter your dreams. Since you experienced the visceral horror of its material form, your sanity should be safe from mere nightmares."

Wilfred sat up a bit straighter, feeling a measure of pride at the distinction. Sitting next to him, Hume looked over at the mortal. Sartre continued, his hand staying on Wilfred's shoulder as he gave a little squeeze. "We could use you. Since we are of the Created, we do not sleep, and cannot dream. That is why Yaggoth has lingered so long in the world; once the nightmare enters the sleeping realm it is beyond our reach. But you, Wilfred...you could find it for us."

His face paling, Wilfred looked down at the carpet. The sight of Socrates laying disabled on the floor after facing Yaggoth was a frightening reminder of the nightmare's power. "It's going to look for Pete, isn't it?" he asked quietly, closing his eyes as he thought of his friend. Wilfred was irritated at the philosophers for having—quite literally—played God with Pete. But he knew that they meant well, and he couldn't sit by while Pete was in danger.

"Yes," replied Sartre simply, nodding. "All of you are safe inside the mansion. Right now we are somewhere yet nowhere in particular; your friends can sleep safely upstairs. Yaggoth will have to look for Pete instead." The three sat in silence for a minute as Wilfred digested the information.

"What would I have to do?" he asked at last, meeting Sartre's eyes with a determined gaze. Wilfred figured that if he had the courage to face Yaggoth back at Ockham's Kegger—even if for only the briefest moment—he could do so again. He owed as much to his friends.

"With my assistance, you could act as a sort of homing beacon. Since you saw Yaggoth's fully manifested form, you could find the nightmare in the dreaming and through that, find its host," Sartre explained, double-checking his plan in his head. "And if we manage to catch Yaggoth while it is hiding in the dreams of a mortal, we can finally destroy it forever."

"But it isn't that simple, right?" Wilfred asked, knowing that hunting an ancient nightmare couldn't be quite so cut and dry.

"Unfortunately not," admitted Sartre, looking away from Wilfred for a moment. Hume was busy inspecting Socrates carefully, not wasting any time in treating his fallen colleague. "Your interaction with Yaggoth in the dreaming world must necessarily be a two-way street. As you find it, it will find you. While your own dreams are proof against Yaggoth's horror, you will have to stand against the nightmare's power as you search the dreams of others."

"Lovely," Wilfred said sarcastically, having seen—and smelled—enough of the creature at the bar to understand the potential obstacles. "How am I supposed to deal with that? I didn't see what happened with Nietzsche and that *thing*, but it put up a hell of a fight."

"Ah," the philosopher replied, smiling widely, "but you will not be fighting anything with your body. You will only have to fight with your mind. Have you ever seen the movie *The Matrix*?"

Wilfred raised an eyebrow, laughing a bit at the seemingly out-of-place reference to a popular film. "Of course I have," he started, pausing as he saw the connection. "It would be like that? I don't know karate in my dreams, though. I mean, sometimes I end up flying, a little bit, but…" He trailed off, looking back at Sartre for an explanation.

"That's when you are dreaming normally," Sartre said, leaning comfortably against the couch. "But I would be able to make it so that in this journey, you are fully lucid. As a lucid dreamer, you will have immense influence over the content and outcome of your dream. You will have power that makes even Nietzsche's feeble influence over reality look insignificant. The danger, however, is that while fully investing your consciousness in a dream should grant you the ability to break through Yaggoth's defenses, death in a lucid dream means death in life."

"Heh. Just like the Matrix, I see," Wilfred said, questioning his ability to handle such a mission. "I've never done anything like that, though," he said before stopping to laugh at the absurdity of his admission. "Haha, well, of course I haven't. But how do you know I'd be able to handle it?" At that, he remembered that he wasn't dreaming yet; he still had a family, and they were almost certainly afraid for him. Wilfred's thoughts turned immediately to his wife and young daughter.

"I don't," Sartre admitted, not about to hide the truth from Wilfred. "You might not be able to withstand Yaggoth's assault. Even then, you could still try to flee back to the waking world. But in all honesty, you may die." He stopped, eyes searching Wilfred's face. "I do know that you had the courage and force of will to face the nightmare before, and that means you at least have the potential for success."

Wilfred's usually stoic demeanor cracked, his eyes starting to water. Clasping his hands tightly together, he held back tears as he thought of his family. "But my wife, my daughter," he said in a shaky voice. "They don't even know where I am right now. Christ, Sophia is probably worried sick." He had gotten too carried away in the excitement of the night.

"I wouldn't ask you if there was any other way, Wilfred," Sartre said, having forgotten for a moment about the ordinary worries of mortal life. "You don't have to do this. I understand—no, I feel—how important your family is to you. But if Yaggoth consumes Pete, all of humanity's nightmares will become real. The whole world will be plunged into madness."

Sensing Wilfred's confusion, Sartre elaborated. "Right now, your friend Pete is little more than a wellspring of power. He will become a full-fledged god in time, but he does not yet have the necessary control or sophistication." Wilfred looked down at the prone figure of Socrates as Sartre continued. "Pete has a great deal of power, Wilfred. A great deal of fuel, if you would, fuel which the dying gods are hungry to have for themselves."

"Dammit," Wilfred said, trying to keep his voice down. He lowered his head, holding it his hands. "Why would you do this?"

Sartre sat in silence, and Hume took his attention from Socrates for a moment as he looked to Wilfred. "New gods would continue to arise even without our interference. It is only a matter of time before one of them falls into darkness; the threat to humanity from Yaggoth and other beings would only be greater had we not interfered. We transformed Pete because it was the only way to exercise some control over the situation," he concluded. The philosopher's words were cold comfort, but they were all he could offer.

Taking slow, deep breaths, Wilfred wiped his watery eyes clear. He was afraid; the fear of losing his life and his family was even worse than the terror of Yaggoth. Yet Wilfred could not simply walk away from the situation if his refusal risked the end of the world. "I'll do it," he said in a level voice, fighting to put the decision and his emotions behind him. "After all the time I've spent talking tough, I can't walk away from this. Pete would never let me live it down." Wilfred smiled at the thought of his friend; he remembered all the happy memories they had shared together. Shivering, a chill ran through his body, as if a fever had broken. "I just want to call my family first, is that OK?"

"Of course," Sartre said, reaching into his jacket and pulling out his cell phone. Flipping the phone open, he handed it to Wilfred. "You'd have a hell of a time placing a call in the middle of the city, but somehow it's always five bars in a dimensional pocket hidden from reality."

"Heh, that figures," Wilfred said, taking the phone before heading off towards the adjoining study. Pulling the door closed behind him, he sank down on to a large, cushioned recliner. While many men had agonized over calling their wives to explain their mysterious absence, few could legitimately claim that they had been out trying to save the world with a team of famous philosophers. Taking a deep breath, Wilfred dialed home.

Within fifteen minutes of their departure, the pair of philosophers were rapidly approaching the center of the planet, a lack of air the only fact sparing Russell from having to listen to Kant complain the entire way down. Russell began to slow their descent; even he did not want to slam into the molten core of Earth at a velocity that put Pete's old fighter jets to shame. The philosophers dropped out of the tunnel into a massive cavern, surrounded by vast pillars of stone reaching down into a pool of bubbling liquid metal.

Gently landing atop a shattered spire, the philosophers looked searchingly around the arching cave. It took little time to spot Nidhogg; wrapped around a particularly massive pillar, the snake was already watching them. Hopping from pillar to pillar, the philosophers approached the beast, prepared for a confrontation.

Yet as they drew near the serpent, it was immediately clear that Nidhogg was not well. His ribs were visible through sagging skin, and it seemed to be all the serpent could do not to slip into the churning heat below. "Have you come," Nidhogg began to ask, needing to muster his strength before continuing, "to watch me die, philosophers?"

Russell and Kant exchanged a concerned look before turning back to the giant before them. "No, we thought..." Kant began before trailing off. "I am sorry. We did not expect to come upon you in such a condition." Nidhogg was one of the few supernatural entities that commanded the philosophers' respect. Long ago appreciating the perversity of his existence, the snake regarded his eventual destruction as necessary for the preservation of humanity. Yet Nidhogg still feared death; the snake was far closer to the mortals than the gods. He was a supernatural creation, but still a living organism, not an angel or demon.

"Our condolences, great serpent," Russell said, bowing his head slightly. "What has happened to you?" he asked, even though he could imagine the answer. The snake was the sole survivor of a long-dead mythology, long divorced from the source of his creation. Nidhogg had lived at the center of the Earth for centuries, gnawing on the roots of the world-tree Yggdrasil. Yet once the Norse pantheon had perished, the world-tree had begun to wither and rot; all that remained of its roots were brittle, dead timbers.

Nidhogg tilted his head a bit as he hung in front of the philosophers. "Yggdrasil has died, and I die with it," he said quietly. Long ago his voice could have shaken the depths of the world; now it was hard to hear him over the bubbling metal beneath them. "The squirrel no longer visits me, and the eagle long ago fell silent. I am...the last." The philosophers shared a confused look with each other; Nidhogg's mythic animal companions had died long, long ago and far before the philosophers had arrived on the world.

Mustering a small laugh, Nidhogg broke the awkward silence. "Do not mourn me, god-killers," he said. "I have waited long for death. Do you know what it is like to lay alone for *centuries*? Once I shared tales with the squirrel; my stories are forgotten. Once the eagle told me of the view from the sky; she would not recognize this world, even if she still lived." The snake took a slow breath, trying to sustain a voice that had been silent for many generations of humanity. "But...perhaps I have one task left. What would you have of me?"

"The angelic brothers—the archangel Michael and Lucifer—took one of our friends, but they were ambushed by some serpent-god. We must find our companion, but...we do not know where to find him," Russell said to Nidhogg, stuffing his hands in his pockets.

"Ah, ahahh," Nidhogg laughed again, shaking his head slightly. He smiled as well as a serpentine leviathan could; few teeth still shone in his mouth. "You flatter me, to think I am still strong enough to track *them*. Malice-striker is little more than a name now; the fallen angels are far beyond my ken." Pausing for a moment, the snake examined the men before him. "Still, that little god...you call him friend and not prey?" Nidhogg asked of them incredulously; he knew well the philosophers' usual purpose.

Kant's eyes widened as the serpent spoke of Pete. "You know of him?" he asked immediately. "How?"

"*How?* I may be old, Immanuel, but I am not yet gone," Nidhogg said, extending his head closer to the pair. "Here, I can feel all which moves upon the face of the world. A god's footsteps resound in the deep; I have been listening to this so-called friend of yours. You were right to think the brothers took him. I listened when their foot-steps joined his, and the cacophony when those fool angels were ambushed."

"Do you know who attacked them, and which party took Pete?" Russell inquired, needing to find a lead on Pete's whereabouts before the trail grew cold.

"He left with the angels, I surmise, but he did not walk. The brothers' steps were heavy, as if they carried a great load," Nidhogg said. The serpent felt more alive—more powerful—than he had in countless years. Being needed, even if only briefly, was enough to help Nidhogg face the coming end. "But as to who fought the angels and lived? That is harder, much harder. It moved upon a mass of tendrils; snakes-but-not, coils without mouths."

"Peculiar..." Russell commented thoughtfully, unable to think of any beings that matched such a description. "And you have not felt its movement before?"

"Heh...heh, indeed," Nidhogg chuckled, unable to shrug due to an acute lack of shoulders. "Whatever it was, it has not walked the earth during my lifetime. It is ancient...older than the brothers, older than even me."

Both of the philosophers frowned, obviously concerned by this revelation. The interference of the angels was already a grave threat; now they would also have to contend with a second, mysterious foe. "Hopefully we will not have to discover anything about that beast ourselves, if we can find Pete before the angels manage to resurrect their dead god Yahweh," Kant said, shaking his head at the thought. "Do you know where the brothers are now?"

"I'm afraid I only know of the earth," Nidhogg replied. "And they are no longer upon the ground. If I could ask the eagle to search the skies, or Jormungandr the seas, but...ah, you know..." The serpent drifted into thought, staring down mournfully at the fate that waited below once his strength failed. In the glimmering white-hot metal, Nidhogg could almost see his kin once more. He thought of his world, and the Ragnarok which had never come; that cataclysmic rebirth had been replaced by a slow, endless rot. "I have…nothing else for you, philosophers," Nidhogg said slowly, his eyes closing. "Thank-you for the company; even an old beast does not want to pass this world unnoticed."

Russell reached back into his memory, trying to think of some appropriate words. He remembered a poem from his boyhood days in school:

> "Yet not to thine eternal resting-place
>
> Shalt thou retire alone, nor couldst thou wish
>
> Couch more magnificent. Thou shalt lie down
>
> With patriarchs of the infant world--with kings,
>
> The powerful of the earth--the wise, the good,
>
> Fair forms, and hoary seers of ages past,
>
> All in one mighty sepulcher,"

Russell spoke somberly as Kant closed his eyes. Nidhogg was no ally of the philosophers; indeed, they would have eventually destroyed the serpent along with the rest of the supernatural world. But the snake was remarkably humane despite his inhumanity. Nidhogg's life, however dangerous to humanity in the long run, was still life. So while he could not live, his death was tragic.

"Your modern poetry has its charms," Nidhogg said appreciatively with a nod, shivers running through his length. "Now please, let me be, while I still have my dignity."

Russell turned immediately, throwing out his right arm towards a nearby stone pillar. Clean lines of force cut through the rock and a thick cylinder separated outwards, falling to land on its one end in the molten core below. Kant turned back to Nidhogg for a final time. "Rest in peace," he said before leaping with Russell down onto the bobbing platform. Focusing once again, Russell guided the cylinder to float underneath of his tunnel to the surface. Kant widened his stance on the precariously wobbling surface, steadying himself for their exit.

With a loud grunt Russell brought both of his hands together firmly in front of him, the cylinder dipping sharply as the metal sea beneath it subsided into a shallow, concave bowl. Going up is, after all, far harder than falling down; Russell had to push his mastery of the elements to the limit in order to ensure a timely return to the world above. The sea below suddenly surged, a flaming spiral lifting the cylinder up towards the ceiling. Accelerating rapidly upwards, the stone platform fit perfectly into the tunnel, driven ever faster by the stream of fire beneath it. Craning his neck to look straight up the tunnel, Kant could not even see the light of the exit, still thousands of miles away. Massive acceleration causing their feet to crack the rock beneath them, the two philosophers rode their magma-driven boulder like a bullet straight from the heart of the world.

Meanwhile, Nietzsche slowly rolled around the battleground at Ashevale Park in his wheelchair; he was as intrigued by the scattered scales on the ground as his colleagues had been earlier. He looked down at his watch, noting that thirty minutes had already passed since he had arrived at the scene. Moving towards the gaping hole in the earth, Nietzsche curiously kicked a small rock into it. Since Russell's car had been parked outside since he arrived, he was certain that his colleagues had gone diving into the Earth on an expedition. Still, it had been awhile, and Nietzsche imagined that Russell was taking his sweet time; even if he was visiting the center of the planet. But as the ground began to tremble beneath him, Nietzsche quickly wheeled himself backwards from the gaping hole.

Flying out of the earth, the half-molten boulder would have looked to a giant like a delightfully entertaining game of Whack-a-Mole. Kant and Russell both dove off the rock before it careened out of the park, landing with a crash and a welcoming symphony of half a dozen car alarms. Russell landed first, smiling at Nietzsche as he ruffled a bit of ash out of his hair. However, Kant landed with his left hand clutched over his head, clearly in pain.

"Do you know how much it hurts to get hit in the eye with a rock while travelling at Mach 10?" Kant hissed angrily, walking over to Nietzsche and leaning over the wheelchair as he stared down at him with his good right eye. "A...LOT." He shook his cane menacingly at Nietzsche, nearly ready to give his colleague some *genuine* disabilities. Cursing under the breath, Kant stormed off to the car and hopped into the passenger's side, slamming the door after him.

"Well, it looks like you're two-for-two with making friends recently, Friedrich," Russell laughed, watching his partner stomp away.

"Ehh," Nietzsche said with a shrug, trying to appear nonchalant despite his genuine disappointment with the situation. He truly wished that the rock had hit Russell instead. "Come up with anything interesting?" he asked, hearing a few police sirens in the distance arriving to respond to boulder-induced mayhem.

Russell turned and walked towards the car, looking down at Nietzsche as he followed alongside him. "Nidhogg is dying, Pete is with the brothers—they're either on water or in the air—and some sort of ancient god is chasing them," he said quickly, not wanting to waste time.

"They aren't in the air," Nietzsche noted, the wheelchair underneath him rapidly transforming into his signature motorcycle.

"Huh?" Russell asked, standing at the driver's-side door of the Aston-Martin.

Nietzsche smiled knowingly, revving the engine of his bike. "Lucifer strictly refuses to do any sort of flying since the Fall, either on angelic wings or commercial air," he explained. "Which means they're on a boat somewhere."

"Ah," Russell said dryly, opening his door to hear another litany of curses from Kant. "I'm glad we're down to only seventy-one percent of the planet, then." Nietzsche idled alongside the car as Russell rolled down his window.

"I'll be waiting for you at the mansion," Nietzsche smirked, giving Russell a mocking wave as he popped a wheelie and blazed off towards the park's exit. Russell's hands tightened on the steering wheel as Nietzsche left in a trail of smoke. The worth of Russell's manhood—no, his very *moustache*—had been called into question. He glanced over at Kant as he turned the wheel sharply, hitting the gas hard.

"You know how I normally feel about your driving," Kant said through gritted teeth, his hand still clasped over his left eye. "But the starry heavens above me and the moral law within me say…*kick his ass*!"

Russell didn't need much motivation. He grinned as they sped perilously down the park driveway after Nietzsche. The car made a sharp left onto the main road with a screech, the local police too distracted by volcanic debris and a massacre in the park to issue speeding tickets. Thankful for the light Saturday-morning traffic, Russell zipped between cars as he made a beeline westwards towards the Philosoplex. Unfortunately, Nietzsche's head start—coupled with his reckless disregard for human life—was paying off. By the time Russell was on the highway the motorcycle was lost in the distance. Seizing his one good chance to close the distance, Russell floored the gas pedal.

Where Nietzsche had an advantage in the city on his bike, Russell knew he could catch up on the freeway. While the German had a hell of a bike, it didn't have a maximum speed anywhere close to that of Russell's top-end British sports-car. Tearing down the highway at nearly two-hundred miles per hour, Russell began to narrow the gap between him and Nietzsche. But even his full speed was not enough to catch Nietzsche; the German's bad habit of sliding sideways under stopped trucks—a trick he likely had picked up from modern action films—had given him too much of a lead downtown. From up on the highway, Russell could see Nietzsche already leaving the exit ramps towards the seemingly normal field which hid the Philosoplex. The desperate situation called for action, and Russell knew he had to dial the amp to eleven.

Calling forth his power yet again, the ground in front of the curving highway buckled and rose, forming a steep fifty-foot ramp dragged out of the earth by sheer force of will. Russell drove straight off the road, hitting the stone ramp and heading for the sky. Still following the winding route down to the field, Nietzsche heard the rumbling and looked up in time to see Russell's car flying high over him. Russell and Kant both thrust their arms out of the side windows, giving Nietzsche the finger in unison as they sailed past him towards the mansion. Slowing the car with a mighty air cushion as it descended, the black sedan settled gracefully in front of the mansion's entrance before Nietzsche managed to cover the remainder of the long driveway.

Chapter Six

Thousands of miles from the philosophers, the harbor of San Juan sparkled in the morning sunlight. From atop the battlements of the old fortress looking over the city, a tourist could see any number of yachts and cruise ships dotting the water. As it happened, the sunny weather of Puerto Rico was attractive not only to exhausted Americans looking for a relaxing vacation. Indeed, amongst the dozens of extravagant yachts belonging to important officials and corporate leaders, the *Paradise Lost* looked perfectly at home. Measuring just over 350', the three-story grey and white pleasure yacht would have suited the tastes of Saudi royalty and Russian oil barons. But whatever one's opinion of the morality of contemporary energy politics, the man standing on the lower rear deck made all the other billionaires in the harbor seem like saints.

Lucifer reached back, slowly running a hand over his smooth head as he surveyed the city around him. Sunbathing in the Caribbean wasn't *exactly* Hell, he thought, but the endless pit also did not have casinos and fine dining establishments. He missed the eternal realms as much as his brother Michael, but Lucifer still appreciated the finer points of mortal life. After all, without the decadence and greed that surrounded him, Lucifer would have far fewer damned souls to turn into living furniture. Adjusting his sunglasses, he winced slightly in pain as he sat up from a wooden lounge chair. He reached down, running his hand tenderly over the bandages on his chest and left leg; his dark skin was punctured and torn in many places. Of course, Lucifer did not mind the pain; he had to resist the urge to dig his fingers into the still-fresh wounds. He dealt in suffering, and agony was his joy. But Lucifer could not afford to let his injuries linger; he would have ample time to explore his masochism once he reigned again in Hell.

And as glorious as the salty water of the bay would feel in gashes that reached far into his body, Lucifer was forbidden from taking a swim. This fact was doubly irritating as Satan had intended to try out his new pair of board shorts. Black and embroidered with red '666's, Lucifer had not been able to resist the stylish yet hilariously ironic shorts when he spotted them on his last shopping trip. The red numbering matched perfectly the shade of the Lord of Hell's favorite casual footwear: bright red Crocs. Despite his still-substantial power, Lucifer had required an unprecedented sacrifice to ensure the awful shoe's commercial success; the soul-for-a-sole bargain had profited the Devil even more than his continued support for the American system of measurement. Standing and resting his hands on the *Paradise Lost's* railing, the fallen angel basked in the glow of the rising sun.

Below deck, the Archangel Michael opened the door to the yacht's second guest bedroom. At present, the room's "guest" was Pete Machal. Michael had bound the new god to the king-sized bed with the same iron shackles which had once held his brother. While not quite as effective as a binding seal, the chains had to suffice in view of the angel's resistance to ruining perfectly good silk sheets with another bloody binding seal. Pete yelled loudly and thrashed as his captor entered the room, the inscribed metal bands around him straining and banging together.

"Release me!" Pete shouted defiantly at Michael as the angel pulled up a chair beside the bed. Sputtering with rage, Pete fell back down to the bed, unable to break chains once forged eons ago by Yahweh himself to bind Lucifer after the Fall. "Fuck you! You're nothing to me!" he spat out, his humanity mixing with the beginnings of divine arrogance.

Michael gave a tired sigh as he pulled off his white fedora, placing it on the table behind him, safely outside the range of Pete's struggling. The angel was wearing khaki shorts and a colorful Hawaiian shirt, white fabric with an assortment of delightful, bright tropical flora. Clasping his hands in his lap, Michael leaned forward to look over Pete. "It pains me to hear you talk like that," the angel said sadly, shaking his head. "It is unbecoming of your new station in this universe."

Panting from exertion, Pete glared over at Michael. Even struggling briefly against the chains exhausted him; the ancient metal sapped his strength and stunted the development of his powers. "I'm not going to help you," he said sternly, staring into the angel's golden eyes.

"I would love if you would, but your *assistance* isn't necessary, so speak," Michael replied, reaching over onto the nightstand beside the bed to pick up a small potted bonsai. Holding the plant on the palm of his hand, he held it out for Pete to see. The bending, perfectly symmetrical branches of the small tree were obviously sculpted. "It is beautiful, isn't it?" The angel asked, reaching his other hand out to stroke a finger gently over the tiny leaves. "It took a bonsai master a great deal of time to grow a plant like this. Every branch had to be bound and trimmed repeatedly to create this shape. By controlling the plant's growth, the master could choose its final form." The angel paused for a moment, letting the implications sink in for Pete. Michael would have preferred to begin shaping Pete's destiny immediately, but for that he needed his brother, and Lucifer's wounds were still too serious for such exertion.

"You're insane," Pete said, subconsciously reflecting on the fact that villains never seemed to take such assertions to heart. "I'm not going to be your god; I'm not going to be the philosophers' god. I will make this world a better place." Over the course of his abduction, Pete had figured out that the angels planned to somehow turn him into a replica of their—he imagined long-dead—Creator, Yahweh. He didn't know how they planned to accomplish such a feat, but Michael's bonsai was enough to instill in Pete a real fear of what such *pruning* might entail.

Michael laughed warmly and smiled, reclining back against his chair. "And what could be a better place than Heaven?" he asked. "With your power, the virtuous will once again look forward to an eternity of splendor; streets paved in gold and life amongst the sainted."

"Yet you would allow your brother to remake Hell!" Pete rebutted angrily. "You want the worst just as much as you want the best. All you care about is being restored to your high throne."

"Oh, not at all," Michael said, still smiling. "You know as well as I do that good is meaningless without evil. Heaven for all would be Heaven for none; Hell is the price that *must* be paid." The angel's face grew sad as he nodded down at Pete understandingly. "But do not mistake me; I weep for the lost and the damned. If it were possible for every soul to enter the Pearly Gates, then I would have it without hesitation."

Pete stared up at the light blue ceiling as he considered Michael's plan. "You don't make any sense, Michael," he replied, trying to appeal to the angel's own sympathies. "How is Heaven truly any different than Hell? Mortals don't experience eternity like you do."

Much to Pete's surprise, Michael frowned but agreed with his assessment. "Your wisdom is already quite great," the angel admitted, looking up from the floor. "In the first Heaven, we left the inhabitants as they were when mortal. We only provided the resources, the absence of pain, and the freedom to explore."

"And they all wanted to die, didn't they Michael?" Pete pressed, already knowing the answer. His mortal experiences with the Luxury Towers elevator had taught him much about the horrors of eternity.

"Yes, yes they did," Michael said, giving a long sigh of frustration. "Some took longer than others; most took a few hundred years before they began to get bored. But as centuries turned into millennia, boredom grew into madness."

Pete shook his head; he did not understand how the angels could have overlooked that fact, but was shocked that Yahweh had not foreseen it. "It didn't strike you that after living long enough to spend a century examining each atom in the material universe, a mortal mind might start to break? You can survive in eternity because a purpose is written into your very being; you are not free." Michael did not disagree; the angels were made to serve their Creator. "Freedom is a great good in life, but it is no better than damnation when it has no end. Truly good people fall into despair and madness simply because they win the lottery and find themselves free of worry. If humans can't handle the Powerball without ending up strung out on cocaine, how did you ever imagine they could handle ten trillion years that would still bring them no closer to death? The choices people make—the purpose they find for themselves—are only meaningful because life is short and fickle."

The angel let Pete finish, hoping his understanding of the complexity of the situation would make Michael's job easier. "I agree, you are quite right," Michael said after Pete finished. "Yahweh, myself, all of us; we all misunderstood the nature of humanity. It is difficult, perhaps impossible, for eternal beings to understand the horror of time. Your unique position gives you valuable perspective, Pete."

"Then why do you want to bring Heaven back?!" Pete asked insistently.

"Why? Because I have developed a new model for Heaven. Yahweh had not anticipated the mortal mind's peculiar aversion to eternal life, but since then I have successfully solved the dilemma which vexed him," Michael explained, fully confident in the solution. "Humans will simply lose a bit of their humanity when they ascend to Heaven; they shall become slightly less mortal and more like me."

Pete looked blankly at Michael, staggered by the stupidity of his explanation. "So you strip them of their free will?" he asked incredulously.

"I don't like to think of it that way," Michael replied, unappreciative of Pete's characterization. "We simply give our wards enough of an ingrained purpose and unshakeable contentment that they can watch the eons pass without getting...restless."

"That sounds a lot like a stoner's plan for getting through senior year in college," Pete said sharply. "Stripping mortals of their free will, drugging them; it doesn't matter what you call it. Turning people into mindless zombies is the only way to get them to appreciate your *great gift* of eternal life."

Pete was not the only one getting angry; Michael did not enjoy his captive's snarky attitude and sardonic tone. "It *is* the greatest gift possible!" he insisted, the agitation clear in his voice. "Since the dawn of time, humans have dreamt of and prayed for eternal life. The virtuous deserve to spend the ages wreathed in glory."

"Please," Pete retorted, "people *dream* of plenty of things! But desire isn't a very good way of measuring moral justice. It's natural—in the most literal sense—for biological creatures to constantly strive for more than they have. Survival is humanity's most powerful primal instinct. What people *want* is not always what people *need*; I would think you would know that much."

Pushing back his chair, the archangel rose to his feet. "Nonsense! Mortals always dream of seeing their family and friends again. All of human life is built up as a bulwark against fear of death.

You've seen their funerals; their grief! I'm saving them from all of that!" he argued breathlessly.

"You can only say that because you're not human and you never were," Pete replied, tiring of Michael's delusions. "I loved both of my parents very much," he added, wincing as he remembered their deaths. "And sure, I'd like to see them again. More than *you* can imagine. But the memories I have of them are special precisely because they were unique, fleeting moments. You're a fool to think anyone would truly enjoy spending eternity with anyone, even their beloved mother." He had to fight back tears at that statement; parts of Pete wanted nothing more in the world than to be safe in his mother's old house. "Time doesn't mean anything to you, Michael. You're right that death defines much of the human experience; but that isn't because death is a wrong to be fixed. Love is nothing without loss, family is nothing without isolation, and joy is nothing without grief. Eternal life is a mockery of everything that makes mortality precious." Pete paused, remembering the angel's words. "You said yourself that good is nothing without evil; can't you appreciate that life is nothing without death?"

"Enough!" Michael shouted, leaning over Pete and shaking his finger accusingly. "Your blasphemy will not stand!" Reaching down, the angel held Pete by his chin. "You *will* remake Heaven in my vision, whelp. We will break you of your insolent humanity and help you appreciate the glory of our divine plan." Michael nearly spat out his last few words, drawing back from the bed as he grabbed his hat off of the desk. Turning sharply, he stormed out of the room, slamming the door behind him.

Pete returned to staring at the ceiling, considering the bizarre series of events that had led up to finding himself chained to a bed in the bottom of a boat. Perhaps the philosophers were right, he thought, having hours ago regretted his rash flight from their compound. He hadn't been himself. Whatever he thought of Hume's plan to annihilate the supernatural, Pete recognized that the angels were far more dangerous. Between Lucifer's love of human suffering and Michael's plan to dismantle free will, the brothers' plans could bring nothing good for humanity. Pete was right to think that the disappearance of Yahweh was somehow tied to the increasingly obvious problems with constructing an afterlife; the pair evidently planned to use him to recreate the worlds that their creator had abandoned. He could not allow himself to be used as a tool in stripping humanity of the dignity of death. But for the moment, Pete could only wait and try to plan an escape.

Sitting by himself in the Philosoplex's darkened study, Wilfred finally pressed the 'Call' button on Sartre's cell. Holding the phone to his ear, he listened anxiously to the ring tone. In the suburbs west of the city, Sophia Behari's phone went off next to her bed. Wilfred's wife had laid alone all night, exhausted but unable to sleep. She had called the local police but had been told—predictably—that she wasn't going to get help searching for a person who was only a few hours late. But for Wilfred, those few hours were exceptional; he was a dedicated family man. Sophia could not remember Wilfred ever disappearing as he had that night, and feared the worst.

She hesitated for a moment before picking up the phone, her eyes glancing at the caller ID. Too shaken to recognize Sartre's name blinking on the small screen, Sophia only knew that it wasn't Wilfred's phone. Bracing herself for the worst, she quickly snatched up the phone and answered after the third ring. "Hello?" she asked urgently.

"Darling, it's me, I'm OK, I'm OK," Wilfred said hurriedly, nearly tripping over his own words as he reassured her. Sophia immediately fell onto her back on the bed, taking a deep breath as her immediate relief gave way to lingering concern and a touch of anger.

"Where on earth are you?" she asked, looking over at the bedside clock. "It's nearly eight in the morning; I've been worried sick about you, Wilfred."

"I'm so sorry, darling," Wilfred replied, knowing that the real bad news was still to come. "There was trouble tonight; Pete got...hurt. Real bad. I've been running around like a madman trying to help him out."

"Oh my god, what happened? Will he be alright?" Sophia asked, curling up with the phone as she spoke. She feared that there had been a fight; Pete and Wilfred were known to get awfully rowdy together. More than once they had gotten into minor altercations while out on the town.

On the other end of the line, Wilfred took a deep breath. He had come to the difficult part of the conversation: telling the truth. Wilfred firmly believed that honesty was the best policy—especially with his wife—and he wasn't about to make up some far-fetched story. That was doubly true when he might not end up coming home to her. "There was, uh," he began, trying to simplify a byzantine series of events. "God, this is going to sound stupid. But the Devil showed up and ran off with Pete."

Sophia simply sat in silence on the other end of the phone, utterly shocked by Wilfred's explanation. Either her husband was on drugs—although he didn't sound it—or he was offering what would possibility be the worst excuse for infidelity *ever*. As he searched for words, Wilfred was moment struck by a peculiarity of faith. While religious individuals held their faith as a point of pride, he found it curious that actually invoking any sort of substantial spiritual experience was almost uniformly considered a sign of insanity. It was exceptionally common for people to earnestly talk about the Devil, but nearly everyone who actually invoked him as an *explanation* was either in jail or an asylum.

"Sophia, I know that sounds completely goddamned ridiculous," he offered against her silence. "But I haven't gone crazy on you. Pete got taken away, and we're all here—Rachel, Patty, Robert and I—with some, uhm, guys that are trying to get him back." Wilfred used his most level, serious voice in an effort to sound less laughable.

"Where is 'here?'" Sophia questioned pointedly. "I'm going to come get you." She had always taken her faith seriously, but Wilfred's story was completely unbelievable. A practicing Buddhist, Sophia was perfectly capable of believing in reincarnation – but not that tale.

Wilfred rubbed his temple with his left hand, his head already throbbing angrily from the tension. "I'm…I'm sorry," he replied, starting to get emotional. "But you can't. I don't know where I am." His wife tried to cut in, but Wilfred had to get it all out. "Wait, please wait. I *have* to help Pete. It's dangerous, but I can't abandon him. You know that. He's my best friend."

Sophia had already begun to cry; tears from fear and tears from helplessness. "I love you, Wilfred, please," she said, begging. "Please come back. Don't abandon *us*; don't abandon your family. I'm so scared." Perhaps it was selfish to ask her husband to leave his friend, but she needed him too.

Tears ran down Wilfred's cheeks as well; he was barely able to handle his wife's grief. "I love you too, Sophia," he whispered back, his voice trembling. "I'll come back to you and Emily, I promise. I promise I will. Just this one thing, for Pete…I have to do it. Try to understand, please. I love you both so much." Sobbing audibly, Sophia pled with him; she told him that he was confused and that everything would be alright – anything to get him to come home. Wilfred knew he couldn't make her understand his position, and his conviction wavered as she begged. "I'm so sorry, love. I'll see you soon," he promised, quickly hanging up the phone as he began to cry uncontrollably.

Fifteen minutes later, Wilfred emerged from the study with his emotions back under control. He found Sartre sitting alone on the couch; Hume and Socrates had left the room. The philosopher turned his attention to Wilfred, looking away from the assortment of strange bottles in front of him. "You don't have to go through with this if you don't want to," he offered, having overheard Wilfred's anguished call from the kitchen.

Wilfred set his jaw, crossing his arms over his chest. "I'm doing it," he said resolutely, looking Sartre in the eye. "After making me put my family through that, you'd better give me the chance to beat the *shit* out of this nightmare."

"Then let's begin," Sartre said, beckoning him to a door on the far side of the room. As the philosopher walked off, his collections of bottles slowly lifted off the table and followed him, wobbling gently in the air. Wilfred paused for a moment before following after the train of beakers, heading to Sartre's study in the west wing of the Philosoplex. Entering the circular room, he saw a well-organized oaken desk in the center of the room, surrounded by famous classical paintings. Sartre's bottles bobbed over toward the desk and neatly arranged themselves into two straight lines. The philosopher picked up the largest bottle, a deep green glass holding a crimson liquid. Pouring a measure of the liquid into a wine glass, he turned to Wilfred.

"First, you need to drink this," he said, handing the glass off before turning back to his desk.

Swirling the glass apprehensively, Wilfred stared down into the liquid. "What is it going to do to me?" he asked cautiously, keenly aware of what happened the last time someone drank one of Sartre's concoctions.

Sartre laughed and faced Wilfred with a smile. "It's just going to relax you a bit so you don't keep asking questions like that all night," he said, nodding down at the source bottle. Somewhat lost in the moment, Wilfred gave Sartre a confused look; he was still under the impression his drink was some sort of magical elixir. "It's just wine, Wilfred. Drink it." Sartre continued, returning to busy himself with the contents of his desk.

Tilting the glass back, Wilfred took a small sip – indeed, as the philosopher has promised, it was wine. Quite good wine, in fact, Wilfred thought as he watched Sartre prepare his equipment. Pulling the chair out from his desk, Sartre deftly spun it around in one hand to face Wilfred. "Have a seat," he suggested.

Wilfred sat down as instructed, looking up to the philosopher. "How is this going to work?" he asked curiously. Admittedly, he was more interested in the part of the journey where he got to break faces, but Wilfred still wanted to have some idea what he was getting in to.

"Ah," Sartre said, twirling a small orange vial between his fingers absent-mindedly. "Have you ever had a dream where you realized you were dreaming?" he asked, looking down at Wilfred.

"Yeah, a few times," Wilfred replied, finishing off his glass of wine.

Sitting on the edge of his desk, the philosopher explained his plan. "Well, what I'm going to do is put you in a dream that is not altogether that different," he said. "You need to be in a state where you are fully aware that you are dreaming: completely lucid. A handful of individuals have lucid dreams without any assistance; they have nearly complete mastery of the course of their dreams. The only difference in your experience will be that I can keep you suspended in such a state, until you find Yaggoth. Ordinary dreamers can still be woken up or shaken from lucidity by a change in mental state." While his explanation sounded complex to Wilfred, Sartre's plan was not very difficult. Compared to the years of effort that went into creating the Existential Dilemma, tinkering with Wilfred's dreams was almost trivially easy. "The only real challenge here lies in convincing your subconscious not to drag you out of lucidity," he explained, realizing some elaboration was in order. "If that happened, you would still be stuck chasing after Yaggoth, but powerless to resist. Simply put, I just need to distract your subconscious for a few hours so it doesn't interfere."

Wilfred raised an eyebrow at him. "Why would it do that?" he asked, wondering what his subconscious had against truly awesome dreams.

"Humans are hard-wired to appreciate the world in certain ways," the philosopher said, turning to gesture at the Monet painting behind him. "While you can consciously imagine that picture coming to life, deep down you instinctively know that it will not. You're capable of great imaginative leaps, but consider moving a car with only your mind, and somewhere a voice inside you says 'no.'" Sartre grinned, remembering an old children's story. "I'm sure you've heard of the Little Engine That Could, oui? 'I think I can' is a great personal motto, but evolutionary history has found it's a poor response to, say, being on fire. People that grew up thinking they could turn a whale into a potted petunia simply by *willing* it didn't last very long."

"That makes sense," Wilfred replied with a nod. "So my brain is hardwired to interfere if I start going about thinking I can suddenly fly, huh. No wonder those dreams never seem to last very long. Why do people end up believing they're Napoleon, then?"

"Heh," Sartre smirked. "Biological systems can screw up in a fantastic number of ways. Some people simply lose the ability to make a distinction between reality and imagination. Individuals that think their sandwich is talking to them end up in therapy; those that think the sky talks to them end up in the ministry."

Wilfred frowned at Sartre's comparison; he was not a particularly religious fellow, but still took offense at the comparison between holy men and lunatics. However, given the evening's events, Wilfred was not about to get into an argument over theology. "So you're going to make me temporarily insane," he concluded somewhat dejectedly, dreading the possibility of life in either an asylum or Congress if he never recovered.

"It's a good kind of insanity, don't worry," Sartre said comfortingly, patting Wilfred's shoulder. "Unlike the real world, in dreams there is nothing wrong with thinking you can fly. That is precisely the kind of ability you'll need, after all. I just have to distract your subconscious with something suitably shiny, so it doesn't jump in and give you a dangerous appreciation for the laws of physics."

"Shiny?"

"The human subconscious is merely a collection of biological directives, the source of your animal instincts, so to speak. Just like with a kitten, all you need to do is wave around something bright and tempting to keep your subconscious busy for hours," Sartre said, stepping around in front of Wilfred. "As a man, a parade of nude waitresses bringing you steaks should do the trick, but let's make sure."

A wide grin spreading across his face; Wilfred appreciated that his mission carried some perks. "I'd chase that laser pointer all night," he said, considering the imagery. "It wouldn't hurt to throw in Eisbrecher rocking out, though." That was his favorite band.

"I'll consider the suggestion, but recall that the entire point of this exercise is to occupy your *subconscious*," Sartre reminded him. "The most you'll get out of it is a lingering desire to ravage your wife at the local steakhouse. Hah!" The philosopher leaned in towards Wilfred, pulling a small metal pen from his breast pocket. Holding it up for him to inspect, Sartre immediately began to melt the pen, metal turning red-hot as it dripped onto Wilfred's lap.

"Holy shit!" Wilfred exclaimed, scrambling and nearly managing to pull himself out of the chair before realizing that the glowing metal was, in fact, perfectly cool. "Talk about screwing with my subconscious; don't drop that there!"

Sartre simply smiled while Wilfred brushed the liquid metal off his lap, drops falling to the ground before quickly solidifying once more. "Exactly the point," Sartre said, putting his half of a pen back into his jacket. "I need to make sure your instincts are working properly, and test their response." He held up his once-empty orange vial, now filled with a murky brown substance. "More importantly, I had to get a sample of your raw emotions in order to get this potion right."

Wilfred leaned forward in his chair, inspecting the bottled emotions. His shock and terror swirled aimlessly within, a product of Sartre's unparalleled mastery of the human mind. The small vial didn't look like much, but it held more Industrial-Strength WTF than even the most disturbing internet fan-fictions. "See? This will do nicely," the philosopher said, heading back to his desk. He popped the cap off of the tube holding Wilfred's emotions and immediately added in a few drops of a bright pink, viscous fluid. Watching the reaction, Sartre followed up with a hefty measure of something green from a largish beaker.

"*Voila!*" Sartre turned back to Wilfred, holding up the now apparently empty vial. "Just the right mixture; you're easy to read." Wilfred had to stare intently at the glass to discern that there was even a substance inside it; the liquid had turned almost perfectly translucent.

"Uh, that's good." Wilfred wasn't entirely sure of that, but recognized that the sooner Sartre finished the less likely he was to have anything else melted onto his lap. Returning to the desk once more, Sartre picked up a clean beer mug and filled it with the same mixture of the two substances. He paused for a moment before grabbing a third ingredient, a small wooden box. Taking off the lid, he tapped the container gently as he sprinkled what appeared to be metal filings into the drink.

"Um," Wilfred asked out loud, giving voice to his instinctive aversion to that particular ingredient.

Sartre glanced back at him, shooting Wilfred a puzzled look. "What? Oh, that. You said you wanted some heavy metal, yes?"

Wilfred blinked, not having imagined that his request for kick-ass music would have entailed taking a shot laced with lead. The addition was not completely unprecedented—people did drink alcohol sprinkled with gold—but he imagined this was a different matter altogether. "And you're sure this is safe?" He didn't want to survive a horrifying mission through the dream world, only to wake up severely disabled by lead poisoning.

"Yes, yes. Remember, all of these things," Sartre said, gesturing over the items on his table. "They're just different emotions and experiences. The physical form is merely symbolic."

Wilfred gave a long sigh; at this point there wasn't any point in trying to make sense of things. Taking the proffered glass from Sartre, Wilfred gave the well-stirred drink a sniff. Grape. That was not a good sign; nothing ever smelt of grapes unless it had something to hide. Other than grapes, that is, but Wilfred had never been entirely sold on them either. Terrible childhood memories of cough syrup and fluoride sprang to mind. Consoling himself with the fact that the drink would supposedly make him something like a cross between Little Nemo and Bruce Lee, Wilfred drank deeply. He nearly gagged; his drink had the nauseating sweetness and grainy texture of grape Kool-Aid that hadn't been properly stirred. Wilfred's eyes watered as he chugged, gasping for air when he finally finished.

"How do you feel?"

Rubbing his eyes clear, Wilfred looked back to Sartre. "Other than that horrific after-taste? I feel fine. No different at all, really."

"Good, good." Sartre reached back into his jacket, pulling out the remnants of his pen. That alone was enough to make Wilfred's hands tighten on the chair's armrests. "I'm not going to melt it, relax. Just tell me if this strikes you as…odd." Once more the philosopher focused on his pen. The melted pieces of pen on the floor and the few still on Wilfred's lap rose up in the air, quickly returning to their source as the pen reconstituted itself seamlessly. "Well?"

"That was weird."

"Weird?" the philosopher questioned.

"I mean, weird that it didn't seem to faze me. I might just be getting used to you guys." After all, Wilfred had spent the better part of his Friday evening watching some admittedly ridiculous stunts.

"Perhaps. But what if I was to say I could transform you into a small, talking lobster?"

Oddly enough, Wilfred didn't find the suggestion at all outrageous. "That seems…plausible," he admitted. "But please don't."

Sartre chuckled, briefly envisioning the tough guy in front of him as a tiny, angry yabby with rubber bands on his claws. "I'm not going to. The formula appears to be working, however. Now try to levitate yourself."

Wilfred furrowed his brow, trying to lift himself out of the chair. After a minute he gave up, shaking his head in exasperation. "It isn't working."

"Of course it isn't; you're not asleep," Sartre explained, pleased with his work. "What is important is that you tried it without hesitation. Your imagination won't help you *here*, but if you did that in the dream world—judging by the expression on your face—you would have shot right through the ceiling."

"Oh, I see," Wilfred said, somewhat embarrassed by his childlike acceptance of the philosopher's suggestion to attempt levitation. Still, he couldn't be blamed for it; his better judgment was thoroughly occupied by steak, breasts, and a pyrotechnic-enhanced performance by Eisbrecher. Somewhere deep in his mind, Wilfred's subconscious was trying to play bass guitar on a sirloin the size of a small table.

Sartre took Wilfred by the arm, helping him out of the chair. "It's time. My elixir won't last forever, so let's get you to your room. A few important points on the way." The two men headed back upstairs, Wilfred following Sartre into his bedroom and soon-to-be battleground. The philosopher took a seat on the edge of the bed, patting the area behind him. As Wilfred kicked off his shoes and lay down, Sartre gave his last pieces of advice. "Remember, you can do nearly anything imaginable once asleep. While your subconscious will not interfere, you will still have to think of what you want in order for it to happen. If you think you are strong, you will be strong. But just as importantly, if you think you are weak, you *will* be weak. You can't die unless you let yourself." Sartre certainly hoped that was true; at the very least, it sounded encouraging.

"I'm still a bit confused on how exactly I'm supposed to find this thing," Wilfred admitted, adjusting his head against the pillow.

"Just think of Yaggoth, and follow your sense of it. Remember, you need to find out where Yaggoth is hiding in the real world. Once we know the identity of the mortal host which the nightmare has possessed, we can track Yaggoth down and destroy it. With any luck, the host's identity will become clear when you are in the same mental space as the nightmare."

"Then what?"

"Return to the point in your dream where your journey began, and you'll be able to wake yourself back up."

Wilfred rightly imagined that wouldn't be quite as easy as the philosopher made it sound. He became suddenly serious, reminding himself that his journey might not include a return trip. "Just promise me one thing," he said as he closed his eyes. "If I don't come back from this…please tell my family. Let them know I wasn't crazy."

Sartre nodded in assent as he stood up, looking back at Wilfred one last time. "Certainly. But I'd rather you tell them yourself," he said, stopping at the doorway. Reaching out, he flicked out the lights. "Never give up." Closing the door behind him, Sartre left Wilfred in the darkened room. He turned and headed down the stairs, imagining that Hume could use his assistance with Socrates. For a few minutes, Wilfred lay alone in bed, slowing his breathing as he closed his eyes. Between Sartre's concoction, the wine, and the fact that it was four o'clock in the morning, he was soon asleep.

Chapter Seven

"*GOTTVERDAMMT!*"

Rachel groaned as her eyes opened, startled awake by the screeching of tires and furious cursing outside. She blinked and looked over at the nightstand; it was barely 8:30 in the morning. While a Pissed-Off Nietzsche Alarm would work well for anyone whose life absolutely depended on getting right the hell out of bed, she had naively hoped to sleep in. Rolling onto her stomach, Rachel pulled a pillow over her head. But the escalating shouting match outside would not be denied an audience, and Rachel rolled out of bed to the tune of a series of increasingly ridiculous and obscene insults.

While Hume hurried outside to break up an impending brawl between Nietzsche and Kant, Rachel and Robert took turns showering and getting dressed in the upstairs bathroom. They had found fresh clothes—remarkably contemporary ones—waiting for them on their dressers. Passing by Wilfred's room and noticing the large 'DO NOT DISTURB. SLEEPING IN.' on his door, they shrugged to each other before heading downstairs.

"Patty!" Rachel exclaimed as they entered the kitchen, rushing over to her friend and nearly toppling her with a hug. "We were all so worried about you, after we heard what happened to Pete."

Giving Robert a warm hug as well, Patty smiled. "I'm OK. This is all just a bit much; I still can't believe it." She was relieved that her friends were safe, especially after Hume had told her over breakfast about the incident at Ockham's Kegger. Incidentally, the philosopher also made one hell of an omelet.

"It sounds like they're done," Robert offered, looking back towards the front entrance. The shouting had stopped. Having seen what the philosophers were capable of, none of the friends wanted to step in the middle of a fight. "Do you think they found Pete?" Not wasting any time on speculation, they all hurried out of the Philosoplex. They found three of the team still outside; Nietzsche had already left to sulk over his defeat. Russell saw them first, waving familiarly to Patty. Hume finished tying a bandage around Kant's head, turning to perform introductions.

"Bertrand Russell, Immanuel Kant," he began, gesturing to the two men in turn. "This is Robert, and Rachel." Kant forced a smile as the group all shook hands. He was only slightly more comfortable now; Nietzsche was gone and Hume had removed the rock from the inside of his skull. Although Rachel was predictably caught up in her enthusiasm to meet more of the philosophers, Patty and Robert both immediately noticed Pete's absence.

"You didn't find him, did you?" Patty asked, fearing the worst. All eyes focused on the philosophers; Rachel felt a pang of guilt for forgetting about Pete. Russell had caught her eye; he was younger than the rest of the philosophers, and had an inscrutable charm.

"Not yet, but we're getting close," Hume admitted, having already been debriefed by Russell on the developments at the park. That response only earned him a barely-decipherable barrage of questions from Pete's three friends. "Wait, wait. We have a lot to discuss and I'd rather not go through this five times. Everyone is meeting in the study promptly; we'll answer your questions there."

As they filed back into the mansion, Robert glanced up at the stairway. "What about Wilfred? Shouldn't we bring him in on this, too?" He knew that his friend wouldn't want to miss any details about Pete.

"Wilfred is doing us—and Pete—a favor," Sartre replied as he came up behind them, followed by a groggy-but-conscious Socrates. "He'll be down later in the day." Wilfred's friends weren't sure whether to be more surprised by his unexpected mission or the appearance of a concious Socrates.

The Greek philosopher approached the three, smiling widely. He still looked like a bit of a mess; it certainly didn't help that Lime had spent the entire night napping on his beard. "Thanks a bunch. I heard you helped save my ass last night," Socrates said, shaking Robert and Rachel's hands firmly.

"That's not exactly what..."

"And nice to meet you, too," he continued, greeting Patty as well before the others could object. Unlike the rest of the philosophers, Socrates seemed surprisingly normal. He favored jeans and a simple t-shirt over a formal suit, not seeing the point in dressing up. "Oh!" he suddenly exclaimed, left hand going to his stomach.

"Grab a seat, I need to get some breakfast before I die." Socrates hurried off to the kitchen, surprisingly nimble for a man that looked like he could successfully wrestle a whale into submission. Arranging themselves around the table as Nietzsche rolled into the study on his wheelchair, everyone took a seat. A minute passed in silence. Then another.

"Would you hurry up?!" Kant yelled in the direction of the kitchen. He was bound to be miserable until his eye healed, and wanted the meeting to be over so he could move on to something more enjoyable—numbing his head in a bucket of ice.

A few hurried noises later, Socrates came rushing back from the kitchen, a massive bowl of cereal in his right hand and Lime nestled comfortably in his left. "Sorry, sorry," he offered as he sat down, letting the kitten scurry under the table to amuse herself with dangling shoelaces.

Robert raised an eyebrow as the Greek philosopher took a seat next to him, setting down what must have been five pounds of cereal-filled ceramic on the table. "I didn't think you guys, uh, needed to eat?" he asked curiously.

"We don't," said Nietzsche dryly, rolling his eyes.

Socrates chuckled, looking over at Robert. "Nah, we don't," he explained. "But god, do I freakin' love Wheaties. Best invention of the last two millennia, honestly." Demonstrating the truth of his love, Socrates immediately and zealously began to dig in to his food. Too busy watching Socrates commit what could only be described as horrific cereal genocide, most of the room did not notice Russell and Rachel eyeing each other across the table.

"Ahem." Hume cleared his throat, bringing everyone's attention back to the slightly more pressing concern of rogue gods using Pete to end the world. "Russell, would you please begin?" he asked, savvy enough to his colleague's reputation to notice the direction of Russell's eyes. Worse yet—and unlike Patty—Rachel actually seemed interested in the philosopher's attention.

"Sure," Russell said, folding his hands in front of him. "I'll be as brief as possible. Somehow the brothers intercepted and abducted Pete. They were ambushed by a third party, but escaped along with Pete. Whoever attacked them left these scales scattered about the park." Reaching into his pocket, he tossed a handful of them on the table for the rest of the group to inspect. "I thought it might have been Nidhogg, so Kant and I paid him a visit. Unfortunately, the wyrm was near death; he couldn't have been there."

"That's a shame," commented Hume quietly, appreciative of the fact that the Nordic serpent had never caused the philosophers any trouble.

"However, he was kind enough to help us discern that the brothers are holding Pete somewhere on the water," he said before being interrupted by Rachel.

"I'm sorry, but who are the brothers?"

"Oh, right! The Archangel Michael and Lucifer are the two angelic brothers. Sorry about that Rachel," he said, smiling with unnecessary charm back at her.

"Thank you," Hume said as he looked around the table. "That leaves us with a few major problems. Where is Pete now? What is this damned snake?" He held up one of the scales between his fingers. "And perhaps most importantly, how did the brothers and Yaggoth react so quickly to our plans?"

"Inside job," said Socrates casually, wiping his mouth and beard clean of Wheaties debris. Everyone at the table was momentarily stunned as all eyes turned to the Greek. "Well, spending half an hour getting your mind digested by that god-forsaken nightmare is quite an intimate experience." Sartre understood Socrates' point immediately. Just as he had told Wilfred the night before, interaction with a nightmare was a two-way street. Yaggoth couldn't have attacked Socrates' mind without making its own thoughts somewhat vulnerable. "I didn't get much in the way of details, just bits and pieces of Yaggoth's memories. But it was definitely tipped off to our plan."

"Tipped off?" Nietzsche asked incredulously. "The only people that knew anything of this idiotic plan are sitting right here."

Socrates shrugged, not having any more of explanation for how Yaggoth had been informed than anyone else. "You're right; I don't have a clue *how* it found out. Still, it wasn't at Ockham's Kegger by pure luck. Someone contacted it shortly after our success with Pete, and it must have gotten to the bar within minutes."

"I don't see how that's possible, nobody here betrayed us. Nobody here *could* betray us, as a matter of fact," Hume explained, shaking his head in confusion. "Correct, Sartre?"

"Indeed," Sartre replied slowly, trying to think through Socrates' startling revelation. "It would take a massive effort for any of us to resist the purpose for which we were created. Even if that was possible—which I sincerely doubt—I would notice immediately. Those kinds of emotions cannot be concealed. Not from me; not at this range."

"More than just us knew; this plan has been in the making for years," Kant reminded them. "All of our fallen brothers knew enough as well."

Noticing the confusion of Rachel and the others, Hume explained. "There used to be more of us. Since our creation, four members of our team have fallen in battle: A.J. Ayer, Plato, Rene Descartes, and Aristotle." He turned back to Kant. "I understand your point, but how is their situation any different? Loathe as I am to imply ill of the dead, Sartre still would have noticed any betrayal on their behalf." Pete's friends suddenly understood the seeming excess of chairs in the hall.

"I did not mean to imply they had betrayed us; I trust in Sartre's abilities," Kant replied. "But we never recovered the bodies of either Ayer or Descartes. It is unlikely, but perhaps they were taken alive to be used against us. If one of them was held far from here, Sartre would not be able to sense a tortured confession, correct?" Sartre grimaced and nodded. Both philosophers had been presumed dead after a cataclysmic assault on the moon half a decade ago. When a trio of weakening lunar deities—Artemis, Diana, and Tsukuyomi—had erected a temple and begun importing worshipers in an attempt to regain their power, the philosophers had no choice but to attack.

Facing the three gods on the source of their power and surrounded by throngs of the Lunar Cult, the philosophers had only narrowly won the ensuing battle. Forced to use the ultimate manifestation of his abilities, Russell had destroyed a third of the moon in a single, terrible blow. While the triumvirate had been defeated as a result, neither Ayer nor Descartes was ever found amongst the pieces of the sundered satellite. Russell still blamed himself for the death of his partner Ayer, with whom he had found a great friendship.

"Even if we assume that much—and it is quite a lot—I cannot see a pattern behind the interference with our plans," Russell added, giving a long sigh. "The brothers and whatever attacked them must have been informed in addition to Yaggoth. But it seems clear that none of those three parties are working together. The nightmare allies with nobody and whatever took place at the park was no staged disagreement."

"There must be a plan," Nietzsche said, lighting another cigarette as he thought. "The facts admit no other possibility. It is impossible that our enemies have struck with such precision through pure luck. I don't see it myself, but there is something behind this chaos."

As it happened, that very *something* was at the moment making her way beneath the earth. Sand crunched under Claudia's sandaled feet as she descended the ancient stone stairwell. Far beneath the desert, the young woman approached one of the last undiscovered sepulchers of Egypt. She wore a modest black skirt and a dark green blouse, her long brown hair pulled back into a ponytail. Adjusting her narrow glasses, she stepped between arching pillars of stone engraved with Grecian script. She walked into the antechamber, the darkened room pulsing with the breath of its massive occupant.

"Claudia Durand," a heavy voice called out, echoing throughout the crypt. "Why do you come before me again?"

She smiled; he had not died in the battle. "Because there is more to be done, my friend." Claudia's voice was sweet and light, out of place in the sweltering dark. "Are you so easily discouraged from your life's work?"

"Heh heh," the old god laughed, shifting on his obsidian throne. Tendrils writhed on the ground before Claudia, serpentine coils that ended in a scorpion's stinger. The two-foot-long blades screeched softly as they dragged across the stone. "I cannot defeat them. The brothers are in their prime compared to me; I am long forgotten by this world. To fight them again would surely be the end of me."

Claudia frowned in disappointment. She had never expected—nor wanted—him to defeat the brothers, but his continued assistance was necessary to her plans. "You do not need to fight them again; the brothers no longer have possession of the little god," she lied smoothly. "Your interference weakened and delayed the angels enough for them to be overtaken by the philosophers. The few of them that survived the encounter returned to their hole with our quarry."

"Oh? The brothers are no more?"

"Indeed. You have outlasted yet another generation of the gods. All that remains is for you to take the power born into that man and reclaim your place in the heavens."

"Hah! Ahahah," he laughed deeply, relishing the thought of the angels' deaths. After all, their followers had long ago wiped out his religion. "And to think they dared to call *me* heresy, to burn *my* temples and slaughter *my* people. Now their wings are crushed into the earth, yet I still live. Foolish insects!" The god rose off his throne, his tentacles arching into the air as they carried him aloft. His vaguely humanoid torso stretched in the shadows as he stared down at the girl before him. "I suppose you have come to tell me how to reach the philosopher's refuge, then? Many have sought for it, but the path lays somewhere beyond even my perception."

"Of course," she said happily. The god's single-minded purpose and overweening pride made him delightfully easy to manipulate. "I can show you the way. Your mighty flail and unyielding shield can do the rest."

"How do you come to know such mysteries, little one?" He asked curiously, pulling a massive silver shield off the wall behind him. "Long have I walked the earth without meeting one such as you. What are you?"

Claudia sniffed dismissively, brushing a strand of hair behind her ear. "My help, freely given, is all you need from me. If I were interested in sharing any more I'd put up a page on Facebook." Putting her hands on her hips, she stared up at the god before her.

"Now should I lead you, or would you rather I leave you to rot under the sand?"

The god chuckled, shaking his head. He did not trust Claudia, but his only alternative to her assistance was a slow death. That day presented his best chance in centuries to rebuild his order. "Rot? I am the Scourge of Power! Lead me, and this world may yet survive." Reaching aside the throne with his right arm, he brought up a seven-tailed flail of living steel. The god hefted his weapon aloft, the metal glimmering in Claudia's brown eyes. "Balance will be restored!"

Wilfred sat bolt upright in his bed, the window flooding his room with light as he blinked and tried to force himself awake. He reached back and stretched his arms behind him, wondering if his friends were already up. Pulling back the sheets and sliding out of bed in his boxers and a white undershirt, his eye caught a note pinned to his door. Walking over, Wilfred examined the note:

"Dear Wilfred,

You are in a dream. In this room, you are still within your own mind. From here—and only here—it is possible for you to send yourself back to reality. Outside of this door lays the rest of the dreaming world, and somewhere therein you will find the nightmare Yaggoth. It will try to destroy you through both force and trickery. Trust nothing outside this room; you have no allies here. REMEMBER: Your power is limited only by your imagination. Good luck – we trust in your strength.

Jean-Paul Sartre

David Hume"

Wilfred jumped back from the door, dropping the note and letting it flutter to the ground. The memories of the last few hours suddenly came flooding back to him: the heart-wrenching conversation with his wife, the tension of watching Sartre conjuring up an elixir. Wilfred sat back down on the edge of his bed, somewhat shaken by the recollection. His eyes flashed upwards towards the door again, focusing on the handle intently. What lay beyond his room? Without a word, he stood tall once more, steeling himself for the battle ahead.

He turned aside towards the closet and pulled it open. Inside the closet hung a single set of clothes; black leather boots, belt, and vest, crisp blue jeans, and a plain grey button-up shirt. Wilfred began to get dressed, pulling on the jeans and shirt before grabbing the belt off the hanger. The buckle seemed to be wrought of silver, and carried the letters 'BAMF' stamped in the metal. His mind had great taste.

"Damn right," he said with a smirk, pulling the belt around him. Slipping into the boots, Wilfred buckled all of the clasps before reaching into the closet for the last item – the vest. Taking the vest off of its hanger, Wilfred immediately noticed the back was inscribed with tiny lettering. Holding it up in front of him, he squinted as he read the words aloud. "Pete. Sophia. Emily. Patty. Rachel. Robert," he said, trailing off as he glanced over the long list of names. The names of all of his friends and family had been printed on the back of the jacket. Wilfred ran his fingers slowly over the names, clutching the vest to his chest for a moment before pulling it over his broad shoulders.

Walking to the door, Wilfred stooped and retrieved the note, folding it neatly and inserting the paper into his breast pocket. He reached out, grasping the door knob deliberately. His fingers tightening, the knob slowly turned until the latch popped open. Taking a deep breath, Wilfred pushed at the door – it did not budge an inch. What was wrong? He blinked in surprise for a moment; his mind was far enough removed from ordinary concerns that it took a good five seconds before he glanced at the door's hinges. The door only opened inward.

Laughing to himself as the tension subsided, Wilfred stepped back and pulled the door open. He jumped as he stared out into space; outside his door the ground disappeared, and he stood before a vast nebula, clouds the size of galaxies embedded with countless points of light. Tentatively peering around the corner of his door, Wilfred could see that the formation circled fully around the floating room. It took him a moment to recompose himself; the accumulation of all the dreams and imagination of every sentient being seemed endless. Once the shock passed, Wilfred's mind turned to how he was supposed to find Yaggoth amongst what must have been countless billions of worlds.

As Wilfred thought, his memory of Yaggoth from Ockham's Kegger fluttered through his thoughts. A thousand howling mouths hanging in a black abyss – the imagery pulled on Wilfred's consciousness. His body turned, following his thoughts as he focused on a particular star in the lower hemisphere of his vision. "There," Wilfred said quietly. As he spoke the world blurred in front of him; his intuition leapt ahead of him as he moved instantly through space. Wilfred abruptly found himself standing in a green field, grass and clovers beneath his feet, the land spotted with occasional trees. The sky was spotted with fluffy white clouds, and a large rainbow hung across the horizon. Not quite what he had expected. Slipping on a pair of sunglasses he suddenly held in his right hand, Wilfred squinted as he looked at the star above. Even though the light was still nearly blinding through his shades, he could see the deep orange star churning malevolently in the sky. Wilfred knew the sun—the world—was evil; he was in the right place after all. He could sense Yaggoth permeating the very atmosphere, its evil giving even the chirping birds a slight, horrifying discordance.

    Wilfred began to walk across the plain, losing track of time as he headed towards the rising peaks in the east. On the surface of the world, it was much harder for Wilfred to precisely locate the nightmare; Yaggoth's presence had become more of a drifting current in a sea of fear, rather than the distinct point it was from far away. The mountains before him now stretching towards the sky, and Wilfred noticed the grass beginning to fade away into rock in the miles ahead. Soft sounds of a gentle breeze were cut through by a loud whinny, and Wilfred spun around quickly, taking a wide stance with his fists up. His eyes widened in surprise as a sparkling white unicorn came trotting into sight, heading in his direction. Remembering the philosophers' advice, Wilfred didn't let his guard down at the horse slowly approached him.

    The unicorn sniffed at Wilfred curiously, just a few feet from the man as it seemed to look him over. It slowly stepped forward, attempting to nuzzle him with its soft nose. Wilfred hopped back immediately, trying to come up with an appropriate response. He didn't trust the creature, but even Wilfred didn't have the sheer nerve to cold-cock a goddamned *unicorn* without provocation. Wilfred tried cautiously taking a few steps further away from the unicorn, but it persistently stepped after him. He sighed in frustration; the mythical beast seemed like a lost kitten. "Ok," he said, peering at the horse. "I'll rub your head, but then you need to leave me alone, alright?" The unicorn gave a soft whinny in response, seeming to understand Wilfred as it approached him once more.

Pressing its nose against Wilfred's left arm, the unicorn sniffed contently as Wilfred rubbed its head and admired the impressive horn. "My daughter Emily would have a fit if she saw this, you know," he said with a laugh. She loved unicorns, as many young girls did. The horse continued nuzzling its face against his arm, taking in his scent. "These clothes must have used a hell of a fabric softener," he commented, looking away from the unicorn for a moment as he smelled his own right shirt-sleeve. "Weird, I don't smell a thing," he continued, wondering what was so interesting about him. Wilfred's curiosity was immediately rewarded; the unicorn's jaw unhinged grotesquely, four rows of razor-sharp teeth glimmering in the sunlight before slamming down around Wilfred's arm like a vise.

"AAAUUUUGGHH!" Wilfred screamed as his bone shattered from the force of the creature's bite. His upper arm already shredded by the grinding motion of the unicorn's mouth, Wilfred struggled to stay on his feet as the horse thrashed back and forth, trying to tear his limb free. It only took a moment before the unicorn succeeded, sending Wilfred flying with a shake of its head as his last tendon snapped. Clutching helplessly at his stump of a left arm, Wilfred watched in horror as the unicorn dropped his severed arm to the ground. The creature's mouth hung open, his blood splattered across the unicorn's once-pristine white coat. Lowering its head, the unicorn prepared to deliver a fatal charge. Wilfred sprung to his feet, leaping far over the unicorn's head with only moments to spare, flying in a wide arc and landing behind it. At the last second, he had remembered Sartre's words of advice: "You can't die unless you let yourself. Never give up."

Fighting through the pain, Wilfred focused first on reconstituting his arm. It took only a second to convince himself that such regeneration was possible *there*, and with that mental hurdle cleared Wilfred's arm soon returned. He gave a happy sigh, flexing his left arm – back to its un-chewed state, a clean shirt and all. The unicorn gave a startled look between Wilfred and his original, still-warm arm lying nearby in the grass. It was immediately clear that the intruder was no ordinary dreamer; most mortals would have disappeared back to reality by this point, screaming and drenched in a cold sweat.

Nevertheless, the first of Yaggoth's guardians was not so easily deterred. Many restless minds had stumbled upon the nightmare within the dream-world, but less than half a dozen had made it past those emerald fields. Digging its hooves into the dirt, the unicorn howled an unearthly cry. Wilfred braced himself against the conal shockwave, dirt and grass flying into his face. When the debris cleared the unicorn was already upon him at a full charge, only a few feet from Wilfred. This time, however, Wilfred was prepared for the attack. Pivoting his weight onto his right foot, Wilfred met the creature with a devastating uppercut. His fist slammed into the unicorn's lower jaw, the creature's misshapen maw painfully forced shut as it was lifted off the ground by the force of Wilfred's blow. "Shoryuken!" It seemed natural, and profoundly satisfying.

Quickly becoming accustomed to his almost effortless power in the realm of imagination, Wilfred watched the unicorn fly upwards in slow motion. In a flash of creativity, he summoned forth a shoulder-mounted rocket launcher, the device falling conveniently in place as he targeted the monstrosity. Squeezing the trigger, Wilfred saw the weapon belch flame as it launched a speeding projectile towards the falling unicorn.

The rocket struck the beast with a flash, delivering an explosive payload usually reserved for tanks, small aircraft, or physics homework. The unicorn crashed to the ground and slid backwards, leaving a trail of flattened and charred grass. Wilfred tossed his spent weapon aside, registering a note of surprise as the unicorn immediately staggered back to its legs. It was unharmed. "You're a resilient bastard," Wilfred muttered, keeping a steady watch on his enemy.

Adding an entirely new level of creepiness to the situation, the unicorn laughed. "Ahhahah. The same could be said of you," its raspy voice responded. "However, I am eternal and unbreakable. You cannot win." It might take quite a beating fighting Wilfred, but the unicorn could not be unmade even by his power. Yaggoth had been characteristically clever in building its defenses; so long as countless children held it in their thoughts, the unicorn would always exist.

"Really?" Wilfred asked, appreciating the invitation to test the limits of his destructive capability. "Let's see about that." He dashed straight at the unicorn, predicting its response as he leapt to the right. As a second sonic blast flew harmlessly past him, Wilfred closed on the unicorn in a second. Approaching from the side faster than the beast could react, Wilfred kicked with enough force to send the unicorn flying up into the air, its chest caving in from the impact. With a blink, he was in front of the unicorn, already hundreds of feet above the ground. He grabbed the unicorn by its horn with both hands, spinning the helpless creature in an accelerating circle. Letting go of his handle suddenly, Wilfred hurdled the unicorn with blinding speed towards the looming mountain range.

The subsequent impact echoed across the plains with a resounding boom; the sound of a malefic unicorn crashing straight through a mountain was both unique and awesome. Able to see clear through to the other side of the shattered precipice, Wilfred gave a satisfied smile and dropped back to the ground. The unicorn had to be at least a few miles away, and none too happy. Yet the moment he touched the ground Wilfred was blown forward by another of the unicorn's terrible shrieks; he tumbled roughly across the ground, his head throbbing in pain from the assault.

"Heh heh heh..." the unicorn chuckled, watching Wilfred scramble to his feet. Despite being nearly split in half by his kick, the horse now appeared perfectly healthy. "Whatever you break will simply grow anew. Give up." It was not simply boasting; the unicorn had been guarding Yaggoth for centuries, and knew that convincing a dreamer that the situation was hopeless was the fastest way to strip their power.

Wilfred laughed loudly, throwing back his head. In that moment, he felt in his element; a battle to the death against an implacable foe. Comfortable as he was with mere violence, Wilfred was not so simple. Even in the waking world, he had an unsurpassed talent for destroying things. And that required more than just force; he possessed a brutal intelligence and a fine eye for weakness. "Give up? HAH!" he snorted, a maniacal grin spreading across his face. "You're already dead!" The last time Wilfred had been told to give up he had ended up in the hospital, proudly reading aloud an apologetic letter from the company that had dared claim their cookware was unbreakable.

The unicorn was unaccustomed to such bravado. "What?" it questioned as Wilfred stretched out his right arm, air shimmering in front of him. A gigantic fire axe appeared in his hands, its bright steel edge gleaming in the light. "You think *that* can kill me? That toy?" Attempting to charge Wilfred again, the unicorn took the butt of the axe's handle in the side of its head, staggering it in its tracks.

Hauling back his two-handed axe for a mighty swing, Wilfred grunted and brought his weapon to bear on the stunned unicorn. The blade sung as it cut through the long horn, the severed bone falling to the side. Bringing the axe back quickly, Wilfred again struck the unicorn with flat side of the axe-head, knocking it over. Dropping his weapon, Wilfred deftly grabbed the long horn off the ground, diving onto the beast before it could get back up. Wrestling with the unicorn, he used his left hand to restrain its head, dodging its kicking legs as best as he could and taking the blows he couldn't. At the first opportunity, Wilfred drove the unicorn's own horn down into its chest, tearing through flesh before burying the tip solidly in the creature's spine.

Dizzy from a few too many hoof-blows to the head, Wilfred hopped off the unicorn and got a bit of distance. Recovering from an amount of blunt force brain trauma that made boxing look like a friendly hug, he saw the unicorn writhing as his vision cleared. He grinned again, happy that his theory had been borne out. Walking over to the twitching and disabled monster, he looked down over it. "So is it still OK to call you a unicorn?" Wilfred quipped, looking between the horn that had re-grown on its head and the one still buried deep in its chest. As he had anticipated, the unicorn could not easily handle being impaled with its own horn. Recovering from its injuries quickly would require dissolving part of itself, a feat to which the unicorn's near immortality was ill-adapted. The beast was surely not dead; it would eventually free itself when the horn was pushed out slowly by the healing process. However, that achievement would be gradual and agonizing, giving Wilfred time enough to proceed undisturbed.

Quickly tiring of the unicorn's sputtering cries, Wilfred turned to walk away from the emerald fields once again. Pressing onwards, the plains slowly vanished from behind him as he passed through stony foothills. The rocks moved under his feet, shifting with a deliberate instability. Many people curse the stone that accidentally trips them, but few other than Wilfred had ever experienced such fickle ground. More worrisome to Wilfred, his slow progress upwards also marked the gradual weakening of his power. As he came closer to the heart of the nightmare, his mastery of the outside world diminished. While at first he had soared over the pernicious rocks, Wilfred was soon grounded by the crushing gravity of Yaggoth's presence. He had survived the first trial, but his friends in the waking world did not know of his success.

"Wasn't Pete enough?!" Robert asked angrily, staring across the table at Sartre. "How could you even ask that of Wilfred?" Rachel held her head in her hands, depressed by the news. Patty had reacted less dramatically to the news of Wilfred's mission; she had already resigned herself to accept her friends' necessary involvement at this point. Pete wasn't going to bring himself back.

"The choice was his," Sartre replied solemnly. "Would you rather he had stood idly by though able to help, watching the end of the world?" Robert gritted his teeth; he knew that Wilfred would never accept such an outcome.

Socrates looked to Robert as well, trying to console him. "Yes, perhaps he will die. But there is no greater glory in this world or the next than placing your life on the line for duty and virtue."

Robert turned quickly to the philosopher; talk of glory is little consolation to the friends and family of the dead. "And he never would have had to make that choice if you hadn't decided it would be good fun to fuck with our lives!" Raising her head up, Rachel gave her friend a shocked look. She couldn't remember the last time she had heard Robert swear like that.

"Hey, I'm not going to deny dragging all of you into this was a dick move," Socrates admitted, shaking his head.

"A necessary 'dick move,' thank you Socrates," Hume interjected.

The Greek shrugged; he had never been comfortable with involving the lives of so many mortals in their struggle. "I know that none of you asked for this. But *bravery* is standing tall against a world you did not choose. Your doubt and your anger can't bring Pete back." Robert snorted angrily in response, crossing his arms in front of his chest and fuming quietly.

"Then what can?" Patty asked the table, looking over the assembled philosophers. "All we know is that he's somewhere on the water, and that isn't exactly a lot of help." With her usual flawless timing, Lime hopped up onto the conference table. Giving a small meow, she stretched and looked straight at Sartre.

Sartre stared back for a moment, his eyes slowly widening. "What a smart kitten..." he whispered, smiling. "*She* can lead us to Pete! She was made by his power; his essence is still a part of her. We would simply have to follow the stream back to its source." Approving of the philosopher's quick thinking, Lime ran across the table and nuzzled her head against his hand.

"And how long would that take?" Nietzsche asked skeptically, looking down at the small animal. "They could be halfway around the world by now. It would take a week for her to lead us back to just the city." Lime mewed helplessly, looking over at Nietzsche. He was right; even a magical kitten could only run so fast.

"Unless..." Russell mused aloud, having been lost in thought about his late friend Ayer. "Perhaps we could modify the PDE combat suit to work with a cat?"

"The *what*?!" Rachel asked, raising an eyebrow at him.

"Ayer foresaw that this mission would inevitably require the involvement of mortals. I worked with him to design an armored combat system that would allow a human to work with us, without requiring constant protection. It is incomplete, but..."

"And you're ready to put a kitten in a weapon with enough firepower to level a city?" Kant asked, shaking his head.

"We could always disable the tactical nukes? AH!" Sartre yelped as Lime bit his finger; she clearly wasn't going to put up with that kind of talk.

Russell looked down at Lime, beckoning her over to him. She trotted across the table, looking up at the philosopher expectantly. He smiled, reaching out a finger to scratch behind her ear. "It could work. She's clearly no ordinary cat; I believe that I could adjust the system's neural interface. And fixing the restraints is trivial; the only difficulty is reworking all of the input formulae."

Looking over at him, Robert's mood seemed to improve slightly. "I could help you," he offered. "Maybe." Just like Wilfred, he wasn't going to pass up the chance to try and save Pete. "My doctoral thesis was on solving boundary problems in AI routines." Russell smiled widely, clapping his hands together.

"That's excellent! We shouldn't waste any time; every second counts while Pete is with them." He pushed his chair back from the table, standing up with Lime in his hands. Russell also knew they had to start quickly, before the rest of the team could veto his plan. "The suit is back in Launch Bay Four, let's get moving." Robert flashed his friends a smile, hurrying off to catch the philosopher.

Walking down the back hallways of the Philosoplex, the comfortable décor gave way to concrete walls and stark lightning. Robert walked alongside Russell, glancing left and right as they quickly moved along. "So how big is this thing?" Robert asked, the pair passing by the first of the building's gargantuan launch bays. As the hall curved to the left, the numbered door to the fourth bay came into view.

"Big," said Russell simply, approaching the twelve-foot blast door. "The machine was designed to allow a mortal to face the Created without getting instantly stomped." Pressing the green button next to the doorframe, the reinforced steel gate slid open, revealing a cylindrical hanger nearly ten stories high. Robert's jaw dropped, standing in the threshold as he stared into the center of the room.

"And there she is, the PDE-1." Robert didn't need to ask about the name; 'Philosophy Delivery Engine' was printed in large block letters around the wall. He looked up at the bulky machine, blown away by its size. When Robert had heard "combat suit," he had imagined something like an outsized set of plate armor. But the PDE-1 rose nearly sixty feet into the air; the machine was larger than many buildings. Smiling to himself, Russell walked over to the armor, running his hand slowly along a dusty, gun-metal foot. "Just to give you an idea of the specifications," he said, turning back to Robert. "She's 58' tall, weighing in at approximately 50 tons depending on armaments. Powered by two independent fusion reactors, she reaches top speed on land at 310 miles per hour and Mach 3 in flight. While she is equipped for long-range combat with an assortment of conventional missiles and tactical nuclear weapons," he gestured up at the large, box-like protrusions on the machine's shoulders and behind the head. "The PDE-1 was primarily designed for melee engagement. A novel field containment system allows for the generation of defensive shields and—more importantly—the operation of the suit's close-combat weaponry."

Robert walked slowly forward, craning his neck up at the machine. For her part, Lime had already leapt from Russell's hands and now clambered over the PDE-1's feet with an enthusiasm most kittens reserved for empty boxes. "Close combat weaponry?" Robert repeated, nearly speechless.

The philosopher went to a nearby workbench, pushing aside piles of paper before finding a laptop buried underneath. Booting up the system, Russell glanced over at the PDE-1 as he initiated long-dormant activation protocols. A surprisingly soft hum filled the chamber as the unit's reactors came online, dust falling away as energy coursed through the metal body. "Each arm contains a specially-designed blade. Their unique physical structure allows for transformation to a plasma state, while retaining physical cohesion and striking force." Russell looked over at Robert, who still appeared thoroughly flabbergasted. "Ah, um. Think of knives that are *made out of the sun*. Put these on." He tossed the mortal a pair of thick industrial strength sunglasses, which Robert quickly donned over his usual glasses.

Turning his attention back to the laptop, Russell prepared to give his new partner a demonstration. "Performance test utilities engaged." The PDE-1's voice made Robert jump from surprise; even a gentle female voice could be startling when coming from a gigantic war engine. Russell's fingers danced on the keyboard, old memories flooding back to him as he worked. It didn't seem like a decade since he had last seen Ayer, but it had been far too long. "Plasma blade test for a duration of fifteen seconds active in five, four…" The unit's three-fingered hands clenched into fists as ten-foot-long black metal blades shot out from the wrist-guards, and locked in. "Two, one." The blades began to melt in place, quickly going from a deep red to blinding white in a fraction of a second. "Zero. Test active." Robert staggered backwards, feeling the intense heat of the weapons even through their containment fields. The blades seemed to ripple in front of his eyes, waves of heated air rising off of them.

"Test concluded." The blades quickly faded to black then retracted into the unit's arms once more. Robert wiped the beaded sweat from his brow, pulling off the safety glasses and looking over at Russell. "Holy shit," he breathed out, shaking his head in disbelief. "We're going to put a kitten in that?" Lime meowed affirmatively.

Russell didn't hear him at first; he blinked his eyes clear and recomposed himself. While he had helped create the materials and mathematics behind the PDE-1, the machine was the brainchild of A.J. Ayer. Seeing it come alive again had reminded him too much of his late partner. "Yeah," he finally replied, forcing a smile. "I don't see how it could go wrong. Lime just wants to get Pete back, too." The kitten ran back over to Russell, leaping up on the desk and staring intelligently at the laptop's display.

"You don't see how it could…"

"Anyways, it isn't like we have much to lose at this point. Sure, the PDE-1 was put on the back burner because of concerns about collateral damage, but things are too far in the shitter to worry about that now. If someone else manages to take control of Pete's power, having Lime accidentally roll over a few suburbs will be the least of humanity's worries." The philosopher looked down at the kitten before him, rubbing her head once more. "And you're a good kitty, aren't you? Aren't you? Yes you are!" Lime purred affectionately. "You're not going to blow up any cities!"

Chapter Eight

Michael grumbled to himself, heading to the back deck of the *Paradise Lost*. There he found his brother, reclining on a chair and sipping a beer. "You realize we're on a timeline here, yes?" The archangel asked, the agitation clear in his voice. Lucifer slowly turned his head over towards Michael with a pronounced laziness that could only be intended to irritate.

"Really?" He asked sarcastically, adjusting the stylish sunglasses on his face. "And here I thought we were just out on vacation." Michael opened his mouth, only to shut it again quickly as Lucifer pulled aside some of the bandages on his chest. His wounds had healed substantially; the Devil no longer felt like he was in danger of simply breaking in half. But the gashes had not yet fully closed; the force of the blows and the poison they carried took time to undo. "And I'm sure *you* realize we only have one chance to get this right, brother. Another day and I should be ready to begin."

"I hope you haven't been picking at them."

Lucifer's nostrils flared with a hint of fire. "I have not been picking at them!" he exclaimed, shaking his beer at Michael. "And maybe if you had done some of the dirty work I wouldn't be laying here looking like a pile of strip streaks."

The archangel rolled his eyes. "I was under the impression that you *like* getting hit, Lucifer. Or do you just say that because you end up getting beaten all the time, either way?" Michael snickered softly; his brother would never forget his defeat at the end of the War in Heaven. Lucifer simply glared at Michael, biting his tongue. He wanted to kill—to torture—his self-righteous brother more than almost anything in the world. Almost anything: but not at the expense of his one chance to reclaim his throne in Hell.

Nearby on the banks of San Juan's harbor, a lone tourist watched two of the world's most powerful entities bicker like children in the back seat for a long car ride. Lowering his binoculars, Charles ran a hand through his hair. It was remarkable enough that his hair was clean; days ago he had lived in an alleyway, scavenging for food. He had thought that his death was near when the terrible nightmares had overtaken him, robbing him of even the slight comfort of sleep. But then the most curious thing had happened—a mailman had stopped in front of his alleyway, calling his name; a name that he himself had almost forgotten. And Charles received a single envelope, his name hand-printed on the front. Inside he found a one-way plane ticket to Puerto Rico, five thousand dollars in cash, and a note that he had difficulty remembering. But the nightmares stopped, and he found himself in the Caribbean surveying the *Paradise Lost* for no particular reason other than it felt like the right thing to do. Charles was happy for the first time in years, giving a laugh as he went to find a restaurant for the evening.

Deep in the recesses of Charles' mind, Yaggoth was not nearly so relaxed. A being with an eons-long reputation for caution, the nightmare was distinctly uncomfortable in its current position. The same person who had directed it to Ockham's Kegger—advice which ended quite poorly, Yaggoth noted—had managed to find it again inside a new host. Yaggoth possessed the knowledge and wisdom of a thousand generations of humanity, but it knew nothing of Claudia Durand. Doubtless, the name was a pseudonym; if the girl's name had any meaning the nightmare would have discovered it. It had now received two letters from the enigmatic C.D.; letters detailing the philosophers' machinations in careful detail. And while Claudia's other correspondents remained unknown to Yaggoth, the nightmare held over them a substantial advantage; it was not a god or the product thereof. Consequently, it was not at all moved by Claudia's assurances of loyalty or devotion to its aims. The endless nightmare did not have followers—only prey—and knew that C.D. worked for herself. That fact, however, was not going to stop Yaggoth from taking whatever advantage it could of the situation.

There was a still-greater threat to Yaggoth than Claudia's persistent involvement. The nightmare could feel Wilfred searching for it in the dream world; he had defeated the first guardian and now moved closer by the hour. While Claudia's intentions remained a mystery, Yaggoth had no difficulty discerning Wilfred's plan. The mortal from the bar—surely at the philosophers' behest—planned to discover the identity of Yaggoth's possessed mortal host. Still terribly weakened from Nietzsche's assault, the nightmare was at present unable to flee through dreams. If discovered while trapped inside Charles, the nightmare would have no choice but to manifest itself again in the real world and run the great risk of direct confrontation with the philosophers. Yaggoth concluded that the mortal threat posed by Wilfred's success required its full attention, despite Pete—such a tempting prize—resting so nearby. The nightmare had not survived so long in the darkness by gambling on its own existence; the searching dreamer had to be annihilated.

Wilfred relaxed slightly as he passed the last of the unstable foothills; the mountains now rose up directly before him, ascending to the clouds. Surveying the rock face in front of him, he did not see any obvious entrance. Yet Wilfred knew he was getting closer. There must be a path, he thought, and then there was: an archway stood in front of him, stairs winding downwards into the deep. Wilfred gulped; he had enough common sense to know that shadowy roads into the underworld rarely ended in flowers and delicious cake. Within the nightmare, even that improbable outcome was no less dangerous: the cake would be only a lie, an excuse for flowers waiting to devour his heart. Steeling himself against the onslaught sure to come, Wilfred stepped forward and disappeared within the mountains.

The smooth stairs curved to the left as Wilfred descended, coiling downwards as he summoned enough light to guide his steps. Yet even that was unnecessary; the path offered no obstacles to his progression. If the precarious ground before had indicated the nightmare's displeasure with Wilfred's presence, the stairs conveyed calm certainty: that way lead only to the maw of death. It seemed like just a minute before Wilfred was far underground, the stairs ending in front of him and straightening out into a short hallway. Pressing forward, the tunnel opened into a vast and oddly square cavern. He stepped forward into the room and with that, the path behind him disappeared back into solid stone. At once the cave was flooded with light. In the center of the room stood a simple wooden chair, and in that chair sat a large man, head in his hands. He straightened up as Wilfred approached.

"Who are you?" Wilfred asked, his eyes scanning over the figure. The man was tall and stocky, dark-skinned and possessed of a bone structure that humanity had left in the dust of geological time.

The man sat silently, staring back at Wilfred. He wore a blue suit, once a fine outfit but now shredded and frayed. Unwilling to be ambushed yet again, Wilfred prepared to attack.

The man spoke. "I am the First of Many. You may call me that if you wish, Wilfred. Now, no need to look so shocked. As you learn about us, so we learn about you." The second guardian of Yaggoth rose to his feet, stretching slowly. Wilfred had already brought his hands up in front of him in a defensive position, eyes narrowing with focus. "Why are you so eager to fight? Time has no meaning here."

"And waiting serves no purpose," Wilfred replied. He had already sprung into action as he replied, dashing towards the First. Swinging, he found only air where the man once stood. It was not that his target was simply not there; it felt to Wilfred as if he had never been there to begin with. Hearing the First chuckle from behind him, Wilfred spun around and faced him again.

"Now, as I was saying. I am the First. I am the original dreamer; I was the one who conceived of Yaggoth. My mind gave birth to the essence of nightmares, and it devoured me. So here I wait, protecting the thing that killed me." The First gestured far back behind his chair, towards a plain door carved in the rock. "It is, after all, the only thing that sustains me. If the nightmare ends, I end with it."

Wilfred was not in the mood to listen to the damned soul's life story. Changing his strategy, he summoned forth his power into an orb of light that swelled between his hands. The energy churned and grew; a small, red sun built towards a cataclysmic supernova. In a moment the sphere broke apart, force radiating outwards from Wilfred as a potent blast-wave. The stone shattered as the blast passed over it, rubble not even returning to the ground before the attack moved past. Creaking quietly, the First's chair tipped over to the floor, its owner looking back at it as his hair fluttered gently in what could have been mistaken for a gentle summer breeze. "Oh, hm, my chair." Leaning back, he tilted his seat upright again. "Still, you are the first one to manage that much. I suppose I should congratulate you." He smiled, clapping heartily for Wilfred, the noise echoing around the cavernous room.

Even in the cool depths, Wilfred felt himself begin to sweat. This thing was nothing like the unicorn earlier, he thought; it didn't even seem to *care* about his attacks. How could he defeat a monster that he couldn't even touch? The unicorn had been resilient, but the First seemed positively invincible. He found himself biting his lip, trying to imagine an attack that might prove more effective. The seemingly genuine applause coming from the First only made Wilfred's situation seem that much more desperate.

"I don't believe you understand, my friend," the First said, pushing his hands into his jacket pockets. "I am the first creature on this planet to have ever dreamt, and since then I have dreamed forever more. What power *you* have comes from your imagination, your ability to conceive the world as it is not. Sartre did a wonderful job ensuring you could do that much without incident." Wilfred swallowed hard. "But for you, imagination is still an act; something you must do to take you beyond the ordinary. For me, there is no need to imagine what might be. I *am* the unreality that surrounds us. Here in the timeless dark, I have sat forever and again; here, I am unbounded."

Wilfred thought of alternatives to combat: perhaps he could collapse the room and evade this guardian, or simply distract him long enough to reach the door. Yet his train of thought was abruptly interrupted as the First stood beside him, putting his hand on Wilfred's shoulder. The nightmare's guardian was there, and he had always been there. Everywhere. Nowhere. "There is little sense in making a further mess of the room," he said, his gentle touch enough to paralyze Wilfred. "Even the swiftest insect cannot run from lightning."

"I..." Wilfred stammered, able to do little more than speak. "I suppose this is the end, then?" Try as he might, he could not even force his body to run from the touch of the First. He knew that accepting defeat would rob him of his power, but even his power was nothing against this opponent.

"The end?" The First laughed again, patting Wilfred's shoulder before putting his hand back into his pocket. "Hardly. I could kill you, true, but what a waste that would be of your remarkable mind! Better to wait for your strength to fade, so that you might join us. We will devour you, as we devoured ourselves." The man smiled widely, and for a moment Wilfred recognized the grin: he had seen it before, one of the many floating in the terrible abyss at Ockham's Kegger.

"Sartre's magic is potent, but here only we are eternal. As his concoction wears thin so too will your resistance, and then," the First snapped his fingers loudly, "you will break."

Pete sighed to himself. Still confined in one of the *Paradise Lost*'s guest rooms, he had done little but stare at the ceiling for what had seemed like days. A humorous situation, Pete thought. If he was to become a god, Pete realized he'd have to get used to sitting around for shockingly long periods of time. After all, gods can't afford to be the sort of people with an itchy trigger finger; poorly-thought through omnipotence had already cursed humanity with a whole host of problems. The last time a god had gotten antsy, disaster struck; the music industry discovered the commercial viability of horrific—yet well-marketed—boy bands, ensuring the perpetual embarrassment of the human civilization for untold decades.

Lying on the bed bound in chains, Pete had nothing to do but think. And as he thought, Pete became less sure of his own convictions. He had at first blown off the philosopher's arguments, certain that it was possible for him to help the world. But after his argument with Michael, Pete couldn't help but admit that the angel also thought *he* was acting for good. Even the archangel's heaven required a heavy sacrifice—an irreversible loss of humanity—that Pete knew many would reject. The real issue was not that Michael wanted to harm people, but that humans simply did not have a uniform conception of a good life. Certainly, some people would trade their humanity for immortality. Others would rather die as mortals then spend eternity hard-wired for happiness. Who was Michael to make that choice for the world?

That line of thought was not only critical, but humbling. If perfect happiness was controversial enough, how could even a god define an appropriate threshold of suffering at some lower level? Pete did not doubt the certainty of his beliefs; he felt the human experience could only be improved by the elimination of pointless natural disasters and crippling illness. Yet it was conceivable to him that others would maintain—not for any love of suffering—that such evil was necessary to a meaningful human existence. At what would point would his *improvement* of the world become *sanitization*? He himself had argued as much in a different context when trying to convince Michael of the inhumanity of heaven. Pete kept returning to the thought that a perfect god might be indistinguishable from a non-existent one.

Any involvement by Pete in changing the mortal world would be a vindication of his own particular moral preferences – his beliefs about what was good and what was evil. What gave him the right to make such decisions? He was a god, of course, but that was little more than a description of his power. Did that power give him the right to force his moral vision on others? "Might makes right" was the creed of tyrants, not saviors. Pete did not want to follow the path of the gods before him, leveling decrees against certain food or practices while demanding special dress and ritual. He was incredulous that some gods—beings that could create an entire galaxy from pure thought—were seriously concerned by what sort of lunch meat mortals had in their hoagies. Even more baffling, many people believed those deities were worthy of eternal adoration.

Yahweh's vendetta against shellfish had already doomed many to a thoroughly unjust afterlife, but human certainty had consequences nearly as terrible. Most of the evil in human history had been done in the name of justice, the inevitable result of confusing preference for moral authority. Humanity as a species seemed to have inordinate trouble distinguishing between personal taste and divinely-mandated morality. With astounding regularity, mortals assure themselves that everything they like is good and everything they dislike is evil.

This was quite puzzling to Pete, for upon deeper inspection there were few larger gaps than that between "what I like" and "what is necessarily good everywhere and at all times." Nevertheless, zealous humans readily translated matters of personal taste—perhaps a dislike of gambling, for instance—into a divine condemnation of the same. The entire structure of religious mythologies encouraged that baffling conflation: if divine beings went completely nuts—on a regular basis—over shockingly petty details of human affairs, was any impulse truly too bizarre for eternal law? If anything, Pete thought, gods should be in the business of encouraging people to respect each other's beliefs, and entertain the notion that they might themselves be mistaken.

Back at the Philosoplex, the meeting had adjourned. As Russell and Robert reprogrammed the PDE-1's neural interface for Lime, Sartre and Hume were upstairs checking on Wilfred's condition. All that remained at the table was Socrates, Rachel, and Patty. Socrates gave a contented sigh, having finished off his gargantuan portion of Wheaties. Patty looked to him, still worried about Pete's predicament. While Hume had made an effort to explain the brothers' plans for Pete, she still had many more questions than answers.

"Er, Socrates?" Patty asked tentatively. "I was wondering...could you tell me more about Michael and Lucifer? And their Creator? I'm still not entirely sure...well, what do they plan to do with Pete?"

"Ah, hrm," Socrates said, resting his arm on the table as he turned to face the two. "The basic problem is pretty simple. The God who created Michael and Lucifer—Yahweh—destroyed himself after his version of heaven...went bad." Patty's eyes went wide; she had a particular interest in the god whom she had worshiped. Or at least thought she had worshiped.

"...went bad?" Patty asked curiously.

Socrates nodded sternly. "People quickly began to go insane in Heaven. Time didn't pass there as it does here; many souls were losing it entirely after a couple thousand years. It was not quite the paradise that either Yahweh or the faithful who went there had imagined."

"Oh," Patty half-mumbled, looking down at the table. "And God...er...Yawheh couldn't make them happy?"

"I'm sure he could," Rachel replied. "He was a god. The question is whether Yahweh wanted to *make* everyone happy."

"Exactly right," Socrates noted. "And Yahweh soon realized the difficulty of his situation: forcing human happiness in Heaven was absolutely no different than forcing human happiness on Earth. Yahweh either had to abandon respect for free will, or forego any further involvement with humanity. He chose the latter."

Patty remained confused, and Socrates explained his reasoning. "You see, it's a pillar of most religions that gods have a good reason not to make the world a perfect place. It was certainly within

147

Yahweh's power to make everyone on Earth happy. Yet he did not—as other gods have not—because doing so would take away humanity's free will." Patty nodded, having spoken at length with Hume about free will. "But if free will is valuable, it must be valuable everywhere: both on Earth and in heaven. But no human being—no mortal with their free will intact—will choose to live forever."

"That's not true," Patty said with a defiant note in her voice. "People all over the world pray for eternal life."

Rachel couldn't help herself but chuckle at Patty's naivety. "Praying for something and experiencing it isn't the same thing, Patty," she chided. "Believers pray for eternity because they have a naïve conception of infinity. You could spend a trillion-trillion years doing every conceivable activity that you enjoy in every conceivable order and you would be no closer to the end of eternity. The only way to fill an infinite amount of time without experiencing infinite periods of absolute, maddening boredom is to have an infinite number of enjoyable activities." Rachel shrugged deeply, reaching up to scratch her head. "And I don't know about you…but I don't think any human being can amuse themselves for eternity."

Patty listened to her friend with a look of frustration on her face; she disagreed with Rachel but didn't feel like she was sophisticated enough to offer a rebuttal. "Maybe this will help," Socrates interjected, pulling over a piece of paper and pen left on the table. "Okay. Now, if you were forced to spend an infinite amount of time without any enjoyable activity in your life…how would you feel?"

"Well…I guess I'd be pretty unhappy," Patty said.

"Haha! Only pretty unhappy?" Socrates responded with a laugh.

Patty thought for a moment before conceding defeat. "Alright. I'd probably try to kill myself before I went totally nuts."

"Yeah, as would any of us," Socrates continued, clicking the pen into place before writing. "So we agree that an eternity of utter boredom would profoundly suck." Patty and Rachel both smiled and nodded. "But look at this," he said as he turned the paper to face Patty. "Infinity minus infinity equals zero, but infinity minus anything other than infinity equals infinity. Let this first infinity be the time you'll spend in heaven, and the second number the number of years for which you could keep yourself amused." Patty immediately understood the argument once it was put in writing. "Unless you can keep yourself busy for an infinite length of time...you're going to end up in the very, *very* bad place of infinite boredom."

Patty looked glum; she was happy that she followed Socrates' argument, but less than pleased to find out the eternal life was, in philosophical terms, infinitely sucky. She thought for a moment, trying to convince herself that she could keep herself happy forever. "Yeah...I see now. Damn. So Yahweh killed himself because heaven failed? Why not just try again?"

"Gods don't take well to failure," Socrates answered. "Especially not Yahweh, and especially not the failure of heaven. That afterlife was supposed to be Yahweh's opus magnum...the most perfect aspect of all creation. And in fairness, I am not sure that it was even possible to make heaven better. What could Yahweh have done other than strip humanity of free will?"

"Yahweh at least had the good sense to kill himself," Rachel said with a deep frown on her face. "His infinite wisdom was useful for that, at least. But Michael and Lucifer...they think they can do better, don't they?" Socrates nodded. "They're going to try and use Pete's power to remake both heaven and hell."

"Undoubtedly," Socrates agreed. "Michael's purpose is to reign in heaven, and Lucifer's is to reign in hell. They do not have free will; they cannot *choose* to abandon their purpose. The brothers will do anything to remake Yahweh's afterlife, even if success means destroying free will and humanity as we know it."

Rachel chewed on her lip thoughtfully. "I can appreciate all of that...but why would Yahweh leave around the brothers to keep screwing with people after he was gone?" Rachel asked. "And not just Yahweh. If gods keep giving up on divinity—as Yahweh did—why haven't any of them had the common sense to just get rid of the supernatural themselves?"

"Zugzwang."

"What?" Patty asked, unfamiliar with the term.

"The word is most commonly used in chess," Socrates explained. "It refers to a position where every move is a bad move.

As it happens, gods go insane by a process of elimination, as they realize how their actions negatively impact the world. When they get to the point where they see no option but resignation—so to speak—even gods fail to notice the possibility of preventing the same game from being played again. Gripped by the realization that their every act undermines free will, they overlook the possibility of a singular, sweeping action eliminating the supernatural entirely." He paused. "Sometimes, even gods can be complete idiots."

"Wouldn't that still destroy free will, though?" Rachel asked skeptically, rolling the idea around in her head. "Existing beings of nominal freedom would be destroyed—like the brothers—and humans would have the future possibility of supernatural interaction foreclosed to them by force."

"Yeap," Socrates shrugged, "it would. And that's precisely why gods—on their own initiative—do not take such a course of action. Before everything went completely FUBAR, we had planned to convince Pete of the necessity of purging the supernatural. By planning and guiding his development, we thought it would be possible to create a god willing to engage in one massive but final violation of free will. If the existence of god necessitates the violation of free will, then it is better to have one final godlike act—destroying all of the supernatural forever—and be done with it."

"How is that any different from what the brothers plan to do with Pete?" Patty asked pointedly. "You're both ready to screw with humanity 'just this once' to accomplish your goals."

"There is an important difference. The brothers wish to force a certain outcome: the creation and acceptance of an eternal afterlife. In contrast, we only want to prevent something from happening."

"That doesn't make any sense, Socrates," Rachel rebutted, hardly able to believe she just said that. "The brothers could just as well say they're only preventing a world where an afterlife does not exist, and that you're forcing a future without gods. Your characterization isn't any more valid."

"Aha, you're almost right. But with free will, there is indeed a difference. Answer me this: would a god that respects free will be required to make every human a god themselves?"

"Er," Rachel paused, "no? Why would they?"

"It seems to me that even if humans are free in some respects—free to choose their flavor of soda, perhaps—they are still to an almost unimaginable extent constrained. Humans are inexorably bound by the laws of the physical world; no person is free to choose to fly about, or grow a tail. Unless everyone is a god in their own universe, they will be unable to do *some* things."

"Respect for free will can't truly imply an obligation for a god to make all things possible," Rachel said, shaking her head.

"Then a god is under no more obligation to ensure that people might experience the supernatural than it is to abolish the fickle laws of physics," Socrates suggested, extending her reasoning.

Rachel tried to think of a response, but didn't get very far. It was hard for her to see any distinction between those two restrictions on human existence. "I, ugh, I don't know," she said, twirling a bit of hair in her finger. "That sounds right, but didn't we already agree that destroying the supernatural was a violation of free will? This entire argument just seems like a train-wreck, honestly."

Socrates laughed in response, smiling happily. "That's the point! What I really think is that the entire concept of 'free will' ends up yielding nonsense when gods are in the picture. If freedom is to mean anything, all of the gods must be destroyed. Pete just needs to be convinced as much, and humanity can finally live without the persistent threat of some *benevolent* god turning everyone into a pleasure-zombie."

Claudia Durand walked between worlds, already frustrated by her difficulty in accessing the Philosoplex. She knew the way—how could she forget?—yet that was little help in light of the fact that Hume's masterpiece held little welcome for unexpected guests. And despite her knowledge, Claudia was most certainly unwelcome there; due to both what she was, and the god that trailed behind her in the astral wake. In constructing the Philosoplex, David Hume had the good sense to scatter the mansion amongst a million places in space and time. Those fragile scraps of reality were held together by a string that only Hume could see. And that string was only pulled taut for those welcome in his world; any intruder would be forced to find and assemble all of the pieces themselves. Even for a being of Claudia's power—one who knew the shape of the final picture, at that—such a task was not easy. Nevertheless, she was making progress; slow progress, but the completion of her gateway was inevitable. Spread throughout the universe, countless images of the girl hunted for the path.

One image, however, was lucky enough to avoid such drudgery. While parts of Claudia dug through primordial fire searching for the scattered pieces, one particular Claudia was enjoying some truly mind-blowing risotto in Old San Juan. "This is amazing, how did you ever find this place?" Charles asked, wiping his mouth before slumping back in his chair. He sat across from Claudia, dining in the outdoor area of a fine Italian restaurant.

Claudia gave a charming laugh, swirling the red wine in her glass aimlessly. "I've been to a lot of places," she said, amusing herself. "Now, this has been a fantastic distraction from my work, but I believe you know who I really want to speak with, Charles."

"Huh?" The man blinked. He was confused, and not entirely because of a few too many glasses of expensive Chianti. "What do you mean? You brought me here; asked to meet me. I don't know anybody…agh!" Claudia's hand was at his collar as she pulled him close, nearly toppling the delicate table.

"I know you're in there. You can either have a chat with me or I can spread your host around the alleyway like confetti." She hissed at the panicked Charles, who should have known that any beautiful woman interested in him was out of her mind. He suddenly convulsed, jumping a bit in his chair as his eyes rolled back into his head. For the moment, Charles gave up the driver's seat.

"You would threaten me in such a way?" Yaggoth spoke, its chorus of voices subdued but still noticeable. "Perhaps you overestimate my weakness, Ms. Durand." She snorted, letting go of Charles' tie. He sat back, straightening out his suit. "I am intrigued by you, but you would be ill-advised to think of me as less than your equal."

Claudia shrugged, adjusting her glasses and taking a sip of her wine. Few beings in the world still spoke with such self-assurance;

even the god she led to the Philosoplex shrunk at the prospect of death. "Perhaps. But I needed to speak with you directly, and you were less than forthcoming." At that moment, Yaggoth might actually pose a threat to her. With her power spread across all existence in preparation to attack the philosophers, the nightmare could be dangerous if incited.

"And you expected me to listen eagerly to your deception?" Charles smirked, looking up at the evening sky. "I have more important concerns than your ham-fisted attempt to manipulate me." Even though Wilfred's intrusion had been successfully nullified by the First of Many, Yaggoth would not rest easy until the threat had been entirely erased.

Setting her glass aside, Claudia stared intently across the table. "There's no sense in lying to you then, eh?" Leaning forward, she set her chin in her hand. "I'm here for Pete, the little sprout in the harbor."

"Really?" Charles asked sarcastically. "What a shock! Here I thought we were in San Juan because of a fantastic discount on flights."

Her face darkened; Claudia would be happy to teach the nightmare a lesson if the circumstances did not demand restraint. She forced a smile and remained calm. "I would like to work with you. Our aims are not altogether that different; we could both benefit from acquiring possession of the godling at an appropriate time."

"You're disappointing me, Claudia. Your *help* is precisely what landed me in my current predicament. You expect me to seek more of the same?" Charles shook his head sadly, fiddling with the tablecloth and almost ready to leave. "Perhaps you truly are as young as you look. I am not like these humans or the pathetic gods that grow out of them."

Taking a deep breath, Claudia kept her cool. "Let me be a little more precise, Yaggoth. I can offer you what nobody else in this world can: lasting power. You are ultimately no different than the brothers, or any other creature crawling around this city. You want to steal Pete's power to sustain yourself against the inevitable decay of this universe and everything in it." Charles nodded slightly, folding his hands on the table and listening. "But I can do far more than that.

I—and I alone—have the ability to turn this new god into a perpetual engine of divine power. You wish to consume him; the brothers hope to break him. Both approaches will crack the perfection of his being, and even if you succeed, it is only a matter of time before you must search for another god to consume." In that, Claudia was correct; even Yaggoth's power would eventually fail against grinding entropy.

Yaggoth was intrigued; even its own subtle plans for Pete were not capable of consuming the god's full power. At most, the nightmare would only bolster itself against the grinding decay of time. Perhaps for a thousand years, perhaps far longer! But even the age of the world seemed brief against the scale of eternity. "And you believe it is possible to secure his power without diminishing it? Once you break the seal of omnipotence the prize is spoiled; only so much can be squeezed from the husk."

She smiled, sitting back and brushing her soft brown hair from her eyes. "So we don't break him. We simply manipulate him."

"Simply? He is useless to either of us until he reaches the height of his power, and you think to manipulate him *then*?"

Claudia was pleased that the nightmare expressed some interest in her suggestions. While she had not yet decided whether she was truly going to work with Yaggoth—most likely she would end up betraying it—the nightmare's assistance would be invaluable. Powerful as Claudia was, she would be not able to execute her plans for Pete under duress. "You could say that deception is my specialty." Finishing her wine, Claudia already relished the thought of working her magic on Pete. "Of course, you are unable to appreciate my talents; you are a truly unique creature in this world. Even I cannot deceive the great nightmare. But humans and gods, with their vulnerable little minds..." She trailed off, a wide grin spreading across her face.

Charles gave a polite chuckle, his eyes going slowly over the girl before him. "I see. But many have made the same claim that you make now. You remind me of Loki, so many centuries ago. He told me the same thing, you see; he promised he could fool the gods themselves. And where is he now? Dead and gone, along with many others."

"I am not Loki; I am not some mortal-turned-god. Like you, I am unique. Nothing like me has ever walked this world. Do not insult me by comparing me to little trickster gods, Yaggoth."

"As you wish, but that only raises the inevitable question: if not a god, what are you? There is no doubt in my mind that you are young; very young by the measure of the heavens. Perhaps you could conceal yourself from me for a short time; perhaps even a few centuries. But no-one is subtle enough to hide from me forever. Nothing lives on this world that is older than I, but...I do not know of you." Charles stared intensely across the table at Claudia. "Yet you heap scorn upon the gods?"

Claudia smiled coyly; she had anticipated this question coming up. Unlike her other 'partners,' Yaggoth's countless minds were not about to pass over such an important consideration. Yet the question bothered Claudia more than she could afford to let on. Before she could formulate an answer, Charles laughed loudly.

"Ahahah!" Charles slapped the table-top lightly as a devious grin spread across his face. "You don't know, do you?" Immediately the blood drained from Claudia's face, confirming Yaggoth's intuition. "Yes, yes..." Charles mused aloud, his eyes flickering over the young woman. "I suspected as much. How appropriate!"

"Appropriate?" Claudia asked through pursed lips.

"You deceive everyone, even yourself. As you hide the truth of the world, you do not know the most basic truth about yourself: what you are, and where you came from," Charles explained confidently. Yaggoth could sense that it held the upper hand, at least for the time being. "It is...quite appropriate. Despite your penchant for deception, it appears that the mystery of your existence bothers you." Charles leaned forward, lowering his voice to a whisper. "Terrifies you."

"Watch your tone, nightmare," Claudia hissed in response. "I do not need to know what I am in order to shred the fragile mortal body in which you are hiding!"

"Of course," Charles said nonchalantly, "but then what would you do? To whom would you turn?" Claudia did not have a ready answer. "I do not doubt your immense power, Ms. Durand. However, it is *precisely* that power which gives me such confidence; you would not be here seeking my aid unless you need me."

"The same can be said of you, Yaggoth," Claudia rebutted, crossing her arms in front of her chest. "It does us no good to bicker; you need me as much as I need you. At this point, we should focus on retrieving the godling from Michael before he damages our prize."

"Ah," Charles said, "I must agree. But you have not yet told me...what precisely *do* you need of me?"

Claudia took another sip of her wine, gingerly setting the glass back down on the table. "Well, it struck me that our powers are perfectly complimentary," she explained, raising her hand and beckoning the waiter over to their table. "I can make people believe anything, but their beliefs are merely that – an illusion. My power to create is...extremely limited. On the other hand, you can transform thoughts into reality; you can take a monster from a mortal's fevered delusions and make it *real*."

"Quite clever," Charles said, rubbing his chin. "You propose to induce nightmares for me to bring in to the world? I admit that I had not considered that possibility. Most dreams are incoherent and fragmentary...difficult things to create, if at all."

"But I could give you an endless supply of humans...tormented by nightmares of unparalleled clarity and unequalled horror."

"I could make an army..." Charles rubbed his hands together.

"Yes," Claudia continued as she handed the waiter the unpaid bill, who thanked her profusely for her generosity before hurrying away. "An army...strong enough to crush the brothers *and* the philosophers. Strong enough to claim this world as our own. Forever."

Robert stared bleary eyed at the computer screen; lines of code raced across the screen as the PDE's revised command program compiled. Startlingly enough, the program did not report any errors. Given the pressing need to get the PDE-1 operational, Robert was thankful that he would not have to go through the onerous debugging process for a seventh time. "It's done; there don't appear to be any problems with our test," he called up to Russell, who nonchalantly hopped the five stories down from the open compartment of the war machine.

The philosopher wiped his brow, tossing aside a few straps and cushions left over from his work on the unit's interior. Russell had left Robert to error-check the code while he had been busy retrofitting the PDE-1 to comfortably hold a kitten instead of a full-grown adult human. Positioning all of the interface nodes on the headset had taken some time, but the rest of the work merely required Russell to provide sufficient cushioning that would protect Lime against the anticipated acceleration and impact forces. Russell walked beside Robert, looking over the results from the compilation and trial run.

It was remarkable that they had managed to re-work the PDE-1's entire pilot program in a few short hours. Fortunately for Robert, the kitten's brain was not altogether that different from a human brain; most mammalian brains have similar components. His real problem had been in fixing all of the algorithms to account for the fact that kittens didn't happen to be bipedal, roughly humanoid creatures. Cats have an entirely different body than humans, and Russell could not build a feline version of the PDE in an afternoon. While it was straightforward enough to translate a person's thought of "lift right arm" into a command for the roughly person-shaped PDE-1, figuring out what to make of "curl right paw" was less than clear.

"Let's put her in and give this a shot, then," Russell said, looking over at Lime. The kitten quickly hopped up and ran about in a circle. The philosopher took over the laptop for a moment, making sure to disable to combat and mobility systems of the PDE-1 before trying an experiment. Comical as it would have been in some situations to have Lime trip over herself while trying to walk, Russell didn't want to roll the dice when dealing with enough fissionable material to punch a hole in space-time itself.

Hoping that Lime wouldn't cause any disasters, Russell took her in his hand and leapt back up into the cockpit. As Robert watched from below, Russell sat Lime in place and tightened her harness, locking the tiny kitten-restraints in place. Russell was confident that Lime wasn't going to fall out of the machine—even if she did, she would land on her feet—so he lowered the helmet onto Lime's head. Kitty ears poked out from two well-positioned holes, the metal helmet and facemask covering her eyes and topped with a thick bundle of wires, leading back into the wall behind her. Standing on the edge, Russell called down to Robert: "Alright, disable the master override and let's see if this works!"

Once Robert released the external locks on the unit's reactors, the PDE-1 began to energize once again. "Please don't break anything...be a good kitty," Russell cooed at Lime as the entire structure began to hum with power. "I'll give you a cheeseburger if this goes through without a disaster," he promised, knowing that was the secret desire of every cat's heart. Lime took a moment to adjust to the virtual world through which she controlled the suit; for a few seconds the arms and torso gave small random twitches of motion. Robert watched, filled with both terror and anticipation. "Is it working?" he called up to the PDE-1, unsure if he could even be heard. There was no response for a brief time, then both of the PDE-1's arms shot out simultaneously as Lime skillfully wiggled the suit's fingers.

"YES!" Russell and Robert both cried out in unison. It didn't take long for the kitten to explore the very limited range of the machine's currently-allowed movements; she could not do much more than maneuver the torso, arms, and head. Russell's eyes darted over the internal readout displays and he rubbed his hands together in enthusiasm; everything was working perfectly. Lime had taken to the PDE-1 like most cats take to a ball of yarn. "Ready to take this for a spin outside?" Russell asked, looking down at Lime inside the cockpit.

"Meee-OW!"

Returning to the ground, Russell gave Robert a huge bear hug. He looked up proudly at the world's most advanced piece of weaponry, manned by a feisty kitten. "I can't believe this, it is almost too much," Robert said, hugging Russell back. His pulse was racing; this was exactly the sort of work he had wanted to do all of his life. With the economy in the dumpster and little demand in the market for mathematicians specializing in AI, he had never imagined doing much besides menial accounting for the evening paper. Glancing at Russell for confirmation, he released the restrictions on the PDE-1's movement, opening the silo cover above to let in the sunlight.

Lime wasted no time, sensing freedom to test the limits of her new kitty toy. The cockpit's cover gave a crisp snap as it closed, sealing Lime inside as the PDE looked up at the exit above. The suit immediately fell into a crouch, one hand on the floor as it bent down. Springing upwards, Lime rocketed upwards and out, igniting her thrusters once clear of the building below. Nodding across the empty room towards a door leading to the exterior, Russell hurried with Robert outside to see their work.

    Hume sung quietly to himself, standing at the kitchen sink while he washed the dishes from breakfast. He had been happy to cook breakfast for his guests at the Philosoplex, and doing the dishes was a remarkably relaxing task for a man normally worried about chasing after rogue gods. Hume looked out the window over the sink and admired the extensive gardens he had laid out beside the living space of the mansion. In that peculiar dimension, seasonal flowers stayed in bloom all year long, giving the philosopher great latitude in design. He looked over the rows of flowers: roses, snap-dragons, lilies and more growing amongst small ponds.

    BOOM. A soapy plate flew out of Hume's hands and crashed onto the floor behind him as Lime slammed the PDE-1 into the decorative garden from above. Water, soil, and petals scattered everywhere as 55 tons of reinforced titanium impacted what was once a picturesque outdoor scene. Hume's mouth hung open as pieces of the ruined garden flew through the air. A single lily smacked into the window in front of him and stuck in place. The flower slowly slid down the glass before Hume's eyes as the debris settled, leaving a view of the PDE-1 standing in a crater of once-living confetti.

    "Son of a bitch!" Hume exclaimed, hurriedly opening the window and retrieving the poor, displaced lily from the pane above. If he had put things in perspective, Hume would have likely been more shocked by the success of Russell's mad plan than the destruction of his garden. At that moment, however, Hume leaned his head out the window, shouting. "What the hell was that?!" The PDE-1 turned slowly towards the voice, cocking its head curiously at Hume and only enraging him further. He could just imagine Lime sitting inside, giving the kind of innocent expression that kittens often deployed after the destruction of a harmless lamp or roll of toilet paper. Cradling the flower in his hands, Hume watched in disbelief as Lime took off again, soaring into the air as she left behind a trail of exhaust and ruined shrubberies.

Moments later Robert and Russell jogged into view of Hume; both of them stared at the crater in shock. "Oh hell...Hume is going to be pissed when he sees this," Russell said to Robert, giving a nervous laugh. Robert swallowed hard as he imagined what Lime could do once she was released in to the outside world.

"You're bloody right I'm pissed!" Hume screamed from the window at them, having to restrain himself from hurling a recently-cleaned teacup at the guilty pair. "Argh!" He stormed off in disgust, hoping to find a vase to salvage at least one of his flowers.

Russell and Robert stood next to each other in the debris of Hume's ruined garden, watching Lime bound here and there in the fields surrounding the Philosoplex. The kitten had achieved almost full mastery of the PDE-1 in a remarkably short period of time; she tumbled, rolled, and dove through the sky effortlessly. Ten minutes later, once Lime had her fill of excitement, she returned to Russell and landed the PDE-1 a few yards in front of him. Landing aside the garden with a careful grace that should have been displayed earlier, the PDE-1 knelt down in front of Russell.

In the short time Russell and Robert had to prepare the PDE-1 for Lime's use, there had not been any chance to reconfigure the combat suit's communication devices. Figuring out how to allow Lime to communicate with the philosophers would have certainly taken far longer than their work on the control systems. Yet Lime was no ordinary kitten, and she wasn't about to be held back by thought-to-speech programs designed for a human mind. Compared to the ordinary house-cat, Lime was a world-class genius; if she had been able to speak English, she would have likely sounded quite distinguished. Yet with her thoughts funneled through the PDE's ill-adapted communication software, her messages came through as a garbled pidgin.

"I am," the PDE said, causing even Russell to jump in surprise. "I am ready to has Pete." The two men looked at each other in shock; neither of them had expected such a remarkable development. Russell knew that Lime was extraordinarily smart, but her speech made him feel uneasy. He wondered if Lime fully understood the perils of piloting the PDE-1.

"Do you understand that this is going to be dangerous? You could die, Lime," he said, unable to send an adorable kitten into battle without an appropriate disclosure.

"Yes," she replied, acknowledging the danger. "But...but...kittehs are tuff! Rawr!" Robert couldn't help but laugh. Inside the device, Lime had some regrets about using the PDE to communicate; her scrambled speech only reinforced humanity's most hurtful stereotypes involving cats and LOLs.

"Ok," Russell said with a chuckle, figuring he couldn't ask for much more from a kitten. He paused in thought for a moment, looking back at Hume's ruined garden. Then, he glanced over at Robert, seeking his opinion. "Do you think it would be safe to enable the unit's combat systems?"

Robert shook his head, laughing nervously. "God no. But if we want to get Pete back, do we have much choice?" After all, even the huge suit would be a sitting duck without means to defend itself from certain opposition.

Turning back to the PDE, Russell addressed himself to Lime. "If we give you full control of the PDE-1, can you control yourself? Flowers are one thing, but I can't have you killing a load of innocent people."

"I be good, promise!" The suit's head nodded slowly. "I listen to ceiling cat! Good kitteh!"

"OK. Then let's head back to the launch bay and we'll get the unit's weaponry online."

"DO WANT!" The PDE bounded excitedly back into the air, thrusters firing as it sailed towards the rear of the Philosoplex and the launch bay. Following after her, Russell and Robert made the final preparations for their desperate plan to rescue Pete.

Chapter Nine

Within half an hour, the entire team had gathered in Launch Bay Four. Satisfied by Russell's assurances that Lime didn't pose a completely new threat to the existence of humanity, the other philosophers had agreed to depart immediately in pursuit of Pete. Due to his unparalleled mastery of the material world, Russell was the only member of the group capable of sustained flight; consequently, he would travel alongside the PDE in pursuit of Pete.

"I'll move with Lime, and provide cover if she is ambushed before we reach Pete," Russell said from a seat behind his desk, legs up as he relaxed after a long day's work.

"And to make sure she isn't reckless," Nietzsche added, still somewhat wary about Lime's involvement in the mission. "We don't have the strength to defeat the brothers by force; we will need to plan the engagement carefully."

"They're that strong?" Rachel asked incredulously; she was hardly able to imagine a foe more terrifying than Yaggoth. "The brothers could beat all of you?"

"Probably not, no," Hume answered, sitting on the edge of Russell's desk. "But we can't afford to send *all* of us. Wilfred's mission is just as important to our success, and we will need to leave some of us behind with him, for the time being."

Kant rubbed his chin thoughtfully; far less grumpy now that his eye had begun to heal. Sporting a stylish black eye-patch in place of soiled bandages, he chimed in. "Still, we should send as much of our strength as we can. While we might not be able to rescue Pete if Wilfred fails to locate Yaggoth, nothing else matters if the brothers manage to turn Pete before we can intervene." Hume nodded. "I suggest that Nietzsche and I follow behind Russell in the jet." Putting the special case of Socrates aside, Nietzsche, Kant, and Russell were the three strongest of the philosophers in direct combat.

"That's fine," Sartre agreed. "I have to stay behind to work with Wilfred when he wakes, and Hume's presence is required to ensure that the Philosoplex remains secure. Socrates can provide the necessary muscle for our group once we leave to deal with Yaggoth."

"You're damned right I can," Socrates chuckled, crossing his thick arms in front of his chest. "Yaggoth may have a thousand mouths now, but when I'm done it'll have a thousand new…"

"We get the idea, Socrates," Hume interrupted. He looked over to the mortals; Patty and Rachel had both gathered with Robert to discuss his afternoon's work with Lime. "Also, we can keep an eye on Pete's friends here."

"I don't think so," Patty spoke up, shaking her head. "I've been sitting in here long enough. Maybe I can't fight, but I'm going after Pete with the rest of them." She pointed at Kant and the PDE-1.

"You'll get in the way," Nietzsche retorted immediately.

"And what if Pete is still pissed off at you for being an asshole earlier?" Patty shot back, glaring at the philosopher. "I think at least one of us should be there when you rescue him. How do *you* expect to convince him to cooperate?"

Sartre had a pretty good idea of how Nietzsche would deal with an obstinate god, and he much preferred Patty's involvement. "She has a point. If we want to get Pete on our side, having some of his friends there would go a long way."

"I want to go too!" Rachel chimed in, bouncing on her feet where she stood. Unsurprisingly, she wanted to see the philosophers in action when they rescued Pete; an atheist for nearly all of her life, Rachel thought that seeing Nietzsche punch out an angel might be the awesomest thing possible. As her eyes lingered briefly on Russell, she found herself wondering if she might have additional, less ideological motives for tagging along.

"Don't they all?" Hume sighed to himself, resigned to the fact that he could do little in the face of Russell's charm. Destroying gods was one thing; protecting women everywhere from his colleague was quite another.

Hearing Hume but not catching the drift of his comment, Robert responded. "Nah, I don't want to go. I'll stay here with you guys. I need to get some rest after all of that programming, and

Wilfred should have one of us here to congratulate him when he wakes up! He's putting his life on the line, too."

"Then it's settled," Russell said, hopping to his feet. He looked between Rachel and Patty, then back to Rachel again with a wide smile. "The five of us should depart immediately; we don't have any time to waste."

"SIX!" Lime shouted through the PDE, startling everyone in the room. She had demonstrated remarkable self-control by sitting through the entire meeting without causing a scene, being as inconspicuous as a 55-ton war machine could.

"Hah…yes, six," Russell amended. "My apologies. I'll go over a few additional details with Lime here while the rest of you get the jet ready." Nietzsche had already wheeled himself out of the room, heading towards another one of the Philosoplex's hangars. Beckoning to the two ladies, Kant waited for them to follow him before leading Rachel and Patty up the hallway towards Launch Bay One. The four remaining men in the room looked amongst themselves.

"Well, I guess I'll go see what I can do about the garden…" Hume said dejectedly.

"I need a nap," Robert added, stifling a yawn.

Sartre looked at his watch; less than an hour remained until his elixir's power began to fade from Wilfred. Even though a real hour amounted to quite some time in the dream world, Sartre had started to worry for Wilfred's safety. "I'll check up on Wilfred again."

Socrates laughed jovially. "And I'm getting some more Wheaties!"

Wilfred stared down at his feet, imagining that he could hear a large clock ticking away the seconds of his life. He had been so confident after his encounter with the unicorn; he had thought that he could face anything that Yaggoth might put before him. But now, he could only think of his wife and his young daughter. What would happen to his body when he was lost to Yaggoth? Would there be a funeral? Perhaps, he thought, the world wouldn't even last that long.

Wilfred knew that was a selfish wish, but he could find little other solace. Twice again he had tried to attack the First without the slightest success; his movements seemed to end before they began.

"You're making even me feel depressed," the First of Many sighed. He was seated again in his red wooden chair, legs crossed like a British professor. "This life isn't so bad, if you look at it the right way."

Wilfred blinked away the tears that swelled in his eyes, staring back at the First with helpless rage. "You think I'm afraid for myself?" he snapped, shaking his head. "I would die a hundred times for my friends. I just…" Wilfred stopped, taking a slow breath. "I just can't stand leaving my family like this. They deserve so much more."

"Ah," the guardian replied, looking up to the smooth ceiling. "I never really had a family, you see. I've seen so many, of course. But back in the Stone Age, I hardly knew my parents. I knew *who* they were, but then our kind were little more than animals. Yaggoth claimed me before I ever had a partner, or a child."

"You can't understand what they mean to me," Wilfred replied, walking forward.

"You are right, but…" the First thought for a moment, and with a snap of his fingers a copy of his red chair appeared across from him. "That is an interesting story. Have a seat, and perhaps I can distract you for a time."

Wilfred approached the chair, looking down at it as he ran his hand over the back. The First of Many watched as he sat down, giving a little chuckle. "Curious about the chair? I suppose it doesn't really fit the rest of the room's décor." Certainly, the cheery red chairs stood out from the stark, smooth-cut stone that composed the rest of the room. "Recently, this fellow had the most amusing nightmare about this chair. He had just acquired a number of do-it-yourself furniture pieces for his new apartment. I can't imagine how the poor man must have suffered trying to assemble this chair; it chased him in his sleep for hours. After that, I had to see if the seat was worth the effort! They are remarkable comfortable for such a simple design, yes?"

The guardian got a blank stare in response; Wilfred wasn't in quite the right kind of mindset for such casual banter. "Yes, it is," he replied at last, leaning forward with his arms on his knees.

"Anyways, the family. As you have seen, I am practically omnipotent here. It was only natural for me to make myself a family: a wife, children, and a home for us all. But you know what? Omnipotence has a damning drawback; I can't make myself truly human. No matter how much I wanted to pretend—and *my god*, did I want to—I just can't get rid of the fact that I am eternal. My family, my love…they were all just little puppets, which I could unmake with a thought."

Wilfred listened in silence, understandably less than sympathetic for the First's problems. "Even with omnipotence, I can't make myself vulnerable. It's not possible to use omnipotence to make myself *truly* mortal, subject to the whims of time and chance. Can you imagine what that does to love, Wilfred? I couldn't fear for my family; nothing could go wrong. I couldn't relish my hours with them; they could exist forever if I wished it. How could I appreciate a world where suffering and hardship could only exist by my own design?" The First of Many uncrossed his legs, looking earnestly across the empty space to Wilfred. "You can't understand it; not yet. But the fact that you're about to lose your family—and they you—is precisely what makes the relationship valuable. The pain is real, but it is also meaningful. I would give all my power to suffer as you do, to face a world beyond my control."

"Will that comfort my daughter or my wife?" Wilfred asked angrily, looking back as their eyes met. "I don't want to be immortal, but I don't want to leave them like this."

"That!" The First exclaimed excitedly, nodding at Wilfred. "That is your greatest treasure; you want what cannot be had. If I was you, and I wanted such a thing, it would *be*. Could you be happy if your future was foretold? Would there be any joy in your life if you knew you would live to old age with your wife, able to see your child grow up happy?"

"Yes. They would be happy," Wilfred replied, only wishing he could guarantee that much for them.

"Maybe, but not you. You would be nothing; less than a man. Nothing you could do or say would ever matter! What reason is there to act in the face of cosmic certainty? You are a noble man, Wilfred, but even you could not live solely on the comfort of knowing your family's happiness was assured. Uncertainty is all that gives you meaning; embrace it! Rejoice in the fact that you're so blessed, as to be able to experience such a tragic end."

"Why do you care?!" Wilfred was irritated; he couldn't stand being told that the impending loss of his entire world was a good thing. Not only a good thing, even—the best possible thing according to the First, that which defined his very humanity. "I didn't know Yaggoth had such a soft, cuddly side."

"Oh, it does not." The First laughed, finding the very notion ridiculous. "But I am not the same thing as the endless nightmare. A rifle may be built for killing, you see, but that does not give its constituent atoms a malice all their own." He paused, looking down over his torn suit. "I am simply the oldest of Yaggoth's victims, only one amongst so very many lost souls. Every day I wish I could have simply died in the distant past; an inconsequential life vanishing in a brutal, ancient world. That fate is lost to me, sadly. All I can do now is serve Yaggoth."

Stifling his grief for the moment, Wilfred began to think. The First of Many had no physical weaknesses; that had already been made more than obvious. But the guardian was not happy with its inhumanity. The First had been robbed of its mortal life, left with a lingering desire that could never be fulfilled. But where there was desire, there was weakness. "Why serve? It took your life from you…your humanity! How could you protect such a monster?"

"What else do I have?" The First questioned, giving a shrug. "This existence is empty, but it is still something. Ever few centuries I run into a person such as you; I can experience your fleeting mortality before it leaves you. It's sadistic, but watching your grief lets me feel a bit less hollow."

"Yaggoth hasn't taken all of your humanity." Wilfred chose his words carefully; he knew that there wasn't much time left for him to make an escape. Most likely, he had only this one chance. "There is still something left that even it cannot take from you." Sartre's magic had already begun to weaken; in the back of his mind, Wilfred could hear the refrain of one of his favorite songs. "Zu sterben fallt so leicht." Oddly fitting, he thought.

"What?" The First of Many sat up straight in his chair, puzzling over Wilfred's words. "There is nothing left for me but a dark eternity. I cannot escape from my fate, just as you cannot escape yours. But if you embrace your grief, perhaps you can find some meaning in the eons..."

"You can't escape, but I can free you," Wilfred offered, not letting his eyes off of the First. "Let me pass and I can give you the vulnerability you seek. I'll give you the last, most important piece of your humanity: death." The cavern filled with a tense silence, the only noise was the faint echo of Wilfred's last word.

The First of Many was thunderstruck by Wilfred's suggestion; never before had one of his opponents suggested such an agreement. All that had come before Wilfred had struggled in vain to destroy him, but the First could not be destroyed. He could not even commit suicide as such; tied in to the essence of Yaggoth, the First was not able to obliterate himself. Yet if he simply let this man pass, he could enable the destruction of the nightmare itself, the only thing that anchored him to existence. How could he have not considered this plan before? The First swallowed hard as he considered the possibility that he might be afraid. His jaw trembled as a terrible, euphoric fear passed over him; mouth opened in a small gasp. If he let Wilfred through, he would not know how long he might last. Perhaps Wilfred's efforts would prove futile, and the First would linger. But perhaps the philosophers would find Yaggoth! Perhaps they would destroy the nightmare, and with it, him.

"Yes!" The First of Many exclaimed, bolting to his feet. "I have been afraid for so long, Wilfred. Afraid to end a life that I never had, I kept thinking that perhaps a few more centuries would give me an answer. But I've been such a cowardly hypocrite. You are right; it is better to die as a mortal than live as a god!"

Wilfred was taken aback by the success of his suggestion. He had thought it might be difficult to convince the First of Many to embrace the end of eternity. But it appeared that all that the First needed was someone else to give voice to that terrible thought. Mortals contemplate the meaning of "death with dignity," but for the tormented undying, death *was* dignity. "Then let's bury you with the rest of mankind." Wilfred extended his hand to the First. The immortal guardian suddenly seemed so very weak, his arm trembling as he reached out to grasp Wilfred's hand.

Unaware of Wilfred's success, Rachel peered out the side window of the philosophers' jet. The front gate opened slowly in front of the plane and it began to taxi towards the runway. Once outside, she could see the PDE-1 lifting off from the bay west of them; Russell seemed tiny standing on the suit's shoulder. Kant and Nietzsche manned the plane's two pilot seats, while Rachel and Patty sat strapped in behind them. Nobody knew where they were going; the plane could only follow Lime as she tracked down Pete's location.

Ascending quickly into the air, Russell looked downwards at the plane as it began rolling down the runway. Lime didn't have a bearing on her creator yet; first, the party would have to depart the Philosoplex and re-enter the real world. His eyes turned back towards the mansion, hoping that Wilfred would be successful in his mission. Not only because the rescue effort would be vastly more complicated with Yaggoth in the picture, but he knew Wilfred's demise would be a heavy blow to his friends. If everything went according to plan, the rest of the party—Socrates, Sartre, Hume, Wilfred, and Robert—would follow behind them and deal with subduing Yaggoth. The plane now airborne and circling below the PDE-1, Russell patted the side of the machine's head. "OK, we're ready to go," he said, subconsciously opening the way out of the pocket dimension. "Keep it below Mach 1 so the jet can stay with us, and don't get too close to Pete. We just want a visual so we can come up with a plan."

"Rawr!" Lime responded affirmatively, the combat suit spinning in mid-air and heading towards the horizon of the Philosoplex. The boundary made temporarily malleable by Russell's will, the PDE-1 rocketed out into the atmosphere of the physical world. With the jet following behind at a safe distance, Lime quickly got her bearings on Pete. Pivoting to the south-east, she fired the thrusters and took off. It didn't take long for the kitten's resolve to be tested. Only a few miles into their journey, a flock of birds flew near the party. Moving below Lime and off to her left, radar warnings went off inside the suit only moments before her keen kitten instincts sensed the birds. "Flying noms!!" she shouted excitedly, quickly slowing the machine down.

Behind the PDE-1, Nietzsche eased up on the throttle as Lime suddenly decelerated. Soon a warning sounded in the cockpit. "PDE combat systems engaged, transferring targeting data." A holographic projection of the flying birds glowed on the screen, seconds counting down until Lime's missile batteries achieved a target lock. Kant put his palm to his face, giving an exasperated groan. At Nietzsche's command, the plane banked sharply to the right, hoping to avoid the impending destruction.

"LIME! NO!" Russell shouted against the wind, smacking the PDE hard enough to leave a small dent in the suit's titanium shell. Lime relented for a moment, the missile pods sitting idle. "We're after Pete, focus! Not now!" The birds drew closer to the machine and Russell imagined that if it weren't for Lime's flight restraints, the kitten would be wiggling her rear in the typical pre-pounce motion. A tense minute passed before Russell let out a deep breath of relief, watching the birds continue safely on their way past the philosophers. "That's a good kitty; I'll get you a nice treat once we find Pete." He looked back at the plane and gave a thumbs-up, able to see Nietzsche's scowl even from such a distance.

Claudia Durand had felt the party pass by her, their movement creating a slight ripple in the image of the Philosoplex held in space before her. But with Hume still in the mansion, none of the departing philosophers had the proficiency necessary to sense Claudia waiting between worlds. The girl paused for a moment, considering her options. She had planned to assist her "partner" in demolishing the philosophers, but Claudia could not risk giving half of the party free reign to find Pete. While Yaggoth had expressed some interest in assisting her, she knew well enough that direct combat was not the nightmare's forte. Even if she could convince it to stave off the approaching philosophers—she doubted that—she knew it could not prevail against so many.

"Change of plans," she said, turning to Abraxas. "Half of the philosophers just left their refuge; they may be fleeing with Pete. I will follow them while you secure the mansion." Claudia knew that the best lies always had a grain of truth; the ancient being could vaguely sense the passing philosophers, even though he could not know if Pete was amongst them.

"Well enough, I will have no problems dealing with this little fortress." He chuckled, somewhat pleased with the development. The old god was strong—perhaps the strongest single entity still on the world—but he appreciated a divided enemy nonetheless. "Are you prepared to open the way?"

"Yes." Claudia called back all of her images, a dozen copies of the young girl appearing around her. Each held what appeared to be a colorful shard of glass, the last few missing pieces of the window into the Philosoplex. One by one the images set the pieces into place, vanishing as their task was finished. Completed at last, the hard, glassy window began to ripple. Taking on a fluid appearance, Claudia's entrance to the Philosoplex stood ready. She stepped aside, holding out an arm towards the picture. "I will contact you once I've located the rest of the philosophers. Hopefully, Pete is still inside and we won't have to make any further journeys."

"Indeed, it would be good to put a swift end to this." The god drew himself up, moving forwards through the astral dark. Tentacles writhing below him and his shield held high, he entered the philosopher's sanctum.

Hume stood in the ruins of his once-beautiful garden, trying to replant the few flowers that had not been either smashed or scorched by Lime's brief visit. At the moment, he was down on his knees, attempting to get an azalea back into the ground. Suddenly, the sky crackled and split, white clouds splintering as the Philosoplex's defensive barrier was breached. Jumping to his feet, Hume pulled off his gardening gloves as his mind spun. How could anyone have accessed his hidden dimension? Even if someone had tortured the requisite knowledge out of one of his lost companions, they would have to possess near-omnipotence to assemble a gateway.

Alarms immediately sounded inside the mansion, jolting Robert awake and bringing Hume's partners running. Sartre sprinted out of Wilfred's room, nearly tripping on his way down the stairs as he met up with Socrates. His half-eaten bowl of cereal still on the kitchen counter, the Greek rushed towards the front door.

The wooden door knocked clean off the hinges in Socrates' hurry, both men ran towards Hume. Sweat was already pouring down the Scotsman's face, his hands clasped tight and eyes shut in focus. He had compacted reality around the mansion, an opaque bubble of force surrounded the building. Hume was a master of inter-planar manipulation, and the Philosoplex was his *opus magnum*. But unlike Russell or Nietzsche, Hume's medium was far more receptive to subtlety than force; he was weak without time to prepare. Despite his inhuman effort, the dimensional tide pushing outwards from the mansion could only slow the invader's progress.

"Shit, who is it?" Socrates asked, unable to make out more than a blurred shape through Hume's barrier.

"WHO?" A voice thundered as Hume's defense began to crumble. "I...AM...ABRAXAS!" The god cried as the shield split open, torn asunder by the blows of his living flail. Hume gave a defeated gasp, collapsing to his hands and knees in exhaustion. Before the three philosophers stood the god Abraxas, last of the ancient Gnostic pantheon. All told, he stood nearly twenty feet tall, the torso of a giant human carried upon a writhing mass of tendrils. His head was that of a rooster, bright plumage which descended to his neck, and eyes that glowed with power. As Abraxas breathed, billowing clouds of foul purple smoke issued from his beak, dissipating into the air around him. "Bring him to me, and I may spare your lives!"

Sartre and Socrates looked between each other in confusion as Hume trembled on the ground, still too weak to stand. Abraxas had been presumed dead for centuries; his name had not even been whispered for many generations of humanity. It was startling enough that the old god still lived, but why would he assault the philosophers? A god of balance, Abraxas represented both good and evil. If anything, Abraxas was a god sympathetic to their goals; he called himself the Scourge of Power, and he had worked for centuries to maintain a delicate balance in the world. "Who do you want? We have taken nothing from you!" Sartre shouted, already backing away slowly. Abraxas was not only alive, but exceptionally deadly.

"LIES! You seek to take everything from me," Abraxas shouted, another cloud of smoke rising from his beak. "Bring me your little god, and with his power I can still secure this world!"

"Are you crazy?!" Socrates asked, remembering enough of the god to understand that this behavior was wildly out of character. "You decided to stop protecting the world from consolidation of power…in order to seek it yourself?" Not only was Abraxas' demand bizarre, the venting purple smoke was a disturbing addition to his usual appearance. Sartre and Hume were doubly concerned; the maddened god seemed touched by the same disease that had earlier plagued Pete.

"Do not try to deny me!" Abraxas howled, his tentacles moving beneath him as the god stormed forwards. Sartre wasted no time, quickly grabbing Hume and pulling him backwards. Socrates had already moved in front of them, pulling off his t-shirt to reveal a block of Greek text tattooed down his muscled back. Sartre had never mastered Greek, but he knew the famous quotation on Socrates' back. A line from Socrates' late friend Aristotle's *Ethics*, the tattoo read:

"But we must not follow those who advise us, being men, to think of human things, and, being mortal, of mortal things, but must, so far as we can, make ourselves immortal, and strain every nerve to live in accordance with the best thing in us; for even if it be small in bulk, much more does it in power and worth surpass everything."

"Let me…help…" Hume panted, slowly recovering as he stood on his own.

Socrates looked back over his shoulder, shaking his head. "I can't let you do that, David," he said with a smile. "You know that even Pete cannot complete his task without your help. Get him back inside, please." Sartre nodded solemnly at Socrates, their eyes meeting.

"Don't use *her* unless you have to, mon amie." Sartre trembled at the thought, hefting Hume's arm around his shoulder and turning back towards the mansion. Sartre did not want to see *that* terrible power, but against Abraxas was there any other option? Looking out of his second story window, Robert saw the two hurrying back towards the mansion as Socrates stood alone against the maddened god. His hands trembled on the window sill, and he could not help but wish he had gone with the others. He ran downstairs.

Socrates managed to dodge the first few tentacles, snapping one of the serpentine limbs with his strong arms. Yet Abraxas bore down on him relentlessly, shield and flail swinging between his stabbing tendrils. The god was much faster than Socrates, and he strafed in a circle around the philosopher. Socrates struggled to keep up, narrowly avoiding a flurry of blades as he tried to stay out of range of Abraxas' flail. But the beast was soon behind Socrates, his tentacles surrounding the philosopher while he struck. Only managing to turn halfway from the blow, Socrates cried out in pain as the flail lashed against him. The metallic ropes cut like blades, shredding Socrates' side and knocking him through the air. He came to a sudden stop in mid-air, and his body jerked as one of Abraxas' stingers plowed through Socrates' chest. Lifting the philosopher up and slamming him face-first into the earth, Abraxas laughed victoriously.

Socrates took advantage of the slight opening to swing backwards with his right hand. His fist hit the flat side of the stinger lodged in his body, snapping the chitin blade where it attached to Abraxas' coil. Rolling quickly to the side and leaping backwards, Socrates shuddered as he dragged the remainder of the poisoned spike from his chest. The philosopher wasn't fatally wounded—not yet—but he knew that pursuing his current line of attack would get him dead quickly. Unable to manage even a purely defensive position while at full strength, Socrates recognized that with a gaping hole in his chest it was would only take a minute for Abraxas to finish him.

Robert stood with the two philosophers, staring out the foyer's window at Socrates' plight. "He shouldn't have to go like this, not again," Hume whispered, his hands pressed against the glass. He knew that if Socrates couldn't defeat Abraxas in physical combat, neither he nor Sartre could provide anything in way of aid. Both of them understood that there was only one chance to defeat the old god. Robert looked away, covering his mouth in horror. He couldn't bear to the see Socrates torn apart, blood running down his back and sides.

Sartre's hand came to Robert's shoulder, firm but comforting. "Don't look away."

Robert looked up at the Frenchman, his eyes watery with fear. "What?"

"You might say it's the most beautiful thing in the world, Robert." Sartre began to cry, joining in Hume's grief. His kept his hand on Robert, facing him towards the window as they waited for the inevitable.

Socrates bolted backwards from Abraxas, buying himself distance and a few second's time. Holding his right hand over his chest, the philosopher could already feel poison coursing through him, weakening him further. What a familiar sensation, he thought, even if it was not quite hemlock. He looked back towards the mansion, smiling for the last time at his friends and partners. Fate certainly had a sense of irony, he thought. Socrates turned to the howling god as it thundered towards him, Abraxas' bloody, thirsty flail held high in the air.

"If duty requires my death, then I die happily." Socrates exhaled a long, calm breath as he brought both of his arms up, palms open and facing the sky. "Let virtue be my weapon." The earth trembled around the philosopher as light began to rise from his skin, luminous beads swirling and coalescing above his hands. As energy poured forth from Socrates, he aged with terrifying speed; his muscles shrunk away and wrinkles spread across his face. In front of his bent and frail body, the essence of his life swelled to humanoid form. A woman hovered a foot above the ground, wearing a simple white dress and wreathed in brilliant light. She looked at Socrates, sadness crossing her young face as she put a hand to the old man's withered cheek. The philosopher said nothing, placing his hand on top of hers as he gave a small nod. He had no regrets. With that, Socrates' life slipped away.

"Stop!" The girl ordered, spinning and holding out a hand against Abraxas. The god shuddered as a wave of force slammed into him, dirt scattering around him as he was nearly brought low. "It is not your place to be here, Abraxas."

"Who?" Robert asked softly, eyes locked on the lady before him. She was what he had always imagined an angel would look like.

"Eudaimonia. Perfection."

Abraxas scrambled to recover, bringing his shield back in front of him. He blocked the second blast with it, the metal crumpling and tearing from the blow. "Something is inside you, old one," Eudaimonia said, walking forwards upon the air. "I will make it right." His flail descended upon her, but the weapon whisked through the girl, as if she was little more than a mist. Abraxas howled incoherently, the purple smoke billowing out of his beak uncontrollably as Socrates' spirit approached. He tried to back away, but soon Eudaimonia floated before his chest. She leaned forward, passing her arms inside him. A frown crossed her face; it was too late for her to save Abraxas from the corruption within. Yet the disease had to be excised. And so it was. Abraxas convulsed and dropped his armaments, hands grabbing his head as Eudaimonia poured her power out into him. Smoke vented violently from the whole of his body, hissing as it gathered into a dissipating cloud above.

"AAAAUUUUGGGGGH!!!" The god's screams shook the mansion itself, his terrible cries lasting for minutes until Abraxas fell silent. At last he collapsed to the ground, too weak to even lift his head as it lay sideways in the dirt. "Not...possible..."

Rushing out through the empty doorframe, the three men ran up towards Socrates' prone body. Sartre fell to his knees, cradling the Greek's head in his lap as he sobbed. Hume looked down at Socrates, pressing his eyes shut for a few moments of silence as he paid his respects. Robert stood a few feet behind him, feeling too much a stranger to the terrible scene. Eudaimonia came to Hume, her form already beginning to shimmer as it faded into the wind. "It is the death he would have wanted," she offered comfortingly, giving Hume a hug. Moving to Sartre, she knelt and hugged him as well. She stopped, reaching a hand down to run over Socrates' lifeless brow. "Goodbye." The light of her form lingered for only a few seconds more as she faded from the world.

"Ahh...ack..." Abraxas coughed as he rolled his eyes towards the philosophers in front of him. "I...am...sorry, little ones. I was not myself..." The god's eyes closed for a moment as he tried to stay conscious. Eudaimonia's forceful exorcism had broken him; it was only a question of time before he passed.

Wiping his eyes, Hume turned towards the fallen god. "Who could have done this to you, Abraxas?" The philosopher glanced up towards the sky, watching the last traces of the purple taint vanishing. He took a shaky breath, trying to steady himself. Despite Socrates' noble sacrifice, their situation had only grown worse. Even though Abraxas had been stopped, they faced a foe stronger yet; powerful enough to manipulate the old god and open a gateway to the Philosoplex.

"Claudia...Durand," Abraxas replied between short gasps, fingers clenching in the dirt. "When...did she do this...to me? How long...was I under her spell?" He pounded a fist into the ground with feeble rage. "How...how..."

"What? Who?" Sartre asked, trying to compose himself as he laid Socrates' head back to the ground. He looked over to Hume; the Scotsman shook his head in response, equally confused. "A being strong enough to break you, yet we haven't even heard of her?"

"She is...yoooung...AH!" Abraxas convulsed, struggling to speak. "Younger than...even you..."

"A new god that we overlooked?" Hume asked incredulously; the philosophers' monitoring system should not have been able to miss such an event.

"No...nooo. Not a god...she was...she was..." He struggled to speak, his mind clouding with flashes of nothingness. "Dark...so dark..." The god could hold on no longer, and with a soft whimper, he lay still.

"What is she?" Sartre wondered aloud, shaking his head.

Hume leaned down over Abraxas, giving a pained sigh once he confirmed that the god had died. They had not learned nearly enough, he thought. "Damn it, I have no idea. Who could be strong enough to corrupt Abraxas?" Yet raw strength alone would not be enough; Hume could not understand how anyone could have breached the Philosoplex. He looked back at his fallen comrade.

Not human in anything but appearance the philosophers—like most of the Created—rapidly disintegrated once their lives were spent. Socrates' body began to evaporate before their eyes, his figure disappearing until all that remained was a single blank scrip of papyrus. Sartre reached out, gently picking up the piece and holding it briefly against his chest.

"What is that?" Robert asked quietly, afraid to disturb the hallowed silence.

"When we were created, each of us was made from one of our works," Sartre explained, carefully tucking the papyrus into his jacket for safe-keeping. "Those objects served as the touchstone for our existence." Robert did not appear to be any less confused. "But

Socrates never wrote anything, at least not anything that still exists. All that survived for history were accounts of him by others. So…his paper is blank." Robert gave a slight nod, finally understanding the significance. He stood with the philosophers, walking alongside of them as they returned inside the mansion.

Hume pulled out his cell as he strode into the foyer of the mansion, pacing back and forth on the carpet as he dialed out to Kant. "Are you alright?" he asked as soon as his colleague answered, fearing that the enigmatic Ms. Durand may have orchestrated a second attack.

"What? Yes, we're fine," Kant replied. He was surprised by Hume's unusual anxiety, and knew that something had gone wrong. "What happened?"

"We came under attack, and Socrates had to summon Eudaimonia."

"He's…dead, then," Kant said quietly, eliciting gasps from Patty and Rachel in the back of the jet. He turned back towards them, trying to listen to Hume and calm Wilfred's friends at the same time. "Not Wilfred, Socrates…I…dammit, Hume, I am putting you on speaker."

Hume's voice filled the cabin. "Before he died, Abraxas named another: Claudia Durand. It is apparent that she opened the way for Abraxas, and that she was the one controlling him."

Nietzsche raised an eyebrow. "Control Abraxas?" he asked. "How is that possible? We had thought him long gone from the world, but he was no weakling…"

"It is worse than that, I'm afraid," Hume continued. "Abraxas was afflicted by the same purple smog as Pete…before he fled from us and was abducted by the brothers. Claudia Durand, as Abraxas called her, seems to have been manipulating us from the start."

"And just who the hell is she?" Kant asked to nobody in particular, his injured eye suddenly throbbing with irritation. "She discovers our plan for Pete…manipulates him away from us…and now she brazenly attacks the Philosoplex using Abraxas as a pawn? How is that possible? Did you see her?"

"I don't know," Hume replied, glancing around the foyer. "I did not see her. But since she did not linger here – I assume she thought Abraxas would be enough to kill us all – she must have more pressing business elsewhere. I suspect that business is Pete and all of you."

"Powerful or not, if this girl just opened an astral gate into the Philosoplex, it will be some time before she can fully return to our world. Correct?" Nietzsche asked.

Hume nodded. "Perhaps not long, but it will take some time, yes. She forced her way in from between dimensions; the return journey won't be immediate. Where are you now?"

"Just heading southeast off of the Gulf Coast," Nietzsche replied, eyes scanning over the navigational controls. "Lime seems to be making a straight line for the Caribbean."

"A logical choice, if the brothers are on the water," Kant added.

"Okay." Hume took a deep breath and steadied himself. "As soon as Wilfred wakes up, we'll follow after you. Be careful! I can't imagine how strong this girl must be, if she could manipulate Abraxas and Pete both."

Nietzsche smirked at the prospect of finally running into a real challenge. A woman, no less, he thought. How ironic. "Ja. Get here as quickly as you can; without Socrates you're all vulnerable."

"We are well-aware of that. I'll stay in contact." Hume hung up the phone, tossing it sideways onto the couch. Nietzsche was right; with Claudia able to access the Philosoplex and Socrates dead the group was nearly defenseless. "Would it be possible to move Wilfred onto the jet while he is still dreaming?" Hume asked, looking to Sartre.

Sartre shook his head. "I'm afraid not; I had to create a number of seals in the bedroom to ensure he wouldn't be disturbed. If he were accidentally woken while his mind was still chasing Yaggoth, he'd likely slip into a coma." Sartre couldn't see any alternative to waiting for Wilfred to wake; attempting to move him now would almost certainly sever his mind from his body. He glanced at his watch again: only fifteen minutes remained. "He's almost out of time. If Wilfred can't get back in fifteen minutes, there won't be anything left to risk in moving him." They could only wait, and hope.

Chapter Ten

The First of Many walked towards the back of his chamber, squeezing Wilfred's hand tightly. With fear and excitement consuming his mind, the First had forgotten about the obvious problem with their plan until it was already upon them. "...it's a poster," Wilfred mumbled, peeling back the edge of the paper sheet on which the door was painted. It was a remarkably well-done poster; from the center of the room it was impossible to know that the door wasn't real.

"Oh!" The First jumped, brought back to reality as Wilfred let go of his hand and stared over at him. "I had completely forgotten about that. You know, I hadn't left that chair in so long…" He stopped, rubbing his head. "It was just a prop, sadly."

"Then how am I supposed to get through?" Wilfred asked, attempting to punch the sturdy rock wall with little success. "Where is Yaggoth?"

"Well, we are in Yaggoth. Myself, the chair, this entire world; we're all just an extension of its form. But if you want more…" The First put a finger to his lip, puzzling over that question. Nobody had ever moved past him; he wasn't even terribly sure where to look for what Wilfred sought. He could not look outside of himself.

Wilfred himself had no more of an idea as to where he could find the core of Yaggoth. While his instinct had led him this far, that sensation had appeared to be nothing more than a ploy to draw him towards the First. "Fucking wonderful," he cursed, punching the wall again. "You don't even know?"

"Wait, wait," the First said, giving a nervous little laugh. "I suppose I'm not sure what exactly you're looking for. Everyone that has ended up here," he gestured around the room, "came looking to destroy Yaggoth. I don't have the faintest idea how you'd even go about doing that from here. It's probably impossible, to tell the truth. But is there something *particular* you wanted to find?"

"All I need to know is the identity of the host!" Wilfred said in exasperation, even as he realized that fact probably should have been mentioned earlier. "I'm not here to fight Yaggoth; god knows that isn't going to work. I only have to find out the host, so I can take that information back to Sartre."

"*Oh.*" The First opened his ragged jacket, digging around inside for a couple of seconds. "Here we are!" He pulled a small green business card out, handing it to Wilfred. The card read "Charles. Nightmare Host," the neat text situated next to a picture of the host. Underneath Charles' name and job title sat a street address. Wilfred blinked in surprise; after a moment, the block number on the address changed to indicate Charles' new position. Flipping the card over, the reverse had a simple and eerily friendly comic logo of four disembodied mouths suspended in space.

"Thank y..." Wilfred was cut off as the wall to their left exploded inwards, the far corner of the room crumbling as three figures stepped through.

"What the hell do you think you're doing, old man?!" The 71,284th was pissed. She was a young African-American lady, dressed in sharp, contemporary clothes. Two men stepped out on either side of her. The 2,907th was an old Indian man, dressed in simple robes. The 653rd appeared as a middle-aged, balding Asian man, wearing thick glasses and a bathrobe. Wilfred quickly stuffed the card into his pants' pocket, wishing his entrance hadn't disappeared. He realized that the "Many" was not just a figure of speech.

"Maybe some of us still have things to do," the 653rd offered, annoyed that a sauna that had been going perfectly well for over seventy years had been interrupted. It would take a least a decade to get the humidity right again.

"But you couldn't be content moping around by yourself, could you?" The 2,907th waved his finger accusing at the First. "Thought you'd kill yourself off and take us—all of us—with you? How selfish."

"Have some perspective!" The First rebutted, stepping in front of Wilfred. "Perhaps some of you can still amuse yourselves for a few millennia longer. But what then? What is that compared to an eternity of suffering? Die now while you still can!"

"Man, you just need to get laid." The 71,284th shook her head, tossing her braided hair back. "You shouldn't have gotten rid of that cute family you made for yourself."

The First of Many looked back at Wilfred, taking a moment to appreciate how he had gotten in to such a position. The dreamer had very little time left, the First realized, and the Many were all beginning to wake. If Wilfred didn't escape before his power expired, even the First could not protect him against the hungering dark. "Run!" He shouted, a faint crack echoing across the chamber as the tunnel from which Wilfred entered opened once more. Wilfred hesitated, wanting to thank the First. "No! *RUN!*"

"You'll wish you *could* die after this, traitor!" Space shattered between the First and his opponents, the force of their wills tearing apart reality itself. The three of the Many were no match for the First, but they were not alone. Everyone was coming. Wilfred wasted no time; he ran towards the exit. The walls blurred by him as he raced up the stairs, but he could still make out mouths moving in the stone. Yaggoth reacted quickly to the First's betrayal, and even the world's oldest dreamer could only stand for so long against a legion of nearly one hundred thousand foes. The First's control began to slip; some of the Many moved past his defenses. As Wilfred ran breathlessly out of the mountain, an old woman stepped in front of him; she wore gypsy clothing and bore a staff of brambles that cut at her hands.

The 95th was quite old, but she was not a prodigy like the First. Her attack missed, the grasping thorns broke the earth where Wilfred no longer stood. He had already dodged around her, pushing off into the air and gaining distance. Wilfred knew that he didn't have time to fight; he could already feel a lingering sense of doubt as to how he was managing to fly. The music was only getting louder in his mind; that fact was strangely both worrisome, yet appropriately climactic. The ground below him teemed with life; thousands rose from the dirt, setting after Wilfred to protect their immortality. Even as he blazed through the atmosphere and the nightmare world grew small behind him, the howling cloud gained on him. A few of the Many drew near to Wilfred only to disappear, dragged back by the furthest reaches of the First's power. Soon the whole of the universe behind him was lost in the flock of tens of thousands. They were getting close—dangerously close—even as Wilfred's room came into view. As their claws tore at his heels, Wilfred's hand grasped the doorknob. It turned.

"AH!" Wilfred bolted upright in bed, his heart pounding in his chest. Panting as sweat poured off his body, he blinked his eyes and adjusted to the waking world. Across from him sat Hume and Robert, while Sartre leaned over the foot of the bed and examined him. "Shitshitshit..." Wilfred repeated, trying to adjust to his newfound reality.

"Two minute to spare," Sartre commented, looking up from his wristwatch and across the bed to Wilfred. "You had us worried." Despite Wilfred's success, the philosophers still looked positively dismal.

"Holy shit, you did it, man!" Robert ran to the side of the bed, slapping Wilfred heartily on the back. His friend deserved some measure of enthusiasm upon on return, after all. Reaching up to clasp Robert's shoulder, Wilfred noticed that the accountant seemed even paler than usual.

Hume smiled and gave a little sigh, pleased that there hadn't been a second tragedy that afternoon. He wiped a hand slowly across his face. "Good job. Did you find it?" Happy as he was that Wilfred survived, the harrowing journey—and Socrates' sacrifice—would mean nothing without the name of Yaggoth's host.

"Ah, uh, um," Wilfred stammered, patting his hands over his chest and legs. Needless to say, his pajamas did not have the same convenient pockets as his attire in the dream world. "There it is!" The green business card fluttered out of his one shirt-sleeve, falling to the bed before Wilfred snatched it up. He offered the card to Sartre, hand trembling from exhaustion.

Sartre took the business card from him, and Hume stepped in close as the pair examined it. "Wonderful," Sartre said quietly, running his thumb slowly over the paper. "You may have just saved the world, Wilfred." Hume nodded in agreement, looking up at Wilfred as the man slouched back onto the bed.

"It feels like I haven't gotten an hour of sleep," Wilfred said, giving a little groan. Tired as he was, he had entirely legitimate worries about falling back asleep. "Is it safe for *real* sleep, now?"

Hume shook his head. "No, not here. It isn't safe. You can sleep on the plane." Walking forward, he helped Wilfred out of bed.

The mortal's stocky frame sagged as Wilfred got to his feet, and Hume threw an arm around his back before Wilfred toppled to the ground.

"Uggh," Wilfred groaned. "Isn't safe? What happened?" He grabbed some clean clothes out of the dresser and rubbed his eyes. Suddenly, Wilfred stood up straight, spinning around to face the philosophers once more. "Did something happen to Pete?"

"No," Sartre replied, shaking his head, "not that I know of. The rest of our team and your friends went after him, but the Philosoplex came under attack. We have to go," Sartre said, some urgency in his voice. "*Now*. Let's get to the plane."

Wilfred clumsily pulled on a pair of jeans, stumbling out the door after Robert with Hume behind him. "Attacked?" He looked between the two philosophers, their usual easygoing demeanors overwritten by stress. "By what? Who?"

"An ugly bastard of an old god," Robert explained. "Socrates is dead." The four men hustled down the stairs, making haste for the rear wing of the Philosoplex.

Wilfred's eyes opened wide as they passed through the foyer; Abraxas' massive body still lay in the wreckage of the mansion's front lawn. Where the Philosoplex's front door once stood was instead a massive, Socrates-shaped hole. "Dead?" He wondered if the philosopher had ever woken from his encounter with Yaggoth. The last Wilfred had seen of the philosopher, he had been unconscious from the battle at Ockham's Kegger. "You couldn't revive him?"

"We need to hurry," Sartre hissed.

As he followed his colleague towards the back hallways and the second launch bay, Hume breathlessly summarized the afternoon's chaotic events. "He was fine; Yaggoth had only disabled him. But Socrates had to sacrifice himself to stop that thing you saw outside—Abraxas."

"I'm sorry," Wilfred said, feeling shaken by the revelation.

"As am I, Wilfred," Hume said while patting his shoulder. "But right now there is no time for grief. We need to get out of here before anything else arrives and finds us defenseless." The door before them hissed open, revealing a second plane.

"Shit..." Wilfred commented quietly. He hadn't gotten a chance to meet Socrates while the philosopher was conscious. From Wilfred's perspective, the Greek had gone from a coma straight to death. Some people just couldn't catch a break, it seemed. Wilfred followed Sartre on to the plane, heading to the passenger section as the philosopher took up his position at the controls.

Taking a seat, Wilfred buckled in and immediately reclined his chair. His eyes had closed before Sartre had even shut the cabin door, drifting into a mercifully dreamless sleep. He had many questions, but they would have to wait. Robert glanced over at his friend as the plane began to taxi towards the runway.

"Should we tell him about everyone else?" He knew that Wilfred would want to know about Pete and the rest; he was just too tired to think straight.

"Let him sleep, for now," Sartre said, looking backwards at the two men. "He needs his rest, and he can catch up later." The plane began to pick up speed, Hume piloting while Sartre dialed out to the rest of the philosophers.

"Wilfred?!" Patty and Rachel asked in unison over the intercom. Their outburst made the nervous crew of the second plane jump in surprise, and Sartre quickly turned down the volume.

"He's fine, just resting now," Sartre replied, hearing Wilfred snore softly behind him. Patty and Rachel gave each other a jubilant high-five. "Where are you now?"

"Approaching Puerto Rico." Kant looked out of his window, surveying the deep blue ocean below. "Where is Yaggoth?"

"*Wonderful.*" Sartre frowned as he checked the card. "The host is in San Juan. That means Yaggoth is already there, the brothers are holding Pete, and this Claudia girl must be on her way." The philosophers were short on firepower before they had lost Socrates; the brothers alone were a match for Russell, Nietzsche, and Kant combined.

Russell was no more pleased with the situation. "As convenient as it is for the gods to gather for us," he added, the intercom crackling with static as wind rushed past him atop the PDE's shoulder, "these bastards seem to be playing us for fools. Ockham's Kegger was compromised, Pete ran away from us, and now this."

"Regrettably, we should reconsider the possibility of betrayal from within." Hume stared forlornly out of his window, watching his prize creation fade into the distance. "Nietzsche may have been correct."

"Shocking," Nietzsche grumbled.

Hume brushed off his colleague's sarcasm. "I cannot fathom any other explanation for all of this. Nothing could have breached the Philosoplex without inside knowledge, at least not in any practical amount of time." He took a deep breath. "Still, it is shocking that any of our deceased brethren may still live, no less that they would betray us."

"There are only so many possibilities, right?" Rachel piped up, earning a nasty glare from Nietzsche who thought she had no business in a serious conversation. "I mean, I don't want to offend anyone, but it doesn't seem so far-fetched to me that one of your friends that you thought dead has been turned against you. At least, it isn't any more far-fetched than any of *you* being alive right now."

"Yes, but that does not solve our dilemma," Kant replied. "While it is entirely possible that any of our fallen could have be reborn by a sufficiently powerful god, any being of that strength would not need to play games with us. Even assuming that a god on the cusp of omnipotence could have hidden from us, what use would such a god have for these games? Why bother with Pete or manipulating Abraxas?"

Hume nodded thoughtfully. "I agree. These ploys bespeak a degree of caution in our adversaries. Whatever her relation to our fallen brothers or our own creation, Claudia Durand is not strong enough to simply take what she wants by force. At the very least, she needs Pete—or Pete's power—for something, and that need is a weakness."

"Then we know she isn't omnipotent," Nietzsche said with a slight smile. "That means I can kill her after all."

"I truly hope that we all live long enough to see that, Frederich," Hume said. "We all have a lot to think about. Until we meet in San Juan, then. Hume out." He clicked off the radio and leaned far back in his seat, staring up at the blinking lights of the cockpit.

Charles threw on his clothes, hurrying about the room. He had slept in late—far later than usual—but still felt nothing even resembling relaxation. The notion that he had to meet with his ladyfriend Claudia—again—was so insistent as to be nearly painful. Something was very wrong, but for the life of him, Charles couldn't figure out *what*. Charles almost thought that he heard voices in his head; he dismissed that notion as ridiculous. He had simply taken in too much wine and too much sun, after all. But still it came: Claudia. Claudia. NOW.

Pulling on a light jacket, Charles jumped in surprise when a knock rapped on his door. "Who is it?!" He didn't have time to deal with room service, likely coming to bring him more bottled water. The quality of the tap water notwithstanding, Charles already had something inside him far worse than anything he'd catch from the sink faucet.

"Who do you think it is? Open the door." Claudia tapped her foot impatiently, glancing back and forth down the hallway. The door sprung open, Charles standing inside the room.

"I was just thinking about y—aaaaAAAHH!" Charles collapsed to the floor as his knees gave out, convulsing violently as Yaggoth roughly took control. Claudia smiled and closed the door behind her; she was pleased that the nightmare wasn't wasting time.

"I have a problem," Claudia said, taking a seat on top of the nearby desk and crossing her legs.

Charles staggered back to his feet, smoothing out his hair. "What a fortunate coincidence." Yaggoth was uncharacteristically panicked, but it tried to stay calm. "I have run into problems of my own. These difficulties make our cooperation even more appealing."

"Why, you're a mind-reader," Claudia laughed, watching as Charles took a seat on the edge of his bed. She knew Abraxas had failed; the corruption that Eudaimonia had purged from the old god was just a small part of Claudia's being. "The philosophers are all coming for Pete; this situation has gotten out of hand."

"And they come for me." Yaggoth knew that the philosophers didn't want the identity of its host to add Charles to their Christmas card list. It was still too weak to flee to another body or into the void; Nietzsche had sapped much of the nightmare's strength. "You are no longer the only one with a disturbing ability to find me."

"Then we can destroy the philosophers together," Claudia said, reaching out and putting a hand on Charles' shoulder. "For the time being, they must not be allowed to interfere with the brothers' work."

"Ah." Charles looked down at the hand on his shoulder, then into Claudia's eyes. "I suspected that the brothers' involvement was your doing, as well." Claudia gave a coy smile, reaching up to flick some of her hair backwards.

"Of course," she replied, "they just don't know that they are doing my bidding. I led them to the philosopher's little godling; I expected that they would betray me and take him for their own. It is easier if they think that they are in control." Claudia looked out the hotel room's window towards the harbor beyond. "Lucifer's treacherous instincts are predictable, and Michael is more like his brother than he would care to admit. We will reacquire our prize in time…but for now, the brothers cannot be disturbed."

"What exactly do you need from the angels?" Charles asked, following Claudia's eyes out the window. "Can we not do without them?"

Claudia shook her head. "Unfortunately not," she explained. "Alone, we do not have the necessary talents in order to control the godling. Great as my power is, I cannot deceive a truly omnipotent god…" She hopped down from the desk and turned back to Charles. "Unless I have a back door into his mind, that is. The brothers are gifted with the powers of creation, and they will surely use that power to shape the godling's mind into a replica of their dead creator, Yahweh. They will open the door for me."

"And once they have created a direct path into his mind…" Charles mused aloud.

"Then we can slaughter the brothers and use that path to bind the godling to our will," Claudia continued. "But they have not yet completed the pathway into his mind. It is difficult magic, even for them, and we must buy the brothers time."

"Very clever," Charles remarked. "But how do I know that you will not simply kill me as well? Once you have the full power of a god at your command, my assistance will no longer be of use to you. Indeed, you have already used me once…you directed me to the philosopher's bar as a ruse. You intend to kill the brothers once they have outlived their usefulness, and I do not doubt that there are still others that you have betrayed. Perhaps my interests would be better served by the brothers; surely Lucifer would have room for me in Hell, and he is a man of his word."

Claudia laughed; she did not believe Yaggoth's bluff. "And you would be content to *serve* in Lucifer's realm?" She shook her finger at Charles, scolding him playfully. "Please. You would rather *die* than kneel before a weakling like him. You will aid me because there are no other options left for you."

"You make a compelling argument," Charles conceded. "But still, you will not succeed if I abandon you now. If I am to die either way, then perhaps I should first see that you fail. Do not forget that you have already betrayed me once." Yaggoth paused, collecting its thoughts. "Yet I am willing to overlook that mistake on one condition. Give me a good reason to believe you will not turn on me again. Why would you let me live?"

"Unlike the brothers, you are like me," Claudia said, stepping closer to Charles. "To you and me, mortals are prey. Little toys for us to seduce, confuse, and devour. But for the brothers—even Lucifer—mortals are subjects to be ruled. The brothers exist to make and execute rules; the angels have an irritating attachment to order. Heaven and Hell may be in many ways the opposite, but both have more codes and regulations than a law library." She reached her left hand up, running a single finger down Charles' cheek. "On the other hand…*we* are chaos, and chaos always serves itself. Your ends are mine, and mine yours."

"I will accept that," Charles answered. "Then what is our next move, partner?"

Claudia giggled playfully. "Oooh. Well, I trust that you recall our earlier conversation? Before we confront the philosophers, I want you to call forth a lesser nightmare to assist us." She closed her eyes and tilted her head forward, kissing Charles deeply. Claudia broke the kiss, whispering to Charles. "Are you ready to be a father?"

Charles wiped his mouth clean of Claudia's lipstick, unmoved by her charms. "Your theatrics are unnecessary," he said dryly. "If you can provide me with a nightmare to use, then I will give it life. But I still require this body for the time being; we will have to find another mortal to use."

Two sharp knocks sounded on the door, eliciting a broad smile from Claudia. "I took the liberty of ordering out," she said, patting Charles' cheek before spinning to run and answer the door.

"You called for room service?" The maid was a lanky teenage girl, dressed in a drab blue apron.

"Yes, thank you," Claudia said politely, holding open the door and beckoning her inside. "Please come in."

The maid walked inside and looked around the nearly spotless room. She turned back to Claudia as she heard the lock click into place behind her. "What do you need?" she asked, her polite tone cracking with a note of fear.

"You," Claudia said, striding towards her prey.

"...what? No...*stop*!" The maid protested, backing away from Claudia. "I'll scream!"

"Please do." Claudia laughed cruelly and reached forward, grabbing the girl by the wrist and dragging her towards the bedroom. The girl screamed herself hoarse until she was thrown onto the bed next to Charles. He sat on the edge of the bed with his hands folded in his lap, staring at his victim with a hungry, inhuman grin.

Before the maid could struggle to her feet, Claudia leapt on top of her, pinning her down onto the bed. The young girl shrieked and struggled, but Claudia's hands were like iron clasps around her wrists. "NOOOO! HELP!" she screamed, tears running down her face as she cried in vain. "Stop, stop, oh god, STOP!"

Claudia gave a long, satisfied moan and breathed a cloud of purple smoke into the girl's face. The maid coughed and shook her head back and forth, trying in vain to clear the air. Through her tears and the smoke, she swore that the shadows on the bed were moving around her. Charles' hand swung down to grab her forehead, and he spoke the last words she would ever hear. "Keep screaming." The shadows laughed and laughed.

Only a few miles away, Lucifer slowly sat up in his chair. Looking down, he prodded gently at the now-closed wounds on his sides. The cuts were still tender, but they no longer threatened to reopen. Setting aside his drink and slipping back into his red Crocs, Lucifer headed downstairs into the *Paradise Lost* to find his brother. Michael was not difficult to locate; he emerged from the rear cabin as soon as he heard footsteps. Lucifer simply nodded at him, turning to enter Pete's guest room. Pete tilted his head up as the door opened. The Devil walked into Pete's room followed immediately by his brother. Pete knew that their joint appearance could only mean that the time had come for his trial. For a moment, Pete considered saying something cliché and defiant—"you'll never succeed," perhaps—but thought better of it.

Pete simply closed his eyes as they moved to either side of him around the bed. The brothers raised their hands over him, chanting slowly in Latin as they began the ritual. White and black magic swirled in the air over his body, blending together into glimmering grey light. Words and symbols shimmered and faded before they gained sudden clarity and arced downwards into Pete's head. His body jerked against the chains as he tried to resist, Pete squeezed his eyes shut and tears ran down his face as the spell bore into his mind. Arcane veins spread slowly throughout his consciousness, creating a doorway into Pete's mind that the brothers could use in order to transform him into Yahweh.

Far above the *Paradise Lost*, Lime waited in low geosynchronous orbit. At Russell's request, she kept the PDE-1 far out of range until the philosophers had time to formulate a plan. Russell had discretely returned to the ground before she had taken off, and for the moment he waited outside the San Juan International Airport. Nietzsche's plane soon dipped from the clouds, finally cleared for landing. It had taken some persuading to convince Nietzsche to circle the airport for half an hour awaiting authorization; he had been of a mind to land the plane whenever he damned well pleased. Kant only managed to win him over by appealing to their need for secrecy. As much as Nietzsche would love leading authorities on a chase through the city on his motorcycle, such a spectacle would surely destroy any chance of surprising the brothers. The plane touched down, slowing before taxiing over towards Russell.

The plane's exit opened as soon as the plane rolled to a halt, and Rachel was the first one out of the plane. She stopped a few feet away from him, feeling a bit awkward getting off of a plane without any luggage. The two smiled widely at each other, standing off to the side of the runway. "Have a good flight?" Russell asked, hands in his pockets.

"Sure, but I bet yours was a lot more fun," she replied, stepping closer. "I think you still have some clouds on you." Rachel reached out and slowly brushed off his shoulder, glad to have an excuse to touch him. Their eyes met for a moment before her hand slipped off of him. Rachel gave him a playful smile and walked away towards the airport terminal.

"Glad you're staying focused on the mission," Nietzsche said, walking down the plane's stairs before re-summoning his wheelchair and taking a seat. He rolled himself past Russell, followed closely by Kant and Patty.

Kant looked back to the sky. "Hume should be here within half an hour. I'm going to stay behind and wait for them; we can't be too cautious at this point." Russell nodded at him, pleased that he would be able to head into town with Rachel and the others. Mostly Rachel, he thought. "We'll meet you at the Hilton as soon as they get in. Until then," Kant coughed suggestively, "I think you should keep yourself occupied with *work*." He pulled a slip of paper from his lapel; on it he had copied down a brief description of Charles, and his location as of five minutes prior. "I'm sure you're capable of checking up on our friend Yaggoth discretely, Bertrand. We can't afford a confrontation quite yet."

"Ah, hah, of course." Russell took the paper, glancing down at it before putting it into his jacket. "I'm a master of discretion, you know." Kant gave Russell a dire stare with his one good eye, shaking his head.

At the Hilton hotel only a few blocks from Claudia and Yaggoth, Russell rested outside on the small deck. Overlooking the Atlantic Ocean—the north side of Puerto Rico—the philosopher sat in a small plastic chair as he watched the waves. From his perch, he thought he could see Nietzsche down in the surf below. After being told by the desk staff about a floating trampoline, the German had insisted upon a brief trip to the beach. Russell couldn't really object; how often did a once-crippled man have such a chance? For Nietzsche, it was just another chance to demonstrate that he could live up to the virtues of his super-man philosophy. Indeed, simply climbing onto a gigantic, floating contraption was not difficult enough. Nietzsche faced the additional challenge of hauling along a moustache that, when water-logged, weighed as much as most compact cars.

Turning his attention away from the beach, Russell put his hands out onto the white plastic table before him. As he concentrated, the plastic between his fingers started to bubble and rise. The door slid open beside him; Patty and Rachel stepped out to see what he was doing. Both women had—quite wisely—decided not to follow Nietzsche to the beach. They looked down at Russell, watching silently as two tennis-ball sized globes of white plastic rose up from the surface of the table. Extending a hand over each, Russell began to shape the matter. The plastic began to ripple and shift; four legs and a tiny tail grew slowly from each of the orbs. Patty couldn't help but notice the difference between Russell's work and when Pete had created Lime. His creation had been almost effortless, and nearly instantaneous, while Russell labored slowly, needing to consider every manipulation in turn.

In less than a minute, Russell had sculpted the once-indistinct pieces of plastic into two tiny white lizards. The creatures dropped down to the now-misshapen top of the table; the result of what was surely gross disregard for the hotel's policies on use of furniture. They moved slowly—artificially at first—before the lizards began to seem lifelike, their surface taking on fine detail and darkening to shades of green. Russell slowly exhaled as he began to relax, his two creations wandering aimlessly around the top of the table. He glanced back at his guests with a smile. "Do they look right?"

Patty and Rachel both leaned forward, inspecting the lizards carefully. Try as they might, neither of them could distinguish Russell's creations from the real lizards that scurried constantly through the bushes of San Juan. "Looks fine to me," Patty said, nodding in approval.

"Are they alive?" Rachel asked curiously, looking over to Russell.

"Oh, hah, no." The philosopher chuckled, shaking his head. "They're just very lifelike puppets. Lime puts my dabbling in this art to shame, I'm afraid."

"Well, you still have to name them," Patty insisted. Puppets or not, the tiny lizards were simply too cute to remain anonymous.

"Uh," Russell shrugged, looking between the two of them. "I don't think that's my forte. Do either of you have any suggestions?"

Rachel and Patty looked between each other, then back at the reptilian puppets. Suddenly, the one lizard gave a little shake, opening its mouth wide as it gave a truly adorable belch. A small, slightly opaque bubble of plastic rose from its mouth, popping within seconds. Russell shrugged; he must have forgotten to remove some of the excess air inside that lizard. "Oh my GOD!" Rachel exclaimed, clapping her hands together. "That's perfect!" Patty and Russell both waited with anticipation. "You have to call them Bub and Bob!"

The philosopher raised an eyebrow, the reference totally lost on him. However, Patty was quick to see Rachel's meaning. "You're right, that IS perfect!" She laughed and gave her friend a light hug. "We're such dorks, seriously." Russell cleared his throat, hoping to be cued in on their inside joke.

"Oh, you didn't grow up in the eighties," Patty laughed, waving her hand at Russell. "There was this early video game called Bubble Bobble, with two little lizards that ran around eating candy and blowing bubbles to capture their enemies."

"Bub and Bob it is, then," Russell conceded, somewhat regretting that he had grown up in an era long before video games. He had once played a game called 'Dance Dance Revolution' at a mall, and found it thoroughly enjoyable. Unfortunately, he had to depart when the mall security arrived to investigate reports of a strange man in a business suit taunting children at the arcade.

"Are they going to find Pete?" Patty asked curiously, reaching down to pet the docile creatures.

"No, we already know where he is," Russell said, glancing up towards the clouds in Lime's general direction. "These two fellows are going to keep an eye on Yaggoth, until Sartre arrives to deal with it. Off you go!" At Russell's command, the two lizards hopped in unison, eliciting a giggle from Rachel. Scampering off the table, they ran from the deck and straight down the hotel's outer wall. Charles' address was only a few blocks westwards; Russell was sure that his little spies would find him in no time at all.

Russell could see through the lizard's eyes as they darted between cars and trees, running with a speed that was impressive even for notoriously fast creatures. They located Charles' hotel, scaling up the wall and through an open window. Running along the hallway ceiling, the lizards searched for Room 308. Finding his destination, Russell guided his toys back outside to find the room's window. Yaggoth and Claudia could not have noticed the two new lizards that sunned themselves on the window; the creatures were a fixture on most warm, flat surfaces.

Positioning his lizards on the hotel room's window, Russell peered inside. A man sat on the bed next to two young women; Russell presumed that the fellow was the host named Charles. Of the two women, one was dressed like a tourist while the other wore a maid's uniform. The maid's hair was tousled and she sat perfectly still on the bed, staring down at the carpet while Charles conversed with the other lady. Focusing his attention, Russell listened in on the discussion.

The woman in glasses and a green skirt laughed loudly, looking over at Charles. "Now wasn't that fun?" she asked before clapping her hands together. "If only we could keep on doing that, then we would have an army in no time!"

Charles made an exhausted noise, shaking his head. "Unfortunately, my power is spent for now..." he replied, eliciting a loud laugh from Claudia.

"Oh, isn't that *always* the case with men?" she teased, reaching over to pat the maid's head. "But it was good for you, wasn't it?" The girl said nothing and continued to stare resolutely at the floor. "As serious as your father, huh?"

"She will only respond to my commands," Charles said with a satisfied smile. "I thought that would be a wise safeguard, given your...proclivities, Claudia." At that, Russell swallowed hard. He had trouble believing that the slight, playful girl was the Claudia Durand responsible for both Socrates' death and Pete's disappearance.

"Oh, that's fine," Claudia responded, waving her hand dismissively at Charles. "What are you going to name her, hmm?"

"...name her?" Charles asked curiously, tilting his head to look between the two women. "I had not planned on it. She is a weapon, not a *pet*. She does not need a name."

Claudia Durand frowned, shaking her head vigorously. "No, no, no," she objected, studying the maid closely. "She needs a name. I'm not going to have you treating our child like some sort of thing. How about Re?"

Charles made an exasperated noise and looked up at the ceiling. "Fine, her name is Re," he conceded. Yaggoth concluded that it would be faster and less aggravating if it simply went along with Claudia.

"...Re," the girl said softly, looking up from the ground and over at Charles. "Thank-you, father."

"Really?" Charles asked, covering his face with his palm. "You're going to have this thing call me father? Do you think this is funny?" For a moment, Yaggoth considered whether being betrayed by Claudia—and being rid of her, one way or another—would be such a terrible thing.

Claudia laughed again. "Yes, I think this is hilarious," she said, stifling another giggle. "The look on your face when she called you father...hah! However," she continued, "this also serves a purpose. If Re follows you around out in the city looking like some sort of drugged-out mental case, you are going to attract unwanted attention."

"Fine," Charles agreed, looking back to Re. "Act a bit more…human, please," he commanded, nodding in approval as Re immediately perked up. "Thank you."

"Anything, father," Re said, reaching up to straighten her messed hair. "It is just so hard to feign interest in…this world. When can I start killing, father? Please tell me it will be soon, please…" Russell grimaced. It was clear to him that whatever Yaggoth and Claudia had done to the poor girl, she was no longer human.

"Yes, soon," Charles said. "Now, Claudia, how are we to proceed? The philosophers have doubtless arrived by now…"

"They have," Claudia agreed, adjusting her glasses on her thin nose. "However, they are not all together. Not all of the philosophers are potent fighters, and are taking care of a number of their godling's mortal friends. If I know them well—and I do—then they will divide into at least two groups." Charles nodded and listened. "Furthermore, I still have some worries that the brothers' work on Pete may attract unwanted attention; either from other gods or idiot mortals."

Charles raised an eyebrow. "Is the Damocles Organization aware of this?" he asked.

"No," Claudia answered. "But the human psychics have an irritatingly persistent interest in the work of the gods. Certainly, if they learned of the brothers' work they would be…ah…less than pleased." She waved her hand dismissively. "I would not worry about them in particular. Still, I would like you and Re to watch over the brothers while I kill off the remaining philosophers."

"Are you certain that you are not underestimating their strength?" Charles questioned, crossing his arms in front of his chest.

"Quite certain," Claudia reassured Charles. "I know full well their power. Taking on all of them will be a challenge, albeit a manageable one. You should know well enough that this body is a poor indication of my true strength." She rose to her feet, bouncing on the balls of her feet. "Now, we need to get going. It will take me a short while to locate the philosophers, so the sooner we start the better."

"Then let's begin," Charles said as he stood alongside Re and Claudia.

Russell snapped his attention back from his lizard pets, the grim look on his face bothering both Rachel and Patty. "Well, there she is…" Russell mumbled, now seated inside in one of the suite's comfortable chairs.

"She?" Patty asked. She had seen the way Russell had reacted to her—and even more so towards Rachel—and considered the sort of mischief a man like him could get into with those lizards.

"Our dear friend Claudia, who let Abraxas into the Philosoplex. She's having a conversation with Yaggoth's host in his hotel room," Russell explained. And while he kept quiet about it, Russell was impressed that Claudia Durand was remarkably attractive for such a malefic, calculating entity. A moment's reflection convinced Russell that his latter observation was not as surprising as it had at first seemed. Nietzsche would have doubtless agreed; great evil and female beauty were often indistinguishable, according to him.

"What does Claudia look like?" Rachel asked, wishing that she could also see through the eyes of Russell's pets.

Russell looked at the two women. "She's young, white…long brown hair in a ponytail, glasses, and a thin face. I wouldn't say she looks more than eighteen or so," he explained. "But it matters very little. If she is as powerful as we think she is, then it's likely that she can assume whatever form she pleases."

"Why is she working with Yaggoth?" Patty chimed in. "What does she want?"

"Oh, that's easy," Russell said jovially. "She just wants to kill us all and take Pete's power for herself. Nothing too complicated."

"That isn't funny." Patty glared at Russell seriously.

"Perhaps not, but I am pleased to be one step ahead of the game, for once," Russell replied, not appearing very apologetic. "I'd rather know that she is planning to come after us than nothing at all. That being said, I need to get in touch with Kant and the others." He pulled out his cell phone, dialing out to the rest of his colleagues. They answered almost immediately.

"Hey, I've got some great news for you guys," Russell said into the phone. "I found Claudia Durand! …yes, with Yaggoth. Uh-huh." He looked at Rachel, making a blah-blah-blah gesture with his hand.

She snickered softly. "Look, let me get to the good news before you start into that. They're working together, but I can track both of them. They made a thrall out of some poor maid, and Yaggoth is going with that girl to the harbor. Meanwhile, Claudia said she's coming to kill us! ...I know, exciting, right?" Patty sighed in exasperation. "I'm going to collect Nietzsche from the beach and meet all of you at the airport. Have a chat with Hume before I get there; we need to figure out how to distract Claudia long enough for us to rescue Pete. ...yeah, cya." Russell snapped his phone shut and put it back into his jacket pocket.

"Are they here?" Patty asked, still worried for Wilfred's safety after the attack on the Philosoplex.

Russell nodded. "Mhm. We need to go find Nietzsche and meet the others."

"Finding him shouldn't be too hard..." Rachel chuckled; she had seen his bathing suit before he went out to the beach.

"Quite. Let's get going," Russell said, cracking his neck and rising to his feet. He opened the door for Rachel and she walked towards the elevators with Patty. After a brief journey downstairs in the elevator, they exited into the hotel's open-air lobby. Immediately, they heard shouts coming from the parking lot. Everyone quickly—but incorrectly—assumed that Nietzsche was to blame. On investigation, they found an elderly Hispanic man, seated in a portable deck chair with a large poster-board sign that simply read "REPENT!"

"Oooh!" Rachel gave an excited squeal, her eyes widening. She loved street evangelists.

"Lovely," Russell said, glancing back towards the beach as the man called out to them. "I'm going to find Friedrich. Don't hurt his feelings!" He playfully wagged a finger at Rachel, grinning. Turning around, he strolled back through the lobby to get Nietzsche off of the beach and dressed.

"What are we repenting for?" Rachel asked, approaching the man. She had made a habit of arguing with street-preachers during her college days, practicing what was arguably the only real-world skill conferred by a philosophy degree.

"Wha..." The preacher stopped short, looking up at the two women. "What are you repenting for?! Your *sins*, girl! What else?"

He narrowed his eyes at Rachel, realizing that he was probably being mocked. It was common, of course, but he was often too earnest in his beliefs to notice. Patty tried not to pay him much attention, making a valiant effort of staring off into the nearby garden. She was no more of a fan of sidewalk evangelism than most people, but she didn't think he needed to be harassed.

"But I like my sins!" Rachel gave a lazy shrug. "Why should I give them up? Do you have any idea how many billable hours come on my Sundays? Lawyers are like sharks; if we stop litigating, we drown!" The preacher made a horrified expression. It was bad enough to work on the Sabbath, but to do so practicing law? That only added insult to injury.

"Young lady, you should not mock the Lord! Your sins will only be repaid with fire! What use will your money be in the bowels of Hell?" Had Lucifer been present, he could have helpfully explained at least two dozen uses for money in hell—especially coinage—most of which would have made everyone quite nauseous. There was never a shortage of the greedy in Hell, and Lucifer felt that torture done well should always incorporate some artistic irony.

"Oh, *him*." Rachel smiled, brushing her fingers through her hair. "I don't believe in god, why should I?" That statement was not entirely true in view of the past few days, but Rachel didn't want to have a ranting preacher think *she* was crazy. Besides, she thought, demanding positive proof of god's existence from a street-preacher was the surest route to the sort of tragicomic arguments that would have her laughing for weeks.

"Why *should* you? Why not?" The preacher leaned back in his chair, shaking his head. He had been evangelizing for quite some time, and was savvy enough to know not to take Rachel's invitation. Demonstrating the existence of the All-Mighty was a task not well-suited to a street-side conversation. "What does it cost to you have faith and be wrong? Nothing! But if you reject the Lord and find yourself mistaken…there is no worse fate!"

Rachel was surprised. She had never before run into a street preacher ready to resort to the argument known as Pascal's Wager. Most others would respond to her with some patently ridiculous proof of god's existence; once, Rachel had been told that flowers proved the existence of not simply *any* god, but specifically Jesus Christ. "So you're saying I should gamble on the existence of god?" She wanted to make sure she was hearing him correctly.

"Call it that if you wish, but why would you ever choose not to believe? If God does not exist, you end up the same whether you believe or not. But if God does exist, your belief makes all the difference in the world!" He grinned widely, holding up his hands as if they were scales for dramatic effect.

"Hardly. How can you say that belief in god costs nothing? It costs time, money in tithes, emotional energy. Look at you; you've probably spend countless days just sitting out here in service of your belief!" Rachel paused, shaking her head sadly. "Just think of what you could have done with your life—for humanity!—if you put all of that time to another use."

"I'd like to think I've done a great deal for humanity," he countered. "But that's beside the point, really. Belief doesn't require any of that time or money to be spent. I think it may suggest it, but…it isn't necessary. Belief itself costs nothing."

"Oh, really?" Rachel smiled deviously; the preacher was walking right into her trap. "So you're saying that I can believe in god—and do absolutely nothing to reflect that belief—and I'll still get in to Heaven?" He stopped, furrowing his brow; that conclusion isn't what he wanted.

"I was a bit hasty. There is a cost to belief, yes. A genuine belief in the Lord means you at least have to try to bide by His commandments and law. But what is *that* cost compared to the cost of Hell?" Eternal damnation was a staple of fundamentalist evangelizing, a fact which would have surprised an observer unaccustomed to that peculiar game. After all, "do as I say or else" was an argument normally used by gangsters; it was curious to see allegedly pious men nakedly engage in the same practice. In nearly any other context, the suggestion that refusal would be met with horrible tragedy would be either offensive or laughable; for instance, while the slogan "Buy or DIE!" had experienced a brief spurt of popularity amongst toaster companies, it had otherwise seen little use.

Rachel decided to put aside her more nuanced objection; she had questions about the weighing of an absolutely certain small cost (incident to belief) against a wildly speculative but terrible cost (that of Hell.) "At least we can agree on that. But even then, you think a just, good god would give people eternal happiness simply because they made a calculated bet that paid off? Or that he would torture people eternally for making a poor gamble?"

"That's, ah..." The preacher was a bit taken aback by her framing of the issue. It certainly didn't seem like either Heaven or Hell were particularly just outcomes for a mortal gambling in the face of insufficient evidence. "Well, you're a clever girl, aren't you?" He reached back, rubbing his mostly bald head. "Maybe you're right about that. Perhaps you do need something more—some proof—but I can offer that, too!"

Jumping slightly as a thoroughly bored Patty elbowed her side, Rachel turned to see Russell returning from the beachfront with Nietzsche. Both ladies turned a bright shade of red and looked away; Nietzsche was wearing a blue Speedo that almost certainly concealed less of his body than his facial hair. "I...I have to go," she explained to the preacher, offering to shake his hand. "It was nice arguing with you."

He took Rachel's hand, shaking it awkwardly as he looked up at her. "You should think about these things; you're a smart young lady." The preacher smiled a toothy grin. "And polite, too. Just don't wait until the end of the world to accept the Lord; then it's too late!"

"I may have less time than you think!" Rachel gave a playful laugh, joining up with her friends. As the four walked towards the elevators, Russell noticed that the two ladies kept their eyes away from Nietzsche. Reaching over, Russell tugged on the towel that the German had casually draped over his shoulder and coughed suggestively.

"Would you mind covering up?" Russell asked politely. Nietzsche had taken his reincarnation as the 'superman' literally, and his choice of swimwear made that fact substantially more awkward.

Nietzsche smirked, giving a shrug as he pulled the towel off and wrapped it around his waist. Crowded into the elevator, everyone stood in silence as the car rose towards their floor. Wrinkling his nose, Nietzsche shook his head, trying to dry out his legendary moustache.

Water flew everywhere, giving the distinct impression of a dog shaking itself clean.

"Oh, EW! Seriously!" Patty recoiled, pressing herself against the back of the elevator car. Rachel simply shook her head; she was not surprised. Not surprised at all. The elevator dinged cheerfully as it reached the fourth floor, eliciting a sigh of relief from both Patty and a chuckle from Nietzsche.

"I appreciate the company, but shouldn't you be downstairs rustling up a taxi while I get ready?" Nietzsche knew all along they didn't mean to follow him up; he attributed their forgetfulness to his magnetic personality. Stepping out of the car alone, he immediately whipped off his towel in a dramatic fashion. Throwing the cloth back over his shoulder, Nietzsche strode majestically down the hallway. The elevator car gave another happy chirp as the door closed, silencing Russell's grumbling.

Chapter Eleven

He laughed again, his voice echoing around the deep. The pain would have been unbearable, were it not so magnificent. "Ahh…hah! Do you think *this* is torture?!" The First of Many hung suspended in his cavern, a thousand barbed chains pulled through his body. "Time has been crueler than anything you could…aaaccck…cck…" The bonds shifted through him, tearing flesh and bone. The First panted as his head reconstituted itself. Below him stood a teeming crowd, the strongest of the Many assembled in judgment of their wayward brother.

"Your suffering is only for our benefit," the 3rd replied, sitting in one of the room's two red chairs. "It is merely amusement while we decide how to deal with you and this threat to our paradise." He rubbed his temples, his power not enough to stop a throbbing headache. The 3rd of Many was a young African boy, looking no more than ten. He wore bright traditional garb over his ebony skin, the only hint of his immense age the lines in his face.

Seated across from him in the other chair, the 2nd looked up at their prisoner. She gave a frustrated sigh, hands folded neatly in her lap. In truth, the 2nd was somewhat sympathetic to the First's aims. Time and freedom had begun to bore her; this betrayal marked the only remotely interesting development in the last century. Yet death seemed to be a fool's escape; if Yaggoth was destroyed, none of the Many would have an opportunity to reevaluate the wisdom of the First's plan. That was the aggravating thing about death: it stubbornly refused to allow for any sort of trial period. Restless or not, the 2nd could not condone such a rash decision. She stood, pulling her straight black hair into a ponytail. "Can't you appreciate our frustration with this situation?"

The First gazed downwards at the stocky, middle-aged Asian woman below him. "Of course I can," he replied. "You have yet to reach the limit of your enjoyment with this life. The power we have here can provide much, certainly more than the thread-bare immortality of Heaven…"

"And you decided to kill us all anyways?!" The 3rd shot back. "A hundred thousand souls have found peace, yet you would slaughter them all to satisfy your selfish nihilism? What kind of a monster are you?" The choir of the Many roared supportively, the irony entirely lost on them.

"Someday...you...all of you!" the First shouted, addressing the whole of the crowd below, "will be as I am now! What good are a few millennia of paradise compared to an eternity of suffering?" Unfortunately for the dreamer, all of the Many had once been human. As a species, humanity had notorious difficulty weighing long-term disadvantages against short-term gains. Given the demanding constraints of survival over evolutionary time, it was perhaps understandable that humans had an unshakeable commitment to selfish, short-term gains. The tribe that didn't go to war over dwindling food sources rarely had descendants attending peace rallies a few millennia down the road, after all.

Still, such perfectly reasonable explanations for humanity's behavior made achieving mutually beneficial consensus no easier. All of the Many would eventually want to die; that was an inescapable truth of eternal life. But at the same time, nobody wanted to extinguish their existence before they had exhausted their opportunities for enjoyment. This led to an impossible dilemma: since Yaggoth took victims much faster than the Many grew bored with life, the majority will of the collective would forever stand squarely behind continued survival.

All of the Many got a bad deal out of Yaggoth's ongoing existence; each and every one of the dreamers would get some measure of happiness before an eternity of maddened boredom. Yet since every one of them—except the First, who had already exhausted himself—wanted to reach the limit of their enjoyment before dying, the Many would never agree to betray Yaggoth. While such problems of collective action were common in the mortal world, the nightmare's victims were in a particularly unfortunate position. Human nature drove the Many to accept not only a bad result, but the worst possible result that could ever be conceived.

Meanwhile, Russell's lizards skittered along the outside wall, Bub and Bob splitting up as they covertly waited on the awning over the hotel's lobby. Charles and Claudia soon stepped outside, enjoying the late afternoon's cool breeze. "All you need to do is keep an eye on the brothers. Make sure that their work continues uninterrupted," she instructed. Charles nodded in response beckoning for Re—now dressed in a pair of shorts and a tank top—to follow him towards the harbor.

"Will you be able to handle all of the philosophers by yourself?" Yaggoth asked through Charles. "I could still send Re with you..."

"No, save your strength. I need you to ensure that the brothers complete their lattice, and if necessary, that they go no further than that. The remaining philosophers aren't a match for me."

"As you wish. Meet me at the harbor's edge once you have dealt with them." Yaggoth wondered if Claudia Durand could truly handle the philosophers alone; the demon was either insanely strong or utterly insane. Even if it gambled the whole of its existence, the nightmare thought that it would be little more than an even match for Nietzsche alone. While Sartre and Hume were negligible elements in a conflict, Yaggoth knew that Russell and Kant were extremely dangerous in their own right.

Claudia waved goodbye to Charles, humming a discordant melody as she strolled off to the east. She did not know precisely where the philosophers were, but she reasoned that they could not be far from Pete's location in the harbor. Expanding her mind, Claudia gave a happy sigh as she took in the emotions of the surrounding population. So much doubt, so much fear; Claudia loved cities. With upscale dining, famous landmarks, and the ill-contained horror of modern life, what more could a demon want? As she wandered past one of San Juan's slums, a haggard man approached her.

"Could you spare some change?" He begged, holding out a beaten metal coffee tin. "My father is in the hospital, and I don't have any money to..."

"You poor man! Of course I can!" Claudia stopped, pulling her purse around as she dug through it. Given her disappointment with the beginning of the day and Abraxas' failure, she felt justified in taking a moment to enjoy the little pleasures of life. "I hope this helps; it's all I have on me!" She pressed two $50 bills into the man's outstretched hands, having to bite her lip to keep from moaning in excitement.

"Oh, bless you, bless you! You're a saint!" The man looked down at the large bills, carefully slipping them inside his money-tin. Perhaps he would eat well tonight; maybe even afford a decent jacket for the coming winter. Unlikely, of course; both bills were obvious forgeries, kept around by Claudia for precisely such occasions. Possessed of poor eyesight and too desperate for skepticism, the beggar couldn't have noticed the problems. But any cashier surely would, if Claudia managed to find a bit of luck.

Trembling slightly as she exhaled, Claudia smiled widely at the beggar. "It's the least I can do. Please, buy yourself something nice!" She knew that visiting an expensive store would only increase his chance of being arrested for using forged bills. She waved, turning to head on her way, lost momentarily in excitement. Such a delightful payoff for a simple act of deception! Claudia felt a bit dizzy as she imagined the man being hauled off by the police, his mind spinning when he finally understood her deceit. Extending a hand to hold the guard-rail, Claudia rested for a moment; not noticing the small lizard that trailed behind her on the sidewalk. She could not afford to indulge too deeply; the philosophers would demand her full attention. But once she slaughtered them and took control of Pete, Claudia would be able to bind the whole world with her lies.

It took a good twenty minutes of wandering for Claudia to get a bearing on the philosophers. Her tracking ability worked in a way analogous to Russell's; acutely sensitive to doubt, she simply looked for bubbles of calm, untroubled thinking. The philosophers did not avoid all doubt, instead, they embraced it. Wise men that knew that they knew nothing; the philosophers were not troubled by uncertainty. It did not haunt them as it did weaker minds, those that yearned for consistency.

Claudia crested a hill overlooking one of San Juan's busy commercial districts, her eyes searching through the teeming crowd before her. She knew she was close. Claudia was not disappointed; as she stepped down the stone stairs towards a large mall, she caught sight of the gathered philosophers and their mortal wards. It was pleasantly convenient that they were all together; Claudia worried about Yaggoth's ability to withstand any determined interference. But with the philosophers under control, the ancient nightmare would surely be able to deal with any meddlesome outsiders that decided to pry into the brother's business.

Skipping down the stairs with barely-contained glee, Claudia moved to catch up with her prey. The crowd worked to her advantage and she imagined that she could strike before being noticed. Weaving between the bustling tourists, Claudia hoped to dispatch Nietzsche first. The German wheeled himself along at the rear of the group; if she could kill him immediately, Claudia felt that her job would be substantially easier.

The crowd grew more hectic as she closed with the philosophers, following them inside one of San Juan's larger malls. People bumped and pressed against Claudia, forcing her to occasionally lose sight of her targets. She became increasingly irritated as she pushed through the mobbed floor of the complex; the philosophers seemed to be gaining distance on her. Trying to squeeze between two tables, Claudia found herself stuck behind an elderly Hispanic woman. The lady inched forward, leaning heavily on her metal walker as she navigated the crowd at a snail's pace. "Excuse me, please," Claudia asked, trying to get around. She couldn't afford to make a scene—not yet—and lose her advantage. "Excuse me!"

The lady stopped in her tracks, looking back at the irritated woman behind her. "Excuse *this*!" She arched backwards, pulling her walker up over her head as she bent in the precise opposite direction of the way old ladies were meant to bend. The metal bars of her walker swung down around Claudia's torso, pinning her arms to her side. The grandmother spun on her heel, delivering a punch straight at the young girl. Claudia narrowly avoided it, her mind reeling as she tried to make sense of the situation. Her train of thought was interrupted Claudia was tackled to the ground, brought low by a couple that had been enjoying their lattes at the table to her right. Her field of vision suddenly went dark as a nearby infant vaulted from his crib, body-slamming Claudia's face.

Claudia felt the rest of the mall's occupants dog-piling on top of her, a disconcerting hail of fists, knees, and elbows pushing her down. So much for the element of surprise, she raged to herself, realizing that for once she had been the one deceived. Easily snapping the metal bars around her, Claudia Durand sprung to her feet, sending the piled bodies on top of her flying.

"*Enough!*" she cried, her face dark with anger. The mall patrons rushed straight back at her with single-minded resolve, but Claudia was done being subtle. She counter-attacked, easily evading the clumsy mortals as she struck back, her thin arms delivering blows capable of liquefying bone. But there was no bone to be found; when Claudia's fist met the grandmother's face, only pieces of clay and stone scattered across the room. The mob pressed in on Claudia, every fallen attacker proving to be yet another earthen golem.

Despite the crowd's persistent assault, it took less than a minute for Claudia Durand to destroy nearly one hundred of the earthen statutes. She stood knee-deep in the wreckage of dirt and clay, the deserted mall floor looking like the work of a genocidal sculptor. A quarter of the length down the floor, a lone man sat casually on the edge of an indoor fountain. He hopped down to his feet, straightening his cravat as he smiled cheerfully. "Pleased to make your acquaintance, Ms. Durand. That was quite a show, don't you think?" Bertrand Russell's eyes locked with Claudia's as they stared each other down. It had begun.

"And you're sure he won't notice?" Wilfred asked, looking down at the glass in his hand. Against all good judgment, he had agreed to drink yet another of Sartre's magical concoctions. Patty looked to Wilfred for confirmation; he had at least some experience with Sartre's work. She was understandably worried about the consequences, but Sartre had insisted that he needed two of the mortals to help him. With Robert asleep in the hotel room, the philosopher had tried to convince Patty and Rachel to help him. Rachel, however, had been too upset over the philosophers' decision to send Russell to delay Claudia for as long as possible. Wilfred had agreed to take her place; he was actually enthusiastic to play a direct role in sealing Yaggoth's fate. He owed it to Pete. And to the First.

"Yes," Sartre explained, "its mortal host won't notice the magic. And I will stay far enough back so that Yaggoth does not pick up on my involvement. All you have to do is get Charles to drink." The philosopher pointed at the cluster of beers in the bottom-left most corner of the large cooler. He had given each of the mortals a potion that would alter their appearance by making others perceive them as they were not. That trick would be enough to get Wilfred and Patty close to Charles; he trusted in the host's human instincts to do the rest.

"Let's do this," Wilfred said, throwing back his head and chugging the shot of purplish goo. Patty grimaced for a moment then followed suit, looking back at Sartre.

"I don't feel any different..." Patty looked down at her hands.

"You shouldn't. The potion isn't changing anything about you, per se; it's simply making other perceive you as colored by wildly favorable emotions." Sartre smiled; nodding out of the alleyway towards the harbor-front ahead. "Beauty is in the eye of the beholder, after all. I don't need to change you to make others see you differently."

In fact, the rest of the mortals out by San Juan's harbor would see two young and attractive people, dressed up in sporty outfits covered in flashy beer logos. Wilfred looked down at the copy of Charles' picture for a final time, peering out across the road. The host hadn't left his position in quite some time; he leaned against the railing, staring idly out over the water. All he had to do was make his way down the waterfront with Patty, offering tourists free beer as part of a promotional campaign. "Ok, we'll shut the cooler and start heading back once we've helped out our friend Charles," Wilfred said, lifting up the handle and rolling out of the alleyway.

"But who is that girl?" Patty worried aloud. "You're sure that isn't Claudia?"

Sartre shook his head. "No, that isn't her," he replied as her peered out at Re from inside the alley. "Still, I don't know what Claudia and Yaggoth did to her. Russell indicated that she is dangerous, and that is why it is imperative that once you give Charles the drink you get out of there as quickly as possible." Both Wilfred and Patty nodded.

Watching the two mortals head out in to the crowd, Sartre pulled out his phone. He had set up a conference call between himself, Nietzsche, Kant, Hume and Lime; they were waiting for Yaggoth and

Claudia to be disabled before they struck at the *Paradise Lost*. "They're off. I'll give you the signal as soon as Yaggoth has been taken care of."

Nietzsche was impatient. "Ja."

"Alright." Hume's attention was focused on assisting Russell as he delayed Claudia.

Lime wanted to blow something up. "Mrraaaaawr!"

Sartre glanced at the lizard sitting on his shoulder; Bub had proven crucial to getting one step ahead of Claudia's machinations. Without Russell's pets, the philosophers would not have been able to set traps for their two foes. Wilfred and Patty started their route a safe measure away from Charles, working their way through the crowd with smiles and jokes. Yaggoth would be immediately suspicious if his host was singled out in a crowd; the pair would have to take their time getting to him.

David Hume stood tall on the roof, wind swirling around him as he rushed to complete his work. While the philosophers still did not know who – or *what* – Claudia Durand was, they rightfully feared that Russell would not be able to delay her alone. Despite the pleasant November weather, beads of sweat ran down Hume's face; he had to weave a trap around Claudia before Russell fell in combat against the girl. Hume did not harbor any illusions of being able to subdue her for very long. There was nothing that Hume could create in a few minutes that would rival the defenses he had erected—and which Claudia had shattered—around the Philosoplex. His magic swirled around the mall like countless shimmering clouds, the only visible signs of Hume's dimensional cage. *Faster*, Hume thought, faster – faster! Claudia Durand had already destroyed the army of golems, and the time was running out on Russell's life.

"Oh! That was just wonderful!" Claudia exclaimed, brushing flecks of clay and dirt from her blouse. "What a delight to be the one deceived, even if only for a moment..." She looked around the rubble surrounding her, smiling as she tugged her purse out from beneath one of the sundered golems. "I'm not going to lie – hah! – I'm impressed that you managed to control so many of these statues with such skill.

So life-like, too..." Claudia reached inside her purse and her fingers closed around cold metal. She pulled out an onyx black butterfly knife, holding it up for Russell to see. "That's as far as you're going to get, though. If you thought you could beat me, you wouldn't be wasting time with diversions." She tossed her purse back into the rubble, skillfully flicking her knife open and shut, open and shut with a crisp snap-snap-snapping noise.

"Perhaps I just wanted to make a grand entrance for a pretty lady!" Russell laughed, fixing a steady gaze on Claudia. Despite his outward calm, Russell was unsettled by how quickly Claudia had destroyed his army. "A pleasure to make your acquaintance, in any event. My name is Bertrand Russell, and I'll be your host for the evening."

"The evening?" Scoffed Claudia, her knife snapping open once again. "You're awfully ambitious. I don't give you more than five minutes to live."

Russell frowned in disappointment, fearing that her assessment would prove accurate. "Perhaps I should defer to your judgment on that," he said with a nod of his head. "But before you kill me, might I perhaps know who you are? I have to admit that I'm terribly curious..."

"Not a chance," Claudia answered humorlessly. She realized that Russell was almost certainly playing for time while his colleagues tried to rescue Pete. "Goodbye, Russell." Before Claudia could move, Russell brought his fists together in front of him with a dull thud. The clay and stone which made up Russell's broken golems surged towards him along the ground. Russell fluidly absorbed the tons of earth, employing his strongest defensive technique as he increased his density a thousand-fold. Tiles cracked under Russell's feet as he assumed a fighting stance; he hoped that his body would hold out long enough for Hume to finish.

Unimpressed by Russell's display, Claudia Durand dashed forward with staggering speed. Russell was unable to follow her movement with his eyes; at the last second, he felt Claudia's approach rippling through the air in front of him. "Gnuh!" Russell grunted as he caught Claudia's right arm by her wrist, the black blade stopping only inches from his neck. She twisted acrobatically in the air, transforming her forward momentum into a new attack. Claudia brought her left knee up and around in a blinding arc, connecting with Russell's face and sending him stumbling sideways. Russell's head swam from the impact of Claudia's knee, disorienting him as he turned and threw the girl away from him. He knew that he had to gain distance until he could see straight; Claudia was too fast for him. Far too fast.

Claudia flew through the air towards the glass displays of ground-level stores, pivoting in midair before landing against the thin glass with cat-like grace. The glass shivered but did not break, and Claudia laughed loudly as slipped back to the ground and onto her feet. "Do all philosophers have such thick skulls?" she teased, watching Russell try to shake his head clear. Her attack had put a sizeable dent in the side of his head, and Russell grimaced as he repaired his stone body.

Blinking as his vision returned, Russell assessed his desperate situation. Claudia Durand was unbelievably strong, and while Russell knew that he could absorb nearly any amount of blunt-force trauma, Claudia's knife was a different matter altogether. With her strength behind a sturdy blade, Russell feared that a single, clean blow might be enough to finish him. Russell kept a steady gaze on Claudia, holding his position on the floor. He simply had to *survive* until Hume finished.

Claudia Durand giggled softly, shaking her head in amusement. "Suddenly you're all serious, Mr. Russell," she said to him. "I'm afraid five minutes might have been a *very* generous assessment on my behalf." Her butterfly knife snapped open again as Claudia cut at her left hand; blood rushing from the deep gash in her palm onto the floor. As Russell looked on surprise, Claudia's blood turned to a deep purple mist as it hit the floor, swirling and spreading. Preparing himself for her next attack, Russell narrowed his eyes in concentration.

She was gone. Russell blinked in surprise and shook his head again, searching frantically back and forth in the billowing, growing smoke. He turned from side to side, reacting to little flashes in the mist, a thousand tiny lights dancing about him like Will-O-Wisps. Russell knew that she coming for him, but…from where? He didn't have the time to find her again, and Russell decided he would have to strike everywhere at once. "Shatter!" Russell commanded, sending forth his power into the earth below him. The earth came to his aid, and the entire mall shook as a dense forest of spikes shot up from the ground in all directions around Russell. Nothing. Russell didn't sense an impact. Had he missed her, somehow?

"Again!" He yelled as the stone pillars sent spikes out laterally, surrounding Russell in a wall of dense nettles teeming with purple smoke. His breath was the only noise to break the tense silence, and Russell suddenly feared that perhaps Claudia had left. Hume's name was on his lips as Russell looked upwards, ready to call out to his partner. If Claudia reached Hume alone, then – "AUGH!" Russell screamed as he fell forward, feeling his back splinter as Claudia's knife drove home. He swung blindly, flailing as he tried to get the agile girl away from him.

Claudia ducked and weaved; her blade darted back and forth as she sliced Russell apart. It had taken three blows before he had snapped out of her illusion, and the philosopher was already gravely wounded before he cleared the area with a deafening burst of air, forcing Claudia to temporarily disengage. Russell struggled to reconstitute himself, panting and gasping in pain as he looked up at Claudia. She stood ten yards in front of him, leaning against one of the few half-formed spires jutting from the floor. "But…shit…" Russell's attack had never gone through – was he hallucinating? How? His eyes went to twisting purple smoke.

"Isn't perception a funny thing?" Claudia twirled the knife back and forth amongst her fingers, the blade covered in bits of stone. "Once you convince yourself that something is real, it's terribly difficult to get out of that trap." She was right, after all. Claudia may well have been thwarted if she had tried to conjure up illusions of herself. But even Russell was quick to believe his own thoughts, and she had turned his expectations against him. "But if you can't trust yourself…who can you trust?"

Blood continued to leak from Claudia's hand, the mist only growing darker around Russell. He dashed forward, hoping to keep Claudia busy and prevent her from tricking him yet again. He was close; just a few feet more! The philosopher felt a faint impact against his stomach, metal tearing as he drove through the second floor balcony's railing. Russell thought he had been on the ground floor – when had he moved? Had he even moved? Russell had no time to think before Claudia kicked him hard in the chest, sending Russell crashing backwards to bounce off the crumbling balcony before falling. She appeared below him and drove her knee into his stomach, splintered pieces of stone breaking away. The knife flashed in Russell's field of vision. Both of Claudia's hands tightened around her blade's handle as she swung it hard into Russell's face, catching him as he tumbled through the air.

Russell's head nearly split in half, an overwhelming wave of pain shooting through his body. The ground, he thought; he needed to get back to the ground. Called forth by his power, the floor split and heaved upwards, tossing Claudia into the air while it rose to meet Russell. "Urrgh!" He grunted as the rising floor hit his falling body. The impact hurt, but Russell knew he couldn't afford to stay in the air. His dense and massive form was ill-suited to aerial combat; Claudia could simply keep juggling him. A testament to his remarkable endurance, the fact that Russell's head was split wide open was not enough to decide the fight. He panted heavily; even as his head slowly reformed itself, stone meeting stone, Russell knew he was reaching his limit. It was hard enough for the philosopher to maintain his defensive technique; having to constantly repair his body was quickly sapping his power.

"Two minutes," Claudia Durand called out, her legs dangling and swinging back and forth as she sat on the edge of the balcony above. "Your beliefs are wearing you out, Bertrand. Give up your hope, and let me put you to rest. Only in the stillness of death can you find true certainty; from nothing, nothing comes." The philosopher struggled to his feet beneath her, his wounds repaired at a great cost. Russell hoped that Hume was ready—he hadn't lasted very long—but Russell would soon be too weak to unleash his most terrible ability. If Hume's shield was incomplete, the attack would punch a hole in the Earth. But there were not any alternatives; if Russell could not fully subdue Claudia for a short time, all was lost.

Bertrand Russell smiled back up at the girl, running a hand over his head. This time, he thought, if he had any luck, she would attack him again. Even though his ultimate attack was instantaneous, the closer Claudia was to the source the better Russell's chances of success. "Certainty is a foolish wish," he replied, trying to readjust the mess that was his tie. "I'm content to just keep doing what I can."

"A pity that is so very little!" Claudia dove towards the philosopher, knife snapping open once again. In reality, she was not above Russell at all—the philosopher had surmised as much—but behind. It did not matter to him which direction she came from; only that she came. His vision blurred as he felt Claudia's knife slam into the base of his spine, the shockwave reducing much of his body to rubble. At least, he thought, he would go out with a bang.

"Collapse!" Russell commanded, pushing his mastery of the natural world to the limits. There was a howling, snapping noise as a black hole opened in the center of Russell's body, too small for anyone to see. It was, after all, a singularity; a single point in space packed with unbelievable mass. Compared to the larger black holes in the universe—or even his desperate attempt on the moon a decade past—Russell's singularity was not particularly impressive. It was tiny for a black hole; the anomaly would soon crumble from its own instability. But the philosopher did not need or want to engulf the planet; he wisely set his sights on the more modest goal of the shopping center. Caught within the black hole's event horizon and unable to escape, both Russell and Claudia were soon dragged inside, pulled through the infinitesimally small hole. The mall soon followed, local space-time bending as all nearby matter was rapidly accelerated into the gravitational well.

Outside of his semi-opaque shield, Hume watched as the massive complex was pulled inwards towards a single point. Countless tons of stone vanished in a flash as the mall imploded into nothing at all. A shudder ran through the entire structure as the black hole collapsed and dissipated, the remnants of the ravaged building snapping and crashing to the ground. Russell didn't have long; Hume had already begun the manipulations necessary to shut the barrier into a cage. Five tense seconds passed before the philosopher's earthen form emerged from the central pile, staggering away from the middle with all possible speed. Russell had created the black hole and knew well its intricacies; still, extracting himself in time had cost the philosopher the last of his power. The moment Russell crossed the threshold, Hume slammed shut the dimensional door. Russell collapsed to the ground, broken.

As Hume sealed his cage around Claudia, the illusion he had cast over the mall dispersed. The mortals outside the mall gasped and gawked as the mall shimmered and disappeared, replacing in a flash by a smoking pile of rubble. Dozens of people stopped in their tracks on the sidewalk, pulling out their phones to take pictures or, alternatively, call the police. Between the quickly-swarming crowd, arriving police, and a general sense of hysteria, nobody noticed Hume helping Russell away from the back of the ruins.

"This is pretty decent!" The young woman said, nodding appreciatively at Wilfred. She looked down at the bottle in hand, reading the label on the free beer.

"I know this is a rum town; we're fighting an uphill batter!" Wilfred laughed with Patty, bantering with the group of tourists. "But a bit of variety is always good." Charles was only a few paces to their left, but they could not rush.

"Would you consider drinking it again sometime?" Patty asked, rifling through her bag for a few promotional buttons and stickers. The crowd gave a mixed although generally positive response. Even those who didn't particularly like the beer, however, were more than eager to take some free merchandise. Once their present audience had taken their fill of the stickers, Wilfred and Patty were ready to move on.

"You look pretty tense, sir," Patty offered to Charles, pulling his special drink out of her cooler. "Would you care for a cold beer?" The host looked at the two of them; he had been too engaged in his observation of the *Paradise Lost* to notice much else.

Re narrowed her eyes at the drink in Patty's hand. "We're busy; get lost," she said sharply. Patty forced herself to exhale and smile politely; she used all of her will to keep the bottle from shaking wildly in her hand. The malice exuding from Re was palpable, and Wilfred quickly spoke up before Patty lost her nerve.

"And I have some buttons for you too, little lady!" Wilfred held up a colorful assortment of buttons, trying to repress the thought of Yaggoth or its companion actually *wearing* them. Re fixed him with a withering glare. "It's all free; we're just trying to make a splash out here and get some buzz going about our fall selection!"

"Sure." Charles took the bottle from Patty, screwing off the top. Yaggoth's host had been getting fidgety standing in place all afternoon, and the job of discrete observation precluded the nightmare from taking direct control. Yaggoth could dominate Charles' mind at will, but if it stayed in for control too long the host would start to deteriorate. Insidious psychological manipulation could only keep Charles in line for so long; Yaggoth decided that beer would provide a temporary solution. Tilting the bottle back, Charles took a slow drink. Patty and Wilfred both held their breath in anticipation. Charles smiled. "That's great," he said before taking another pull on the drink. "There isn't much good beer like this, out here on the islands."

"Well...thanks! I'm glad you like it!" Wilfred replied, offering his selection of pins. "Take a button or two!" Charles obliged, picking out a red one and pinning it onto his lapel. Re did her best to ignore all of them, staring out towards the harbor and grumbling to herself. Patty clapped a few times, smiling broadly as Charles put on the pin. While in reality the button had some catchy slogan about "genuine taste," it would have more appropriately read "owned." Exchanging goodbyes with Charles, Wilfred and Patty continued on their way down the waterfront. Pulling out a few more beers and offering them to the next group of tourists, Wilfred repeated his sales pitch as Patty shut the cooler.

Sartre immediately snapped out his phone, thrusting his fist in the air for a second. "Success! Yaggoth should be completely disabled, now. Proceed with the attack." He grinned widely, ready to give the two mortals a huge hug when they returned.

"Should be?" Nietzsche's voice crackled over the phone. "We don't have room for a mistake."

"And we can't afford to wait any longer, Yaggoth or not," Kant replied, in position on the far side of the harbor. "If the brothers even begin to corrupt Pete before we get there, we'll have no choice but to kill him too."

Sartre grimaced, even as he knew they were right. "Just go. There's no way to know if my solution worked until Yaggoth tries to emerge again. Provoke a confrontation!" As he hung up the phone, Sartre heard the noise of a sirens build into a deafening wail to his southwest. Charles glanced nervously behind him, looking in the direction of the growing noise as the tourists around him gossiped and took out their phones, checking for information. Sartre could only hope that Hume and Russell had been equally successful; in a few moments, there would be no turning back from the final battle.

Back in the hotel room, Rachel stared at the television screen in front of her. Apparently, a large shopping mall had been hit by a terrorist attack. At least, that's what the broadcasters were calling it; Rachel could tell that the oddly-shaped rubble was not the result of an explosion – an implosion, if anything. The reporter on the television stated that no bodies had been found, and he seemed a little bit disappointed by that fact. Rachel breathed a small sigh of relief, but could not stop worrying.

Less than a block from the ruined mall, Hume had quickly given up on finding a taxi. Between the small streets, teeming crowds and the arrival of half of the city's emergency services personnel, the streets were gridlocked. Even if Hume had flagged down a taxi, they were not going to get anywhere. Hume looked between Russell and the chaos in the streets, biting his lips. He had not wanted to use any more of his power, especially not to travel just a few blocks. But Russell was not going to be walking anywhere, and Hume couldn't treat him in an alleyway without quickly attracting attention. Hume gathered Russell in his arms, preparing to walk between worlds. Teleportation was Hume's most rarely-used ability precisely because it was so wildly inefficient. Environmentalists rightly decried using a car for short commutes; the energy waste was atrocious. But compared to teleportation, commuting seemed positively ascetic. With Russell's life dwindling away, Hume had no choice but to expend more of his power. It took only a second for Hume to remember their hotel room, drawing the location out of his mind before blinking himself and Russell between worlds.

"*Whatthefuck!!*" Rachel screamed and fell off the side of the bed. Hume had appeared next to her in a flash, Russell hanging off of him like a ragdoll. Rachel quickly snapped out of her shock and she covered her mouth as she saw the Russell's condition. Russell's body looked like a half-finished sculpture, cracks running through him and pieces of stone flaking off with every movement. Even that grim sight looked like the picture of health once Hume turned him over, laying Russell down face-first on the mattress. Claudia's final blow had nearly broken the man; a shattered crater sat where his upper back should have been, deep crevices trailing away from the point of impact along Russell's entire spine. Rachel ran to the side of the bed; Russell stared blankly off to the side, his eyes a dull marble color. "No, no," she whispered, tears welling in up her eyes.

"There is no time for grief! Call the others!" Rachel felt Hume's phone bounce off of her chest, landing on the bed beside Russell. "Tell them they need to go, NOW!" His voice snapped with urgency; Hume had already turned to attend to his colleague. She tried to clear her eyes, grabbing for the phone with trembling hands.

Rachel steadied herself as Sartre answered her call. "Hume says you need to go now, quickly!" she said urgently, her eyes tracing every crack that ran through Russell's body. "...no. I don't know if he's okay. He looks...awful." Rachel looked to Hume, but he could not spare a second of his concentration. "Just get Pete back to us in one piece, alright? Good luck." She closed the phone and sat it on the nightstand.

There wasn't anything Rachel could do; she wasn't a doctor or a sculptor. Even mastery of those professions would not have been of much help to Hume. His healing worked in a peculiar way; in fact, the term 'healing' was not entirely accurate. Hume searched through alternate universes for uninjured instances of his patients, replacing 'what is' with 'what might have been.' In a way, his work was much like that a surgeon grafting on fresh skin; the philosopher had to find a compatible dimension.

Unfortunately, Hume's method was no more effective than more traditional regeneration magics. While it was true that an ordinary scrape would be just as easy to replace as a tumor, the philosopher rarely had the luxury of working with mundane, physical wounds. Supernatural attacks cut more than just flesh; their destruction spanned many levels of existence. Hume was finding it difficult to locate another world in which Russell had *not* been fatally wounded; Claudia's blow had been ruthlessly precise. Adding to the difficulty, he was racing against time. It took all of the little power Russell had left to sustain his hardened form; if he returned to a normal state while so severely injured, his death would be instantaneous. For just a moment, Rachel found herself wishing that prayer actually worked. She shook off the thought; Russell's life lay entirely in the hands of David Hume. It would be an insult to his diligent care to pretend otherwise.

Chapter Twelve

Michael and Lucifer's power had diminished greatly since Yahweh's death, but their ears were still keen enough to pick up the sound of dozens of sirens sounding deep in the city. Lucifer opened his eyes, looking up at Michael as he spoke for the first time since their ritual began. "We have a problem." Below them, Pete had problems of his own; he twitched and shuddered on the bed as the brothers' magic bored into his mind.

The Archangel Michael frowned and growled in frustration. It would only be another half an hour—maybe less—before they managed to break through the last of Pete's defenses. The arcane bands around the young god's head had grown intricate and dense, thousands of twisting lines of energy rooted in Pete's mind. Reaching deep into his consciousness, the brothers' spell-work was the psychic equivalent of open heart surgery. Michael bit his bottom lip hard, nearly drawing blood as he fought back the impulse to say something profane.

"Perhaps this disturbance does not involve us?" Lucifer wondered out loud, looking out the port-hole window in Pete's room. Michael shook his head; as much as he hoped Lucifer was right, he feared that other forces were at work in San Juan.

"Unlikely..." Michael replied. "My power of premonition is not what it used to be, but I suspect that Claudia may have found us."

"I suppose that is not *too* surprising," Lucifer conceded, moving away from the bed and opening the cabin door. "Still, I thought we had successfully eluded her." The brothers had abducted Pete at Claudia Durand's suggestion, but they had subsequently ignored the rest of their pact with the girl. Claudia offered the brothers refuge in the frozen north; instead, the angels had snuck their prize away to the Caribbean. It was only natural that they assumed Claudia had come looking for them. True, she had come, but their treachery had been anticipated. Neither of the angels recognized that they were still performing their part admirably.

Pete groaned incoherently beneath them; he surely would have offered a snarky comment about their difficulties if he did not have magical brain-washer jammed into his skull. Still, he could appreciate that they had stopped, and for a moment, he could rest. Pete didn't hear the door of his guest room slam shut, or his captors storming up to the top deck of the *Paradise Lost*.

Once they reached the upper deck of the yacht, the brothers saw multiple helicopters to their northeast, swarming over the source of the disturbance. Michael flicked on the radio; he found that every local station carried the same story.

"...no injuries have been reported. Onlookers report seeing the mall closed for construction, even as the owners deny that there was any work scheduled. Police have cordoned off the area, and are increasing their presence in the San Juan area. Residents are advised to stay alert, and report any suspicious activity." *Click*. The archangel changed the channel; he needed to know more about what had happened.

"We can confirm reports that the wreckage does not—repeat, not—appear to be the result of an explosion. Authorities have closed media access to the site, but multiple videos have already spread across the internet. Copies have been made available on our website, but we urge listeners to remain calm..." *Click*.

Lucifer stroked his chin and furrowed his brow. "If Claudia was coming to, ah, discuss the terms of our agreement...why not come for us directly?"

"She is not the only one looking for us."

"Hmm...the philosophers," Lucifer said with a chuckle. "They must have run in to Claudia before they could reach us. That battle can only benefit us, no matter who emerges as the victor."

Michael nodded in agreement. "If they are fighting each other...perhaps we have time to make a timely exit?"

"No." Lucifer shook his head, pulling his shades from his pocket and putting them on. If he was going to battle, then he wanted to be sure he did so looking sharp. "We can't run away from Claudia or the philosophers...at least, not on a boat. And our prize is in far too delicate of a position now to be moved by magic. If the philosophers have come looking for their toy, they will surely be reluctant to strike in the middle of a city. Best that we let our pursuers weaken each other, and then destroy them here."

Both Michael and Lucifer were tired from their work on Pete; breaking into the mind of a god was an arduous process. Remaining in San Juan would provide some replenishment of the brother's powers; both angels thrived on the faith of mortals. Despite its luxurious tourism industry, the city natives were resolutely Catholic. That had been one of the prime reasons for Michael's choice of harbor in the first place; the massed faithful bolstered his already-formidable powers.

Michael sighed. "Regrettably, you are right. We will simply have to wait and see what—if anything—comes." Michael still hoped to avoid direct conflict. Despite his peculiar sense of ethics, Michael would rather not use a city of the faithful as a shield. His concern was only amplified by the recognition that his brother would be positively thrilled to inflict as much collateral damage on the city's believers as humanly—demonically—possible. "Hold off on summoning our defenses until we are certain of an attack. We may still be misreading the situation; it is possible that this is a fight that does not involve us."

Lucifer shrugged nonchalantly. His brother could be right; it wasn't completely unheard of for supernatural entities to lose their cool and make a scene. And it had been awhile since the last major flare-up; the Tunguska Event was the most recent of such catastrophes. It was a little-known fact that behind the "Pepsi or Coke?" challenges of the 1990s lay two competing minor deities of food and drink, each having allied themselves to a different company. Such hedonistic gods were notoriously short-tempered, and when clever marketing campaigns had failed to decide the dispute, fists began to fly. The battle had quickly spiraled out of control, the gods tumbling backwards through time as they grappled to the death. An impact that took a good piece out of the early 20th century Russian tundra conclusively settled the rivalry, ushering in new popularity for bottled water and iced tea.

Of course, the gods and the Created did not hide because they were afraid of humanity. True, there were a handful of mortals savvy to the supernatural power struggles and strong enough to interfere. But even the strongest of those groups—the Damocles Organization, a secretive cabal of human psychics—was of little concern to the gods. Only the very worst actors had reason to fear mortal interference, and that threat paled in comparison to potential retribution by other gods.

As diverse as the gods were, nearly all of them needed humanity; even the most bloodthirsty god of slaughter required a ready supply of victims. With humanity—and the human experience—parceled out over countless domains and religions, the supernatural world was in a state of perpetual cold war. All of the gods wished to increase their influence, but none could risk a world-destroying catastrophe that would wipe out the very purpose of their existence.

The philosophers could not trust in mutually-assured destruction as an effective deterrent. Too many times, humanity had come far too close to extinction because of an errant deity. There was only one reliable solution: to get rid of the weapons, to eliminate the gods themselves. Kant snapped out of his contemplations, startled by the guide whom had appeared behind him on the ramparts of El Morro, San Juan's largest coastal fort.

"Excuse me, sir, are you alright?" Sandra, as her name tag read, seemed like a nice lady, Kant noted; she probably in her early 30s. Helping tourists through the old fortresses of San Juan did not pay well, but Sandra got a killer tan while doing what she loved.

"Oh!" Kant smiled, nodding at her. "I'm quite alright; it's just a lovely view of the harbor from up here on the battlements." The philosopher leaned back against the stone walls, looking up into the cloud-spotted sky. Lime should be starting the engagement any minute now; Kant and Nietzsche would move in once the kitten tested the yacht's defenses with a long-ranged attack.

"That's why they built the fortress here," Sandra teased, looking out into the harbor herself. "So the residents could keep pirates and other undesirables out." She did not have an inkling that the port's bloody history was not yet over. "Do you need any water? It's awfully hot out here; I know I have to keep getting a drink." The guide had begun worrying about Kant after she had seen the elderly gentleman standing in place for nearly an hour, his cane resting against the wall as he stared out over the water. More than once, visitors had suffered heat stroke climbing about the exposed fortress, and it was part of Sandra's job to keep such medical emergencies to a minimum.

"Perhaps in a bit. But...thank you for your concern. I'm tougher than I look, young lady." Kant smiled widely; Sandra didn't know the half of it.

Still, Sandra persisted; she didn't want him passing out and dying during her shift. "How about I go get you a cup of water? Would that be alright, sir?"

"I couldn't refuse such an offer, thank you." Kant tipped his head appreciatively. He had no use for a drink, but he would rather such a polite lady be safely underground fetching some water when the trouble started. Precision targeting computers or not, Kant did not fully trust Lime's accuracy with the PDE-1's missile batteries.

"I'll be right back!" Sandra waved, her tan uniform disappearing into the stairwell as she hurried off towards the water fountain below. It was only a few seconds before Sartre's voice came over Kant's earpiece.

"Get ready, here we go."

Even though nobody was there to hear it, the PDE-1's mechanical voice roared loudly in the high atmosphere as Lime cut loose. Half a dozen guided missiles streamed out of the combat suit's shoulder pods, at first appearing as a faint glimmering in the sky above San Juan's harbor. The missiles flew downwards, howling as they broke through the clouds and descended towards the *Paradise Lost*. Kant and Nietzsche were the first to notice the projectiles; they had kept their eyes peeled on the sky. But the brothers did not need any forewarning in order to quickly spot the missiles.

"Now, that's a surprise," Lucifer commented, squinting through his sunglasses as he stared up at the missiles. Honestly, who was trying to attack them with *that*? Even the mortals in the Damocles Organization knew better than to waste conventional armaments against the gods. Another diversion, perhaps? The Devil cracked his neck slowly, taking a deep breath before spitting forth a ball of crimson flame. The flaming orb separated into strands, each piece spinning away as they raced upwards to intercept the approaching missiles. Each fiery line struck its mark, the yacht shaking in the water as the heavy explosives detonated in mid air.

As the sky thundered and blossomed in flame, San Juan began to descend into panic. Lucifer felt the city buzzing with fear and anxiety; he drew power from the growing chaos. Inside the city center, people ran through the streets, meals were left unfinished, and more than a few public employees wondered why that kind of shit always happened when *they* were on-call. Soon enough, all hell—and heaven, for that matter—would break loose in the harbor.

Immanuel Kant gnawed on his lip as he watched Lucifer destroy Lime's missiles. He knew that Michael would be waiting for him out on the water; Kant had a score to settle with the archangel. Perhaps the philosopher would vindicate himself against his old foe. A smirk slowly spread across Kant's face as his favorite tune flitted through his head. He was ready. "Hammerzeit!" Kant said quietly, grabbing a hold of his cane as he crouched. The stone floor snapped under Kant's feet and he launched himself upwards into the air, leaping towards the water from the fortress' highest parapet. At the same time on the other side of the harbor, Nietzsche dashed across the water towards the *Paradise Lost*.

On the top deck of the yacht Michael shook his head, rubbing his temples. He saw the two philosophers approaching; the brothers were not going to get away without a fight. "No choice now, then. Let's bring in the help," Michael concluded aloud, turning to his brother. When they existed, Heaven and Hell both had well-deserved reputations for militarism; each realm supported legions of fanatics ready for war, always on guard against the other. Those armies had long ago fallen, but the brothers had kept to themselves some tiny remnants of their once-great forces. Not much—they would not have even been worth a mention in the *old* days—but enough to deter the philosophers, perhaps.

Lucifer did not need to be asked twice; the Lord of Hell was more than pleased to summon demons into the heart of a human city. He muttered a few words in an indecipherable tongue, rolling his thumb over the ruby and gold signet ring on his right hand. Even though the seal denoted authority over a vanished kingdom, there were still many that would bow to Lucifer's command. Three twilight rifts flashed around the yacht, carrying forth their dread occupants to battle. The boat trembled in the water as the summoning finished, a trio of gargantuan horrors standing guard around the *Paradise Lost*, waist-deep in the harbor. Nearly eighty feet tall, the massive but roughly humanoid demons had crimson skin covered with deep purple markings. Each wore a broad, leather trophy sash across its chest, dozens of stitched faces drawn taut and dried. The beasts had no mouths; consumption was not among the privileges of their rank. They were silent watchers—the last of Lucifer's elite guard—demons with lidless eyes and unmatched strength.

When Robert had last been awake, the world had still been perfectly sane. That had changed. He awoke with a start as he heard screams in the hall outside his hotel room. Perhaps, he wondered, bad things would stop happening if he just stayed awake; that was the second time Robert had woken up to some sort of catastrophe.

Lime's missile strike on the *Paradise Lost* and the arrival of Lucifer's demons had pushed the residents of San Juan into a blind panic. There were hurried footsteps outside Robert's room as people rushed madly, heading for a single airport that was already hopelessly overwhelmed. Quickly pulling on some clothes, he walked to the next room, finding the door unlocked as he walked inside. There in the bedroom, he found Hume, Rachel, and a still-barely-alive Russell. Unable to watch Hume's agonizingly slow work, Rachel stood at the far window, looking into the streets below.

"What happened?!" Robert looked between Russell and Rachel. Despite Russell's ghastly condition, the philosopher looked better now than when he had arrived with Hume.

Rachel turned back to look at him, a pained expression on her face. Chaos swirled in the city below; she knew that it was only a matter of time before people started to get hurt. She couldn't help but wonder how the street preacher felt. Vindicated? Terrified? "The end of the world, I think," Rachel replied at last, meeting her friend in the middle of the room to give Robert a tight hug. "They're going in after Pete right now."

Meanwhile, Wilfred leaned against the alleyway next to Patty, both of the mortals trying to catch their breath. They had only narrowly escaped death just moments ago. Not because Sartre's plan had gone wrong; indeed, Charles and Re seemed blissfully unaware of Sartre's work. Yet when the demons materialized in the middle of the harbor the waterfront had quickly turned into a death-trap. Hundreds of terrified people stampeded away from the water, trampling the slow or unlucky under foot as they fled. Only Sartre's timely intervention had saved the two from being knocked over in the chaos.

"What the hell are those?" Patty asked breathlessly, staring around the corner of the alley into the water. The huge beasts flexed their muscle-bound arms; they had wrists the size of a bus.

"Just demons." Sartre was less concerned with the developments in the bay than the results of his plan. If his potion had failed to work as intended, a few summoned bodyguards were going to be the least of their worries. Yaggoth was still weak, but the nightmare could do worse than Lucifer's guards. Much worse.

Patty grabbed Sartre's arm, giving him an insistent shake. "Just demons?!" She repeated incredulously, gesturing at the towering beasts. "They're going to destroy the whole city!"

"Alright, *big* demons," Sartre corrected himself. "You don't need to worry about them; Kant and Nietzsche are more than capable of dealing with a few distractions. We have to stay focused on..." He stopped, all eyes suddenly turning to look across the harbor-front. The last of the crowd had escaped, leaving a handful of broken bodies strewn across the grown, the fruits of the mob's panic. Only two people remained standing amongst the dead and injured: Charles and Re.

"*YOU!*" Yaggoth bellowed with a thousand voices, fully in control of Charles for the time being. The fingers of his human host clawed at his face for a moment, leaving bloody scrapes on Charles' cheeks. "What have you *done* to me?!" Re stood in a stupor at Charles' side, staring blankly at the ground.

"What *did* you do to it?" Wilfred asked, glancing across at Sartre as the man charged towards them.

Sartre grinned in satisfaction. If Yaggoth was limited to raging madly through its host, then Sartre's concoction had worked. "That drink cut Charles off from the rest of the dreaming world. Yaggoth is trapped in the host's mind; unable to escape or tap into any of its otherworldly power." Even better, Yaggoth's loss of power had disabled Re; Sartre had feared that the girl might still transform into whatever had been put inside of her. Charles screamed madly, hands flailing in the air as he approached. Sartre was quite pleased with his work. "With a reaction like that, you'd think I gave him *actual* American beer."

Sartre and Wilfred stood shoulder-to-shoulder, ready to intercept Charles. Feet dragged on the dirty stone pavement as they fought to subdue Yaggoth's host. The struggle was fierce but one-sided.

"ARrrrRrrgGGghhHH! DIE! DIE!" Charles twisted and writhed as Wilfred and Sartre pinned him up against the wall. They didn't want to unnecessarily injure Charles, whose possession by Yaggoth was suffering enough for the poor man. Still, Yaggoth was not making things easy. Charles strained furiously against the two; each of the men had taken one of his arms and one of his legs, holding him back. The host did not begin to calm down until Yaggoth recognized that if it gave Charles a heart attack, it might actually manage to kill itself.

"You should have picked a beefier host if *that* was your backup plan." Wilfred smirked as Charles relented. Even after a few days in paradise to recover his strength, the small and recently-homeless man could have been pinned down by Wilfred alone.

"Or someone that knew kung-fu. That was pretty sad," Patty added as she stood behind Wilfred. "Hell, I could probably beat your ass." Sartre laughed, nodding in agreement. He looked back out of the alley; Re was still staring blankly at the ground.

"I'm...ahh..." Charles tried to catch his breath; the nightmare wasn't used to the intolerable constaints of a mortal body. "I'm...going to...devour you all..." Despite the threat, Yaggoth gave up its resistance, fully aware of its helplessness.

"You could sure use it, beanstalk," Wilfred mocked, giving Charles' nearly non-existent bicep a squeeze. Yaggoth hissed in response.

Patty and Wilfred both took a step back as Charles was let free, Sartre standing between him and the mortals. "Last time we fought on your terms," he said, remembering his defeat at Ockham's Kegger. "It doesn't look like you were so lucky this time, eh?" He felt vindicated; despite his lack of real combat ability, Sartre was not to be underestimated.

"And what are you going to do with me now?" Charles wiped the sweat from his forehead, staring back at Sartre. "You're too *soft* to kill this fool; we both know it. I will find a way out of this little trick eventually."

"Of course you will; it was never intended to be a permanent solution." Sartre moved in close, his eyes narrowing behind his glasses as he grabbed Charles' chin. "But believe me," he said softly, "if I can't come up with anything else, don't doubt I'll kill one man to save thousands more." Wilfred and Patty were both taken aback by Sartre's cold logic. The philosopher laughed off the tension, leaning back. "However, for now you're just going to hang out with us at the hotel."

"What about her?" Patty asked, gesturing to Re.

Sartre looked to Re again, then back to Charles. "Tell me what you did to her," he ordered. Charles laughed loudly, and Sartre cuffed him sharply in the mouth.

"Acck," Charles coughed, spitting up some blood. "What do you *think* I did to her? I have a pretty limited repertoire."

"What does he mean?" Wilfred asked, studying the motionless girl.

"Ugh." Sartre did not want to deal with any further complications. "He transformed whoever that poor girl was into a nightmare that was inside her. She is human in appearance only, and just for the time being. I suspect that she is dependent on Yaggoth to function."

"Well, we can't just leave her there. Can we?" Patty asked.

Sartre rubbed his temple in frustration. He had no doubt in his mind that Re was exceptionally dangerous. She would be a liability if he brought her with Charles and a public hazard if he left her alive in the middle of San Juan. "No. No, we can't." Sartre turned to Wilfred. "Hold on to Charles while I go take of her."

"Wait!" Patty cried, grabbing Sartre's arm once again. "What the hell do you mean 'take care of her?'" Sartre closed his eyes and took a deep breath.

"She isn't human, Patty. She's never going to be human again," he explained. "Whoever that poor girl was…she's already dead."

"But…but!" Patty protested, tears welling up in her eyes. "Can't you…do something for her? Help her?"

"All that anyone can do now is put her body to rest," Sartre said through gritted teeth. Patty tried to protest again, but Sartre cut her off angrily. "We don't have any choice!" Covering her face in her hands, Patty stepped away from Sartre.

"Just do it fast," Wilfred counseled Sartre. The philosopher nodded grimly and walked out of the alley. Patty closed her eyes as Sartre strode towards Re. Wilfred said a quiet prayer under his breath. The silence was broken by a sharp snapping noise. Yaggoth couldn't control itself any longer, and Charles laughed cruelly.

"Such a pity! Such a pretty girl!" Charles mocked Wilfred as Sartre walked back towards the alley. Behind the philosopher, Re lay flat on the ground. Sartre had been quick and quiet with his work.

"Shut the fuck up!" Wilfred yelled, pulling back from Charles. The host staggered a few inches away from the wall, looking up at Wilfred in surprise. *Crack!* Wilfred's right fist connected squarely with Charles' bottom jaw, breaking bone as Yaggoth's mortal host collapsed unconscious to the ground. "Fuck!" Wilfred exclaimed again, trembling with anger as he turned away from Charles. Patty stared at her friend in shock; she hoped that Wilfred hadn't accidentally killed the poor man.

Sartre knelt over Charles, checking the host's pulse and giving Wilfred an irritated look. "You're carrying him," Sartre said. He couldn't really blame Wilfred, though. Wilfred reached down and picked up Charles' prone figure, pulling the man's arms over his shoulders to bring him along. Walking back out into the open, all three of them paused once they saw that the situation in the harbor had only grown more intense. In addition to Lucifer's guards, seven pillars of golden light beamed up into the sky, surrounding the *Paradise Lost* in a ring. "We definitely need to get back to the hotel," Sartre said and hurried to help Wilfred carry Charles. Patty looked for one last time at Re's dead body as they rushed back towards the hotel.

"*Veni*, Seraphim," the Archangel Michael intoned as he held his own signet ring aloft, the emerald-studded silver band glittering in the afternoon's light. His servants came to answer their master's call; seven angels appeared in the holy light, white wings spread wide. Alabaster white and perfectly shaped, the androgynous figures all wore a simple linen robe, wielding a silver sword in hand. "Destroy the interlopers!" Michael commanded with a ringing cry. The lesser angels saluted Michael with their swords, pausing only to glance at their demonic allies below.

None of the summoned creatures were particularly keen about working with their millennia-old foes; it had taken some work to persuade even those loyal servants of the necessity. Still, all had assented after they had been promised that if the angels and demons cooperated for now, they would all be allowed to kill each other later. That plan had received high marks all around; the eternal war was all that mattered to the brothers' soldiers.

Immanuel Kant picked up speed as he fell through the air towards the *Paradise Lost*. Despite its size, the large yacht was almost totally obscured behind the brothers' assembled host. Yet Kant smiled to himself, for he knew that Michael and Lucifer would not have summoned in allies without good cause. Had their corruption of Pete's power taken such a toll on the brothers' strength? Kant shook his head and cleared his mind of the fear that they may have succeeded in breaking Pete. Even if Michael and Lucifer were weakened by their efforts on Pete, Kant could not afford anything short of total concentration.

Immanuel Kant had an old and bitter score to settle with Michael that went far beyond the angels' abduction of Pete Machal. The philosopher had clashed once before with the Archangel Michael; a war of words in the highest council of Heaven. His loss there had ensured Yahweh's death and set Michael loose on the mortal world. Kant would not fail again, and he swore that his blade would set Michael right where his reason could not.

His old and gnarled hands both gripped the ash-wood cane he held out before him, and Kant's eyes snapped shut in concentration. It took only a second for the philosopher to undo the magical safeties laced around his cane, unleashing Michael's doom into the world. "*Schrei, Armageddon!*" Kant screamed into the rushing wind as his cane howled with energy and expanded outwards in a burst of crackling energy.

The seraphim that had risen up to meet Kant faltered in their approach, eyes wide in terror. Immanuel Kant broke through the storm of light and sound immediately above his foes wielding a four-foot long claymore and a terrible expression that bespoke a single motive: retribution. His great blade, *Armageddon*, was masterfully engraved with an image of a great oak tree split by lightning and the gleaming metal thrummed with the power.

Kant spun deftly in the air, bringing his weapon to bear as he dropped through the cloud of stunned angels. The nearest of the seraphim parried Kant's blow with remarkable speed, but discovered that even divine steel would offer little protection. The seraphim's sword snapped in half with a deafening *crack* only moments before the angel himself was cleaved apart in a shower of golden blood and scattered, white feathers. Defying gravity, Kant moved laterally through the sky as he watched the other angels rise about him, their wings beating furiously to match his new course.

Kant knew it would be troublesome to fight all six of the remaining seraphim at once, especially in mid-air where their wings gave them a substantial advantage in maneuverability and speed. Yet before he could even formulate a strategy, two of the angels to Kant's left disappeared in a terrific barrage of explosions. The rest of the angels scattered in confusion, dodging wildly as the air around Kant blossomed with balls of flame. *She has good timing – for a kitten,* Kant thought with a laugh. Lime had joined the fray.

"You get Pete!" Lime exclaimed as she brought the PDE-1 to hover in mid-air near Kant, the suit's spent missile pods still coughing smoke. "I can haz big flying noms, nao!" She turned the PDE-1 to face the bewildered angels and roared fearsomely through the war machine's speakers. "RAAAAAAWWWRRR!"

Kant grinned at the wonderful absurdity of it all and wished that he had the luxury of watching the angels struggle against Lime's fury. He called out to the PDE, pointing his sword at the two hulking demons which strode through the water towards them. "Think you can handle them, too?"

"Yes, yes! Do want!" The PDE nodded at Kant enthusiastically as Lime deployed the combat suit's close-combat weaponry. "Iz a big kitteh – you get Pete!" Both of the PDE's fusion blades white-hot, Lime roared again as she fired the thrusters and went after the remaining angels. "Angry cat…IZ ANGRY!" Kant did not doubt her in the slightest as he quit the melee and sped towards the *Paradise Lost*, narrowing his eyes at the sight of Michael watching him from the yacht's upper deck.

Approaching from the other side of the harbor, Friedrich Nietzsche was in his element. All that stood between him and the *Paradise Lost* was one of Lucifer's towering guards, striding through the deep water towards the philosopher. Nietzsche drew forth his power as he sprinted across the water's surface; sparks arced over his body and the sound of thunder rolled through San Juan's harbor.

With a loud *snap*, the racing electricity coalesced into a weapon, a whip-like coil of charge around the philosopher's right arm. The grotesque horror before Nietzsche was surely not as hateful as a woman, he thought, but his lash would serve all the same. Suddenly he dove to the side and water erupted where he had stood seconds ago, one of the demon's immense fists plowing downwards into the harbor.

Nietzsche casually threw his arm out and the whip of electricity unwound, hissing as it cut through the falling water and sliced across the monster's forearm. Flesh split and burnt where the whip struck, but the demon did not care. It turned and punched again, forcing Nietzsche to duck and dodge away a second time through the shower of saltwater.

He raced sideways, circling the demon as it struggled to turn and face him. Dancing on the water, Nietzsche was far faster than the lumbering beast could hope to match. He leapt up from the churning water and ran upwards over the demon's back, feeling Lucifer's guard twisting as it tried to reach him. In a flash, Nietzsche was atop of the demon's broad back, watching with a smile as his foe's hands approached from both sides.

"Give me some leverage, you stupid beast!" he yelled, evading the demon's hands as they swatted clumsily at him. Nietzsche cast out his whip a second time, aiming for the demon's left arm as it drew back for another blow. That time, however, he did not seek to cut – the lash doubled in length as it arced outwards, wrapping tightly around an immense wrist.

Nietzsche hopped far to the right, onto the other side of the demon's head, drawing the band of electricity taut. "Auf wiedersehen!" he called out mockingly, focusing his attention on a point far below, near the water. There was a loud clash of thunder as Nietzsche surged forward with all the speed of a lightning strike; he pulled the whip downwards in a single fluid motion, his weapon still anchored to the demon's wrist.

The sparking cord of energy cut through muscle and bone alike, lopping off the demon's head as Nietzsche reappeared in a flash above the water. He called his weapon back to him, disengaging it from the demon's wrist as the creature's huge head toppled downwards into the water with a deafening splash. Moments later the body followed its wayward head into the harbor, sagging sideways below collapsing into the seawater of the harbor.

Nietzsche raced towards the *Paradise Lost*, feeling the sea churn beneath him as the titanic corpse hit the water. Massive waved raced and crashed around him, buffeting the brothers' yacht. Leaping upwards from the churn, Nietzsche flipped forward and landed on the rear deck in a crouch.

Lucifer and Michael stood only a few yards away from him across the polished wood floor; the former had an amused smile on his face. While Lucifer was not exactly pleased by Nietzsche's arrival, he was thankful that his opponent would be the philosopher – and not Claudia Durand. He had only met the girl once before, but Claudia had a power that frightened even the Lord of All Hell; not an easy feat, to be sure.

"Welcome, welcome to our home away from home!" Lucifer exclaimed, clapping his hands together before spreading his arms wide. "To what do we owe this honor?" he asked as the *Paradise Lost* rocked on the subsiding waves below. Nietzsche did not answer right away; he stared quietly at the two angels, and the silence was only punctuated by the distant roar of the PDE-1's missile batteries.

At last, Nietzsche spoke. "You know why I'm here," he said quietly, taking his eyes off of the brothers only to note Kant's approach from their rear.

"Oh, of course we know," Lucifer retorted with a sigh, shaking his head. "But I wanted to hear you *say* it." He held up his left hand, making a silly voice as he pretended to speak through it. "Like this...'I'm Friedrich Nietzsche, and I'm here to save the life of a god!' You don't mind, do you?"

Nietzsche fixed Lucifer with a deadly glare. "He can live or die, it is no matter to me. We can always make another." He rose to his feet, straightening himself out. "I'm just here to make sure *your* god stays dead, and send you both to join him."

Lucifer laughed loudly. "Unlikely, I'm afraid." Lucifer wagged a scolding finger at Nietzsche. "I appreciate the sport, but you're far too weak to threaten me." Nietzsche let him speak – Kant was nearly upon the angels from behind, his claymore heaving backwards for a lethal strike. Suddenly, Michael spun with dizzying speed and pulled a sword from thin air, his blade meeting *Armageddon* in the air with a ringing clash of noise. Kant quivered from the force of Michael's parry as he hopped backwards onto the deck.

Michael swung his consecrated blade through the air and the gleaming silver long-sword shimmered with a warm, golden flame. "Did you really think you could sneak up on me, *heretic*?" The archangel's voice dripped with distain as he locked eyes with Kant.

"It's been awhile, Michael." Kant stared unflinchingly back. "We're going to settle this. Now."

"I couldn't agree with you more," Michael hissed, ignoring his brother and Nietzsche entirely as he strode towards Kant. "Your death is long overdue."

Of all the philosophers, only Kant had—upon his original, mortal death—ended up in the Christian heaven. Once there, he had experienced firsthand the horror of eternal life. A renowned thinker, he had been called to sit in council amongst the angels when Yahweh sought to repair his broken paradise. Back then, Kant advocated a sort of limited heaven; humans would be able to live for as long as they liked, but would be free to permanently end their existence. Kant had thought that to be the most equitable plan for Heaven: allowing the righteous dead to lead new, fulfilling lives for as many centuries as they would have it.

His suggestion had not been received kindly by the heavenly host; the angels felt that Kant's heaven would be pointless—why not simply make mortals live longer?—and Yahweh had worried over the sanctity of life. Admitting that it was only humane to allow inhabitants of *Heaven* to end their lives raised difficult questions about long-standing policies towards the mortal inhabitants of a much less forgiving world. Kant's solution had been no more absurd than any of the others—Michael's included—and in that sat the real challenge. Frustrated to the point of madness, Yahweh had annihilated himself rather than struggle with the insoluble difficulties of his own theology.

In some ways, that end had been particularly tragic. Yahweh generally meant well; his short stint as Jesus still received positive reviews from most critics. But he had become a god long before the great developments of the Enlightenment. Like every other human of his era, Yahweh had gone into godhood with a multitude of awfully silly beliefs about the universe. A poor concept of eternity was only one of many problems—including an abysmal lack of scientific acumen and what was on balance a hideously oppressive moral worldview—that had plagued Yahweh's work. Understandably stubborn about changing with the times—he *was* a god, after all—the collapse of Yahweh's eternal paradise had been the last straw. In a colossal fit of pique, Yahweh obliterated himself and left the rest of his creation to slowly unravel.

Both Kant and Michael blamed each other for Yahweh's cataclysmic exit. Each felt that if they had presented a unanimous plan before the god, he could have been persuaded to take a less drastic course. Undoubtedly, their interminable arguments over the problems with Heaven had only convinced Yahweh that the situation was unsalvageable. Kant—and the other humans in Heaven—had thought Michael's plan to be positively malefic; the angels rejected the humans' suggestions as impious nonsense. Over five-hundred billion souls had been lost forever when Heaven and Hell collapsed; neither Kant nor Michael would settle for anything less than the other's death.

"Sooo…" Lucifer said slowly, breaking the awkward silence. Kant and Michael continued to glower at each other; only Nietzsche turned to look at the Devil. "I suppose it's going to be you and me, huh?" The philosopher gave him a solemn nod. "Wonderful!" Lucifer clapped his hands together excitedly. "Now, it's a bit early for any pale moonlight…but you just won a dance with the devil!" He laughed at the reference; Lucifer always did enjoy the clever lines that humanity had written about him. Still, not every mortal stereotype about Lucifer was true: in fact, the Lord of Hell was positively inept at playing the fiddle, and usually left his lawyers—of which he had *plenty*—to deal with "the details." Yet some of the folk tales were still accurate; a rough iron pitchfork fell into Lucifer's hands, its ever-burning metal a comforting sensation on his skin.

"For the glory of God!" Michael cried as he launched himself upwards at Kant, broad wings appearing from nowhere as the angel took off. The sharp crashes of blade against blade soon echoed around the yacht.

The Devil rolled his eyes, spinning the pitchfork back and forth in his hands as he sized Nietzsche up. "Everything has to be so dramatic with him, you know?" Lucifer complained, wincing as he heard his brother chanting the Lord's Prayer between strokes. "As soon as this business is done, the first thing I'm going to do is…." He stopped, thinking. "No, the *first* thing will be going to Disney World. Seeing the devices people force terrified children to ride is an inspiration for my work. Marvelous stuff. But the *second* thing I plan to do will be stabbing that pious idiot in the throat."

"That's a small comfort," Nietzsche chuckled. "If you beat me, at least I can die knowing one of you will get what you deserve, ja?"

Lucifer made a tsk-ing noise with his tongue, shaking a finger at the philosopher. "*If* I beat you?" The Devil shook his head sadly. "You don't have a snowball's chance in hell of surviving this fight."

"I suppose you would know, heh."

"You'd be surprised how many smart-asses ask me that," Lucifer replied, his right hand tightening on the shaft of his weapon. He put his free hand to his cheek, asking in a mocking voice. "Oh, Mr. Devil, what is a snowball's chance here?" Satan licked his lips. "Want to know what I say?"

Nietzsche narrowed his eyes. "What?"

"I say, 'more of a chance than you!'" Lucifer guffawed loudly. "Then I have the poor bastard eaten alive by a snowman!" The Devil wiped a tear from his eye, blown away by his own magnificent sense of humor. "Oh, ahahah. Ahhhhahahahah!"

Nietzsche stared at him, dumbstruck by Lucifer's utter lack of concern about the imminent battle. "Which one is the torture? The snowman...or your sense of humor?"

Lucifer straightened up, sniffing indignantly as he cleared his nose. "Now *that* was below the belt." He dug his feet in to the floor. "Have at you!" The *Paradise Lost* shook from the force as Lucifer launched himself forward. Yet as fast as the Devil was, his weapon was even faster; the three prongs of the pitchfork extended with blinding speed. The razor points pierced through Nietzsche's body, the resultant impact enough to let the Devil know something was wrong. Lucifer stopped as fast as he could, the floorboards snapping underfoot as Nietzsche's figure detonated, the resultant shockwave annihilating a sizable piece of the ship's aft. Thrown backwards from the explosion, Lucifer saw the philosopher moving beside him; Nietzsche tried to take advantage of his simulacrum's destructive finale by moving behind Lucifer.

Lucifer's pitchfork retracted as he swung backhandedly at Nietzsche, exhaling a torrent of flame in the philosopher's direction. As it struck the flame, the Devil's weapon fanned the fire into a snapping wave of destruction. Nietzsche had no time to dodge; he opted to block with his face, his legendary moustache sizzling at the ends as the philosopher absorbed the impact. He was tossed into the half-exposed belly of the yacht, flying embers setting fire to anything not as bad-assed as Nietzsche; that is to say, everything. The Devil spun his pitchfork like a baton, pleased with his work. Somewhere in the now-burning yacht below, Nietzsche coughed out smoke.

Suddenly, there was a loud crash from behind the Devil; the noise of shattering glass and truly obscene German swears leading directly to the conclusion that his brother had kicked Kant through the deck windows. "What the *hell* are you doing?!" Michael reappeared above Lucifer, his usually pristine figure marred by a number of slight cuts, dripping golden blood.

"Is that a trick question?" Lucifer craned his head to look upwards at his brother. "You want me to fight, and then you're surprised by fire? Honestly…" The archangel glared daggers at Lucifer.

"If you hit the godling—argh!" Michael was cut off as Kant charged at him on the roof, their swords meeting once again. With a mighty heave, the archangel threw Kant backward and tried to catch his breath. "Any…damage to Pete…*disastrous!*" It was only a moment before Kant was upon Michael again, his greatsword dancing with impossible speed.

Distracted by his brother—and selfishly hoping he might see Michael injured—Lucifer barely had time to duck as a fiery chunk of seraphim whizzed over his head. Glancing to the side, he saw that the PDE-1 was putting up one hell of a fight; the last of Michael's seraphim rained down upon the *Paradise Lost*'s deck in well-seared pieces and both of Lucifer's remaining demons were direly wounded. "Nice!" He called out towards the PDE, giving a thumbs-up and deeply inhaling the scent of roasted angel. "Now that really takes me back…" Lucifer mused aloud as a pained expression crossed his face. "So many Christmases with Baalzebub and Maamon around the fire-pit, savoring some poor angel I plucked from the reaches of Heaven…" He sighed deeply.

In the burning engine room downstairs, Nietzsche frowned as he considered his options. He had expected his explosive illusion to at least harm Lucifer; that technique had taken quite some time to perfect. Still, Nietzsche recognized that he could not put too much stock in his ability to harm Lucifer at a distance. His foe was too strong to be disabled by an electrical impulse and impervious to any sort of burning. Nietzsche sighed as he glanced up out of the flames, and concluded that he could do nothing but grapple at close range. Surely, Lucifer was waiting for him to jump up – Nietzsche needed a new exit. He waggled his moustache, shrugged, and promptly punched a gaping hole through the *Paradise Lost*'s hull.

Chapter Thirteen

In the heart of San Juan, mere mortals proved more than capable of calling forth their own fire without godly assistance. Stores and cars burned as panicked mobs ran in the streets, fleeing from the otherworldly war raging in the harbor. The city's residents were already on-edge after Russell imploded the Mall of the Americas; Lucifer's demons pushed San Juan from terror to blind, pants-shitting panic.

Rachel gazed out over the city from her high perch on the hotel balcony, grimly wondering how many lives would be lost before the day was through. As dangerous as the gods were, she couldn't help but recognize that humanity was often its own worst enemy. To the best of her knowledge, the philosophers had not involved many mortals in their battles with Claudia and the brothers – and the demons in the harbor made no effort to attack the city. More people probably died today from car accidents than the supernatural, Rachel thought, watching as mass hysteria spread through San Juan.

The city's descent into madness was even stranger to Rachel in view of the fact that most of the citizens, in their everyday lives, comfortably asserted that the creatures running about in the harbor actually existed. Still, she was forced to admit that even if you were the sort of person who believed wholeheartedly in the existence of demons, having three of them appear from thin air would be a bit of a surprise. Rachel couldn't really blame people for being afraid, she concluded, but it bothered her that so many would die because of that fear.

Rachel craned her neck outwards, looking down into the hotel's open-air lobby far below. From her vantage point, she saw piles of abandoned luggage, a large cage full of what must have been terribly confused parrots and the entrance to the hotel's fancy Italian restaurant. The detailed glass doors and polished wood looked out of place amidst the rest of the chaos, and Rachel found it remarkable that nobody had tried to loot the restaurant for food.

At that moment a haggard man wandered into Rachel's view; he was disheveled and Rachel guessed he had seen rough times long before the present. Rachel narrowed her eyes, trying to get a better look at the new arrival. He looked unkempt and tired, clutching a money-tin in his hands as he shuffled forwards. The man stopped beside a pile of leather-bound, expensive, and clearly abandoned bags. He stared at the luggage for a moment, rubbing his messy, graying beard. Then he shook his head dismissively and walked to the door of the hotel restaurant. Leaning forward, he pressed his face against the locked glass doors, eyes searching around the darkened interior. Unable to see anyone within, he reached out and knocked sharply a few times on the glass. Still without an answer from inside the restaurant, he sat and waited, cradling his money protectively in his lap.

Rachel wondered what the man thought of the howling sirens and general hysteria that consumed San Juan. Apparently he had not. He sat down in front of the host's stand, legs crossed and the tin resting in his lap. For a moment, Rachel considered calling out to him, but then thought better of it. Bizarrely enough, he was handling the apparent coming of the apocalypse better than most of the city. Whether he was crazy or not, she didn't want to disrupt his tranquility. All he seemed to want was some pasta.

The rest of San Juan was not nearly so serene; while Rachel could not hear it herself, more sensitive ears than her own could pick up the terrible rhythm of panicked masses running in the crowded streets. Nidhogg shuddered painfully, straining to hear past the reverberations of mortal panic. He could not hear their screams or their prayers, but there was no need for that. The citizens of San Juan were terrified, Nidhogg knew that much. By why? They were running from something in the harbor, he surmised, but it was difficult for Nidhogg to see past the obscuring layer of water. Suddenly, Nidhogg's vision flickered black for a moment, and he gasped. Uncontrollable chills ran through the serpent despite the blistering heat of the Earth's core, and Nidhogg felt his body slowly numbing.

Desperately, he listened to the city, trying to follow the philosophers with the last of his failing strength. Nidhogg had heard Kant's thunderous departure from the Earth, but no return. What fate had they met upon the waters? If only he had a bit longer, Nidhogg thought, just a few more minutes. Then he could see to the end of the story. Once again, the great serpent's sight went black – but that time, it did not return. His grip on the earthen spire slipped a bit, rocks fell and splashed into the twisting fire below.

Many centuries ago, the Nidhogg would have seen nothing of value in just a few minutes. But now, the world would go on without him; that recognition cut through Nidhogg like a knife. What would come of the world above? It was absurd, he thought. One of the great Created, suddenly brought low by the little, fatal ticks of the passing seconds! He laughed. Time could be so fickle. Then, he fell.

On the roof of the *Paradise Lost*, both Michael and Kant felt the boat began to list to the side as it took on water. Unbeknownst to them, they shared a thought as Lucifer and Nietzsche were each blamed by their partner for such recklessness. Kant pushed off his right foot and dodged behind one of the yacht's antennae clusters, trying to gain some distance on his opponent. Kant's weapon was longer and heavier; he had the advantage fighting at the maximum reach of his blade. The Archangel Michael had quickly recognized as much and kept Kant on the defensive at close quarters.

Overcoming his usual aversion to property damage, Michael bore forward and hacked through the electronics between him and Kant. He had come to terms with the fact that with the yacht both on fire and flooding; further damage couldn't possibly make things worse. Even if the brothers had bothered to acquire an insurance policy for their expensive boat, they still would be out of luck; "acts of god(s)" weren't covered to begin with. Still, Michael was determined that if the *Paradise Lost* was to sink, then he would bury Kant with it beneath the waves.

Despite Michael rushing towards him through the sparking equipment, Kant coolly assessed the situation. He thought that the archangel would be stronger. Michael was far more agile than him, and had the advantage of untold eons of practice in martial combat. But despite all his skill and his burning hatred for Kant, Michael fought with surprising caution. He took few risks in order to attack Kant; loathe taking a chance in order to seize the advantage, Michael had done little but force a stalemate.

Unlike the angel, Immanuel Kant did not have the slightest interest in living forever. As the *Paradise Lost* tilted precipitously beneath him, Kant suddenly changed direction – he sprung forward at Michael and swung *Armageddon* downwards in a reckless, overhead arc. The archangel half-stumbled and rolled to the side, only barely managing to find his footing before Kant pressed the attack. Still off-balance, Michael did not have time to dodge again and swung his blazing longsword to meet Kant's attack.

Kant planted his feet firmly on the yacht's roof and poured his very soul into *Armageddon* as he unleashed its final power. If Michael did not fall, Kant knew he would not be able to stop the certain counter-attack. The air snapped with weird energy and the two blades sang furiously as they met. Michael's entire body shook from the impact, but he had stopped Kant's attack. "Ack! ...*w-what?!*" Michael choked in pain. The angel's golden blood sprayed forth as a massive gash opened across his chest, far behind Kant's blocked sword. Michael found himself falling backwards off the roof, desperately trying to spread his wings again.

Kant wasted no time trying to follow after Michael; his last trick had already been revealed. Summoning his focus once again, the philosopher brought the sword back around, slicing through the air in Michael's direction. Kant's epic claymore—*Armageddon*—could cut far more than what it simply touched. A paper-thin sheet of force shot outwards from Kant's stroke, slamming into Michael's falling body. The archangel screamed incoherently as he spun and lost blood, his cries finally drowned out as he fell into the harbor with a loud crash. Kant grinned wickedly and leapt down into the water after Michael. "Hammerzeit!"

Despite his cool assessment of the situation, Kant was not entirely responsible for his surprising advantage. As panic spread through San Juan, Michael's strength faltered while Lucifer's grew. Mass hysteria amongst the city's faithful was sapping the archangel's power, weakening him as the population sought safety in riot police and paramedics, not pews. Already exhausted from hours of effort spent on Pete, Michael struggled against an opponent who—in ideal conditions—he could easily crush.

On the contrary, Lucifer was riding high as the city teemed with chaos. While he too had expended a great deal of energy working on Pete, a couple hundred thousand humans losing their minds in terror was more than enough to compensate. The Paradise Lost tilted beneath Lucifer, rousing him from his reminiscence on the home-cooked angel of Christmases past. "Oh, what the *hell*! Michael is going to blame me for that!" Lucifer cursed as he saw water erupt into the rooms below, dousing Nietzsche as surely as it began to flood the yacht. He angrily thrust his pitchfork forward and the weapon extended once again as it punched through the lower decks – but not quite quickly enough.

Nietzsche was already gone; he had exited through his ragged hole and emerged from the side of the *Paradise Lost*. Retracting his pitchfork, Lucifer blinked in surprise as he saw Michael falling from the roof covered in blood and Kant diving after him. While he would ordinarily be pleased by the sight, Lucifer knew that he would be unable to control Pete alone. He had to finish the fight quickly, before his brother got himself killed.

Lucifer turned to his right as three Nietzsches leapt on to the deck from the water below. Two—or maybe all—of them were fakes, Lucifer knew, but there was only one way to find out. The Devil shrugged and stabbed the central Nietzsche as they closed on him; Lucifer had always been a gambling man. Lightning crackled around his pitchfork, and Lucifer braced himself for a blast that never came. Instead, the mirage twisted into a copy of Nietzsche's whip and coiled around Lucifer's weapon, attempting to tear it from his grasp. Before Lucifer could react, the second Nietzsche barreled head-first into him and exploded violently, throwing the Devil backwards across the charred deck and away from his pitchfork. Fanning away the flames to clear his vision, Lucifer found Nietzsche—presumably the real one—leaping at him with his fist pulled back for a devastating punch.

Lucifer laughed and snapped his fingers with imperceptible speed. Nietzsche's eyes went wide, but it was far too late from him to turn from his momentous charge. With a sickening ripping noise, Nietzsche came to an abrupt stop on the waiting prongs of Lucifer's pitchfork. The philosopher twitched then sagged noticeably but Lucifer did not relent, swinging his weapon sideways to slam Nietzsche forcibly against the walls of the *Paradise Lost*'s main cabin. Lucifer kept Nietzsche impaled against the shattered wall for a moment before pulling back his pitchfork and letting Nietzsche collapse to the deck in a bloody pile.

Lucifer spun the weapon in front of himself, watching Nietzsche's blood boil as it ran down the length of his sizzling metal prongs. "As I was trying to tell you before, you were a bit optimistic to think you could beat *me*." He stepped forward and gave Nietzsche a little kick. The philosopher gurgled. "It was a good effort though, I'll give you that. Your mistake was thinking that I could be separated from my weapon. But this," he shook his pitchfork demonstratively, "this is part of me. God Almighty himself couldn't take it from me, although I promise you he tried."

Below Lucifer in the bottom of the yacht, Pete had not noticed the smoke which filled his room or the rising heat from the fire which was burning down his door. Only faintly aware of the outside world, Pete's first inkling that things were seriously wrong came as his bed slipped across the sloping floor into deep, cool water. Still chained in place as he sunk along with the yacht, Pete writhed for a few minutes until he got used to the distinctly uncomfortable sensation of having his lungs filled with water. It was small consolation Pete that he wasn't *actually* drowning; that fact made the sensation no less horrifying. However, everyone else didn't know that Pete would be more or less safe sinking to the bottom of the harbor inside a ruined yacht.

"Pete!! Noooo!" Lime exclaimed, the PDE-1's badly damaged speakers crackling with static as she cried out. Lime waded towards the *Paradise Lost* through a grisly stretch of water; the two demons laid cut asunder in the bay, floating amongst scattered pieces of roasted angel. The PDE had suffered serious damage itself; one of the suit's arms rested somewhere on the bottom of the harbor after being torn off in the kitten's titanic struggle against the hell-spawned behemoths. "Kitteh is coming! Please to not die!!" Limed tried to fire the dented machine's thrusters only to find the propulsion units inoperable. She waded awkwardly through the deep water, struggling to reach Pete before either he died or the PDE-1 failed entirely.

Lucifer looked away from Nietzsche's body, raising an eyebrow at the approaching PDE-1. He was honestly surprised that a giant toy had managed to defeat two of his guards; whatever the crackling weapon on the unit's remaining left arm was, Lucifer could tell it was potent. "You know what they say about curiosity and cats," the Devil called out, turning to face Lime. He could sense the small living creature at the core of the war machine – it would be a simple matter to destroy it. Lucifer lifted up his pitchfork, aiming the killing blow. Yet again his weapon extended outwards, the three bloodied prongs racing for Lime – only to glance off the PDE's shoulder as Lucifer was suddenly dragged backwards.

As Lucifer fell and turned towards him, Nietzsche released his control over the whip and grabbed the Devil firmly by both shoulders. Only a few inches from the philosopher, Lucifer saw nothing but Nietzsche's blood-shot eyes and a moustache that bristled with untold fury. The Devil's vision exploded into a cascade of bright stars and his ears rang as Nietzsche swung his entire body forward and delivered a cataclysmic, world-ending head-butt. The *Paradise Lost* slipped another two meters under water, Lucifer forgot his middle name, and seismographs throughout the Caribbean registered a small earthquake.

So close to Pete, Lime sensed her creator's dangerously weakened state. Using the PDE-1's remaining plasma blade—as delicately as one could use a weapon designed for cutting buildings in half—Lime opened up the center of the *Paradise Lost*. Bracing the PDE-1 against the yacht's torn hull, she held the boat afloat and deactivated the weapon. Lime reached inside the flooded lower deck of the boat, searching awkwardly for Pete.

Close by on what remained of the *Paradise Lost*'s rear deck, Nietzsche grappled desperately with Lucifer, able to do little more than soak blows as he held the Devil back. His terrifying head-butt saved Lime's life, yet it did little but temporarily stun Lucifer. Nietzsche spent the last of his energy wrestling with Lucifer, hoping to buy Lime enough time to extract Pete. While Nietzsche succeeding in keeping Lucifer from using his pitchfork to land a finishing attack, the philosopher could only grit his teeth as he took strike after brutal strike from an enraged Lucifer.

Lime rummaged through the ruins of the Paradise Lost, blindly searching for Pete. After an agonizing minute she found him and the PDE's hand closed around the bed which held Pete Machal. Pulling him from the watery depths, Lime looked at her creator's pitiful state; Pete was soaked, coughing up sea water, and bound securely to a queen-sized bed. All of that she understood. But Lime did not understand the crystalline magic around Pete's head which glimmered and hummed weirdly. One of the PDE's fingers brushed against the spellwork curiously; Lime was not sure if the sparkling veins were even corporeal at all.

With a sudden, ringing *pop* the brothers' magical lattice shattered. Pete's eyes flew open in a heartbeat, and he screamed a horrifying, soul-wrenching noise. Shards of wild magic tore through Pete's mind, tearing at the very essence of his being. "NOO! Kitteh iz sorry!" Lime cried out as her adorable kitten eyes welled up with tears inside the PDE's cockpit. "Did not mean to hurt!" Shimmering magic dissipated into the air as Pete's godhood collapsed in upon itself.

"NO! You stupid—*uunfff!*" Lucifer never finished his sentence as Nietzsche threw him back to the deck.

Beneath the *Paradise Lost*, Michael too felt the shockwave as his magic broke. Were he not trying to avoid Kant within the shadows of the yacht's sinking wreckage, he would have let off a litany of words so profane that only angels were deemed safe to know them. Making a snap decision, Michael hid his glowing sword and white wings, bolting underwater for the entrance to the harbor. Pete would be *useless* to him after having the careful magic sundered so recklessly; Michael knew that omnipotence would now be far beyond the man's reach, if he even survived. He presumed that his brother would quickly reach the same conclusion, and join him in flight. There would be other gods, in time; continuing to fight the philosophers over Pete's spent husk was a pointless exercise.

Howling in agony as he thrashed against the chains which bound him, Pete tried to salvage his mind from the trauma of the brothers' shattered magic. The pieces spun wildly through his consciousness; Pete could feel his potential—and his sanity—being shredded with every passing second. He would need what power he had left to stop the damage from spiraling out of control; power that he couldn't access still bound within Yahweh's chains. "BREAK THE CHAINS!" Pete screamed up to the PDE-1. If he was not released soon, Pete knew that he would surely die.

Lime hesitated for a split second as she stared helplessly down at her creator. The PDE was barely operational; her only chance to free Pete might be the plasma blade. Maybe—*maybe!*—the chains would break, but what of the man inside them?

Pete twisted violently against his bonds, yelling once again. *"DO IT!"* His command struck Lime as if it were a physical blow; she could not question the judgment of her creator. Lime closed her eyes as she heaved the PDE's remaining arm upwards, throwing Pete and his bed straight towards the sky. The air crackled as Lime's energy blade snapped into place and charged to full power. From the deck of the *Paradise Lost*, Nietzsche watched through a haze of blood as the glowing weapon arced through the air to meet Pete's fall. Something from beyond the world snapped apart, and reality itself trembled. Pete remembered something about an elevator. Then he fell, wreathed in smoke and flame until he struck the dark water below.

Kant rocketed out of the water and landed on what little of the *Paradise Lost* remained afloat. He could only stare in horror as Lucifer lifted Nietzsche above his head with both arms and brought him down to his knee with a sickening crack. Already a mass of bruises, Nietzsche slumped against the bloody deck bent in half. He gurgled something unintelligible then lay still. Lucifer stepped over the broken philosopher and his eyes glittered with rage. His best chance to reclaim the throne of Hell in nearly two millenia – ruined by a band of weak fools!

Lucifer seethed. "I…am…" He took a deep breath, channeling the hate which boiled within him. "I am going to make you suffer in *unimaginable* ways, old man." Lucifer knew that his brother had already taken flight far behind him, but he did not care. There would be time enough to rejoin Michael after butchering Kant and the idiotic cat, Lucifer thought. He would not suffer disappointment graciously.

Kant readied *Armageddon* before him, blinking away the mix of sweat and seawater that ran down his face. He was exhausted from battling Michael, and Lime was too obsessed with her search for Pete's body to be of any use. "You *will* die," Lucifer said as he called his pitchfork back into his hand. "But before you die, you are going to tell me what you know of the girl." Kant gave him a confused look. "Claudia Durand! *What* is she? *Where* is she? I am going to serve that meddlesome bitch's head on a platter!" Still, Kant stared silently. But he was not staring at Lucifer; he was staring past him.

The Devil felt it too, and he turned slowly towards a power more terrible than any he had faced since the Fall. As he watched, the dark waters parted before him and issued forth a thousand dancing tendrils of black lightning. Pete Machal rose from the depths, an awful scar smoldering on his chest as he locked his eyes on Lucifer. He raised a quivering arm and pointed a single finger at the Devil. Pete's lips parted as he spoke a word of unmaking, and most of Lucifer's torso vanished in a swirl of shadow and driven ash. The storm around Pete vanished, and he collapsed into the PDE's waiting hand.

Lucifer sank to his knees beside Nietzsche, looking down at the blackened hole that had only moments ago been his chest and right arm. "Nobody…*uses* me…like this…" The Devil coughed up a mouthful of ash that had once been his chest and collapsed. He shuddered and turned his head to the side, staring at Nietzsche. "I…know…that you…aren't dead…" Lucifer trembled from the joyous, overwhelming pain. He reached his withered left arm out towards Nietzsche, straining to reach him as Kant charged from behind with his sword raised high.

Nietzsche's eyes opened and he called out to Kant through the pain. "Hold!" Kant skidded to a halt beside Lucifer, *Armageddon* poised to strike a final blow. "Let him be." Kant lowered his blade and watched curiously at Lucifer pressed two of his fingers to Nietzsche's forehead. With the dust of his own obliterated body, Lucifer drew a small glyph.

"There…" Lucifer shuddered and dropped his hand to the deck, nodding at his work approvingly. "Take…*that*…and kill her! Kill her…and tell her…" He grabbed Nietzsche's lapel with what little remained of his strength. "Tell her…that nobody…*nobody*…uses Lucifer." The Devil closed his eyes for the last time. "Now…let me…enjoy this. It's been…*so* long…in coming…" He moaned once in ecstasy. Then Lucifer Morningstar, First of the Fallen and Lord of All Hell disappeared forever.

Nietzsche grunted and rolled over onto his shattered back, looking up at Kant. "It's done," he whispered. A grin spread under the bruised contours of his face.

"It is…" Kant replied slowly, looking up from Nietzsche to where Lime waited with Pete in hand. "What did he give you?"

"The power…he could never wield," Nietzsche said cryptically as he stared over Kant's shoulder towards the blazing sun. "The light."

Kant nodded and dismissed *Armageddon*, then knelt down beside Nietzsche. Small waves lapped against Nietzsche's body as Lime waded close to the ruins of the *Paradise Lost* with Pete's prone figure in hand. Kant slowly stood to his feet and carried Nietzsche aloft in his arms, turning to look back towards the shoreline of San Juan.

Sartre gave a long, shaky sigh and mopped the beaded sweat from his face. "They're bringing him back," he said quietly. He couldn't make eye contact with Pete's assembled friends – all of them stared at Sartre intently, full of palpable worry. Sartre had felt the instant Pete's power snapped; the moment when his experimental god collapsed in a final flash. He did not know whether Pete survived the ordeal. But alive or not, the man would not be able to complete his part in the philosophers' grand plan.

Patty opened her mouth only to close it again immediately, eyes watering with tears. Then she cried out and began to weep, burying her head in Wilfred's chest as he embraced her.

"You bastards…" Robert muttered as he pulled off his glasses, wiping his eyes. "He didn't deserve this."

"It…I…" Sartre stumbled as he tried to find the right words, looking to Hume for assistance. "He…might…still live. From here it is hard to know, but they will be here soon."

Hume held up his hand towards Sartre, stopping his colleague. He turned to Pete's friends and placed a hand on Patty's shoulder. She choked back another sob and looked up at him. "I'm sorry," Hume said, giving Patty a gentle squeeze before letting go of her shoulder. "For Pete, and for all of this." He looked sideways towards Robert. "None of you deserved this, and I'm sorry."

Rachel stood from beside Russell's bed. "You did what you had to do," she said to Hume, earning an angry glare from Wilfred. "That's all that *anyone* can ever do, god or not. I'm going downstairs to welcome Pete back." Rachel glanced down at Russell before turning to walk away, and he smiled back. Russell was flesh and bone once again, saved—if only barely—by Hume's tireless work.

Joining Hume and Rachel as they walked towards the door, Sartre cast his eyes around the room. Russell was bedridden but alive. Yaggoth stewed with silent rage inside Charles, bound to a chair in the far corner. Socrates gave his life to stop Abraxas and Claudia Durand would soon come looking for them. Sartre bit his lip hard enough to draw blood. He would have to make another Existential Dilemma. They needed another god.

Hume put his arm around Sartre as they walked side by side towards the waiting elevator. He too knew that they would have to try again. The philosophers had escaped total disaster only by the narrowest of margins, and lost much of their strength in the process. Hume's stomach churned at the thought of tricking another mortal into godhood, but he could not imagine that anyone would serve willingly after what happened to Pete.

"I'm not going to hold the door all day," Rachel teased, her eyes holding Hume's for a long moment.

Hume nodded and stepped inside the elevator with Sartre. The rest of Pete's friends squeezed in beside, unsure whether they were going to a homecoming or a funeral. Perhaps, Hume thought, Pete might yet live. His friends deserved a rest from worry and fear. But David Hume could not rest – not so long as the gods still walked the earth. For him, the end was yet to come.

Made in United States
Orlando, FL
24 August 2025